THE
BASIL AND JOSEPHINE
STORIES

BY F. SCOTT FITZGERALD

NOVELS

THE LAST TYCOON *(unfinished)*
with a foreword by Edmund Wilson and notes by the author
TENDER IS THE NIGHT
THE GREAT GATSBY
THE BEAUTIFUL AND DAMNED
THIS SIDE OF PARADISE

STORIES

BITS OF PARADISE
uncollected stories by Scott and Zelda Fitzgerald
THE BASIL AND JOSEPHINE STORIES
edited with an introduction by Jackson R. Bryer and John Kuehl
THE PAT HOBBY STORIES
with an introduction by Arnold Gingrich
TAPS AT REVEILLE
SIX TALES OF THE JAZZ AGE AND OTHER STORIES
with an introduction by Frances Fitzgerald Smith
FLAPPERS AND PHILOSOPHERS
with an introduction by Arthur Mizener
THE STORIES OF F. SCOTT FITZGERALD
a selection of 28 stories, with an introduction by Malcolm Cowley
BABYLON REVISITED AND OTHER STORIES

STORIES AND ESSAYS

AFTERNOON OF AN AUTHOR
with an introduction and notes by Arthur Mizener
THE FITZGERALD READER
with an introduction by Arthur Mizener

LETTERS

THE LETTERS OF F. SCOTT FITZGERALD
with an introduction by Andrew Turnbull
LETTERS TO HIS DAUGHTER
with an introduction by Frances Fitzgerald Smith
DEAR SCOTT/DEAR MAX
edited by John Kuehl and Jackson Bryer

AND A COMEDY

THE VEGETABLE
with an introduction by Charles Scribner III

F. SCOTT
FITZGERALD

THE

BASIL

AND

JOSEPHINE STORIES

Edited with an Introduction by
JACKSON R. BRYER *and* JOHN KUEHL

A Scribner Classic

COLLIER BOOKS
MACMILLAN PUBLISHING COMPANY
New York

Macmillan Publishing Company
866 Third Avenue, New York, N Y 10022
Collier Macmillan Canada, Inc.

Library of Congress Cataloging-in-Publication Data
Fitzgerald, F. Scott (Francis Scott), 1896-1940.
The Basil and Josephine stories.
(A Scribner classic)
Reprint. Originally published: New York : Scribner,
1973.
I. Bryer, Jackson R.   II. Kuehl, John Richard,
     1928-   III. Title.
PS3511.I9B37   1987   813'.52   86-31703
ISBN 0-02-019870-1

First Scribner Classic/Collier Edition 1987

10   9   8   7   6   5   4   3   2   1

Printed in the United States of America

CONTENTS

Introduction

Sometime in March of 1928, when he was having great difficulty writing his fourth novel, F. Scott Fitzgerald suddenly and
quite surprisingly reached back into his childhood and began
a series of stories about his life from 1907 at age eleven in
Buffalo, New York, to 1913 at age seventeen, when he entered
Princeton University. Transparently concealing himself behind the alias Basil Duke Lee, Fitzgerald wrote eight of these
stories between March 1928 and February 1929. The *Saturday
Evening Post,* which was then paying him three thousand five
hundred dollars a story—and literally sustaining him during
the financially lean years between novels—published all eight
between April 28, 1928, and April 27, 1929.

A ninth story, whose date of composition is not clear, "That
Kind of Party," was apparently rejected by the *Post* because,

according to Arthur Mizener, "its editors did not care to believe that children of ten and eleven played kissing games." In an effort to sell this story apart from the series, Fitzgerald changed the protagonist's name to Terrence R. Tipton; but his attempts to market it were unsuccessful. The story did not appear in print until Mizener published it in the Summer 1951 issue of the *Princeton University Library Chronicle*. In his brief introductory note, Mizener indicated that the story belonged chronologically second in the Basil series. A comparison of details in the story with notes in Fitzgerald's autobiographical *Ledger*, however, unmistakably locates it as describing events of 1907, thus putting it first, and that is where we have placed it.

Between January 1930 and June 1931, with his novel *Tender Is the Night* still uncompleted, Fitzgerald wrote five stories about Basil's female counterpart, Josephine Perry. With his price now at four thousand dollars a story, the *Post* published these, starting with "First Blood" on April 5, 1930, and concluding with "Emotional Bankruptcy" on August 15, 1931. The Josephine stories take her from "just sixteen" to "a month short of eighteen."

Almost as soon as the Basil stories began to appear in print, Fitzgerald's Scribner's editor, Maxwell Perkins, expressed admiration for them. After having seen the first three, he wrote the author on June 28, 1928, that he had "read them with great interest," expressed the hope that "you will be doing some more," and asked, "Won't you have a book of them sometime?" In a similar vein, Fitzgerald's agent, Harold Ober, wrote him on August 8, 1928, after reading the first four of the group: "I think you will have to write two or three more of these stories for I shall never be satisfied until I hear more about Basil, and I think everyone who reads the stories feels the same way. They will make an exceedingly interesting book, I think." Replying to Perkins in July 1928, Fitzgerald had indicated that he did plan the series as a book, "a nice *light* novel, almost, to follow my novel in the season *immediately* after, so as not to seem in the direct line of my so-called 'work.'"

Fitzgerald toyed with this idea for the next six years, intermittently considering publishing the Basil and Josephine stories as a book in order to lower the amount of advance money he owed to Scribners, but ultimately rejecting this idea because he felt that to do so before publishing his novel would both cheat the public and also lower his reputation as a serious writer. But, in May of 1934, with *Tender Is the Night* now in print, Fitzgerald offered four plans for a fall book. Plan Two was as follows:

> The Basil Lee stories, about 60,000 words, and the Josephine stories, 37,500—with one or two stories added, the last of which will bring Basil and Josephine together—making a book of about 120,000 words under some simple title such as "Basil and Josephine." This would in some ways look like the best commercial bet because it might be taken like Tarkington's "Gentle Julia," "Penrod," etc. almost as a novel, *and the most dangerous artistically for the same reason*—for the people who buy my books might think that I was stringing them by selling them watered goods under a false name.

Perkins replied immediately:

> We are all strongly in favor of Plan #2, Basil and Josephine. The only point against it might be that of the time you would need to get it right. If you feel confident about that not being too great,—not more than six weeks say— we are very strongly for it. I see the danger of misleading the public into thinking of it as a novel in the same sense that "Tender Is the Night" is, and we ought to be sure that there is no mistake made. I think we could surely do it with safety and I believe the book would be very much liked and admired.

But Fitzgerald's enthusiasm for the idea waned and, abandoning it in favor of a selection of the short stories he had published since 1926, he outlined his reasons to Perkins on May 21: the Basil and Josephine stories were "not as good as I thought" (he had marked his tear sheets of several of them "never to be republished"); they were "full of Tarkington" and might invite disadvantageous comparisons; they "would require a tremendous amount of work and a good deal of new invention to make them presentable"; their "best phrases and ideas" had been used in *Tender Is the Night*. His principal misgiving, hinted at as early as his July 1928 letter to Perkins and reiterated in his outline of Plan Two by the words "almost a novel, *and the most dangerous artistically for the same reason*," was now explained more fully:

> . . . I have not quite enough faith in the Business Department to believe that they would not exploit it to some extent as a novel . . . and any such misconception would just ruin what position I have reconstituted with the critics. The ones who like "Tender" would be disgusted; the ones who were baffled by it or dislike my work would take full advantage to goose-pile on me. It's too damn risky and I am too old for such a chance and the penalty might be too high. What it amounts to is that if it is presented as a novel it wrecks me and if it were presented as short stories then what is the advantage of it over a better collection of short stories?

Fitzgerald's dread lest "Basil and Josephine" seem a novel is understandable. He had not produced a full-length piece of fiction since *The Great Gatsby* (1925) and he hoped *Tender Is the Night* (published on April 12, 1934) would revive his reputation for serious long fiction. By 1934, most readers knew of him only as a popular writer who contributed stories like the Basil and Josephine series to the *Post* and other mass circulation magazines. These readers might very well regard a book of Basil and Josephine as "watered goods." Fitzgerald, who regarded the story—with its hack-work connotations and its literal potboiling function in his life—as less "artistic" and "serious" than the novel, was thus understandably uneasy. When *Taps at Reveille* appeared in March 1935, it included only five Basil stories ("The Scandal Detectives," "The Freshest Boy," "He Thinks He's Wonderful," "The Captured Shadow," and

"The Perfect Life") and three from the Josephine sequence ("First Blood," "A Nice Quiet Place," and "A Woman with a Past"). Three additional Basil stories ("A Night at the Fair," "Forging Ahead," and "Basil and Cleopatra") were later reprinted by Arthur Mizener in *Afternoon of an Author* (1957).

But now that Fitzgerald's reputation as a serious novelist is more than secure, his misgivings and objections are irrelevant; and the two series deserve to appear in a single volume. They deserve this partly because Fitzgerald's assessment of "Basil and Josephine" as a novel is not so far-fetched since both sequences reflect novelistic form in the same way *Winesburg, Ohio* does. Each portrays a central character among recurrent characters undergoing a process of development dependent on time and place; and each emphasizes the role of society and sex. Each should be read sequentially. And, if we heed Fitzgerald's remark that he planned "one or two" additional stories, "the last of which will bring Basil and Josephine together," we will also wish to read them in juxtaposition.

That Fitzgerald saw at least the Basil series as a cohesive and carefully plotted unit is indicated by the presence in his papers, now at Princeton University, of a long sheet of paper on which he handwrote a plan for these stories. He has the characters arranged under headings such as "St. Paul," "school," "male," and "female." The sheet also contains his outline for the eight *Post* stories:

I	Scandal Detectives	(Age 14)	Gentleman Burglar
II	A Night at the Fair	(" 14)	Long Pants
III	The Freshest Boy	(" 15)	Fresh-New York
IV	He Thinks He's Wonderful	(" 15)	Conceit —Talking
V	The Captured Shadow	(" 15)	1st Success
VI	The Perfect Life	(" 16)	Priggishness
VII	"Forging Ahead"	(" 16)	Work
VIII	Basil and Cleopatra	(" 17)	Love

At the top of this list could be added:

That Kind of Party   (Age 11) Kissing

This plan shows that Fitzgerald designed these stories to present Basil encountering different experiences and hardships so that, in the words of critic Matthew J. Bruccoli, "he gradually comes to achieve self-control through an understanding of his own assets and liabilities of personality." A measure of his success in attaining this goal is how interdependent thematically and structurally the Basil stories are. Bruccoli has shown convincingly that each of them, except "The Captured Shadow," employs "a duplicate action structure in which Basil is involved twice in substantially the same situation." His second response to the situation often is different from his first and the reader thus gets a keener understanding of whether or not he has matured.

In "Basil and Cleopatra," for example, there are two country club scenes. In the first, Basil is completely dazzled by Minnie Bibble and crushed by her attentions to Littleboy Le Moyne. He yearns "to be older, less impressionable, less impressed." By the second country club scene, after the football game in which Basil has starred in defeating Le Moyne's Princeton freshman squad, Basil is able to handle his awareness that she has lost all feeling for him. He realizes now that there is "nothing left except to escape with his pride." The similar settings of these two scenes and the presence in both of the same three major characters (Le Moyne's drunken and love-stricken burst into the post-game dance is a gesture worthy of the Basil of earlier stories) serve to heighten the contrast between Basil's different responses. In a similar way, two parties in "That Kind of Party," two actions with Hubert in "The Scandal Detectives," two visits to the fair in "A Night at the Fair," two train rides in "The Freshest Boy," two unsuccessful encounters with girls in "He Thinks He's Wonderful," two conversations with Jobena Dorsey in "The Perfect Life," and two statements by his mother in "Forging Ahead" all serve either to re-emphasize a personality trait in Basil or a development within that personality.

The Basil stories are also linked inextricably in other ways, ways which make a reading of them in sequence obligatory. At least three major motifs or symbols run through the entire sequence. One, the gentleman burglar, which is introduced in "The Scandal Detectives" with Basil's plot against Hubert Blair, reappears in "The Freshest Boy" in Basil's dream on the train, and culminates with Basil's successful production of "The Captured Shadow." There is obviously an internal progression within the motif itself here in that, in its first two appearances, Basil either cannot bring off his scheme or merely dreams about it, whereas in its third appearance he not only brings it off—albeit as part of a play—but does so with a great deal of flair.

Similarly, the motif of athletic prowess runs through several of the stories. In the early ones, Basil admires Hubert Blair's "virtuosic athletic ability," has a second dream on the train of being sent into a close game in the last seconds, follows Yale football star Ted Fay and his girl friend to an intimate rendez-vous in a New York restaurant, and is impressed by the presence in Evelyn Beebe's living room of Andy Lockhart, golf champion and captain of the Yale freshman baseball team. Then, in two of the last three stories, Basil achieves the same sort of fulfillment of his athletic dream as he achieves with his gentleman burglar fantasy. In "The Perfect Life," he stars in a losing cause for St. Regis; and, in "Basil and Cleopatra," he realizes his fondest hopes. Sent in to quarterback the Yale freshmen against Princeton when the starting quarterback is injured, he engineers a winning drive which defeats not only Princeton but also his rival in love, Littleboy Le Moyne.

Another recurrent motif or symbol is that of the automobile and the kind of romantic promise and social prestige its possession conveys. This is introduced in "A Night at the Fair," when Basil and Riply Buckner watch enviously as Speed Paxton drives away in his Blatz Wildcat with a beautiful blonde. It reappears in "He Thinks He's Wonderful" as Margaret Torrence tells Basil that her family is going to get a car, when Basil realizes that "the great thing . . . was to own an automobile," and when, at the end of the story, he triumphantly takes Imogene Bissel for a ride in his grandfather's electric. In "The

Introduction

Perfect Life," Basil first encounters Jobena Dorsey in what he notes is the first "long, low, English town car" he has ever seen. And, finally, in "Forging Ahead," the symbol surfaces again when Minnie Bibble asks Basil to visit her in the evenings and he replies, "I haven't got a car."

Fitzgerald also uses recurrent characters to link many of the stories. Unless one reads them in sequence as a unit, the casual mention or brief appearance of a character is often meaningless. The presence of Lewis Crum in the front seat of Joe Gorman's car in "He Thinks He's Wonderful" subtly links Basil's humiliations in St. Paul to the similar experiences he has had at St. Regis in "The Freshest Boy," a story in which Crum plays a major role. Similarly, in "Basil and Cleopatra," Fitzgerald notes in passing that Basil is rooming at Yale with Brick Wales and George Dorsey. This detail is an indication of how far Basil has come in attaining his goal of social acceptance; for it was Brick Wales who took away Basil's roommate in "The Freshest Boy" and now he is rooming with him himself. And George Dorsey, of course, is a principal witness to Basil's eccentric behavior in "The Perfect Life." In "A Night at the Fair," when Elwood Leaming suggests that Basil and Riply join him for the evening, it recalls the fact that the same Elwood Leaming was the subject of one of Basil and Riply's entries in their Book of Scandal in "The Scandal Detectives." Clearly, Basil and Riply have come a long way in a year.

The recurrent appearances of two more prominent characters have even greater importance. The first of these is Hubert Blair. In both "The Scandal Detectives" and "A Night at the Fair" Basil seemingly triumphs over Hubert only to have Hubert reappear a second time and turn defeat into victory. Significantly, though, while Hubert is central to the first story, he is introduced very close to the end of "A Night at the Fair." Apparently, Fitzgerald intends that we remember Hubert from the earlier story; and he depends upon that memory for the impression that his reappearance in the second story will make. Hubert's other major appearance is in "The Captured Shadow," and the situation there parallels that in "The Scandal Detectives": both involve a drama conceived by Basil in which Riply and Bill Kampf are given parts and in which Hubert is also assigned a role which he ultimately refuses to play. But, again, the difference between the two situations is the key to Basil's development. Hubert's second refusal to play his part does not defeat Basil as the first one does; in the second instance, Hubert's defection hardly bothers Basil and the play succeeds without him.

The second major character whose successive appearances have major thematic implications is Ermine Gilberte Labouisse Bibble. Minnie Bibble first charms Basil in "He Thinks He's Wonderful." Then, in "Forging Ahead," Rhoda Sinclair casually mentions to Basil that she's heard that he thinks he's wonderful. This is the first reference to Basil's unfortunate reputation since "He Thinks He's Wonderful," and, since there have been two intervening stories, we wonder why this phrase reappears. When, about two pages later, Minnie is reintroduced, we realize that Rhoda's remark was a foreshadowing device. Minnie's return is thematically necessary because, as with Hubert, we must observe Basil's second response to a similar situation in order to see how or whether he has changed. And, almost immediately, there is a difference: as Minnie tries to get him to kiss her, he jumps to his feet "in a curious panic," thinking, he "couldn't possibly kiss her like this —right at once. It was all so different and older than a year ago." Here Basil's new dream of success, as it has been developed in "The Captured Shadow" and "Forging Ahead," has come into conflict with his old romantic dreams, which the Minnie of "He Thinks He's Wonderful" represents. By the end of "Forging Ahead," Basil is still unable to choose and his "moments of foresight alternated with those when the future was measured by a day." The opening passages of "Basil and Cleopatra" clearly express his continued fascination with Minnie. But, at the end of that story, Basil's maturation has reached a significant point. This is made clear in the very last paragraph:

> There was a flurry of premature snow in the air and the stars looked cold. Staring up at them he saw that they were his stars as always—symbols of ambition, struggle and glory. The wind blew through them, trumpeting that

high white note for which he always listened and the thin-blown clouds, stripped for battle, passed in review. The scene was of an unparalleled brightness and magnificence, and only the practiced eye of the commander saw that one star was no longer there.

A "commander" now, Basil possesses a "practiced eye" to tell him Minnie and what she stands for was just "one" of several "stars." Because the others, which signify male "ambition, struggle and glory," are still "his," unlike many Fitzgerald protagonists, Basil has transcended destructive femininity.

If this symbolic triumph is unusual in Fitzgerald's fiction, many other aspects of both series are not. One such aspect is his view of and emphasis on social class. When he reviewed *Penrod and Sam* for a 1917 issue of the *Nassau Literary Magazine*, Fitzgerald observed:

Mr. Tarkington has done what so many authors of juvenile books fail to do: he has admitted the unequaled snobbishness of boyhood and has traced the neighborhood social system which, with Penrod and Sam at the top, makes possible more than half the stories.

These words apply just as accurately to Fitzgerald's own juvenile stories; for his Basil series captures "the neighborhood social system" and the Josephine sequence "unequaled snobbishness." But Tarkington *focuses* on such matters, while Fitzgerald places them in a larger context. "Only comfortable," Basil embodies the insecure American middle class; "almost very rich," Josephine embodies the insulated American upper class. Two stories—one about each—show that their author thought class even more a psychological than an economic condition.

After Basil's mother loses several thousand dollars in "Forging Ahead," her son must earn money or attend the drab state university instead of glamorous Yale. He consults Horatio Alger's *Bound to Rise*, then seeks a job. At newspaper offices, door-keepers, office boys, and telephone girls insult him; at the Great Northern car shops, his efforts are criticized, his overalls stolen, his services terminated. As "a last resort," Basil visits great-uncle Benjamin Reilly, who insinuates, "Your mother can't afford to send you, eh?" and "Spent all her money?" Working for the Reilly Wholesale Drug Company means becoming an unappealing cousin's constant companion and seeing little of the desirable Minnie Bibble. Though "Forging Ahead" ends on a happy note with his mother "solvent" and Basil "engaged" to Minnie, he has been spiritually damaged by his precarious social position.

"A Snobbish Story" bears a double-edged ironic title, since soon after its poor artist expresses contempt for the wealthy, their representative, Josephine, flees the sordidness he represents. Having unceremoniously approached her during the Lake Forest tennis tournament, handsome, shabby reporter-turned-playwright John Boynton Bailey takes her to the little theater which is considering his play, *Race Riot*. She finds out he is married, but accepts a part. Bailey meets Mr. Perry and the latter offers financial support for the play, only to have the local constable interrupt with the news that Bailey's wife has tried to kill herself. Josephine quickly abandons him, deciding "That any value she might have was in the immediate, shimmering present—and thus . . . she threw in her lot with the rich and powerful of this world forever."

Like a good deal of Fitzgerald's fiction, the Basil and Josephine stories are about dominating life through sexual magnetism. If, like Tarkington, Fitzgerald portrayed "snobbishness" and "the neighborhood social system" in his juvenile stories, he also added an important element which Tarkington had left out, the adolescent's growing awareness of sex and its power. Usually in Fitzgerald's fiction, the theme of sexual magnetism involves a victorious upper-class female (*femme fatale*) and a vanquished middle-class male (*homme manqué*), who define each other as if they were alter egos. With Basil and Josephine, however, the rejecter fails and the rejected succeeds because unambitious Josephine functions *exclusively* among men— "the only thing she cared about in the world was being in love and being with the person she currently loved"—while ambitious Basil *intermittently* manages to transcend the feminine universe. This is seen most clearly in the final passage from

"Basil and Cleopatra" quoted above. Since Josephine's conquests produce ultimate defeat and Basil's seeming defeats lead to potential triumph, the juxtaposition of the two sequences is ironic.

If the development within the Basil series is toward an increasing maturity, with Josephine it is more a matter of awareness. And, if the Basil stories are linked by similar scenes which show Basil often responding differently, the Josephine sequence features the central character going through the same basic situation five times, with the same results on all but one occasion. The only difference which occurs is in her deepening understanding of what has happened. In each story, Josephine ignores men who desire her and instead pursues a handsome glamorous outsider whom she ultimately wins, only to discover that she doesn't want him after all. It is in her comprehension of why she doesn't want him that the development within the series occurs. The only exception to this pattern is "A Woman with a Past," where "for the first time in her life" she tries for a man, Dudley Knowleton, and fails. In this story and in the last one in the sequence, "Emotional Bankruptcy," Josephine evidences considerable understanding of her dilemma. From Dudley Knowleton, she learns, "There were two kinds of men, those you played with and those you might marry." This leads to her "first mature thought": "One mustn't run through people, and, for the sake of a romantic half-hour, trade a possibility that might develop."

But the final recognition doesn't take place until "Emotional Bankruptcy." After she has experienced nothing when she repeats the same old pattern and runs through several men on a Princeton weekend, Josephine meets the perfect man, Edward Dicer, only to discover that even *his* kisses are meaningless. "What have I done? What have I done?" she wails, realizing that "One cannot both spend and have," and that "The love of her life had come by, and looking in her empty basket, she had found not a flower left for him—not one."

The title of this last story, defined in Josephine's cry of dismay, could well describe the Josephine series as a whole; but because only the first three of the sequence were published in *Taps at Reveille*, readers of that volume are unable to view the important culmination of Josephine's gradual disintegration. In a similar way, the Basil series is certainly thematically incomplete without "Forging Ahead" and "Basil and Cleopatra," both omitted from *Taps at Reveille.* And emotional bankruptcy, which is introduced explicitly in the Josephine series for the first time in Fitzgerald's work, becomes, as Arthur Mizener notes, "the most pervasive idea he ever had." It is essential to an understanding of Dick Diver in *Tender Is the Night* and Monroe Stahr in *The Last Tycoon;* and "The Crackup" essays are generally conceded to be an autobiographical expression of the same concept.

Juxtaposing the two sequences also shows that, while superficially romantic Josephine lives in "the immediate, shimmering present," authentically romantic Basil lives in "the future, always glowing like a comfortable beacon." This future, which holds "achievement and power," includes much besides women for "fiercely competitive" Basil, whose "fantastic ambition" embraces being "a great athlete, popular, brilliant and always happy." To attain such goals, he must enter "the fabled world":

> Yale was the faraway East, that he had loved with a vast nostalgia since he had first read books about great cities. Beyond the dreary railroad stations of Chicago and the night fires of Pittsburgh, back in the old states, something went on that made his heart beat fast with excitement. He was attuned to the vast, breathless bustle of New York, to the metropolitan days and nights that were tense as singing wires. Nothing needed to be imagined there, for it was all the very stuff of romance—life was as vivid and satisfactory as in books and dreams.

As with Nick and Gatsby, Basil is Fitzgerald's "Young Man from the Provinces" come East, in his case to begin his conquest of "the successive worlds of school, college and New York."

Without any future, without any destiny, Josephine is also without moral sense. "A Nice Quiet Place" concludes when she compromises her sister's groom just before the wedding as an excuse to return to Island Farms and Sonny Dorrance. Basil behaves badly too, but he invariably suffers private remorse. In "That Kind of Party," where he commits "insolence and forgery" and assaults "both the crippled and the blind," he chants several "Now I lay mes" and "Our Fathers"; in "The Scandal Detectives," after waylaying Hubert Blair, he feels "morally alone"; and in "The Captured Shadow," when he exposes little Ham Beebe to the mumps for selfish private reasons, he cannot savor his public success.

Although Josephine has some theatrical experience (midsummer vaudeville) and seeks more (*Race Riot*), she is even less the prospective artist than the confirmed moralist. Basil embodies both. His imagination, like his conscience, derives from his special middle-class background. Apparently fatherless after "That Kind of Party," and spoiled by a mother who enjoys a prominent role throughout, he grows egotistical, as such titles as "The Freshest Boy" and "He Thinks He's Wonderful" and such epithets as "conceited," "Bossy," "ultraconfident," and "stuck-up" indicate. Basil, the egotist, manipulates things with considerable skill, organizing a party, terrorizing a friend, eluding a date, directing a play, avoiding a dance, preventing a marriage, etc. However, since egotism and its concomitant manipulation have often made him unpopular and penitent, he finally realizes "others had wills as strong as his, and more power." What he does not realize, but what the stories imply, is that egotism become a sense of self and manipulation become a sense of design are creative tools. Indeed, Basil has already employed them when composing The Book of Scandal, which records "deviations from rectitude on the part of . . . fellow citizens," and "The Captured Shadow" or "A Melodramatic Farce in Three Acts." While Josephine will probably remain a mere narcissistic schemer, Basil could well metamorphose into a professional playwright. His series, then, could represent Fitzgerald's "Portrait of the Artist as a Young Man."

Josephine, whose name suggests "empress," is the prototypical *femme fatale*, and, except for the *homme manqué*, this vampiric destroyer was the most important figure Fitzgerald ever drew. She germinated in prep-school and college stories to appear over and over again in the later work. Though always rendered believable by a creator who once observed, "I am half feminine—at least my mind is. . . . Even my feminine characters are feminine Scott Fitzgeralds," her psychological make-up exhibits less complexity than that of the *homme manqué*. She has an independent existence, yet she functions primarily as a foil, the persistent and powerful barrier to his success. Thus, Josephine, like other fatal women, seems superficial when compared with Basil, whose middle name "Duke" also conveys nobility. He emerges triumphant, escaping the fate of Amory Blaine, Anthony Patch, Jay Gatsby, Dick Diver, and Monroe Stahr, all victimized by females. Why? Because Basil possesses the "vitality" this passage from "He Thinks He's Wonderful" claims for him:

> He lay on his bed, baffled, mistaken, miserable but not beaten. Time after time, the same vitality that had led his spirit to a scourging made him able to shake off the blood like water not to forget, but to carry his wounds with him to new disasters and new atonements—toward his unknown destiny.

Would even "vitality" have been enough, however, had Basil, an aristocrat of the world of spirit, and Josephine, an aristocrat of the world of matter, come "together" as Plan Two described? Perhaps the answer lies in the relationship between their real-life models, Scott Fitzgerald and Ginevra King.

Fitzgerald's *Ledger* outlines his college romance with her through a series of short statements whose very matter-of-factness lends them poignancy: January 1915: "Met Ginevra"; June: "Ritz, Nobody Home and Midnight Folie with Ginevra. . . . Deering: I'm going to take Ginevra home in my electric"; August: "No news from Ginevra"; October: "Dinner with Ginevra in Waterbury"; November: "Letters to G.K."; February 1916: "Long letters to Ginevra"; March: "Ginevra fired from school"; April: "Ginevra & Living on the train. A fascinating story"; August: "Lake Forrest. Peg Carry. Petting Party. Ginevra. Party"; November: "Ginevra and Margaret Cary to Yale game"; January 1917: "Final break with Ginevra"; June:

Ginevra engaged?"; September: "Oh Ginevra"; July 1918: "Zelda. . . . Ginevra married."

When Fitzgerald met her, Miss King was sixteen, a junior at Westover, and already popular with the Ivy League boys. Mizener has summed up their relationship:

> For Ginevra, he became for a time the most important of her many conquests. As she said herself many years later, ". . . at this time I was definitely out for quantity not quality in beaux, and, although Scotty was top man, I still wasn't serious enough not to want plenty of other attention!" . . . To the end of his life he kept every letter she ever wrote him (he had them typed up and bound; they run to 227 pages). Born and brought up in the best circumstances in Chicago and Lake Forest, Ginevra moved for him in a golden haze.

The duration and depth of Fitzgerald's feelings toward the girl are shown in a remark from a letter of November 9, 1938, to Frances Turnbull: "In *This Side of Paradise* I wrote about a love affair that was still bleeding as fresh as the skin wound on a haemophile." That he returned to this romance in the Josephine series is confirmed by Ginevra King Pirie's observation, in a letter to Mizener: "I was too thoughtless in those days & too much in love with love to think of consequences. These things he has emphasized—and over-emphasized in the Josephine stories, but it is only fair to say I asked for some of them."

Had Basil met Josephine it is probable she would have undermined his "vitality," but not simply because Ginevra undermined Fitzgerald's. For Basil, resembling the prototypical *homme manqué*, combines a particular flaw *of* middle-class American society with general superiority *to* that society. This flaw involves sex, the disastrous attraction toward fickle rich girls like Gladys Van Schellinger, another of the important recurrent characters in the Basil series, whose "vague unexciting quality . . . was more than compensated for by her exquisite delicacy, the fine luxury of her life." Yet, though he contains the seeds of failure, Basil emerges triumphant from the nine tales Fitzgerald actually told. And, again, this pattern for the sequence as a whole is reflected in many of the individual stories. Beginning in "That Kind of Party" and continuing through such others as "The Scandal Detectives," "He Thinks He's Wonderful," and "The Perfect Life," Basil does superficially awful things or loses a girl but in the end is wiser or with an even better girl or both.

If Josephine is based on Ginevra King, Basil and the Basil series have an even firmer basis in Fitzgerald's own boyhood experiences. One has only to glance at the notes in the *Ledger* to see how very closely he followed his self-model. If we look at the page headed "Ten Years Old," we find three details which he transferred intact into "That Kind of Party": September 1906—"He told Miss McGraw at Narden's that Mexico City was *not* the capitol of Central America"; January 1907—"He went to the charity ball and to the Mack's party at the country club where he wore his juvenile tuxedo and was chased by a cripple named Sears McGraw whom he loathes to this day"; June 1907—"collected cigar bands." The central incident of "The Scandal Detectives" is suggested by two entries about his fourteenth year: March 1911—"The founding of The Scandal Detectives"; and April 1911—"The Scandal detectives go after Reuben." The events of "A Night at the Fair" originated in an incident recorded for September 1911: "Attended state fair and took chicken on roller coaster." Other entries which certainly formed the basis for fictional material include an October 1911 entry, "Bill Agar says I'm Fresh," two July 1912 notations, "Began to feel lack of automobile" and "growing unpopular," and an August 1912 reference, "Wrote and gave The Captured Shadow." But such extensive autobiographical connections as these and the others which previous commentators have noted —e.g., the fictional Riply Buckner, Hubert Blair, and Bill Kampf are modeled after the real Cecil Read, Reuben Warner, and Paul Ballion—while interesting for what the stories reveal about their author's adolescent years, are nonetheless less significant than the control Fitzgerald exercises over them.

Many American critics have agreed that Fitzgerald's ability to participate in a story and to analyze that participation simultaneously gives his work maturity and power. This "double vision," best illustrated by *The Great Gatsby*, where he acts as

Introduction

Gatsby and observes as Nick, characterizes the Basil and Josephine stories. The fact that, as we have seen, these stories are so closely based on his own adolescent experiences, however, makes the use of the "double vision" here of even more note than in *Gatsby*. Thus, we find Fitzgerald softening a basically condemnatory attitude toward Josephine when in "First Blood," we learn, "There would have been no use saying the simple truth—that she could not help what she had done, that great beauty has a need, almost an obligation of trying itself, that her ample cup of emotion had spilled over on its own accord, and it was an accident that it had destroyed [Anthony Harker] and not her." In the Basil series, Fitzgerald often uses irony to undercut his hero's more idealistically romantic moments. In "A Night at the Fair," when it appears that Basil's new long trousers will not arrive in time for him to go to the fair, he feels that "all his life . . . he would look back with infinite regret upon that irretrievable hour"; but Fitzgerald adds quickly, "Like most of us, he was unable to perceive that he would have any desires in the future equivalent to those that possessed him now."

Another kind of authorial intrusion in the Basil series not only shows Fitzgerald subtly controlling his material but also shows him evoking a time and place, what it was like to grow up in America in the decade before World War I. Sometimes he does this with direct statements, as in this marvelously witty passage on the dance crazes of the day:

> Only in certain Paris restaurants where the Argentines step untiringly through their native coils does anything survive of the dance craze as it existed just before the war. At that time it was not an accompaniment to drinking or love-making or hailing in the dawn—it was an end in itself. Sedentary stockbrokers, grandmothers of sixty, Confederate veterans, venerable statesmen and scientists, sufferers from locomotor ataxia, wanted not only to dance but to dance beautifully. Fantastic ambitions bloomed in hitherto sober breasts, violent exhibitionism cropped out in families modest for generations. Nonentities with long legs became famous overnight, and there

were rendezvous where they could renew the dance, if they wished, next morning. Because of a neat glide or an awkward stumble careers were determined and engagements were made or broken, while the tall Englishman and the girl in the Dutch cap called the tune.

And sometimes he does it within the framework of the story itself, by the manner in which he describes the actions of a character, as in this account of Basil's second shave:

> For the second time in his life he shaved, completing the operation by cutting a short straight line under his nose. It bled profusely, but on the advice of Hilda, the maid, he finally stanched the flow with little pieces of toilet paper. Quite a number of pieces were necessary; so, in order to facilitate breathing, he trimmed it down with a scissors, and with this somewhat awkward mustache of paper and gore clinging to his upper lip, wandered impatiently around the house.
>
> At six he began working on it again, soaking off the tissue paper and dabbing at the persistently freshening crimson line. It dried at length, but when he rashly hailed his mother it opened once more and the tissue paper was called back into play.

These are not simply evocations of a time and place; they also contain in their carefully chosen wording Fitzgerald's mixture of nostalgia and ironic humor, a mixture which could well be used to describe the tone of the Basil and Josephine stories. Older and wiser now in middle age than he had been when he wrote about his college years in *This Side of Paradise* (1920), Fitzgerald could recapture his youth and view it with ironic detachment as well. The stories contain all the remembered details of the era. Basil's "favorite clothes" are "white duck knickerbockers, pepper-and-salt Norfolk jacket, a Belmont collar and a gray knitted tie." He owns "eight color reproductions of Harrison Fisher girls" and knows about Horatio Alger, Weber and Fields, and James J. Hill. Josephine reads Alan Seeger, *Smart Set,* and *Snappy Stories.* Popular songs of the day—"By the Light of the Silvery Moon," "Oh, My Darling Clementine," "Peg of My Heart," "On Moonlight Bay," "Oh, You Beautiful Doll," and "Chinatown"—and dances like the tango, the Castle Walk, and the maxixe, permeate their lives. But the author is not so immersed in reminiscence as not to be able to step back and observe that Basil is "sitting with disarming quiet upon the still unhatched eggs of the mid-twentieth century" and that Josephine is "an unconscious pioneer of the generation that was destined to 'get out of hand.'"

These are not uniformly excellent short stories, especially those in the Josephine series, but they benefit enormously from being read as two series and as ironically juxtaposed sequences. Presented together and fully for the first time, "The Basil and Josephine Stories" convey what it was like growing up way back then and there; and they do so with all the skill that a mature and fully developed literary artist could bring to bear on his material.

Textual Note and Acknowledgments

For the eight stories which appeared in *Taps at Reveille*—
"The Scandal Detectives," "The Freshest Boy," "He Thinks
He's Wonderful," "The Captured Shadow," "The Perfect
Life," "First Blood," "A Nice Quiet Place," and "A Woman
with a Past"—we have used the texts in the 1935 Scribner's
edition. In two instances, on page 93 in "He Thinks He's Wonderful," and on page 192 in "First Blood," we have rejected
readings from this edition as being confusing and have substituted for these readings from the original *Saturday Evening
Post* texts of the stories. In the first instance, we have substituted "For all the candor of this smile, its effect, because of
the special contours of Minnie's face and independent of her
mood, was of sparkling invitation" for "For all the candor of
this smile, the effect—because of the special contours of Min-

nie's face and independent of her mood—was sparkling invitation." In "First Blood," we have used the *Post* reading "she waited as he burned darkly," instead of the later "she wailed as he burned darkly."

In a few instances also, we have corrected what we felt were obvious typographical errors in the texts of stories from the 1935 edition of *Taps at Reveille.* These are as follows: p. 75, line 2—she appears as She in 1935 edition; p. 88, line 28—Imogene appears as Imagine in 1935 edition; p. 102, line 20—strawberries appears as straw in 1935 edition; p. 104, line 6—imbibing appears as imbiding in 1935 edition; p. 105, line 4—striking appears as strikeing in 1935 edition; p. 128, line 6—George appears as Keorge in 1935 edition; p. 208, line 8—lie appears as die in 1935 edition; p. 221, line 28—Josephine appears as Rosemary in 1935 edition; p. 242, line 15—there is no period after heart in 1935 edition. We have not corrected mistakes which we felt were due to Fitzgerald's poor spelling.

For "A Night at the Fair," "Forging Ahead," "Basil and Cleopatra," "A Snobbish Story," and "Emotional Bankruptcy," we have used the texts of the *Post* printings, the last Fitzgerald saw in print, and have made no silent corrections or emendations at all. In the case of "That Kind of Party," all that apparently survives is a carbon of Fitzgerald's typescript, corrected in Fitzgerald's hand (one very significant correction occurs when Fitzgerald corrects Basil to read Terrence). Due to the kind cooperation of Professor Arthur Mizener, we have been able to obtain a copy of this carbon and the text we have used is that text, again without any corrections or emendations.

Besides Professor Mizener, we wish to acknowledge the assistance and cooperation of Alexander Clark and Wanda Randall of the Princeton University Library, Mrs. Joanne Giza, and Professor Matthew J. Bruccoli. Professor Bruccoli was most helpful in putting at our disposal both his forthcoming edition of *F. Scott Fitzgerald's Ledger* (Washington, D.C.: NCR Editions, 1972) and a copy of his unpublished thesis, " 'A Handful, Lying Loose'—A Study of F. Scott Fitzgerald's Basil Duke Lee Stories" (University of Virginia, 1955). The latter remains the best piece of criticism done to date on the Basil series; and we have drawn heavily upon Professor Bruccoli's insights in our

Introduction. Other material relating to the Basil and Josephine stories which we have found useful includes Constance Drake's article, "Josephine and Emotional Bankruptcy," in the 1969 *Fitzgerald/Hemingway Annual;* John A. Higgins' *F. Scott Fitzgerald—A Study of the Stories* (Jamaica, N.Y.: St. John's University Press, 1971); Kenneth Eble's *F. Scott Fitzgerald* (New York: Twayne, 1963); Robert J. Sklar's *F. Scott Fitzgerald —The Last Laöcoon* (New York: Oxford University Press, 1967); and Matthew J. Bruccoli and Jennifer McCabe Atkinson's edition of the Fitzgerald-Ober correspondence, *As Ever, Scott Fitz-* (Philadelphia: J.B. Lippincott, 1972).

J.R.B. and J.K.

College Park, Md.
Princeton, N.J.
November 20, 1972

THE
BASIL AND JOSEPHINE
STORIES

I. *Basil*

That Kind of Party

I

After the party was over a top-lofty Stevens Duryea and two 1909 Maxwells waited with a single victoria at the curb—the boys watched as the Stevens filled with a jovial load of little girls and roared away. Then they strung down the street in threes and fours, some of them riotous, others silent and thoughtful. Even for the always surprised ages of ten and eleven when the processes of assimilation race hard to keep abreast of life, it had been a notable afternoon.

So thought Terrence R. Tipton, by occupation actor, athlete, scholar, philatelist and collector of cigar bands. He was so exalted that all his life he would remember vividly coming out of the house, the feel of the spring evening, the way that Dolly

Bartlett walked to the auto and looked back at him, pert exultant and glowing. What he felt was like fright—appropriately enough for one of the major compulsions had just taken its place in his life. Fool for love was Terrence from now, and not just at a distance but as one who had been summoned and embraced, one who had tasted with a piercing delight and had become an addict within an hour. Two questions were in his mind as he approached his house—how long had this been going on, and when was he liable to encounter it again?

His mother greeted a rather pale, tow-headed little boy with the greenest of eyes and thin keen features. How was he? He was all right. Did he have a good time at the Gilrays'? It was all right. Would he tell her about it? There was nothing to tell.

"Wouldn't you like to have a party, Terrence?" she suggested. "You've been to so many."

"No, I wouldn't, Mother."

"Just think—ten boys and ten little girls, and ice-cream and cake and games."

"What games?" he asked, not faintly considering a party but from reflex action to the word.

"Oh, euchre or hearts or authors."

"They don't have that."

"What do they have?"

"Oh, they just fool around. But I don't want to have a party."

Yet suddenly the patent disadvantages of having girls in his own house and bringing into contact the worlds within and without, like indelicately tearing down the front wall—were challenged by his desire to be close to Dolly Bartlett again.

"Could we just be alone without anybody around?" he asked.

"Why, I wouldn't bother you," said Mrs. Tipton. "I'd simply get things started, then leave you."

"That's the way they all do." But Terrence remembered that several ladies had been there all afternoon, and it would be absolutely unthinkable if his mother were anywhere at hand.

At dinner the subject came up again.

"Tell Father what you did at the Gilrays'," his mother said. "You must remember."

"Of course I do, but ——"

"I'm beginning to think you played kissing games," Mr. Tipton guessed casually.

"Oh, they had a crazy game they called Clap-in-and-clap-out," said Terrence indiscreetly.

"What's that?"

"Well, all the boys go out and they say somebody has a letter. No, that's post-office. Anyhow they have to come in and guess who sent for them." Hating himself for the disloyalty to the great experience, he tried to end with: "—and then they kneel down and if he's wrong they clap him out of the room. Can I have some more gravy please?"

"But what if he's right?"

"Oh, he's supposed to hug them," Terrence mumbled. It sounded so shameful—it had been so lovely.

"All of them?"

"No, only one."

"So that's the kind of party you wanted," said his mother, somewhat shocked. "Oh Terrence."

"I did not," he protested, "I didn't say I wanted that."

"But you didn't want me to be there."

"I've met Gilray downtown," said Mr. Tipton. "A rather ordinary fellow from upstate."

This sniffishness toward a diversion that had been popular in Washington's day at Mount Vernon was the urban attitude toward the folkways of rural America. As Mr. Tipton intended, it had an effect on Terrence, but not the effect counted on. It caused Terrence, who suddenly needed a pliable collaborator, to decide upon a boy named Joe Shoonover, whose family were newcomers in the city. He bicycled over to Joe's house immediately after dinner.

His proposition was that Joe ought to give a party right away and, instead of having just a few kissing games, have them steadily all afternoon, scarcely pausing for a bite to eat. Terrence painted the orgy in brutal but glowing colors:

"Of course you can have Gladys. And then when you get tired of her you can ask for Kitty or anybody you want, and they'll ask for you too. Oh, it'll be wonderful!"

"Supposing somebody else asked for Dolly Bartlett."

"Oh, don't be a poor fool."

"I'll bet you'd just go jump in the lake and drown yourself."

"I would not."

"You would too."

This was poignant talk but there was the practical matter of asking Mrs. Shoonover. Terrence waited outside in the dusk till Joe returned.

"Mother says all right."

"Say, she won't care what we do, will she?"

"Why should she?" asked Joe innocently, "I told her about it this afternoon and she just laughed."

Terrence's schooling was at Mrs. Cary's Academy, where he idled through interminable dull grey hours. He guessed that there was little to learn there and his resentment frequently broke forth in insolence, but on the morning of Joe Shoonover's party he was simply a quiet lunatic at his desk, asking only to be undisturbed.

"So the capitol of America is Washington," said Miss Cole, "and the capitol of Canada is Ottawa—and the capitol of Central America——"

"—is Mexico City," someone guessed.

"Hasn't any," said Terrence absently.

"Oh, it must have a capitol," said Miss Cole looking at her map.

"Well, it doesn't happen to have one."

"That'll do, Terrence. Put down Mexico City for the capitol of Central America. Now that leaves South America."

Terrence sighed.

"There's no use teaching us wrong," he suggested.

Ten minutes later, somewhat frightened, he reported to the principal's office where all the forces of injustice were confusingly arrayed against him.

"What you think doesn't matter," said Mrs. Cary. "Miss Cole is your teacher and you were impertinent. Your parents would want to hear about it."

He was glad his father was away, but if Mrs. Cary telephoned, his mother would quite possibly keep him home from the party. With this wretched fate hanging over him he left the school gate at noon and was assailed by the voice of Albert Moore, son of his mother's best friend, and thus a likely enemy.

Albert enlarged upon the visit to the principal and the probable consequences at home. Terrence thereupon remarked that Albert, due to his spectacles, possessed four visual organs. Albert retorted as to Terrence's pretention to universal wisdom. Brusque references to terrified felines and huge paranoiacs enlivened the conversation and presently there was violent weaving and waving during which Terrence quite accidentally butted into Albert's nose. Blood flowed—Albert howled with anguish and terror, believing that his life blood was dripping down over his yellow tie. Terrence started away, stopped, pulled out his handkerchief and threw it toward Albert as a literal sop, then resumed his departure from the horrid scene, up back alleys and over fences, running from his crime. Half an hour later he appeared at Joe Shoonover's back door and had the cook announce him.

"What's the matter?" asked Joe.

"I didn't go home. I had a fight with Albert Moore."

"Gosh. Did he take off his glasses?"

"No, why?"

"It's a penitentiary offense to hit anybody with glasses. Say, I've got to finish lunch."

Terrence sat wretchedly on a box in the alley until Joe appeared, with news appropriate to a darkening world.

"I don't know about the kissing games," he said. "Mother said it was silly."

With difficulty Terrence wrested his mind from the spectre of reform school.

"I wish she'd get sick," he said absently.

"Don't you say that about my mother."

"I mean I wish her sister would get sick," he corrected himself. "Then she couldn't come to the party."

"I wish that too," reflected Joe. "Not very sick though."

"Why don't you call her up and tell her her sister is sick."

"She lives in Tonawanda. She'd send a telegram—she did once."

"Let's go ask Fats Palmer about a telegram."

Fats Palmer, son of the block's janitor, was a messenger boy, several years older than themselves, a cigarette smoker and a blasphemer. He refused to deliver a forged telegram because he might lose his job but for a quarter he would furnish a blank and get one of his small sisters to deliver it. Cash down in advance.

"I think I can get it," said Terrence thoughtfully.

They waited for him outside an apartment house a few squares away. He was gone ten minutes—when he came out he wore a fatigued expression and after showing a quarter in his palm sat on the curbstone for a moment, his mouth tightly shut, and waved them silent.

"Who gave it to you, Terrence?"

"My aunt," he muttered faintly, and then: "It was an egg."

"What egg?"

"Raw egg."

"Did you sell some eggs?" demanded Fats Palmer. "Say, I know where you can get eggs——"

Terrence groaned.

"I had to eat it raw. She's a health fiend."

"Why, that's the easiest money I ever heard of," said Fat, "I've sucked eggs——"

"Don't!" begged Terrence, but it was too late. That was an egg without therapeutic value—an egg sacrificed for love.

II

This is the telegram Terrence wrote:

> *Am sick but not so badly could you come at once please*
> *Your loving sister*

By four o'clock Terrence still knew academically that he had a family but they lived a long way off in a distant past. He knew also that he had sinned, and for a time he had walked an alley saying "Now I lay me's" over and over for worldly mercy in the matter of Albert Moore's spectacles. The rest could wait until he was found out, preferably after death.

Four o'clock found him with Joe in the Shoonover's pantry where they had chosen to pass the last half hour, deriving a sense of protection from the servants' presence in the kitchen. Mrs. Shoonover had gone, the guests were due—and as at a signal agreed upon the doorbell and the phone pealed out together.

"There they are," Joe whispered.

"If it's my family," said Terrence hoarsely, "tell them I'm not here."

"It's not your family—it's the people for the party."

"The phone I mean."

"You'd better answer it." Joe opened the door to the kitchen, "Didn't you hear the doorbell, Irma?"

"There's cake dough on my hands and Essie's too. You go Joe."

"No, I certainly will not."

"Then they'll have to wait. Can't you two boys walk?"

Once again the double summons, emphatic and alarming rang through the house.

"Joe, you got to tell my family I'm not here," said Terrence tensely. "*I* can't say I'm not here, can I? It'll only take a minute to tell them. Just say I'm not here."

"We've got to go to the door. Do you want all the people to go home?"

"No, I don't. But you simply got to——"

Irma came out of the kitchen wiping her hands.

"My sakes alive," she said, "why don't you tend the door before the children get away?"

They both talked at once, utterly confused. Irma broke the deadlock by picking up the phone.

"Hello," she said. "Keep quiet Terrence, I can't hear. Hello —hello. . . . Nobody's on that phone now. You better brush your hair, Terrence—and look at your hands!"

Terrence rushed for the sink and worked hastily with the kitchen soap.

"Where's a comb?" he yelled. "Joe, where's your comb?"

"Upstairs, of course."

Still wet Terrence dashed up the back stairs, realizing only at the mirror that he looked exactly like a boy who had spent most of the day in the alley. Hurriedly he dug for a clean shirt of Joe's; as he buttoned it a wail floated up the front stairs——

"Terrence, they've gone. There's nobody at the door— they've gone home."

7

Overwhelmed the boys rushed out on the porch. Far down the street two small figures receded. Cupping their hands Terrence and Joe shouted. The figures stopped, turned around— then suddenly they were joined by other figures, a lot of figures: a victoria drove around the corner and clopped up to the house. The party had begun.

At the sight of Dolly Bartlett Terrence's heart rose chokingly and he wanted to be away. She was not anyone he knew, certainly not the girl about whom he put his arms a week ago. He stared as at a spectre. He had never known what she looked like, perceiving her almost as an essence of time and weather —if there was frost and elation in the air she was frost and elation, if there was a mystery in yellow windows on a summer night she was that mystery, if there was music that could inspire or sadden or excite she was that music, she was "Red Wing" and "Alice Where art thou going?" and the "Light of the Silvery Moon."

To cooler observers Dolly's hair was child's gold in knotted pigtails, her face was as regular and as cute as a kitten's and her legs were neatly crossed at the ankles or dangled helplessly from a chair. She was so complete at ten, so confident and alive that she was many boys' girl—a precocious mistress of the long look, the sustained smile, the private voice and the delicate touch, devices of the generations.

With the other guests Dolly looked about for the hostess and finding none infiltrated into the drawing room to stand about whispering and laughing in nervous chorus. The boys also grouped for protection, save two unselfconscious minims of eight who took advantage of their elders' shyness to show off, with dashings about and raucous laughter. Minutes passed and nothing happened; Joe and Terrence communicated in hissing whispers, their lips scarcely moving.

"You ought to start it," muttered Terrence.

"You start it. It was your scheme."

"It's your party, and we might just as well go home as stand around here all afternoon. Why don't you just say we're going to play it and then choose somebody to go out of the room."

Joe stared at him incredulously.

"Big chance! Let's get one of the girls to start it. You ask Dolly."

"I will not."

"How about Martha Robbie?"

Martha was a tomboy who had no terrors for them, and no charm; it was like asking a sister. They took her aside.

"Martha, look, would you tell the girls that we're going to play post-office?"

Martha drew herself away in a violent manner.

"Why, i certainly will not," she cried sternly. "I most certainly won't do any such thing."

To prove it she ran back to the girls and set about telling them.

"Dolly, what do you think Terrence asked me. He wanted to——"

"Shut *up!*" Terrence begged her.

"——play post-"

"Shut up! We didn't want anything of the sort."

There was an arrival. Up the veranda steps came a wheel chair, hoisted by a chauffeur, and in it sat Carpenter Moore, elder brother of that Albert Moore from whom Terrence had drawn blood this morning. Once inside Carpenter dismissed the chauffeur and rolled himself deftly into the party looking about him arrogantly. His handicap had made him a tyrant and fostered a singular bad temper.

"Greetings and salutations, everybody," he said. "How are you, Joe, boy?"

In a minute his eye fell on Terrence, and changing the direction of his chair he rolled up beside him.

"You hit my brother on the nose," he said in a lowered voice. "You wait till my mother sees your father."

His expression changed; he laughed and struck Terrence as if playfully with his cane.

"Well, what are you doing around here? Everybody looks as if their cat just died."

"Terrence wants to play Clap-in-and-clap-out."

"Not me," denied Terrence, and somewhat rashly added, "Joe wanted to play it. It's his party."

"I did not," said Joe heatedly. "Terrence did."

"Where's your mother?" Carpenter asked Joe. "Does she know about this?"

Joe tried to extricate himself from the menace.

"She doesn't care—I mean she said we could play anything we wanted."

Carpenter scoffed.

"I'll bet she didn't. And I'll bet most of the parents here wouldn't let them play that disgusting stuff."

"I just thought if there was nothing else to do——" he said feebly.

"You did, did you?" cried Carpenter. "Well just answer me this—haven't you ever been to a party before?"

"I've been to——"

"Just answer me this—if you've ever been to any parties before—which I doubt, which I very seriously doubt—you know what people do. All except the ones who don't behave like a gentleman."

"Oh, I wish you'd go jump in the lake."

There was a shocked silence, for since Carpenter was crippled from the waist down and could not jump even in a hypothetical lake, it fell on every ear like a taunt. Carpenter raised his cane, and then lowered it, as Mrs. Schoonover came into the room.

"What are you playing?" she asked mildly, "Clap-in-and-clap-out?"

III

Carpenter's stick descended to his lap. But he was by no means the most confused—Joe and Terrence had assumed that the telegram had taken effect, and now they could only suppose that Mrs. Schoonover had detected the ruse and come back. But there was no sign of wrath or perturbation on her face.

Carpenter recovered himself quickly.

"Yes, we were, Mrs. Schoonover. We were just beginning. Terrence is 'It.'"

"I've forgotten how," said Mrs. Schoonover simply, "but isn't someone supposed to play the piano? I can do that anyhow."

"That's fine," exclaimed Carpenter. "Now Terrence has to take a pillow and go into the hall."

"I don't want to," said Terrence quickly suspecting a trap. "Somebody else be It."

"You're It," Carpenter insisted fiercely. "Now we'll push all the sofas and chairs into a row."

Among the few who disliked the turn of affairs was Dolly Bartlett. She had been constructed with great cunning and startling intent for the purpose of arousing emotion and all her mechanism winced at the afternoon's rebuff. She felt cheated and disappointed, but there was little she could do save wait for some male to assert himself. Whoever this might be something in Dolly would eagerly respond and she kept hoping it would be Terrence, who in the role of lone wolf possessed a romantic appeal for her. She took her place in the row with ill will while Mrs. Schoonover at the piano began to play "Every Little Movement has a Meaning all its Own."

When Terrence had been urged forcibly into the hall Carpenter Moore explained his plan. The fact that he himself had never participated in such games did not keep him from knowing the rules, but what he proposed was unorthodox.

"We'll say some girl has a message for Terrence, but that girl won't be anybody but the girl next to you, see? So whoever he kneels to or bows to we'll just say it isn't her, because we're thinking of the girl next to her, understand?" He raised his voice, "Come in, Terrence!"

There was no response and looking into the hall they found that Terrence had disappeared. He had not gone out either door and they scattered through the house searching, into the kitchen up the stairs and in the attic. Only Carpenter remained in the hall poking tentatively at a row of coats in a closet. Suddenly his chair was seized from behind and propelled quickly into the closet. A key turned in the lock.

For a moment Terrence stood in silent triumph. Dolly Bartlett, coming downstairs, brightened at the sight of his dusty, truculent face.

"Terrence, where were you?"

"Never mind. I heard what you were going to do."

"It wasn't me, Terrence." She came close to him. "It was Carpenter. I'd just as soon really play."

"No, you wouldn't."

"I bet I would."

It was suddenly breathless there in the hall. And then on an impulse as she opened her arms and their heads bent together, muffled cries began to issue from the closet together with a tattoo on the door. Simultaneously Martha Robbie spoke from the stairs.

"You better kiss her, Terrence," she said tartly. "I never saw anything so disgusting in all my life. I know what I'm going to do right now."

The party swarmed back downstairs, Carpenter was liberated. And to the strains of Honey Boy from the piano the assault on Terrence was renewed. He had laid hands on a cripple or at least on a cripple's chair and he was back at dodging around the room again, followed by the juggernaut, wheeled now by willing hands.

There was activity at the front door. Martha Robbie, on the telephone, had located her mother on a neighboring porch in conference with several other mothers. The burden of Martha's message was that all the little boys were trying to embrace all the little girls by brute force, that there was no effective supervision and that the only boy who had acted like a gentleman had been brutally imprisoned in a closet. She added the realistic detail that Mrs. Schoonover was even then playing "I Wonder Who's Kissing Her Now" on the piano, and she accounted for her remaining at such an orgy by implying that she herself was under duress.

Eight excited heels struck the porch, eight anxious eyes confronted Mrs. Schoonover, who had previously only encountered these ladies in church. Behind her the disturbance around Terrence reached its climax. Two boys were trying to hold him and he had grabbed Carpenter's cane; attached by this to the wheelchair the struggle swayed back and forth wildly, then the chair rocked, rose startlingly on its side and tipped over, spilling Carpenter on the floor.

The mothers, Carpenter's among them, stood transfixed. The girls cried out, the boys around the chair shrank back hurriedly. Then an amazing thing happened. Carpenter gave an extraordinary twist to his body, grasped at the chair and with his over-developed arms pulled himself up steadily until he was standing, his weight resting for the first time in five years upon his feet.

He did not realize this—at the moment he had no thought for himself. Even as he stood there with the whole room breathless, he roared, "I'll fix you, confound it," and hobbled a step and then another step in Terrence's direction. As Mrs. Moore gave a little yelp and collapsed the room was suddenly full of wild exclamations:

"Carpenter Moore can walk! Carpenter Moore can walk!"

IV

Alleys and kitchens, kitchens and alleys—such had been Terrence's via doloroso all day. It was by the back door that he left the Schoonovers', knowing that he would be somehow blamed for Carpenter's miraculous recovery; it was through the kitchen that he entered his own home ten minutes later, after a few hasty Our Father's in the alley.

Helen, the cook, attired in her going-out dress, was in the kitchen.

"Carpenter Moore can walk," he announced, stalling for time. And he added crypticly, "I don't know what they're going to do about it. Supper ready?"

"No supper tonight except for you, and it's on the table. Your mother got called away to your aunt's, Mrs. Lapham. She left a letter for you."

This was a piece of luck surely and his heart began to beat again. It was odd that his aunt was sick on the day they had invented an illness for Joe's aunt.

> Dearest Boy—
> I hate to leave you like this but Charlotte is ill and I'm catching the trolley to Lockport. She says it's not very bad but when she sends a telegram it may mean anything. I worried when you didn't come to lunch, but Aunt Georgie, who is going with me, says you stopped by and ate a raw egg so I know you're all right.

He read no further as the knowledge of the awful truth came to him. The telegram had been delivered, but to the wrong door.

"And you're to hurry and eat your supper so I can see you get to Moores'," said Helen. "I've got to lock up after you."

"Me go to the Moores?" he said incredulously.

The phone rang and his immediate instinct was to retreat out the door into the alley.

"It's Dolly Bartlett," Helen said.

"What does she want?"

"How should I know."

Suspiciously he went to the phone.

"Terrence, can you come over to our house for supper?"

"What?"

"Mother wants you to come to supper."

In return for a promise to Helen that he would never again call her a Kitchen Mechanic, the slight change of schedule was arranged. It was time things went better. In one day he had committed insolence and forgery and assaulted both the crippled and the blind. His punishment obviously was to be in this life. But for the moment it did not seem important—anything might happen in one blessed hour.

The Scandal Detectives

It was a hot afternoon in May and Mrs. Buckner thought that a pitcher of fruit lemonade might prevent the boys from filling up on ice cream at the drug store. She belonged to that generation, since retired, upon whom the great revolution in American family life was to be visited; but at that time she believed that her children's relation to her was as much as hers had been to her parents, for this was more than twenty years ago.

Some generations are close to those that succeed them; between others the gap is infinite and unbridgeable. Mrs. Buckner—a woman of character, a member of Society in a large Middle-Western city—carrying a pitcher of fruit lemonade through her own spacious back yard, was progressing across a hundred years. Her own thoughts would have been comprehensible to her great-grandmother; what was happening in a room above the stable would have been entirely unintelligible to them both. In what had once served as the coachman's sleeping apartment, her son and a friend were not behaving in a normal manner, but were, so to speak, experimenting in a void. They were making the first tentative combinations of the ideas and materials they found ready at their hand—ideas destined to become, in future years, first articulate, then startling and finally commonplace. At the moment when she called up to them they were sitting with disarming quiet upon the still unhatched eggs of the mid-twentieth century.

Riply Buckner descended the ladder and took the lemonade. Basil Duke Lee looked abstractedly down at the transaction and said, "Thank you very much, Mrs. Buckner."

"Are you sure it isn't too hot up there?"

"No, Mrs. Buckner. It's fine."

It was stifling; but they were scarcely conscious of the heat, and they drank two tall glasses each of the lemonade without knowing that they were thirsty. Concealed beneath a sawed-out trapdoor from which they presently took it was a composition book bound in imitation red leather which currently absorbed much of their attention. On its first page was inscribed, if you penetrated the secret of the lemon-juice ink: "THE BOOK OF SCANDAL, written by Riply Buckner, Jr., and Basil D. Lee, Scandal Detectives."

In this book they had set down such deviations from rectitude on the part of their fellow citizens as had reached their ears. Some of these false steps were those of grizzled men, stories that had become traditions in the city and were embalmed in the composition book by virtue of indiscreet exhumations at family dinner tables. Others were the more exciting sins, confirmed or merely rumored, of boys and girls their own age. Some of the entries would have been read by adults with bewilderment, others might have inspired wrath, and there were three or four contemporary reports that would have prostrated the parents of the involved children with horror and despair.

One of the mildest items, a matter they had hesitated about setting down, though it had shocked them only last year, was: "Elwood Leaming has been to the Burlesque Show three or four times at the Star."

Another, and perhaps their favorite, because of its uniqueness, set forth that "H. P. Cramner committed some theft in the East he could be imprisoned for and had to come here"— H. P. Cramner being now one of the oldest and "most substantial" citizens of the city.

The single defect in the book was that it could only be enjoyed with the aid of the imagination, for the invisible ink must keep its secrets until that day when, the pages being held close to the fire, the items would appear. Close inspection was necessary to determine which pages had been used—already a rather grave charge against a certain couple had been superimposed upon the dismal facts that Mrs. R. B. Cary had consumption and that her son, Walter Cary, had been expelled from Pawling School. The purpose of the work as a whole was not blackmail. It was treasured against the time when its protagonists should "do something" to Basil and Riply. Its possession gave them a sense of power. Basil, for instance, had never seen Mr. H. P. Cramner make a single threatening gesture in Basil's direction but let him even hint that he was going to do something to Basil, and there preserved against him was the record of his past.

It is only fair to say that at this point the book passes entirely out of this story. Years later a janitor discovered it beneath the trapdoor, and finding it apparently blank, gave it to his little girl; so the misdeeds of Elwood Leaming and H. P. Cramner were definitely entombed at last beneath a fair copy of Lincoln's Gettysburg Address.

The book was Basil's idea. He was more the imaginative and in most ways the stronger of the two. He was a shining-eyed, brown-haired boy of fourteen, rather small as yet, and bright and lazy at school. His favorite character in fiction was Arsène Lupin, the gentleman burglar, a romantic phenomenon lately imported from Europe and much admired in the first bored decades of the century.

Riply Buckner, also in short pants, contributed to the partnership a breathless practicality. His mind waited upon Basil's imagination like a hair trigger and no scheme was too fantastic for his immediate "Let's do it!" Since the school's third baseball team, on which they had been pitcher and catcher, decomposed after an unfortunate April season, they had spent their afternoons struggling to evolve a way of life which should measure up to the mysterious energies fermenting inside them. In the cache beneath the trapdoor were some "slouch" hats and bandanna handkerchiefs, some loaded dice, half of a pair of handcuffs, a rope ladder of a tenuous crochet persuasion for rear-window escapes into the alley, and a make-up box containing two old theatrical wigs and crêpe hair of various colors—all to be used when they decided what illegal enterprises to undertake.

Their lemonades finished, they lit Home Runs and held a desultory conversation which touched on crime, professional baseball, sex and the local stock company. This broke off at the sound of footsteps and familiar voices in the adjoining alley.

From the window, they investigated. The voices belonged to Margaret Torrence, Imogene Bissel and Connie Davies, who were cutting through the alley from Imogene's back yard to Connie's at the end of the block. The young ladies were thirteen, twelve and thirteen years old respectively, and they considered themselves alone, for in time to their march they were rendering a mildly daring parody in a sort of whispering giggle and coming out strongly on the finale: "Oh, my *dar*-ling *Clemen*-tine."

Basil and Riply leaned together from the window, then remembering their undershirts sank down behind the sill.

"We heard you!" they cried together.

The girls stopped and laughed. Margaret Torrence chewed exaggeratedly to indicate gum, and gum with a purpose. Basil immediately understood.

"Whereabouts?" he demanded.

"Over at Imogene's house."

They had been at Mrs. Bissel's cigarettes. The implied recklessness of their mood interested and excited the two boys and they prolonged the conversation. Connie Davies had been

Riply's girl during dancing-school term; Margaret Torrence had played a part in Basil's recent past; Imogene Bissel was just back from a year in Europe. During the last month neither Basil nor Riply had thought about girls, and, thus refreshed, they became conscious that the centre of the world had shifted suddenly from the secret room to the little group outside.

"Come on up," they suggested.

"Come on out. Come on down to the Whartons' yard."

"All right."

Barely remembering to put away the Scandal Book and the box of disguises, the two boys hurried out, mounted their bicycles and rode up the alley.

The Whartons' own children had long grown up, but their yard was still one of those predestined places where young people gather in the afternoon. It had many advantages. It was large, open to other yards on both sides, and it could be entered upon skates or bicycles from the street. It contained an old seesaw, a swing and a pair of flying rings; but it had been a rendezvous before these were put up, for it had a child's quality—the thing that makes young people huddle inextricably on uncomfortable steps and desert the houses of their friends to herd on the obscure premises of "people nobody knows." The Whartons' yard had long been a happy compromise; there were deep shadows there all day long and ever something vague in bloom, and patient dogs around, and brown spots worn bare by countless circling wheels and dragging feet. In sordid poverty, below the bluff two hundred feet away, lived the "micks"—they had merely inherited the name, for they were now largely of Scandinavian descent—and when other amusements palled, a few cries were enough to bring a gang of them swarming up the hill, to be faced if numbers promised well, to be fled from into convenient houses if things went the other way.

It was five o'clock and there was a small crowd gathered there for that soft and romantic time before supper—a time surpassed only by the interim of summer dusk thereafter. Basil and Riply rode their bicycles around abstractedly, in and out of trees, resting now and then with a hand on someone's shoulder, shading their eyes from the glow of the late sun that, like youth itself, is too strong to face directly, but must be kept down to an undertone until it dies away.

Basil rode over to Imogene Bissel and balanced idly on his wheel before her. Something in his face then must have attracted her, for she looked up at him, looked at him really, and slowly smiled. She was to be a beauty and belle of many proms in a few years. Now her large brown eyes and large beautifully shaped mouth and the high flush over her thin cheek bones made her face gnome-like and offended those who wanted a child to look like a child. For a moment Basil was granted an insight into the future, and the spell of her vitality crept over him suddenly. For the first time in his life he realized a girl completely as something opposite and complementary to him, and he was subject to a warm chill of mingled pleasure and pain. It was a definite experience and he was immediately conscious of it. The summer afternoon became lost in her suddenly—the soft air, the shadowy hedges and banks of flowers, the orange sunlight, the laughter and voices, the tinkle of a piano over the way—the odor left all these things and went into Imogene's face as she sat there looking up at him with a smile.

For a moment it was too much for him. He let it go, incapable of exploiting it until he had digested it alone. He rode around fast in a circle on his bicycle, passing near Imogene without looking at her. When he came back after a while and asked if he could walk home with her, she had forgotten the moment, if it had ever existed for her, and was almost surprised. With Basil wheeling his bicycle beside her, they started down the street.

"Can you come out tonight?" he asked eagerly. "There'll probably be a bunch in the Whartons' yard."

"I'll ask mother."

"I'll telephone you. I don't want to go unless you'll be there."

"Why?" She smiled at him again, encouraging him.

"Because I don't want to."

"But why don't you want to?"

"Listen," he said quickly, "What boys do you like better than me?"

"Nobody. I like you and Hubert Blair best."

Basil felt no jealousy at the coupling of this name with his. There was nothing to do about Hubert Blair but accept him philosophically, as other boys did when dissecting the hearts of other girls.

"I like you better than anybody," he said deliriously.

The weight of the pink dappled sky above him was not endurable. He was plunging along through air of ineffable loveliness while warm freshets sprang up in his blood and he turned them, and with them his whole life, like a stream toward this girl.

They reached the carriage door at the side of her house.

"Can't you come in, Basil?"

"No." He saw immediately that that was a mistake, but it was said now. The intangible present had eluded him. Still he lingered. "Do you want my school ring?"

"Yes, if you want to give it to me."

"I'll give it to you tonight." His voice shook slightly as he added, "That is, I'll trade."

"What for?"

"Something."

"What?" Her color spread; she knew.

"You know. Will you trade?"

Imogene looked around uneasily. In the honey-sweet silence that had gathered around the porch, Basil held his breath.

"You're awful," she whispered. "Maybe. . . . Good-by."

II

It was the best hour of the day now and Basil was terribly happy. This summer he and his mother and sister were going to the lakes and next fall he was starting away to school. Then he would go to Yale and be a great athlete, and after that—if his two dreams had fitted onto each other chronologically instead of existing independently side by side—he was due to become a gentleman burglar. Everything was fine. He had so many alluring things to think about that it was hard to fall asleep at night.

That he was now crazy about Imogene Bissel was not a

distraction, but another good thing. It had as yet no poignancy, only a brilliant and dynamic excitement that was bearing him along toward the Whartons' yard through the May twilight.

He wore his favorite clothes—white duck knickerbockers, pepper-and-salt Norfolk jacket, a Belmont collar and a gray knitted tie. With his black hair wet and shining, he made a handsome little figure as he turned in upon the familiar but now reënchanted lawn and joined the voices in the gathering darkness. Three or four girls who lived in neighboring houses were present, and almost twice as many boys; and a slightly older group adorning the side veranda made a warm, remote nucleus against the lamps of the house and contributed occasional mysterious ripples of laughter to the already overburdened night.

Moving from shadowy group to group, Basil ascertained that Imogene was not yet here. Finding Margaret Torrence, he spoke to her aside, lightly.

"Have you still got that old ring of mine?"

Margaret had been his girl all year at dancing school, signified by the fact that he had taken her to the cotillion which closed the season. The affair had languished toward the end; none the less, his question was undiplomatic.

"I've got it somewhere," Margaret replied carelessly. "Why? Do you want it back?"

"Sort of."

"All right. I never did want it. It was you that made me take it, Basil. I'll give it back to you tomorrow."

"You couldn't give it to me tonight, could you?" His heart leaped as he saw a small figure come in at the rear gate. "I sort of want to get it tonight."

"Oh, all right, Basil."

She ran across the street to her house and Basil followed. Mr. and Mrs. Torrence were on the porch, and while Margaret went upstairs for the ring he overcame his excitement and impatience and answered those questions as to the health of his parents which are so meaningless to the young. Then a sudden stiffening came over him, his voice faded off and his glazed eyes fixed upon a scene that was materializing over the way.

From the shadows far up the street, a swift, almost flying

figure emerged and floated into the patch of lamplight in front of the Whartons' house. The figure wove here and there in a series of geometric patterns, now off with a flash of sparks at the impact of skates and pavement, now gliding miraculously backward, describing a fantastic curve, with one foot lifted gracefully in the air, until the young people moved forward in groups out of the darkness and crowded to the pavement to watch. Basil gave a quiet little groan as he realized that of all possible nights, Hubert Blair had chosen this one to arrive.

"You say you're going to the lakes this summer, Basil. Have you taken a cottage?"

Basil became aware after a moment that Mr. Torrence was making this remark for the third time.

"Oh, yes, sir," he answered—"I mean, no. We're staying at the club."

"Won't that be lovely?" said Mrs. Torrence.

Across the street, he saw Imogene standing under the lamp-post and in front of her Hubert Blair, his jaunty cap on the side of his head, maneuvering in a small circle. Basil winced as he heard his chuckling laugh. He did not perceive Margaret until she was beside him, pressing his ring into his hand like a bad penny. He muttered a strained hollow good-by to her parents, and, weak with apprehension, followed her back across the street.

Hanging back in a shadow, he fixed his eyes not on Imogene but on Hubert Blair. There was undoubtedly something rare about Hubert. In the eyes of children less than fifteen, the shape of the nose is the distinguishing mark of beauty. Parents may call attention to lovely eyes, shining hair or gorgeous coloring, but the nose and its juxtaposition on the face is what the adolescent sees. Upon the lithe, stylish, athletic torso of Hubert Blair was set a conventional chubby face, and upon this face was chiseled the piquant, retroussé nose of a Harrison Fisher girl.

He was confident; he had personality, uninhibited by doubts or moods. He did not go to dancing school—his parents had moved to the city only a year ago—but already he was a legend. Though most of the boys disliked him, they did homage to his virtuosic athletic ability, and for the girls his every movement, his pleasantries, his very indifference, had a simply immeasurable fascination. Upon several previous occasions Basil had discovered this; now the discouraging comedy began to unfold once more.

Hubert took off his skates, rolled one down his arm and caught it by the strap before it reached the pavement; he snatched the ribbon from Imogene's hair and made off with it, dodging from under her arms as she pursued him, laughing and fascinated, around the yard. He cocked one foot behind the other and pretended to lean an elbow against a tree, missed the tree on purpose and gracefully saved himself from falling. The boys watched him noncommittally at first. Then they, too, broke out into activity, doing stunts and tricks as fast as they could think of them until those on the porch craned their necks at the sudden surge of activity in the garden. But Hubert coolly turned his back on his own success. He took Imogene's hat and began setting it in various quaint ways upon his head. Imogene and the other girls were filled with delight.

Unable any longer to endure the nauseous spectacle, Basil went up to the group and said, "Why, hello, Hube," in as negligent a tone as he could command.

Hubert answered: "Why, hello, old—old Basil the Boozle," and set the hat a different way on his head, until Basil himself couldn't resist an unwilling chortle of laughter.

"Basil the Boozle! Hello, Basil the Boozle!" The cry circled the garden. Reproachfully he distinguished Riply's voice among the others.

"Hube the Boob!" Basil countered quickly; but his ill humor detracted from the effect, though several boys repeated it appreciatively.

Gloom settled upon Basil, and through the heavy dusk the figure of Imogene began to take on a new, unattainable charm. He was a romantic boy and already he had endowed her heavily from his fancy. Now he hated her for her indifference, but he must perversely linger near in the vain hope of recovering the penny of ecstasy so wantonly expended this afternoon.

He tried to talk to Margaret with decoy animation, but Margaret was not responsive. Already a voice had gone up in the darkness calling in a child. Panic seized upon him; the blessed ìour of summer evening was almost over. At a spreading of the ɡroup to let pedestrians through, he maneuvered Imogene ɪnwillingly aside.

"I've got it," he whispered. "Here it is. Can I take you ʰome?"

She looked at him distractedly. Her hand closed automatically on the ring.

"What? Oh, I promised Hubert he could take me home." At ʈhe sight of his face she pulled herself from her trance and forced a note of indignation. "I saw you going off with Margaret Torrence just as soon as I came into the yard."

"I didn't. I just went to get the ring."

"Yes, you did! I saw you!"

Her eyes moved back to Hubert Blair. He had replaced his roller skates and was making little rhythmic jumps and twirls on his toes, like a witch doctor throwing a slow hypnosis over an African tribe. Basil's voice, explaining and arguing, went on, but Imogene moved away. Helplessly he followed. There were other voices calling in the darkness now and unwilling responses on all sides.

"All right, mother!"

"I'll be there in a second, mother."

"Mother, can't I please stay out five minutes more?"

"I've got to go," Imogene cried. "It's almost nine."

Waving her hand and smiling absently at Basil, she started off down the street. Hubert pranced and stunted at her side, circled around her and made entrancing little figures ahead.

Only after a minute did Basil realize that another young lady was addressing him.

"What?" he demanded absently.

"Hubert Blair is the nicest boy in town and you're the most conceited," repeated Margaret Torrence with deep conviction.

He stared at her in pained surprise. Margaret wrinkled her nose at him and yielded up her person to the now-insistent demands coming from across the street. As Basil gazed stupidly after her and then watched the forms of Imogene and Hubert disappear around the corner, there was a low mutter of thunder along the sultry sky and a moment later a solitary drop plunged through the lamplit leaves overhead and splattered on the sidewalk at his feet. The day was to close in rain.

III

It came quickly and he was drenched and running before he reached his house eight blocks away. But the change of weather had swept over his heart and he leaped up every few steps, swallowing the rain and crying "Yo-o-o!" aloud, as if he himself were a part of the fresh, violent disturbance of the night. Imogene was gone, washed out like the day's dust on the sidewalk. Her beauty would come back into his mind in brighter weather, but here in the storm he was alone with himself. A sense of extraordinary power welled up in him, until to leave the ground permanently with one of his wild leaps would not have surprised him. He was a lone wolf, secret and untamed; a night prowler, demoniac and free. Only when he reached his own house did his emotion begin to turn, speculatively and almost without passion, against Hubert Blair.

He changed his clothes, and putting on pajamas and dressing-gown descended to the kitchen, where he happened upon a new chocolate cake. He ate a fourth of it and most of a bottle of milk. His elation somewhat diminished, he called up Riply Buckner on the phone.

"I've got a scheme," he said.

"What about?"

"How to do something to H. B. with the S. D."

Riply understood immediately what he meant. Hubert had been so indiscreet as to fascinate other girls besides Miss Bissel that evening.

"We'll have to take in Bill Kampf," Basil said.

"All right."

"See you at recess tomorrow. . . . Good night!"

IV

Four days later, when Mr. and Mrs. George P. Blair were finishing dinner, Hubert was called to the telephone. Mrs.

Blair took advantage of his absence to speak to her husband of what had been on her mind all day.

"George, those boys, or whatever they are, came again last night."

He frowned.

"Did you see them?"

"Hilda did. She almost caught one of them. You see, I told her about the note they left last Tuesday, the one that said, 'First warning, S. D.,' so she was ready for them. They rang the back-door bell this time and she answered it straight from the dishes. If her hands hadn't been soapy she could have caught one, because she grabbed him when he handed her a note, but her hands were soapy so he slipped away."

"What did he look like?"

"She said he might have been a very little man, but she thought he was a boy in a false face. He dodged like a boy, she said, and she thought he had short pants on. The note was like the other. It said 'Second warning, S. D.'"

"If you've got it, I'd like to see it after dinner."

Hubert came back from the phone. "It was Imogene Bissel," he said. "She wants me to come over to her house. A bunch are going over there tonight."

"Hubert," asked his father, "do you know any boy with the initials S. D.?"

"No, sir."

"Have you thought?"

"Yeah, I thought. I knew a boy named Sam Davis, but I haven't seen him for a year."

"Who was he?"

"Oh, a sort of tough. He was at Number 44 School when I went there."

"Did he have it in for you?"

"I don't think so."

"Who do you think could be doing this? Has anybody got it in for you that you know about?"

"I don't know, papa; I don't think so."

"I don't like the looks of this thing," said Mr. Blair thoughtfully. "Of course it may be only some boys, but it may be——"

He was silent. Later, he studied the note. It was in red ink and there was a skull and crossbones in the corner, but being printed, it told him nothing at all.

Meanwhile Hubert kissed his mother, set his cap jauntily on the side of his head, and passing through the kitchen stepped out on the back stoop, intending to take the usual short cut along the alley. It was a bright moonlit night and he paused for a moment on the stoop to tie his shoe. If he had but known that the telephone call just received had been a decoy, that it had not come from Imogene Bissel's house, had not indeed been a girl's voice at all, and that shadowy and grotesque forms were skulking in the alley just outside the gate, he would not have sprung so gracefully and lithely down the steps with his hands in his pockets or whistled the first bar of the Grizzly Bear into the apparently friendly night.

His whistle aroused varying emotions in the alley. Basil had given his daring and successful falsetto imitation over the telephone a little too soon, and though the Scandal Detectives had hurried, their preparations were not quite in order. They had become separated. Basil, got up like a Southern planter of the old persuasion, was just outside the Blairs' gate; Bill Kampf, with a long Balkan mustache attached by a wire to the lower cartilage of his nose, was approaching in the shadow of the fence; but Riply Buckner, in a full rabbinical beard, was impeded by a length of rope he was trying to coil and was still a hundred feet away. The rope was an essential part of their plan; for, after much cogitation, they had decided what they were going to do to Hubert Blair. They were going to tie him up, gag him and put him in his own garbage can.

The idea at first horrified them—it would ruin his suit, it was awfully dirty and he might smother. In fact the garbage can, symbol of all that was repulsive, won the day only because it made every other idea seem tame. They disposed of the objections—his suit could be cleaned, it was where he ought to be anyhow, and if they left the lid off he couldn't smother. To be sure of this they had paid a visit of inspection to the Buckners' garbage can and stared into it, fascinated, envisaging Hubert among the rinds and eggshells. Then two of them, at last, resolutely put that part out of their minds and concentrated upon the luring of him into the alley and the overwhelming of him there.

Hubert's cheerful whistle caught them off guard and each of the three stood stock-still, unable to communicate with the others. It flashed through Basil's mind that if he grabbed Hubert without Riply at hand to apply the gag as had been arranged, Hubert's cries might alarm the gigantic cook in the kitchen who had almost taken him the night before. The thought threw him into a state of indecision. At that precise moment Hubert opened the gate and came out into the alley.

The two stood five feet apart, staring at each other, and all at once Basil made a startling discovery. He discovered he liked Hubert Blair—liked him as well as any boy he knew. He had absolutely no wish to lay hands on Hubert Blair and stuff him into a garbage can, jaunty cap and all. He would have fought to prevent that contingency. As his mind, unstrung by his situation, gave pasture to this inconvenient thought, he turned and dashed out of the alley and up the street.

For a moment the apparition had startled Hubert, but when it turned and made off he was heartened and gave chase. Outdistanced, he decided after fifty yards to let well enough alone; and returning to the alley, started rather precipitously down toward the other end—and came face to face with another small and hairy stranger.

Bill Kampf, being more simply organized than Basil, had no scruples of any kind. It had been decided to put Hubert into a garbage can, and though he had nothing at all against Hubert, the idea had made a pattern on his brain which he intended to follow. He was a natural man—that is to say, a hunter—and once a creature took on the aspect of a quarry, he would pursue it without qualms until it stopped struggling.

But he had been witness to Basil's inexplicable flight, and supposing that Hubert's father had appeared and was now directly behind him, he, too, faced about and made off down the alley. Presently he met Riply Buckner, who, without waiting to inquire the cause of his flight, enthusiastically joined him. Again Hubert was surprised into pursuing a little way. Then, deciding once and for all to let well enough alone, he returned on a dead run to his house.

Meanwhile Basil had discovered that he was not pursued and keeping in the shadows, made his way back to the alley. He was not frightened—he had simply been incapable of action. The alley was empty; neither Bill nor Riply was in sight. He saw Mr. Blair come to the back gate, open it, look up and down and go back into the house. He came closer. There was a great chatter in the kitchen—Hubert's voice, loud and boastful, and Mrs. Blair's frightened, and the two Swedish domestics contributing bursts of hilarious laughter. Then through an open window he heard Mr. Blair's voice at the telephone:

"I want to speak to the chief of police. . . . Chief, this is George P. Blair. . . . Chief, there's a gang of toughs around here who——"

Basil was off like a flash, tearing at his Confederate whiskers as he ran.

v

Imogene Bissel, having just turned thirteen, was not accustomed to having callers at night. She was spending a bored and solitary evening inspecting the month's bills which were scattered over her mother's desk, when she heard Hubert Blair and his father admitted into the front hall.

"I just thought I'd bring him over myself," Mr. Blair was saying to her mother. "There seems to be a gang of toughs hanging around our alley tonight."

Mrs. Bissel had not called upon Mrs. Blair and she was considerably taken aback by this unexpected visit. She even entertained the uncharitable thought that this was a crude overture, undertaken by Mr. Blair on behalf of his wife.

"Really!" she exclaimed. "Imogene will be delighted to see Hubert, I'm sure. . . . Imogene!"

"These toughs were evidently lying in wait for Hubert," continued Mr. Blair. "But he's a pretty spunky boy and he managed to drive them away. However, I didn't want him to come down here alone."

"Of course not," she agreed. But she was unable to imagine why Hubert should have come at all. He was a nice enough boy, but surely Imogene had seen enough of him the last three afternoons. In fact, Mrs. Bissel was annoyed, and there was a minimum of warmth in her voice when she asked Mr. Blair to come in.

They were still in the hall, and Mr. Blair was just beginning to perceive that all was not as it should be, when there was another ring at the bell. Upon the door being opened, Basil Lee, red-faced and breathless, stood on the threshold.

"How do you do, Mrs. Bissel? Hello, Imogene!" he cried in an unnecessarily hearty voice. "Where's the party?"

The salutation might have sounded to a dispassionate observer somewhat harsh and unnatural, but it fell upon the ears of an already disconcerted group.

"There isn't any party," said Imogene wonderingly.

"What?" Basil's mouth dropped open in exaggerated horror, his voice trembled slightly. "You mean to say you didn't call me up and tell me to come over here to a party?"

"Why, of course not, Basil!"

Imogene was excited by Hubert's unexpected arrival and it occurred to her that Basil had invented this excuse to spoil it. Alone of those present, she was close to the truth; but she underestimated the urgency of Basil's motive, which was not jealousy but mortal fear.

"You called *me* up, didn't you, Imogene?" demanded Hubert confidently.

"Why, no, Hubert! I didn't call up anybody."

Amid a chorus of bewildered protestations, there was another ring at the doorbell and the pregnant night yielded up Riply Buckner, Jr., and William S. Kampf. Like Basil, they were somewhat rumpled and breathless, and they no less rudely and peremptorily demanded the whereabouts of the party, insisting with curious vehemence that Imogene had just now invited them over the phone.

Hubert laughed, the others began to laugh and the tensity relaxed. Imogene, because she believed Hubert, now began to believe them all. Unable to restrain himself any longer in the presence of this unhoped-for audience, Hubert burst out with his amazing adventure.

"I guess there's a gang laying for us all!" he exclaimed. "There were some guys laying for me in our alley when I went out. There was a big fellow with gray whiskers, but when he saw me he ran away. Then I went along the alley and there was a bunch more, sort of foreigners or something, and I started after'm and they ran. I tried to catch em, but I guess they were good and scared, because they ran too fast for *me*."

So interested were Hubert and his father in the story that they failed to perceive that three of his listeners were growing purple in the face or to mark the uproarious laughter that greeted Mr. Bissel's polite proposal that they have a party, after all.

"Tell about the warnings, Hubert," prompted Mr. Blair. "You see, Hubert had received these warnings. Did you boys get any warnings?"

"I did," said Basil suddenly. "I got a sort of warning on a piece of paper about a week ago."

For a moment, as Mr. Blair's worried eye fell upon Basil, a strong sense not precisely of suspicion but rather of obscure misgiving passed over him. Possibly that odd aspect of Basil's eyebrows, where wisps of crêpe hair still lingered, connected itself in his subconscious mind with what was bizarre in the events of the evening. He shook his head somewhat puzzled. Then his thoughts glided back restfully to Hubert's courage and presence of mind.

Hubert, meanwhile, having exhausted his facts, was making tentative leaps into the realms of imagination.

"I said, 'So you're the guy that's been sending these warnings,' and he swung his left at me, and I dodged and swung my right back at him. I guess I must have landed, because he gave a yell and ran. Gosh, he could run! You'd ought to of seen him, Bill—he could run as fast as you."

"Was he big?" asked Basil, blowing his nose noisily.

"Sure! About as big as father."

"Were the other ones big too?"

"Sure! They were pretty big. I didn't wait to see, I just yelled, 'You get out of here, you bunch of toughs, or I'll show you!' They started a sort of fight, but I swung my right at one of them and they didn't wait for any more."

"Hubert says he thinks they were Italians," interrupted Mr. Blair. "Didn't you, Hubert?"

"They were sort of funny-looking," Hubert said. "One fellow looked like an Italian."

Mrs. Bissel led the way to the dining room, where she had caused a cake and grape juice supper to be spread. Imogene took a chair by Hubert's side.

"Now tell me all about it, Hubert," she said, attentively folding her hands.

Hubert ran over the adventure once more. A knife now made its appearance in the belt of one conspirator; Hubert's parleys with them lengthened and grew in volume and virulence. He had told them just what they might expect if they fooled with him. They had started to draw knives, but had thought better of it and taken to flight.

In the middle of this recital there was a curious snorting sound from across the table, but when Imogene looked over, Basil was spreading jelly on a piece of coffee cake and his eyes were brightly innocent. A minute later, however, the sound was repeated, and this time she intercepted a specifically malicious expression upon his face.

"I wonder what you'd have done, Basil," she said cuttingly. "I'll bet you'd be running yet!"

Basil put the piece of coffee cake in his mouth and immediately choked on it—an accident which Bill Kampf and Riply Buckner found hilariously amusing. Their amusement at various casual incidents at table seemed to increase as Hubert's story continued. The alley now swarmed with malefactors, and as Hubert struggled on against overwhelming odds, Imogene found herself growing restless—without in the least realizing that the tale was boring her. On the contrary, each time Hubert recollected new incidents and began again, she looked spitefully over at Basil, and her dislike for him grew.

When they moved into the library, Imogene went to the piano, where she sat alone while the boys gathered around Hubert on the couch. To her chagrin, they seemed quite content to listen indefinitely. Odd little noises squeaked out of them from time to time, but whenever the narrative slackened they would beg for more.

"Go on, Hubert. Which one did you say could run as fast as Bill Kampf?"

She was glad when, after half an hour, they all got up to go.

"It's a strange affair from beginning to end," Mr. Blair was saying. "I don't like it. I'm going to have a detective look into the matter tomorrow. What did they want of Hubert? What were they going to do to him?"

No one offered a suggestion. Even Hubert was silent, contemplating his possible fate with certain respectful awe. During breaks in his narration the talk had turned to such collateral matters as murders and ghosts, and all the boys had talked themselves into a state of considerable panic. In fact each had come to believe, in varying degrees, that a band of kidnappers infested the vicinity.

"I don't like it," repeated Mr. Blair. "In fact I'm going to see all of you boys to your own homes."

Basil greeted this offer with relief. The evening had been a mad success, but furies once aroused sometimes get out of hand. He did not feel like walking the streets alone tonight.

In the hall, Imogene, taking advantage of her mother's somewhat fatigued farewell to Mr. Blair, beckoned Hubert back into the library. Instantly attuned to adversity, Basil listened. There was a whisper and a short scuffle, followed by an indiscreet but unmistakable sound. With the corners of his mouth falling, Basil went out the door. He had stacked the cards dexterously, but Life had played a trump from its sleeve at the last.

A moment later they all started off, clinging together in a group, turning corners with cautious glances behind and ahead. What Basil and Riply and Bill expected to see as they peered warily into the sinister mouths of alleys and around great dark trees and behind concealing fences they did not know—in all probability the same hairy and grotesque desperadoes who had lain in wait for Hubert Blair that night.

VI

A week later Basil and Riply heard that Hubert and his mother had gone to the seashore for the summer. Basil was sorry. He had wanted to learn from Hubert some of the graceful mannerisms that his contemporaries found so dazzling and that might come in so handy next fall when he went away to school. In tribute to Hubert's passing, he practised leaning against a tree and missing it and rolling a skate down his arm, and he wore his cap in Hubert's manner, set jauntily on the side of his head.

This was only for a while. He perceived eventually that though boys and girls would always listen to him while he talked, their mouths literally moving in response to his, they would never look at him as they had looked at Hubert. So he abandoned the loud chuckle that so annoyed his mother and set his cap straight upon his head once more.

But the change in him went deeper than that. He was no longer sure that he wanted to be a gentleman burglar, though he still read of their exploits with breathless admiration. Outside of Hubert's gate, he had for a moment felt morally alone; and he realized that whatever combinations he might make of the materials of life would have to be safely within the law. And after another·week he found that he no longer grieved over losing Imogene. Meeting her, he saw only the familiar little girl he had always known. The ecstatic moment of that afternoon had been a premature birth, an emotion left over from an already fleeting spring.

He did not know that he had frightened Mrs. Blair out of town and that because of him a special policeman walked a placid beat for many a night. All he knew was that the vague and restless yearnings of three long spring months were somehow satisfied. They reached combustion in that last week— flared up, exploded and burned out. His face was turned without regret toward the boundless possibilities of summer.

A Night at the Fair

I

The two cities were separated only by a thin well-bridged river; their tails curling over the banks met and mingled, and at the juncture, under the jealous eye of each, lay, every fall, the State Fair. Because of this advantageous position, and because of the agricultural eminence of the state, the fair was one of the most magnificent in America. There were immense exhibits of grain, livestock and farming machinery; there were horse races and automobile races and, lately, aeroplanes that really left the ground; there was a tumultuous Midway with Coney Island thrillers to whirl you through space, and a whining, tinkling hoochie-coochie show. As a compromise between the serious and the trivial, a grand exhibition of fireworks, culminating in a representation of the Battle of Gettysburg, took place in the Grand Concourse every night.

At the late afternoon of a hot September day two boys of fifteen, somewhat replete with food and pop, and fatigued by eight hours of constant motion, issued from the Penny Arcade. The one with dark, handsome, eager eyes was, according to the cosmic inscription in his last year's Ancient History, "Basil Duke Lee, Holly Avenue, St. Paul, Minnesota, United States, North, America, Western Hemisphere, the World, the Universe." Though slightly shorter than his companion, he appeared taller, for he projected, so to speak, from short trousers, while Riply Buckner, Jr., had graduated into long ones the week before. This event, so simple and natural, was having a disrupting influence on the intimate friendship between them that had endured for several years.

During that time Basil, the imaginative member of the firm, had been the dominating partner, and the displacement effected by two feet of blue serge filled him with puzzled dismay—in fact, Riply Buckner had become noticeably indifferent to the pleasure of Basil's company in public. His own assumption of long trousers had seemed to promise a liberation from the restraints and inferiorities of boyhood, and the companionship of one who was, in token of his short pants, still a boy was an unwelcome reminder of how recent was his own metamorphosis. He scarcely admitted this to himself, but a certain shortness of temper with Basil, a certain tendency to belittle him with superior laughter, had been in evidence all afternoon. Basil felt the new difference keenly. In August a family conference had decided that even though he was going East to school, he was too small for long trousers. He had countered by growing an inch and a half in a fortnight, which added to his reputation for unreliability, but led him to hope that his mother might be persuaded, after all.

Coming out of the stuffy tent into the glow of sunset, the two boys hesitated, glancing up and down the crowded highway with expressions compounded of a certain ennui and a certain inarticulate yearning. They were unwilling to go home before it became necessary, yet they knew they had temporarily glutted their appetite for sights; they wanted a change in the tone, the motif, of the day. Near them was the parking space, as yet a modest yard; and as they lingered indecisively, their eyes were caught and held by a small car, red in color and slung at that proximity to the ground which indicated both speed of motion and speed of life. It was a Blatz Wildcat, and for the next five years it represented the ambition of several million American boys. Occupying it, in the posture of aloof exhaustion exacted by the sloping seat, was a blond, gay, baby-faced girl.

The two boys stared. She bent upon them a single cool glance and then returned to her avocation of reclining in a Blatz Wildcat and looking haughtily at the sky. The two boys exchanged a glance, but made no move to go. They watched the girl—when they felt that their stares were noticeable they dropped their eyes and gazed at the car.

After several minutes a young man with a very pink face and pink hair, wearing a yellow suit and hat and drawing on yellow gloves, appeared and got into the car. There was a series of frightful explosions; then, with a measured tup-tup-tup from the open cut-out, insolent, percussive and thrilling as a drum, the car and the girl and the young man whom they had recognized as Speed Paxton slid smoothly away.

Basil and Riply turned and strolled back thoughtfully toward the Midway. They knew that Speed Paxton was dimly terrible —the wild and pampered son of a local brewer—but they envied him—to ride off into the sunset in such a chariot, into the very hush and mystery of night, beside him the mystery of that baby-faced girl. It was probably this envy that made them begin to shout when they perceived a tall youth of their own age issuing from a shooting gallery.

"Oh, El! Hey, El! Wait a minute!"

Elwood Leaming turned around and waited. He was the dissipated one among the nice boys of the town—he had drunk beer, he had learned from chauffeurs, he was already thin from too many cigarettes. As they greeted him eagerly, the hard, wise expression of a man of the world met them in his half-closed eyes.

"Hello, Rip. Put it there, Rip. Hello, Basil, old boy. Put it there."

"What you doing, El?" Riply asked.

"Nothing. What are you doing?"

"Nothing."

Elwood Leaming narrowed his eyes still further, seemed to give thought, and then made a decisive clicking sound with his teeth.

"Well, what do you say we pick something up?" he suggested. "I saw some pretty good stuff around here this afternoon."

Riply and Basil drew tense, secret breaths. A year before they had been shocked because Elwood went to the burlesque shows at the Star—now here he was holding the door open to his own speedy life.

The responsibility of his new maturity impelled Riply to appear most eager. "All right with me," he said heartily.

He looked at Basil.

"All right with me," mumbled Basil.

Riply laughed, more from nervousness than from derision. "Maybe you better grow up first, Basil." He looked at Elwood, seeking approval. "You better stick around till you get to be a man."

"Oh, dry up!" retorted Basil. "How long have you had yours? Just a week!"

But he realized that there was a gap separating him from these two, and it was with a sense of tagging them that he walked along beside.

Glancing from right to left with the expression of a keen and experienced frontiersman, Elwood Leaming led the way. Several pairs of strolling girls met his mature glance and smiled encouragingly, but he found them unsatisfactory—too fat, too plain or too hard. All at once their eyes fell upon two who sauntered along a little ahead of them, and they increased their pace, Elwood with confidence, Riply with its nervous counterfeit and Basil suddenly in the grip of wild excitement.

They were abreast of them. Basil's heart was in his throat. He looked away as he heard Elwood's voice.

"Hello, girls! How are you this evening?"

Would they call for the police? Would his mother and Riply's suddenly turn the corner?

"Hello, yourself, kiddo!"

"Where you going, girls?"

"Nowhere."

"Well, let's all go together."

Then all of them were standing in a group and Basil was relieved to find that they were only girls his own age, after all. They were pretty, with clear skins and red lips and maturely piled-up hair. One he immediately liked better than the other —her voice was quieter and she was shy. Basil was glad when Elwood walked on with the bolder one, leaving him and Riply to follow with the other, behind.

The first lights of the evening were springing into pale existence; the afternoon crowd had thinned a little, and the lanes, empty of people, were heavy with the rich various smells of pop corn and peanuts, molasses and dust and cooking Wienerwurst and a not-unpleasant overtone of animals and hay. The Ferris wheel, pricked out now in lights, revolved leisurely through the dusk; a few empty cars of the roller coaster rattled overhead. The heat had blown off and there was the crisp stimulating excitement of Northern autumn in the air.

They walked. Basil felt that there was some way of talking to this girl, but he could manage nothing in the key of Elwood Leaming's intense and confidential manner to the girl ahead —as if he had inadvertently discovered a kinship of tastes and of hearts. So to save the progression from absolute silence—for Riply's contribution amounted only to an occasional burst of silly laughter—Basil pretended an interest in the sights they passed and kept up a sort of comment thereon.

"There's the six-legged calf. Have you seen it?"

"No, I haven't."

"There's where the man rides the motorcycle around. Did you go there?"

"No, I didn't."

"Look! They're beginning to fill the balloon. I wonder what time they start the fireworks."

"Have you been to the fireworks?"

"No, I'm going tomorrow night. Have you?"

"Yes, I been every night. My brother works there. He's one of them that helps set them off."

"Oh!"

He wondered if her brother cared that she had been picked up by strangers. He wondered even more if she felt as silly as he. It must be getting late, and he had promised to be home by half-past seven on pain of not being allowed out tomorrow night. He walked up beside Elwood.

"Hey, El," he asked, "where we going?"

Elwood turned to him and winked. "We're going around the Old Mill."

"Oh!"

Basil dropped back again—became aware that in his temporary absence Riply and the girl had linked arms. A twinge of jealousy went through him and he inspected the girl again and with more appreciation, finding her prettier than he had thought. Her eyes, dark and intimate, seemed to have wakened at the growing brilliance of the illumination overhead; there was the promise of excitement in them now, like the promise of the cooling night.

He considered taking her other arm, but it was too late; she and Riply were laughing together at something—rather, at nothing. She had asked him what he laughed at all the time and he had laughed again for an answer. Then they both laughed hilariously and sporadically together.

Basil looked disgustedly at Riply. "I never heard such a silly laugh in my life," he said indignantly.

"Didn't you?" chuckled Riply Buckner. "Didn't you, little boy?"

He bent double with laughter and the girl joined in. The words "little boy" had fallen on Basil like a jet of cold water. In his excitement he had forgotten something, as a cripple might forget his limp only to discover it when he began to run.

"You think you're so big!" he exclaimed. "Where'd you get the pants? Where'd you get the pants?" He tried to work this up with gusto and was about to add: "They're your father's pants," when he remembered that Riply's father, like his own, was dead.

The couple ahead reached the entrance to the Old Mill and waited for them. It was an off hour, and half a dozen scows bumped in the wooden offing, swayed by the mild tide of the artificial river. Elwood and his girl got into the front seat and he promptly put his arm around her. Basil helped the other girl into the rear seat, but, dispirited, he offered no resistance when Riply wedged in and sat down between.

They floated off, immediately entering upon a long echoing darkness. Somewhere far ahead a group in another boat were singing, their voices now remote and romantic, now nearer and yet more mysterious, as the canal doubled back and the boats passed close to each other with an invisible veil between.

The three boys yelled and called, Basil attempting by his vociferousness and variety to outdo Riply in the girl's eyes, but after a few moments there was no sound except his own voice and the continual bump-bump of the boat against the wooden sides, and he knew without looking that Riply had put his arm about the girl's shoulder.

They slid into a red glow—a stage set of hell, with grinning demons and lurid paper fires—he made out that Elwood and his girl sat cheek to cheek—then again into the darkness, with the gently lapping water and the passing of the singing boat now near, now far away. For a while Basil pretended that he was interested in this other boat, calling to them, commenting on their proximity. Then he discovered that the scow could be rocked and took to this poor amusement until Elwood Leaming turned around indignantly and cried:

"Hey! What are you trying to do?"

They came out finally to the entrance and the two couples broke apart. Basil jumped miserably ashore.

"Give us some more tickets," Riply cried. "We want to go around again."

"Not me," said Basil with elaborate indifference. "I have to go home."

Riply began to laugh in derision and triumph. The girl laughed too.

"Well, so long, little boy," Riply cried hilariously.

"Oh, shut up! So long, Elwood."

"So long, Basil."

The boat was already starting off; arms settled again about the girls' shoulders.

"So long, little boy!"

"So long, you big cow!" Basil cried. "Where'd you get the pants? Where'd you get the pants?"

But the boat had already disappeared into the dark mouth of the tunnel, leaving the echo of Riply's taunting laughter behind.

II

It is an ancient tradition that all boys are obsessed with the idea of being grown. This is because they occasionally give voice to their impatience with the restraints of youth, while those great stretches of time when they are more than content to be boys find expression in action and not in words. Sometimes Basil wanted to be just a little bit older, but no more. The question of long pants had not seemed vital to him—he wanted them, but as a costume they had no such romantic significance as, for example, a football suit or an officer's uniform, or even the silk hat and opera cape in which gentlemen burglars were wont to prowl the streets of New York by night.

But when he awoke next morning they were the most important necessity in his life. Without them he was cut off from his contemporaries, laughed at by a boy whom he had hitherto led. The actual fact that last night some chickens had preferred Riply to himself was of no importance in itself, but he was fiercely competitive and he resented being required to fight with one hand tied behind his back. He felt that parallel situations would occur at school, and that was unbearable. He approached his mother at breakfast in a state of wild excitement.

"Why, Basil," she protested in surprise, "I thought when we talked it over you didn't especially care."

"I've got to have them," he declared. "I'd rather be dead than go away to school without them."

"Well, there's no need of being silly."

"It's true—I'd rather be dead. If I can't have long trousers I don't see any use in my going away to school."

His emotion was such that the vision of his demise began actually to disturb his mother.

"Now stop that silly talk and come and eat your breakfast. You can go down and buy some at Barton Leigh's this morning."

Mollified, but still torn by the urgency of his desire, Basil strode up and down the room.

"A boy is simply helpless without them," he declared vehemently. The phrase pleased him and he amplified it. "A boy is simply and utterly helpless without them. I'd rather be dead than go away to school—"

"Basil, stop talking like that. Somebody has been teasing you about it."

"Nobody's been teasing me," he denied indignantly—"nobody at all."

After breakfast, the maid called him to the phone.

"This is Riply," said a tentative voice. Basil acknowledged the fact coldly. "You're not sore about last night, are you?" Riply asked.

"Me? No. Who said I was sore?"

"Nobody. Well, listen, you know about us going to the fireworks together tonight."

"Yes." Basil's voice was still cold.

"Well, one of those girls—the one Elwood had—has got a sister that's even nicer than she is, and she can come out tonight and you could have her. And we thought we could meet about eight, because the fireworks don't start till nine."

"What do?"

"Well, we could go on the Old Mill again. We went around three times more last night."

There was a moment's silence. Basil looked to see if his mother's door was closed.

"Did you kiss yours?" he demanded into the transmitter.

"Sure I did!" Over the wire came the ghost of a silly laugh. "Listen, El thinks he can get his auto. We could call for you at seven."

"All right," agreed Basil gruffly, and he added, "I'm going down and get some long pants this morning."

"Are you?" Again Basil detected ghostly laughter. "Well, you be ready at seven tonight."

Basil's uncle met him at Barton Leigh's clothing store at ten, and Basil felt a touch of guilt at having put his family to all this trouble and expense. On his uncle's advice, he decided finally on two suits—a heavy chocolate brown for every day and a dark blue for formal wear. There were certain alterations to be made but it was agreed that one of the suits was to be delivered without fail that afternoon.

His momentary contriteness at having been so expensive made him save car fare by walking home from downtown. Passing along Crest Avenue, he paused speculatively to vault the high hydrant in front of the Van Schellinger house, wondering if one did such things in long trousers and if he would ever do it again. He was impelled to leap it two or three times as a sort of ceremonial farewell, and was so engaged when the Van Schellinger limousine turned into the drive and stopped at the front door.

"Oh, Basil," a voice called.

A fresh delicate face, half buried under a mass of almost white curls, was turned toward him from the granite portico of the city's second largest mansion.

"Hello, Gladys."

"Come here a minute, Basil."

He obeyed. Gladys Van Schellinger was a year younger than Basil—a tranquil, carefully nurtured girl who, so local tradition had it, was being brought up to marry in the East. She had a governess and always played with a certain few girls at her house or theirs, and was not allowed the casual freedom of children in a Midwestern city. She was never present at such rendezvous as the Whartons' yard, where the others played games in the afternoons.

"Basil, I wanted to ask you something—are you going to the State Fair tonight?"

"Why, yes, I am."

"Well, wouldn't you like to come and sit in our box and watch the fireworks?"

Momentarily he considered the matter. He wanted to accept, but he was mysteriously impelled to refuse—to forgo a pleasure in order to pursue a quest that in cold logic did not interest him at all.

"I can't. I'm awfully sorry."

A shadow of discontent crossed Gladys' face. "Oh? Well, come and see me sometime soon, Basil. In a few weeks I'm going East to school."

He walked on up the street in a state of dissatisfaction. Gladys Van Schellinger had never been his girl, nor indeed anyone's girl, but the fact that they were starting away to school at the same time gave him a feeling of kinship for her —as if they had been selected for the glamorous adventure of the East, chosen together for a high destiny that transcended the fact that she was rich and he was only comfortable. He was sorry that he could not sit with her in her box tonight.

By three o'clock, Basil, reading the Crimson Sweater up in his room, began giving attentive ear to every ring at the bell. He would go to the head of the stairs, lean over and call, "Hilda, was that a package for me?" And at four, dissatisfied with her indifference, her lack of feeling for important things, her slowness in going to and returning from the door, he moved downstairs and began attending to it himself. But nothing came. He phoned Barton Leigh's and was told by a busy clerk: "You'll get that suit. I'll guarantee that you'll get that suit." But he did not believe in the clerk's honor and he moved out on the porch and watched for Barton Leigh's delivery wagon.

His mother came home at five. "There were probably more alterations than they thought," she suggested helpfully. "You'll probably get it tomorrow morning."

"Tomorrow morning!" he exclaimed incredulously. "I've got to have that suit tonight."

"Well, I wouldn't be too disappointed if I were you, Basil. The stores all close at half-past five."

Basil took one agitated look up and down Holly Avenue. Then he got his cap and started on a run for the street car at the corner. A moment later a cautious afterthought caused him to retrace his steps with equal rapidity.

'If they get here, keep them for me," he instructed his mother—a man who thought of everything.

"All right," she promised dryly, "I will."

It was later than he thought. He had to wait for a trolley, and when he reached Barton Leigh's he saw with horror that the doors were locked and the blinds drawn. He intercepted a last clerk coming out and explained vehemently that he had to have his suit to night. The clerk knew nothing about the matter. . . . Was Basil Mr. Schwartze?

No, Basil was not Mr. Schwartze. After a vague argument wherein he tried to convince the clerk that whoever promised him the suit should be fired, Basil went dispiritedly home.

He would not go to the fair without his suit—he would not go at all. He would sit at home and luckier boys would go adventuring along its Great White Way. Mysterious girls, young and reckless, would glide with them through the enchanted darkness of the Old Mill, but because of the stupidity, selfishness and dishonesty of a clerk in a clothing store he would not be there. In a day or so the fair would be over—forever—those girls, of all living girls the most intangible, the most desirable, that sister, said to be nicest of all —would be lost out of his life. They would ride off in Blatz Wildcats into the moonlight without Basil having kissed them. No, all his life—though he would lose the clerk his position: "You see now what your act did to me"—he would look back with infinite regret upon that irretrievable hour. Like most of us, he was unable to perceive that he would have any desires in the future equivalent to those that possessed him now.

He reached home; the package had not arrived. He moped dismally about the house, consenting at half-past six to sit silently at dinner with his mother, his elbows on the table.

"Haven't you any appetite, Basil?"

"No, thanks," he said absently, under the impression he had been offered something.

"You're not going away to school for two more weeks. Why should it matter—"

"Oh, that isn't the reason I can't eat. I had a sort of headache all afternoon."

Toward the end of the meal his eye focused abstractedly on some slices of angel cake; with the air of a somnambulist, he ate three.

At seven he heard the sounds that should have ushered in a night of romantic excitement.

The Leaming car stopped outside, and a moment later Riply Buckner rang the bell. Basil rose gloomily.

"I'll go," he said to Hilda. And then to his mother, with vague impersonal reproach, "Excuse me a minute. I just want to tell them I can't go to the fair tonight."

"But of course you can go, Basil. Don't be silly. Just because—"

He scarcely heard her. Opening the door, he faced Riply on the steps. Beyond was the Leaming limousine, an old high car, quivering in silhouette against the harvest moon.

Clop-clop-clop! Up the street came the Barton Leigh delivery wagon. Clop-clop! A man jumped out, dumped an iron anchor to the pavement, hurried along the street, turned away, turned back again, came toward them with a long square box in his hand.

"You'll have to wait a minute," Basil was calling wildly. "It can't make any difference. I'll dress in the library. Look here, if you're a friend of mine, you'll wait a minute." He stepped out on the porch. "Hey, El, I've just got my—got to change my clothes. You can wait a minute, can't you?"

The spark of a cigarette flushed in the darkness as El spoke to the chauffeur; the quivering car came to rest with a sigh and the skies filled suddenly with stars.

III

Once again the fair—but differing from the fair of the afternoon as a girl in the daytime differs from her radiant presentation of herself at night. The substance of the cardboard booths and plaster palaces was gone, the forms remained. Outlined in lights, these forms suggested things more mysterious and entrancing than themselves, and the people strolling along the network of little Broadways shared this quality, as their pale faces singly and in clusters broke the half darkness.

The boys hurried to their rendezvous, finding the girls in the deep shadow of the Temple of Wheat. Their forms had scarcely merged into a group when Basil became aware that something was wrong. In growing apprehension, he glanced from face to face and, as the introductions were made, he realized the appalling truth—the younger sister was, in point of fact, a fright, squat and dingy, with a bad complexion brooding behind a mask of cheap pink powder and a shapeless mouth that tried ceaselessly to torture itself into the mold of charm.

In a daze he heard Riply's girl say, "I don't know whether I ought to go with you. I had a sort of date with another fellow I met this afternoon."

Fidgeting, she looked up and down the street, while Riply, in astonishment and dismay, tried to take her arm.

"Come on," he urged. "Didn't I have a date with you first?"

"But I didn't know whether you'd come or not," she said perversely.

Elwood and the two sisters added their entreaties.

"Maybe I could go on the Ferris wheel," she said grudgingly, "but not the Old Mill. This fellow would be sore."

Riply's confidence reeled with the blow; his mouth fell ajar, his hand desperately pawed her arm. Basil stood glancing now with agonized politeness at his own girl, now at the others, with an expression of infinite reproach. Elwood alone was successful and content.

"Let's go on the Ferris wheel," he said impatiently. "We can't stand here all night."

At the ticket booth the recalcitrant Olive hesitated once more, frowning and glancing about as if she still hoped Riply's rival would appear.

But when the swooping cars came to rest she let herself be persuaded in, and the three couples, with their troubles, were hoisted slowly into the air.

As the car rose, following the imagined curve of the sky, it occurred to Basil how much he would have enjoyed it in other company, or even alone, the fair twinkling beneath him with new variety, the velvet quality of the darkness that is on the edge of light and is barely permeated by its last attenuations. But he was unable to hurt anyone whom he thought of as an inferior. After a minute he turned to the girl beside him.

"Do you live in St. Paul or Minneapolis?" he inquired formally.

"St. Paul. I go to Number 7 School." Suddenly she moved closer. "I bet you're not so slow," she encouraged him.

He put his arm around her shoulder and found it warm. Again they reached the top of the wheel and the sky stretched out overhead, again they lapsed down through gusts of music from remote calliopes. Keeping his eyes turned carefully away, Basil pressed her to him, and as they rose again into darkness, leaned and kissed her cheek.

The significance of the contact stirred him, but out of the corner of his eye he saw her face—he was thankful when a gong struck below and the machine settled slowly to rest.

The three couples were scarcely reunited outside when Olive uttered a yelp of excitement.

"There he is!" she cried. "That Bill Jones I met this afternoon —that I had the date with."

A youth of their own age was approaching, stepping like a circus pony and twirling, with the deftness of a drum major, a small rattan cane. Under the cautious alias, the three boys recognized a friend and contemporary—none other than the fascinating Hubert Blair.

He came nearer. He greeted them all with a friendly chuckle. He took off his cap, spun it, dropped it, caught it, set it jauntily on the side of his head.

"You're a nice one," he said to Olive. "I waited here fifteen minutes this evening."

He pretended to belabor her with the cane; she giggled with delight. Hubert Blair possessed the exact tone that all girls of fourteen, and a somewhat cruder type of grown women, find irresistible. He was a gymnastic virtuoso and his figure was in constant graceful motion; he had a jaunty piquant nose, a disarming laugh and a shrewd talent for flattery. When he took a piece of toffee from his pocket, placed it on his forehead, shook it off and caught it in his mouth, it was obvious to any disinterested observer that Riply was destined to see no more of Olive that night.

So fascinated were the group that they failed to see Basil's eyes brighten with a ray of hope, his feet take four quick steps backward with all the guile of a gentleman burglar, his torso writhe through the parting of a tent wall into the deserted premises of the Harvester and Tractor Show. Once safe, Basil's tensity relaxed, and as he considered Riply's unconsciousness of the responsibilities presently to devolve upon him, he bent double with hilarious laughter in the darkness.

IV

Ten minutes later, in a remote part of the fairgrounds, a youth made his way briskly and cautiously toward the fireworks exhibit, swinging as he walked a recently purchased rattan cane. Several girls eyed him with interest, but he passed them haughtily; he was weary of people for a brief moment— a moment which he had almost mislaid in the bustle of life— he was enjoying his long pants.

He bought a bleacher seat and followed the crowd around the race track, seeking his section. A few Union troops were moving cannon about in preparation for the Battle of Gettysburg, and, stopping to watch them, he was hailed by Gladys Van Schellinger from the box behind.

"Oh, Basil, don't you want to come and sit with us?"

He turned about and was absorbed. Basil exchanged courtesies with Mr. and Mrs. Van Schellinger and he was affably introduced to several other people as "Alice Riley's boy," and a chair was placed for him beside Gladys in front.

"Oh, Basil," she whispered, glowing at him, "isn't this fun?"

Distinctly, it was. He felt a vast wave of virtue surge through him. How anyone could have preferred the society of those common girls was at this moment incomprehensible.

"Basil, won't it be fun to go East? Maybe we'll be on the same train."

"I can hardly wait," he agreed gravely. "I've got on long pants. I had to have them to go away to school."

One of the ladies in the box leaned toward him. "I know your mother very well," she said. "And I know another friend of yours. I'm Riply Buckner's aunt."

"Oh, yes!"

"Riply's such a nice boy," beamed Mrs. Van Schellinger.

And then, as if the mention of his name had evoked him, Riply Buckner came suddenly into sight. Along the now empty and brightly illuminated race track came a short but monstrous procession, a sort of Lilliputian burlesque of the wild gay life. At its head marched Hubert Blair and Olive, Hubert prancing and twirling his cane like a drum major to the accompaniment of her appreciative screams of laughter. Next followed Elwood Leaming and his young lady, leaning so close together that they walked with difficulty, apparently wrapped in each other's arms. And bringing up the rear without glory were Riply Buckner and Basil's late companion, rivaling Olive in exhibitionistic sound.

Fascinated, Basil stared at Riply, the expression of whose face was curiously mixed. At moments he would join in the general tone of the parade with silly guffaw, at others a pained expression would flit across his face, as if he doubted that, after all, the evening was a success.

The procession was attracting considerable notice—so much that not even Riply was aware of the particular attention focused upon him from this box, though he passed by it four feet away. He was out of hearing when a curious rustling sigh passed over its inhabitants and a series of discreet whispers began.

"What funny girls," Gladys said. "Was that first boy Hubert Blair?"

"Yes." Basil was listening to a fragment of conversation behind:

"His mother will certainly hear of this in the morning."

As long as Riply had been in sight, Basil had been in an agony of shame for him, but now a new wave of virtue, even stronger than the first, swept over him. His memory of the incident would have reached actual happiness, save for the fact that Riply's mother might not let him go away to school. And a few minutes later, even that seemed endurable. Yet Basil was not a mean boy. The natural cruelty of his species toward the doomed was not yet disguised by hypocrisy—that was all.

In a burst of glory, to the alternate strains of Dixie and The

Star-Spangled Banner, the Battle of Gettysburg ended. Outside by the waiting cars, Basil, on a sudden impulse, went up to Riply's aunt.

"I think it would be sort of a—a mistake to tell Riply's mother. He didn't do any harm. He—"

Annoyed by the event of the evening, she turned on him cool, patronizing eyes.

"I shall do as I think best," she said briefly.

He frowned. Then he turned and got into the Van Schellinger limousine.

Sitting beside Gladys in the little seats, he loved her suddenly. His hand swung gently against hers from time to time and he felt the warm bond that they were both going away to school tightened around them and pulling them together.

"Can't you come and see me tomorrow?" she urged him. "Mother's going to be away and she says I can have anybody I like."

"All right."

As the car slowed up for Basil's house, she leaned toward him swiftly. "Basil—"

He waited. Her breath was warm on his cheek. He wanted her to hurry, or, when the engine stopped, her parents, dozing in back, might hear what she said. She seemed beautiful to him then; that vague unexciting quality about her was more than compensated for by her exquisite delicacy, the fine luxury of her life.

"Basil—Basil, when you come tomorrow, will you bring that Hubert Blair?"

The chauffeur opened the door and Mr. and Mrs. Van Schellinger woke up with a start. When the car had driven off, Basil stood looking after it thoughtfully until it turned the corner of the street.

The Freshest Boy

It was a hidden Broadway restaurant in the dead of the night, and a billiant and mysterious group of society people, diplomats and members of the underworld were there. A few minutes ago the sparkling wine had been flowing and a girl had been dancing gaily upon a table, but now the whole crowd were hushed and breathless. All eyes were fixed upon the masked but well-groomed man in the dress suit and opera hat who stood nonchalantly in the door.

"Don't move, please," he said, in a well-bred, cultivated voice that had, nevertheless, a ring of steel in it. "This thing in my hand might—go off."

His glance roved from table to table—fell upon the malig-

nant man higher up with his pale saturnine face, upon Heath-
erly, the suave secret agent from a foreign power, then rested
a little longer, a little more softly perhaps, upon the table
where the girl with dark hair and dark tragic eyes sat alone.

"Now that my purpose is accomplished, it might interest you
to know who I am." There was a gleam of expectation in every
eye. The breast of the dark-eyed girl heaved faintly and a tiny
burst of subtle perfume rose into the air. "I am none other than
that elusive gentleman, Basil Lee, better known as the
Shadow."

Taking off his well-fitting opera hat, he bowed ironically
from the waist. Then, like a flash, he turned and was gone into
the night.

"You get up to New York only once a month," Lewis Crum
was saying, "and then you have to take a master along."

Slowly, Basil Lee's glazed eyes returned from the barns and
billboards of the Indiana countryside to the interior of the
Broadway Limited. The hypnosis of the swift telegraph poles
faded and Lewis Crum's stolid face took shape against the
white slip-cover of the opposite bench.

"I'd just duck the master when I got to New York," said Basil.

"Yes, you would!"

"I bet I would."

"You try it and you'll see."

"What do you mean saying I'll see, all the time, Lewis?
What'll I see?"

His very bright dark-blue eyes were at this moment fixed
upon his companion with boredom and impatience. The two
had nothing in common except their age, which was fifteen,
and the lifelong friendship of their fathers—which is less than
nothing. Also they were bound from the same Middle-Western
city for Basil's first and Lewis's second year at the same Eastern
school.

But, contrary to all the best tradition, Lewis the veteran was
miserable and Basil the neophyte was happy. Lewis hated
school. He had grown entirely dependent on the stimulus of
a hearty vital mother, and as he felt her slipping farther and
farther away from him, he plunged deeper into misery and

homesickness. Basil, on the other hand, had lived with such intensity on so many stories of boarding-school life that, far from being homesick, he had a glad feeling of recognition and familiarity. Indeed, it was with some sense of doing the appropriate thing, having the traditional rough-house, that he had thrown Lewis' comb off the train at Milwaukee last night for no reason at all.

To Lewis, Basil's ignorant enthusiasm was distasteful—his instinctive attempt to dampen it had contributed to the mutual irritation.

"I'll tell you what you'll see," he said ominously. "They'll catch you smoking and put you on bounds."

"No, they won't, because I won't be smoking. I'll be in training for football."

"Football! Yeah! Football!"

"Honestly, Lewis, you don't like anything, do you?"

"I don't like football. I don't like to go out and get a crack in the eye." Lewis spoke aggressively, for his mother had canonized all his timidities as common sense. Basil's answer, made with what he considered kindly intent, was the sort of remark that creates lifelong enmities.

"You'd probably be a lot more popular in school if you played football," he suggested patronizingly.

Lewis did not consider himself unpopular. He did not think of it in that way at all. He was astounded.

"You wait!" he cried furiously. "They'll take all that freshness out of you."

"Clam yourself," said Basil, coolly plucking at the creases of his first long trousers. "Just clam yourself."

"I guess everybody knows you were the freshest boy at Country Day!"

"Clam yourself," repeated Basil, but with less assurance. "Kindly clam yourself."

"I guess I know what they had in the school paper about you—"

Basil's own coolness was no longer perceptible.

"If you don't clam yourself," he said darkly, "I'm going to throw your brushes off the train too."

The enormity of this threat was effective. Lewis sank back

in his seat, snorting and muttering, but undoubtedly calmer. His reference had been to one of the most shameful passages in his companion's life. In a periodical issued by the boys of Basil's late school there had appeared, under the heading Personals:

If someone will please poison young Basil, or find some other means to stop his mouth, the school at large and myself will be much obliged.

The two boys sat there fuming wordlessly at each other. Then, resolutely, Basil tried to reinter this unfortunate souvenir of the past. All that was behind him now. Perhaps he had been a little fresh, but he was making a new start. After a moment, the memory passed and with it the train and Lewis' dismal presence—the breath of the East came sweeping over him again with a vast nostalgia. A voice called him out of the fabled world; a man stood beside him with a hand on his sweater-clad shoulder.

"Lee!"

"Yes, sir."

"It all depends on you now. Understand?"

"Yes, sir."

"All right," the coach said, "go in and win."

Basil tore the sweater from his stripling form and dashed out on the field. There were two minutes to play and the score was 3 to 0 for the enemy, but at the sight of young Lee, kept out of the game all year by a malicious plan of Dan Haskins, the school bully, and Weasel Weems, his toady, a thrill of hope went over the St. Regis stand.

"33-12-16-22!" barked Midget Brown, the diminutive little quarterback.

It was his signal—

"Oh, gosh!" Basil spoke aloud, forgetting the late unpleasantness. "I wish we'd get there before tomorrow."

II

St. Regis School, Eastchester
November 18, 19—
Dear Mother: There is not much to say today, but I thought I would write you about my allowance. All the boys have a bigger allowance than me, because there are a lot of little things I have to get, such as shoe laces etc. School is still very nice and am having a fine time, but football is over and there is not much to do. I am going to New York this week to see a show. I do not know yet what it will be, but probably the Quacker Girl or little boy Blue as they are both very good. Dr. Bacon is very nice and there is a good phycission in the village. No more now as I have to study Algebra.
Your Affectionate Son,
Basil D. Lee.

As he put the letter in its envelope, a wizened little boy came into the deserted study hall where he sat and stood staring at him.

"Hello," said Basil, frowning.

"I been looking for you," said the little boy, slowly and judicially. "I looked all over—up in your room and out in the gym, and they said you probably might of sneaked off in here."

"What do you want?" Basil demanded.

"Hold your horses, Bossy."

Basil jumped to his feet. The little boy retreated a step.

"Go on, hit me!" he chirped nervously. "Go on, hit me, cause I'm just half your size—Bossy."

Basil winced. "You call me that again and I'll spank you."

"No, you won't spank me. Brick Wales said if you ever touched any of us—"

"But I never did touch any of you."

"Didn't you chase a lot of us one day and didn't Brick Wales—"

"Oh, what do you want?" Basil cried in desperation.

"Doctor Bacon wants you. They sent me after you and somebody said maybe you sneaked in here."

Basil dropped his letter in his pocket and walked out—the little boy and his invective following him through the door. He traversed a long corridor, muggy with that odor best described as the smell of stale caramels that is so peculiar to boys' schools, ascended a stairs and knocked at an unexceptional but formidable door.

Doctor Bacon was at his desk. He was a handsome, red-headed Episcopal clergyman of fifty whose original real interest in boys was now tempered by the flustered cynicism which is the fate of all headmasters and settles on them like green mould. There were certain preliminaries before Basil was asked to sit down—gold-rimmed glasses had to be hoisted up from nowhere by a black cord and fixed on Basil to be sure that he was not an impostor; great masses of paper on the desk had to be shuffled through, not in search of anything but as a man nervously shuffles a pack of cards.

"I had a letter from your mother this morning—ah—Basil." The use of his first name had come to startle Basil. No one else in school had yet called him anything but Bossy or Lee. "She feels that your marks have been poor. I believe you have been sent here at a certain amount of—ah—sacrifice and she expects—"

Basil's spirit writhed with shame, not at his poor marks but that his financial inadequacy should be so bluntly stated. He knew that he was one of the poorest boys in a rich boys' school.

Perhaps some dormant sensibility in Doctor Bacon became aware of his discomfort; he shuffled through the papers once more and began on a new note.

"However, that was not what I sent for you about this afternoon. You applied last week for permission to go to New York on Saturday, to a matinée. Mr. Davis tells me that for almost the first time since school opened you will be off bounds tomorrow."

"Yes, sir."

"That is not a good record. However, I would allow you to go to New York if it could be arranged. Unfortunately, no masters are available this Saturday."

Basil's mouth dropped ajar. "Why, I—why, Doctor Bacon, I know two parties that are going. Couldn't I go with one of them?"

Doctor Bacon ran through all his papers very quickly. "Unfortunately, one is composed of slightly older boys and the other group made arrangements some weeks ago."

"How about the party that's going to the Quaker Girl with Mr. Dunn?"

"It's that party I speak of. They feel that their arrangements are complete and they have purchased seats together."

Suddenly Basil understood. At the look in his eye Doctor Bacon went on hurriedly:

"There's perhaps one thing I can do. Of course there must be several boys in the party so that the expenses of the master can be divided up among all. If you can find two other boys who would like to make up a party, and let me have their names by five o'clock, I'll send Mr. Rooney with you."

"Thank you," Basil said.

Doctor Bacon hesitated. Beneath the cynical incrustations of many years an instinct stirred to look into the unusual case of this boy and find out what made him the most detested boy in school. Among boys and masters there seemed to exist an extraordinary hostility toward him, and though Doctor Bacon had dealt with many sorts of schoolboy crimes, he had neither by himself nor with the aid of trusted sixth-formers been able to lay his hands on its underlying cause. It was probably no single thing, but a combination of things; it was most probably one of those intangible questions of personality. Yet he remembered that when he first saw Basil he had considered him unusually prepossessing.

He sighed. Sometimes these things worked themselves out. He wasn't one to rush in clumsily. "Let us have a better report to send home next month, Basil."

'Yes, sir.'

Basil ran quickly downstairs to the recreation room. It was Wednesday and most of the boys had already gone into the village of Eastchester, whither Basil, who was still on bounds, was forbidden to follow. When he looked at those still scattered about the pool tables and piano, he saw that it was going to be difficult to get anyone to go with him at all. For Basil was quite conscious that he was the most unpopular boy at school.

It had begun almost immediately. One day, less than a fortnight after he came, a crowd of the smaller boys, perhaps urged on to it, gathered suddenly around him and began calling him Bossy. Within the next week he had two fights, and both times the crowd was vehemently and eloquently with the other boy. Soon after, when he was merely shoving indiscriminatively, like every one else, to get into the dining room, Carver, the captain of the football team, turned about and, seizing him by the back of the neck, held him and dressed him down savagely. He joined a group innocently at the piano and was told, "Go on away. We don't want you around."

After a month he began to realize the full extent of his unpopularity. It shocked him. One day after a particularly bitter humiliation he went up to his room and cried. He tried to keep out of the way for a while, but it didn't help. He was accused of sneaking off here and there, as if bent on a series of nefarious errands. Puzzled and wretched, he looked at his face in the glass, trying to discover there the secret of their dislike—in the expression of his eyes, his smile.

He saw now that in certain ways he had erred at the outset —he had boasted, he had been considered yellow at football, he had pointed out people's mistakes to them, he had shown off his rather extraordinary fund of general information in class. But he had tried to do better and couldn't understand his failure to atone. It must be too late. He was queered forever.

He had, indeed, become the scapegoat, the immediate villain, the sponge which absorbed all malice and irritability abroad—just as the most frightened person in a party seems to absorb all the others' fear, seems to be afraid for them all. His situation was not helped by the fact, obvious to all, that the supreme self-confidence with which he had come to St. Regis in September was thoroughly broken. Boys taunted him with impunity who would not have dared raise their voices to him several months before.

This trip to New York had come to mean everything to him —surcease from the misery of his daily life as well as a glimpse into the long-awaited heaven of romance. Its postponement for week after week due to his sins—he was constantly caught reading after lights, for example, driven by his wretchedness into such vicarious escapes from reality—had deepened his longing until it was a burning hunger. It was unbearable that he should not go, and he told over the short list of those whom he might get to accompany him. The possibilities were Fat Gaspar, Treadway and Bugs Brown. A quick journey to their rooms showed that they had all availed themselves of the Wednesday permission to go into Eastchester for the afternoon.

Basil did not hesitate. He had until five o'clock and his only chance was to go after them. It was not the first time he had broken bounds, though the last attempt had ended in disaster and an extension of his confinement. In his room, he put on a heavy sweater—an overcoat was a betrayal of intent—replaced his jacket over it and hid a cap in his back pocket. Then he went downstairs and with an elaborately careless whistle struck out across the lawn for the gymnasium. Once there, he stood for a while as if looking in the windows, first the one close to the walk, then one near the corner of the building. From here he moved quickly, but not too quickly, into a grove of lilacs. Then he dashed around the corner, down a long stretch of lawn that was blind from all windows and, parting the strands of a wire fence, crawled through and stood upon the grounds of a neighboring estate. For the moment he was free. He put on his cap against the chilly November wind, and set out along the half-mile road to town.

Eastchester was a suburban farming community, with a small shoe factory. The institutions which pandered to the factory workers were the ones patronized by the boys—a movie house, a quick-lunch wagon on wheels known as the Dog and the Bostonian Candy Kitchen. Basil tried the Dog first and happened immediately upon a prospect.

This was Bugs Brown, a hysterical boy, subject to fits and strenuously avoided. Years later he became a brilliant lawyer, but at that time he was considered by the boys of St. Regis to be a typical lunatic because of his peculiar series of sounds with which he assuaged his nervousness all day long.

He consorted with boys younger than himself, who were without the prejudices of their elders, and was in the company of several when Basil came in.

"Who-ee!" he cried. "Ee-ee-ee!" He put his hand over his mouth and bounced it quickly, making a wah-wah-wah sound.

"It's Bossy Lee! It's Bossy Lee! It's Boss-Boss-Boss-Boss-Bossy Lee!"

"Wait a minute, Bugs," said Basil anxiously, half afraid that Bugs would go finally crazy before he could persuade him to come to town. "Say, Bugs, listen. Don't, Bugs—wait a minute. Can you come up to New York Saturday afternoon?"

"Whe-ee-ee!" cried Bugs to Basil's distress.

"Whee-ee-ee!"

"Honestly, Bugs, tell me, can you? We could go up together if you could go."

"I've got to see a doctor," said Bugs, suddenly calm. "He wants to see how crazy I am."

"Can't you have him see about it some other day?" said Basil without humor.

"Whee-ee-ee!" cried Bugs.

"All right then," said Basil hastily. "Have you seen Fat Gaspar in town?"

Bugs was lost in a shrill noise, but someone had seen Fat; Basil was directed to the Bostonian Candy Kitchen.

This was a gaudy paradise of cheap sugar. Its odor, heavy and sickly and calculated to bring out a sticky sweat upon an adult's palms, hung suffocatingly over the whole vicinity and met one like a strong moral disuasion at the door. Inside, beneath a pattern of flies, material as black point lace, a line of boys sat eating heavy dinners of banana splits, maple nut and chocolate marshmallow nut sundaes. Basil found Fat Gaspar at a table on the side.

Fat Gaspar was at once Basil's most unlikely and most ambitious quest. He was considered a nice fellow—in fact he was so pleasant that he had been courteous to Basil and had spoken to him politely all fall. Basil realized that he was like that to everyone, yet it was just possible that Fat liked him, as people used to in the past, and he was driven desperately to take a chance. But it was undoubtedly a presumption, and as he approached the table and saw the stiffened faces which the other two boys turned toward him, Basil's hope diminished.

"Say, Fat—" he said, and hesitated. Then he burst forth suddenly. "I'm on bounds, but I ran off because I had to see you. Doctor Bacon told me I could go to New York Saturday if I could get two other boys to go. I asked Bugs Brown and he couldn't go, and I thought I'd ask you."

He broke off, furiously embarrassed, and waited. Suddenly the two boys with Fat burst into a shout of laughter.

"Bugs wasn't crazy enough!"

Fat Gaspar hesitated. He couldn't go to New York Saturday and ordinarily he would have refused without offending. He had nothing against Basil; nor, indeed, against anybody; but boys have only a certain resistance to public opinion and he was influenced by the contemptuous laughter of the others.

"I don't want to go," he said indifferently. "Why do you want to ask *me?*"

Then, half in shame, he gave a deprecatory little laugh and bent over his ice cream.

"I just thought I'd ask you," said Basil.

Turning quickly away, he went to the counter and in a hollow and unfamiliar voice ordered a strawberry sundae. He ate it mechanically, hearing occasional whispers and snickers from the table behind. Still in a daze, he started to walk out without paying his check, but the clerk called him back and he was conscious of more derisive laughter.

For a moment he hesitated whether to go back to the table and hit one of those boys in the face, but he saw nothing to be gained. They would say the truth—that he had done it because he couldn't get anybody to go to New York. Clenching his fists with impotent rage, he walked from the store.

He came immediately upon his third prospect, Treadway. Treadway had entered St. Regis late in the year and had been put in to room with Basil the week before. The fact that Treadway hadn't witnessed his humiliations of the autumn encouraged Basil to behave naturally toward him, and their relations had been, if not intimate, at least tranquil.

"Hey, Treadway," he cried, still excited from the affair in the Bostonian, "can you come up to New York to a show Saturday afternoon?"

He stopped, realizing that Treadway was in the company of Brick Wales, a boy he had had a fight with and one of his bitterest enemies. Looking from one to the other, Basil saw a look of impatience in Treadway's face and a far-away expression in Brick Wales', and he realized what must have been happening. Treadway, making his way into the life of the school, had just been enlightened as to the status of his roommate. Like Fat Gaspar, rather than acknowledge himself eligible to such an intimate request, he preferred to cut their friendly relations short.

"Not on your life," he said briefly. "So long." The two walked past him into the candy kitchen.

Had these slights, so much the bitterer for their lack of passion, been visited upon Basil in September, they would have been unbearable. But since then he had developed a shell of hardness which, while it did not add to his attractiveness, spared him certain delicacies of torture. In misery enough, and despair and self-pity, he went the other way along the street for a little distance until he could control the violent contortions of his face. Then, taking a roundabout route, he started back to school.

He reached the adjoining estate, intending to go back the way he had come. Half-way through a hedge, he heard footsteps approaching along the sidewalk and stood motionless, fearing the proximity of masters. Their voices grew nearer and louder; before he knew it he was listening with horrified fascination:

"—so, after he tried Bugs Brown, the poor nut asked Fat Gaspar to go with him and Fat said, 'What do you ask me for?' It serves him right if he couldn't get anybody at all."

It was the dismal but triumphant voice of Lewis Crum.

III

Up in his room, Basil found a package lying on his bed. He knew its contents and for a long time he had been eagerly expecting it, but such was his depression that he opened it listlessly. It was a series of eight color reproductions of Harrison Fisher girls "on glossy paper, without printing or advertising matter and suitable for framing."

The pictures were named Dora, Marguerite, Babette, Lucille, Gretchen, Rose, Katherine and Mina. Two of them—Marguerite and Rose—Basil looked at, slowly tore up and dropped in the wastebasket, as one who disposes of the inferior pups from a litter. The other six he pinned at intervals around the room. Then he lay down on his bed and regarded them.

Dora, Lucille and Katherine were blond; Gretchen was medium; Babette and Mina were dark. After a few minutes, he found that he was looking oftenest at Dora and Babette and, to a lesser extent, at Gretchen, though the latter's Dutch cap seemed unromantic and precluded the element of mystery. Babette, a dark little violet-eyed beauty in a tight-fitting hat, attracted him most; his eyes came to rest on her at last.

"Babette," he whispered to himself—"beautiful Babette."

The sound of the word, so melancholy and suggestive, like "Velia" or "I'm going to Maxime's" on the phonograph, softened him and, turning over on his face, he sobbed into the pillow. He took hold of the bed rails over his head and, sobbing and straining, began to talk to himself brokenly—how he hated them and whom he hated—he listed a dozen—and what he would do to them when he was great and powerful. In previous moments like these he had always rewarded Fat Gaspar for his kindness, but now he was like the rest. Basil set upon him, pummelling him unmercifully, or laughed sneeringly when he passed him blind and begging on the street.

He controlled himself as he heard Treadway come in, but did not move or speak. He listened as the other moved about the room, and after a while became conscious that there was an unusual opening of closets and bureau drawers. Basil turned over, his arm concealing his tear-stained face. Treadway had an armful of shirts in his hand.

"What are you doing?" Basil demanded.

His roommate looked at him stonily. "I'm moving in with Wales," he said.

"Oh!"

Treadway went on with his packing. He carried out a suitcase full, then another, took down some pennants and dragged his trunk into the hall. Basil watched him bundle his toilet things into a towel and take one last survey about the room's new barrenness to see if there was anything forgotten.

"Good-by," he said to Basil, without a ripple of expression on his face.

"Good-by."

Treadway went out. Basil turned over once more and choked into the pillow.

"Oh, poor Babette!" he cried huskily. "Poor little Babette! Poor little Babette!"

Babette, svelte and piquant, looked down at him coquettishly from the wall.

IV

Doctor Bacon, sensing Basil's predicament and perhaps the extremity of his misery, arranged it that he should go into New York, after all. He went in the company of Mr. Rooney, the football coach and history teacher. At twenty Mr. Rooney had hesitated for some time between joining the police force and having his way paid through a small New England college; in fact he was a hard specimen and Doctor Bacon was planning to get rid of him at Christmas. Mr. Rooney's contempt for Basil was founded on the latter's ambiguous and unreliable conduct on the football field during the past season—he had consented to take him to New York for reasons of his own.

Basil sat meekly beside him on the train, glancing past Mr. Rooney's bulky body at the Sound and the fallow fields of Westchester County. Mr. Rooney finished his newspaper, folded it up and sank into a moody silence. He had eaten a large breakfast and the exigencies of time had not allowed him to work it off with exercise. He remembered that Basil was a fresh boy, and it was time he did something fresh and could be called to account. This reproachless silence annoyed him.

"Lee," he said suddenly, with a thinly assumed air of friendly interest, "why don't you get wise to yourself?"

"What, sir?" Basil was startled from his excited trance of this morning.

"I said why don't you get wise to yourself?" said Mr. Rooney in a somewhat violent tone. "Do you want to be the butt of the school all your time here?"

"No, I don't," Basil was chilled. Couldn't all this be left behind for just one day?

"You oughtn't to get so fresh all the time. A couple of times in history class I could just about have broken your neck." Basil could think of no appropriate answer. "Then out playing football," continued Mr. Rooney"—you didn't have any nerve. You could play better than a lot of 'em when you wanted, like that day against the Pomfret seconds, but you lost your nerve."

"I shouldn't have tried for the second team," said Basil. "I was too light. I should have stayed on the third."

"You were yellow, that was all the trouble. You ought to get wise to yourself. In class, you're always thinking of something else. If you don't study, you'll never get to college."

"I'm the youngest boy in the fifth form," Basil said rashly.

"You think you're pretty bright, don't you?" He eyed Basil ferociously. Then something seemed to occur to him that changed his attitude and they rode for a while in silence. When the train began to run through the thickly clustered communities near New York, he spoke again in a milder voice and with an air of having considered the matter for a long time:

"Lee, I'm going to trust you."

"Yes, sir."

"You go and get some lunch and then go on to your show. I've got some business of my own I got to attend to, and when I've finished I'll try to get to the show. If I can't, I'll anyhow meet you outside."

Basil's heart leaped up. "Yes, sir."

"I don't want you to open your mouth about this at school —I mean, about me doing some business of my own."

"No, sir."

"We'll see if you can keep your mouth shut for once," he said, making it fun. Then he added, on a note of moral sternness, "And no drinks, you understand that?"

"Oh, no, sir!" The idea shocked Basil. He had never tasted a drink, nor even contemplated the possibility, save the intangible and nonalcoholic champagne of his café dreams.

On the advice of Mr. Rooney he went for luncheon to the Manhattan Hotel, near the station, where he ordered a club sandwich, French fried potatoes and a chocolate parfait. Out of the corner of his eye he watched the nonchalant, debonair, blasé New Yorkers at neighboring tables, investing them with a romance by which these possible fellow citizens of his from the Middle West lost nothing. School had fallen from him like a burden; it was no more than an unheeded clamor, faint and far away. He even delayed opening the letter from the morning's mail which he found in his pocket, because it was addressed to him at school.

He wanted another chocolate parfait, but being reluctant to bother the busy waiter any more, he opened the letter and spread it before him instead. It was from his mother:

DEAR BASIL: This is written in great haste, as I didn't want to frighten you by telegraphing. Grandfather is going abroad to take the waters and he wants you and me to come too. The idea is that you'll go to school at Grenoble or Montreux for the rest of the year and learn the languages and we'll be close by. That is, if you want to. I know how you like St. Regis and playing football and baseball, and of course there would be none of that; but on the other hand, it would be a nice change, even if it postponed your entering Yale by an extra year. So, as usual, I want you to do just as you like. We will be leaving home almost as soon as you get this and will come to the Waldorf in New York, where you can come in and see see us for a few days, even if you decide to stay. Think it over, dear.

With love to my dearest boy,
MOTHER.

Basil got up from his chair with a dim idea of walking over to the Waldorf and having himself locked up safely until his mother came. Then, impelled to some gesture, he raised his voice and in one of his first basso notes called boomingly and without reticence for the waiter. No more St. Regis! No more St. Regis! He was almost strangling with happiness.

"Oh, gosh!" he cried to himself. "Oh, golly! Oh, gosh! Oh, gosh!" No more Doctor Bacon and Mr. Rooney and Brick Wales and Fat Gaspar. No more Bugs Brown and on bounds and being called Bossy. He need no longer hate them, for they were impotent shadows in the stationary world that he was sliding away from, sliding past, waving his hand. "Good-by!" He pitied them. "Good-by!"

It required the din of Forty-second Street to sober his maudlin joy. With his hand on his purse to guard against the omnipresent pickpocket, he moved cautiously toward Broadway. What a day! He would tell Mr. Rooney—Why, he needn't ever go back! Or perhaps it would be better to go back and let them know what he was going to do, while they went on and on in the dismal, dreary round of school.

He found the theatre and entered the lobby with its powdery feminine atmosphere of a matinée. As he took out his ticket, his gaze was caught and held by a sculptured profile a few feet away. It was that of a well-built blond young man of about twenty with a strong chin and direct gray eyes. Basil's brain spun wildly for a moment and then came to rest upon a name—more than a name—upon a legend, a sign in the sky. What a day! He had never seen the young man before, but from a thousand pictures he knew beyond the possibility of a doubt that it was Ted Fay, the Yale football captain, who had almost single-handed beaten Harvard and Princeton last fall. Basil felt a sort of exquisite pain. The profile turned away; the crowd revolved; the hero disappeared. But Basil would know all through the next hours that Ted Fay was here too.

In the rustling, whispering, sweet-smelling darkness of the theatre he read the program. It was the show of all shows that he wanted to see, and until the curtain actually rose the program itself had a curious sacredness—a prototype of the thing itself. But when the curtain rose it became waste paper to be dropped carelessly to the floor.

ACT I. *The Village Green of a Small Town near New York.*

It was too bright and binding to comprehend all at once, and it went so fast that from the very first Basil felt he had missed things; he would make his mother take him again when she came—next week—tomorrow.

An hour passed. It was very sad at this point—a sort of gay sadness, but sad. The girl—the man. What kept them apart even now? Oh, those tragic errors and misconceptions. So sad. Couldn't they look into each other's eyes and *see?*

In a blaze of light and sound, of resolution, anticipation and imminent trouble, the act was over.

He went out. He looked for Ted Fay and thought he saw him leaning rather moodily on the plush wall at the rear of the theatre, but he could not be sure. He bought cigarettes and lit one, but fancying at the first puff that he heard a blare of music he rushed back inside.

ACT II. *The Foyer of the Hotel Astor.*

Yes, she was, indeed, like that song—a Beautiful Rose of the Night. The waltz buoyed her up, brought her with it to a point of aching beauty and then let her slide back to life across its last bars as a leaf slants to earth across the air. The high life of New York! Who could blame her if she was carried away by the glitter of it all, vanishing into the bright morning of the amber window borders, or into distant and entrancing music as the door opened and closed that led to the ballroom? The toast of the shining town.

Half an hour passed. Her true love brought her roses like herself and she threw them scornfully at his feet. She laughed and turned to the other, and danced—danced madly, wildly. Wait! That delicate treble among the thin horns, the low curving note from the great strings. There it was again, poignant and aching, sweeping like a great gust of emotion across the stage, catching her again like a leaf helpless in the wind:

> Rose—Rose—Rose of the night,
> When the spring moon is bright you'll be fair—

A few minutes later, feeling oddly shaken and exalted, Basil drifted outside with the crowd. The first thing upon which his eyes fell was the almost forgotten and now curiously metamorphosed spectre of Mr. Rooney.

Mr. Rooney had, in fact, gone a little to pieces. He was, to begin with, wearing a different and much smaller hat than when he left Basil at noon. Secondly, his face had lost its somewhat gross aspect and turned a pure and even delicate white, and he was wearing his necktie and even portions of his shirt on the outside of his unaccountably wringing wet overcoat. How, in the short space of four hours, Mr. Rooney had got himself in such shape is explicable only by the pressure of confinement in a boys' school upon a fiery outdoor spirit. Mr. Rooney was born to toil under the clear light of heaven and, perhaps half consciously, he was headed toward his inevitable destiny.

"Lee," he said dimly, "you ought get wise to y'self. I'm going to put you wise y'self."

To avoid the ominous possibility of being put wise to himself in the lobby, Basil uneasily changed the subject.

"Aren't you coming to the show?" he asked, flattering Mr. Rooney by implying that he was in any condition to come to the show. "It's a wonderful show."

Mr. Rooney took off his hat, displaying wringing-wet matted hair. A picture of reality momentarily struggled for development in the back of his brain.

"We got to get back to school," he said in a sombre and unconvinced voice.

"But there's another act," protested Basil in horror. "I've got to stay for the last act."

Swaying, Mr. Rooney looked at Basil, dimly realizing that he had put himself in the hollow of this boy's hand.

"All righ'," he admitted. "I'm going to get somethin' to eat. I'll wait for you next door."

He turned abruptly, reeled a dozen steps and curved dizzily into a bar adjoining the theatre. Considerably shaken, Basil went back inside.

ACT III. *The Roof Garden of Mr. Van Astor's House. Night.*

Half an hour passed. Everything was going to be all right, after all. The comedian was at his best now, with the glad appropriateness of laughter after tears, and there was a promise of felicity in the bright tropical sky. One lovely plaintive duet, and then abruptly the long moment of incomparable beauty was over.

Basil went into the lobby and stood in thought while the crowd passed out. His mother's letter and the show had cleared his mind of bitterness and vindictiveness—he was his old self and he wanted to do the right thing. He wondered if it was the right thing to get Mr. Rooney back to school. He walked toward the saloon, slowed up as he came to it and, gingerly opening the swinging door, took a quick peer inside. He saw only that Mr. Rooney was not one of those drinking at the bar. He walked down the street a little way, came back and tried again. It was as if he thought the doors were teeth to bite him, for he had the old-fashioned Middle-Western boy's horror of the saloon. The third time he was successful. Mr. Rooney was sound asleep at a table in the back of the room.

Outside again Basil walked up and down, considering. He would give Mr. Rooney half an hour. If, at the end of that time, he had not come out, he would go back to school. After all, Mr. Rooney had laid for him ever since football season—Basil was simply washing his hands of the whole affair, as in a day or so he would wash his hands of school.

He had made several turns up and down, when, glancing up an alley that ran beside the theatre his eye was caught by the sign, Stage Entrance. He could watch the actors come forth.

He waited. Women streamed by him, but those were the days before Glorification and he took these drab people for wardrobe women or something. Then suddenly a girl came out and with her a man, and Basil turned and ran a few steps up the street as if afraid they would recognize him—and ran back, breathing as if with a heart attack—for the girl, a radiant little beauty of nineteen, was Her and the young man by her side was Ted Fay.

Arm in arm, they walked past him, and irresistibly Basil followed. As they walked, she leaned toward Ted Fay in a way that gave them a fascinating air of intimacy. They crossed Broadway and turned into the Knickerbocker Hotel, and twenty feet behind them Basil followed in time to see them go into a long room set for afternoon tea. They sat at a table for two, spoke vaguely to a waiter, and then, alone at last, bent eagerly toward each other. Basil saw that Ted Fay was holding her gloved hand.

The tea room was separated only by a hedge of potted firs from the main corridor. Basil went along this to a lounge which was almost against their table and sat down.

Her voice was low and faltering, less certain than it had been in the play, and very sad: "Of course I do, Ted." For a long time, as their conversation continued, she repeated "Of course I do" or "But I do, Ted." Ted Fay's remarks were too low for Basil to hear.

"—says next month, and he won't be put off any more. . . . I do in a way, Ted. It's hard to explain, but he's done everything for mother and me. . . . There's no use kidding myself. It was a fool-proof part and any girl he gave it to was made right then and there. . . . He's been awfully thoughtful. He's done everything for me."

Basil's ears were sharpened by the intensity of his emotion; now he could hear Ted Fay's voice too:

"And you say you love me."

"But don't you see I promised to marry him more than a year ago."

"Tell him the truth—that you love me. Ask him to let you off."

"This isn't musical comedy, Ted."

"That was a mean one," he said bitterly.

"I'm sorry, dear, Ted darling, but you're driving me crazy going on this way. You're making it so hard for me."

"I'm going to leave New Haven, anyhow."

"No, you're not. You're going to stay and play baseball this spring. Why, you're an ideal to all those boys! Why, if you—"

He laughed shortly. "You're a fine one to talk about ideals."

"Why not? I'm living up to my responsibility to Beltzman; you've got to make up your mind just like I have—that we can't have each other."

"Jerry! Think what you're doing! All my life, whenever I hear that waltz—"

Basil got to his feet and hurried down the corridor, through the lobby and out of the hotel. He was in a state of wild emotional confusion. He did not understand all he had heard, but from his clandestine glimpse into the privacy of these two, with all the world that his short experience could conceive of at their feet, he had gathered that life for everybody was a struggle, sometimes magnificent from a distance, but always difficult and surprisingly simple and a little sad.

They would go on. Ted Fay would go back to Yale, put her picture in his bureau drawer and knock out home runs with the bases full this spring—at 8:30 the curtain would go up and she would miss something warm and young out of her life, something she had had this afternoon.

It was dark outside and Broadway was a blazing forest fire as Basil walked slowly along toward the point of brightest light. He looked up at the great intersecting planes of radiance with a vague sense of approval and possession. He would see it a lot now, lay his restless heart upon this greater restlessness of a nation—he would come whenever he could get off from school.

But that was all changed—he was going to Europe. Suddenly Basil realized that he wasn't going to Europe. He could not forego the molding of his own destiny just to alleviate a few months of pain. The conquest of the successive worlds of school, college and New York—why, that was his true dream that he had carried from boyhood into adolescence, and because of the jeers of a few boys he had been about to abandon it and run ignominiously up a back alley! He shivered violently, like a dog coming out of the water, and simultaneously he was reminded of Mr. Rooney.

A few minutes later he walked into the bar, past the quizzical eyes of the bartender and up to the table where Mr. Rooney still sat asleep. Basil shook him gently, then firmly. Mr. Rooney stirred and perceived Basil.

"G'wise to yourself," he muttered drowsily. "G'wise to yourself an' let me alone."

"I am wise to myself," said Basil. "Honest, I am wise to myself, Mr. Rooney. You got to come with me into the washroom and get cleaned up, and then you can sleep on the train again, Mr. Rooney. Come on, Mr. Rooney, please—"

v

It was a long hard time. Basil got on bounds again in December and wasn't free again until March. An indulgent mother had given him no habits of work and this was almost beyond the power of anything but life itself to remedy, but he made numberless new starts and failed and tried again.

He made friends with a new boy named Maplewood after Christmas, but they had a silly quarrel; and through the winter term, when a boys' school is shut in with itself and only partly assuaged from its natural savagery by indoor sports, Basil was snubbed and slighted a good deal for his real and imaginary sins, and he was much alone. But on the other hand, there was Ted Fay, and Rose of the Night on the phonograph—"All my life whenever I hear that waltz"—and the remembered lights of New York, and the thought of what he was going to do in football next autumn and the glamorous mirage of Yale and the hope of spring in the air.

Fat Gaspar and a few others were nice to him now. Once when he and Fat walked home together by accident from downtown they had a long talk about actresses—a talk that Basil was wise enough not to presume upon afterward. The smaller boys suddenly decided that they approved of him, and a master who had hitherto disliked him put his hand on his shoulder walking to a class one day. They would all forget eventually—maybe during the summer. There would be new fresh boys in September; he would have a clean start next year.

One afternoon in February, playing basketball, a great thing happened. He and Brick Wales were at forward on the second team and in the fury of the scrimmage the gymnasium echoed with sharp slapping contacts and shrill cries.

"Here yar!"

"Bill! Bill!"

Basil had dribbled the ball down the court and Brick Wales, free, was crying for it.

"Here yar! Lee! Hey! Lee-y!"

Lee-y!

Basil flushed and made a poor pass. He had been called by a nickname. It was a poor makeshift, but it was something more than the stark bareness of his surname or a term of derision. Brick Wales went on playing, unconscious that he had done anything in particular or that he had contributed to the events by which another boy was saved from the army of the bitter, the selfish, the neurasthenic and the unhappy. It isn't given to us to know those rare moments when people are wide open and the lightest touch can wither or heal. A moment too late and we can never reach them any more in this world. They will not be cured by our most efficacious drugs or slain with our sharpest swords.

Lee-y! It could scarcely be pronounced. But Basil took it to bed with him that night, and thinking of it, holding it to him happily to the last, fell easily to sleep.

He Thinks He's Wonderful

I

After the college-board examinations in June, Basil Duke Lee and five other boys from St. Regis School boarded the train for the West. Two got out at Pittsburgh, one slanted south toward St. Louis and two stayed in Chicago; from then on Basil was alone. It was the first time in his life that he had ever felt the need of tranquillity, but now he took long breaths of it; for, though things had gone better toward the end, he had had an unhappy year at school.

He wore one of those extremely flat derbies in vogue during the twelfth year of the century, and a blue business suit become a little too short for his constantly lengthening body. Within he was by turns a disembodied spirit, almost unconscious of his person and moving in a mist of impressions and emotions, and a fiercely competitive individual trying desperately to control the rush of events that were the steps in his own evolution from child to man. He believed that everything was a matter of effort—the current principle of American education—and his fantastic ambition was continually leading him to expect too much. He wanted to be a great athlete, popular, brilliant and always happy. During this year at school, where he had been punished for his "freshness," for fifteen years of thorough spoiling at home, he had grown uselessly introspective, and this interfered with that observation of others which is the beginning of wisdom. It was apparent that before he obtained much success in dealing with the world he would know that he'd been in a fight.

He spent the afternoon in Chicago, walking the streets and avoiding members of the underworld. He bought a detective story called "In the Dead of the Night," and at five o'clock recovered his suitcase from the station check room and boarded the Chicago, Milwaukee and St. Paul. Immediately he encountered a contemporary, also bound home from school.

Margaret Torrence was fourteen; a serious girl, considered beautiful by a sort of tradition, for she had been beautiful as a little girl. A year and a half before, after a breathless struggle, Basil had succeeded in kissing her on the forehead. They met now with extraordinary joy; for a moment each of them to the other represented home, the blue skies of the past, the summer afternoons ahead.

He sat with Margaret and her mother in the dining car that night. Margaret saw that he was no longer the ultraconfident boy of a year before; his brightness was subdued, and the air of consideration in his face—a mark of his recent discovery that others had wills as strong as his, and more power—appeared to Margaret as a charming sadness. The spell of peace after a struggle was still upon him. Margaret had always liked him—she was of the grave, conscientious type who sometimes loved him and whose love he could never return—and now she could scarcely wait to tell people how attractive he had grown.

After dinner they went back to the observation car and sat on the deserted rear platform while the train pulled them visibly westward between the dark wide farms. They talked of people they knew, of where they had gone for Easter vacation, of the plays they had seen in New York.

"Basil, we're going to get an automobile," she said, "and I'm going to learn to drive."

"That's fine." He wondered if his grandfather would let him drive the electric sometimes this summer.

The light from inside the car fell on her young face, and he spoke impetuously, borne on by the rush of happiness that he was going home: "You know something? You know you're the prettiest girl in the city?"

At the moment when the remark blurred with the thrilling night in Margaret's heart, Mrs. Torrence appeared to fetch her to bed.

Basil sat alone on the platform for a while, scarcely realizing that she was gone, at peace with himself for another hour and content that everything should remain patternless and shapeless until tomorrow.

II

Fifteen is of all ages the most difficult to locate—to put one's fingers on and say, "That's the way I was." The melancholy Jacques does not select it for mention, and all one can know is that somewhere between thirteen, boyhood's majority, and seventeen, when one is a sort of counterfeit young man, there is a time when youth fluctuates hourly between one world and another—pushed ceaselessly forward into unprecedented experiences and vainly trying to struggle back to the days when nothing had to be paid for. Fortunately none of our contemporaries remember much more than we do of how we behaved in those days; nevertheless the curtain is about to be drawn aside for an inspection of Basil's madness that summer.

To begin with, Margaret Torrence, in one of those moods of idealism which overcome the most matter-of-fact girls, gave it as her rapt opinion that Basil was wonderful. Having practised believing things all year at school, and having nothing much to believe at that moment, her friends accepted the fact. Basil suddenly became a legend. There were outbreaks of giggling when girls encountered him on the street, but he suspected nothing at all.

One night, when he had been home a week, he and Riply Buckner went on to an after-dinner gathering on Imogene Bissel's veranda. As they came up the walk Margaret and two other girls suddenly clung together, whispered convulsively and pursued one another around the yard, uttering strange cries—an inexplicable business that ended only when Gladys Van Schellinger, tenderly and impressively accompanied by her mother's maid, arrived in a limousine.

All of them were a little strange to one another. Those who had been East at school felt a certain superiority, which, however, was more than counterbalanced by the fact that romantic pairings and quarrels and jealousies and adventures, of which they were lamentably ignorant, had gone on while they had been away.

After the ice cream at nine they sat together on the warm stone steps in a quiet confusion that was halfway between childish teasing and adolescent coquetry. Last year the boys would have ridden their bicycles around the yard; now they had all begun to wait for something to happen.

They knew it was going to happen, the plainest girls, the shyest boys; they had begun to associate with others the romantic world of summer night that pressed deeply and sweetly on their senses. Their voices drifted in a sort of broken harmony in to Mrs. Bissel, who sat reading beside an open window.

"No, look out. You'll break it. Bay-zil!"

"Rip-lee!"

"Sure I did!"

Laughter.

> "—on Moonlight Bay
> We could hear their voices call—"

"Did you see——"

"Connie, don't—don't! You tickle. Look out!"

Laughter.

"Going to the lake tomorrow?"

"Going Friday."

"Elwood's home."

"Is Elwood home?"

"—you have broken my heart—"

"Look out now!"

"Look out!"

Basil sat beside Riply on the balustrade, listening to Joe Gorman singing. It was one of the griefs of his life that he could not sing "so people could stand it," and he conceived a sudden admiration for Joe Gorman, reading into his personality the thrilling clearness of those sounds that moved so confidently through the dark air.

They evoked for Basil a more dazzling night than this, and other more remote and enchanted girls. He was sorry when the voice died away, and there was a rearranging of seats and a businesslike quiet—the ancient game of Truth had begun.

"What's your favorite color, Bill?"

"Green," supplies a friend.

"Sh-h-h! Let him alone."

Bill says, "Blue."

"What's your favorite girl's name?"

"Mary," says Bill.

"Mary Haupt! Bill's got a crush on Mary Haupt!"

She was a cross-eyed girl, a familiar personification of repulsiveness.

"Who would you rather kiss than anybody?"

Across the pause a snicker stabbed the darkness.

"My mother."

"No, but what girl?"

"Nobody."

"That's not fair. Forfeit! Come on, Margaret."

"Tell the truth, Margaret."

She told the truth and a moment later Basil looked down in surprise from his perch; he had just learned that he was her favorite boy.

"Oh, yes-s!" he exclaimed sceptically. "Oh, yes-s! How about Hubert Blair?"

He renewed a casual struggle with Riply Buckner and presently they both fell off the balustrade. The game became an inquisition into Gladys Van Schellinger's carefully chaperoned heart.

"What's your favorite sport?"

"Croquet."

The admission was greeted by a mild titter.

"Favorite boy."

"Thurston Kohler."

A murmur of disappointment.

"Who's he?"

"A boy in the East."

This was manifestly an evasion.

"Who's your favorite boy here?"

Gladys hesitated. "Basil," she said at length.

The faces turned up to the balustrade this time were less teasing, less jocular. Basil depreciated the matter with "Oh, yes-s! Sure! Oh, yes-s!" But he had a pleasant feeling of recognition, a familiar delight.

Imogene Bissel, a dark little beauty and the most popular girl in their crowd, took Gladys' place. The interlocutors were tired of gastronomic preferences—the first question went straight to the point.

"Imogene, have you ever kissed a boy?"

"No." A cry of wild unbelief. "I have not!" she declared indignantly.

"Well, have you ever been kissed?"

Pink but tranquil, she nodded, adding, "I couldn't help it."

"Who by?"

"I won't tell."

"Oh-h-h! How about Hubert Blair?"

"What's your favorite book, Imogene?"

"Beverly of Graustark."

"Favorite girl?"

"Passion Johnson."

"Who's she?"

"Oh, just a girl at school."

Mrs. Bissel had fortunately left the window.

"Who's your favorite boy?"

Imogene answered steadily, "Basil Lee."

This time an impressed silence fell. Basil was not surprised—we are never surprised at our own popularity—but he knew that these were not those ineffable girls, made up out of books and faces momentarily encountered, whose voices he had heard for a moment in Joe Gorman's song. And when, presently, the first telephone rang inside, calling a daughter home, and the girls, chattering like birds, piled all together into Gladys Van Schellinger's limousine, he lingered back in the shadow so as not to seem to be showing off. Then, perhaps because he nourished a vague idea that if he got to know Joe Gorman very well he would get to sing like him, he approached him and asked him to go to Lambert's for a soda.

Joe Gorman was a tall boy with white eyebrows and a stolid face who had only recently become one of their "crowd." He did not like Basil, who, he considered, had been "stuck up" with him last year, but he was acquisitive of useful knowledge and he was momentarily overwhelmed by Basil's success with girls.

It was cheerful in Lambert's, with great moths batting against the screen door and languid couples in white dresses and light suits spread about the little tables. Over their sodas, Joe proposed that Basil come home with him to spend the night; Basil's permission was obtained over the telephone.

Passing from the gleaming store into the darkness, Basil was submerged in an unreality in which he seemed to see himself from the outside, and the pleasant events of the evening began to take on fresh importance.

Disarmed by Joe's hospitality, he began to discuss the matter.

"That was a funny thing that happened tonight," he said, with a disparaging little laugh.

"What was?"

"Why, all those girls saying I was their favorite boy." The remark jarred on Joe. "It's a funny thing," went on Basil. "I was sort of unpopular at school for a while, because I was fresh, I guess. But the thing must be that some boys are popular with boys and some are popular with girls."

He had put himself in Joe's hands, but he was unconscious

of it; even Joe was only aware of a certain desire to change the subject.

"When I get my car," suggested Joe, up in his room, "we could take Imogene and Margaret and go for rides."

"All right."

"You could have Imogene and I'd take Margaret, or anybody I wanted. Of course I know they don't like me as well as they do you."

"Sure they do. It's just because you haven't been in our crowd very long yet."

Joe was sensitive on that point and the remark did not please him. But Basil continued: "You ought to be more polite to the older people if you want to be popular. You didn't say how do you do to Mrs. Bissel tonight."

"I'm hungry," said Joe quickly. "Let's go down to the pantry and get something to eat."

Clad only in their pajamas, they went downstairs. Principally to dissuade Basil from pursuing the subject, Joe began to sing in a low voice:

> "Oh, you beautiful doll,
> You great—big——"

But the evening, coming after the month of enforced humility at school, had been too much for Basil. He got a little awful. In the kitchen, under the impression that his advice had been asked, he broke out again:

"For instance, you oughtn't to wear those white ties. Nobody does that that goes East to school." Joe, a little red, turned around from the ice box and Basil felt a slight misgiving. But he pursued with: "For instance, you ought to get your family to send you East to school. It'd be a great thing for you. Especially if you want to go East to college, you ought to first go East to school. They take it out of you."

Feeling that he had nothing special to be taken out of him, Joe found the implication distasteful. Nor did Basil appear to him at that moment to have been perfected by the process.

"Do you want cold chicken or cold ham?" They drew up chairs to the kitchen table. "Have some milk?"

"Thanks."

Intoxicated by the three full meals he had had since supper, Basil warmed to his subject. He built up Joe's life for him little by little, transformed him radiantly from what was little more than a Midwestern bumpkin to an Easterner bursting with *savoir-faire* and irresistible to girls. Going into the pantry to put away the milk, Joe paused by the open window for a breath of quiet air; Basil followed. "The thing is if a boy doesn't get it taken out of him at school, he gets it taken out of him at college," he was saying.

Moved by some desperate instinct, Joe opened the door and stepped out onto the back porch. Basil followed. The house abutted on the edge of the bluff occupied by the residential section, and the two boys stood silent for a moment, gazing at the scattered lights of the lower city. Before the mystery of the unknown human life coursing through the streets below, Basil felt the purport of his words grow thin and pale.

He wondered suddenly what he had said and why it had seemed important to him, and when Joe began to sing again softly, the quiet mood of the early evening, the side of him that was best, wisest and most enduring, stole over him once more. The flattery, the vanity, the fatuousness of the last hour moved off, and when he spoke it was almost in a whisper:

"Let's walk around the block."

The sidewalk was warm to their bare feet. It was only midnight, but the square was deserted save for their whitish figures, inconspicuous against the starry darkness. They snorted with glee at their daring. Once a shadow, with loud human shoes, crossed the street far ahead, but the sound served only to increase their own unsubstantiality. Slipping quickly through the clearings made by gas lamps among the trees, they rounded the block, hurrying when they neared the Gorman house as though they had been really lost in a midsummer night's dream.

Up in Joe's room, they lay awake in the darkness.

"I talked too much," Basil thought. "I probably sounded pretty bossy and maybe I made him sort of mad. But probably when we walked around the block he forgot everything I said."

Alas, Joe had forgotten nothing—except the advice by which Basil had intended him to profit.

"I never saw anybody as stuck up," he said to himself wrathfully. "He thinks he's wonderful. He thinks he's so darn popular with girls."

III

An element of vast importance had made its appearance with the summer; suddenly the great thing in Basil's crowd was to own an automobile. Fun no longer seemed available save at great distances, at suburban lakes or remote country clubs. Walking downtown ceased to be a legitimate pastime. On the contrary, a single block from one youth's house to another's must be navigated in a car. Dependent groups formed around owners and they began to wield what was, to Basil at least, a disconcerting power.

On the morning of a dance at the lake he called up Riply Buckner.

"Hey, Rip, how you going out to Connie's tonight?"

"With Elwood Leaming."

"Has he got a lot of room?"

Riply seemed somewhat embarrassed. "Why, I don't think he has. You see, he's taking Margaret Torrence and I'm taking Imogene Bissel."

"Oh!"

Basil frowned. He should have arranged all this a week ago. After a moment he called up Joe Gorman.

"Going to the Davies' tonight, Joe?"

"Why, yes."

"Have you got room in your car—I mean, could I go with you?"

"Why, yes, I suppose so."

There was a perceptible lack of warmth in his voice.

"Sure you got plenty of room?"

"Sure. We'll call for you quarter to eight."

Basil began preparations at five. For the second time in his life he shaved, completing the operation by cutting a short straight line under his nose. It bled profusely, but on the advice of Hilda, the maid, he finally stanched the flow with little pieces of toilet paper. Quite a number of pieces were necessary; so, in order to facilitate breathing, he trimmed it down with a scissors, and with this somewhat awkward mustache of paper and gore clinging to his upper lip, wandered impatiently around the house.

At six he began working on it again, soaking off the tissue paper and dabbing at the persistently freshening crimson line. It dried at length, but when he rashly hailed his mother it opened once more and the tissue paper was called back into play.

At quarter to eight, dressed in blue coat and white flannels, he drew one last bar of powder across the blemish, dusted it carefully with his handkerchief and hurried out to Joe Gorman's car. Joe was driving in person, and in front with him were Lewis Crum and Hubert Blair. Basil got in the big rear seat alone and they drove without stopping out of the city onto the Black Bear Road, keeping their backs to him and talking in low voices together. He thought at first that they were going to pick up other boys; now he was shocked, and for a moment he considered getting out of the car, but this would imply that he was hurt. His spirit, and with it his face, hardened a little and he sat without speaking or being spoken to for the rest of the ride.

After half an hour the Davies' house, a huge rambling bungalow occupying a small peninsula in the lake, floated into sight. Lanterns outlined its shape and wavered in gleaming lines on the gold-and-rose colored water, and as they came near, the low notes of bass horns and drums were blown toward them from the lawn.

Inside Basil looked about for Imogene. There was a crowd around her seeking dances, but she saw Basil; his heart bounded at her quick intimate smile.

"You can have the fourth, Basil, and the eleventh and the second extra. . . . How did you hurt your lip?"

"Cut it shaving," he said hurriedly. "How about supper?"

"Well, I have to have supper with Riply because he brought me."

"No, you don't," Basil assured her.

"Yes, she does," insisted Riply, standing close at hand. "Why don't you get your own girl for supper?"

—but Basil had no girl, though he was as yet unaware of the fact.

After the fourth dance, Basil led Imogene down to the end of the pier, where they found seats in a motorboat.

"Now what?" she said.

He did not know. If he had really cared for her he would have known. When her hand rested on his knee for a moment he did not notice it. Instead, he talked. He told her how he had pitched on the second baseball team at school and had once beaten the first in a five-inning game. He told her that the thing was that some boys were popular with boys and some boys were popular with girls—he, for instance, was popular with girls. In short, he unloaded himself.

At length, feeling that he had perhaps dwelt disproportionately on himself, he told her suddenly that she was his favorite girl.

Imogene sat there, sighing a little in the moonlight. In another boat, lost in the darkness beyond the pier, sat a party of four. Joe Gorman was singing:

> "My little love—
> —in honey man,
> He sure has won my——"

"I thought you might want to know," said Basil to Imogene. "I thought maybe you thought I liked somebody else. The truth game didn't get around to me the other night."

"What?" asked Imogene vaguely. She had forgotten the other night, all nights except this, and she was thinking of the magic in Joe Gorman's voice. She had the next dance with him; he was going to teach her the words of a new song. Basil was sort of peculiar, telling her all this stuff. He was good-looking and attractive and all that, but—she wanted the dance to be over. She wasn't having any fun.

The music began inside—"Everybody's Doing It," played with many little nervous jerks on the violins.

"Oh, listen!" she cried, sitting up and snapping her fingers. "Do you know how to rag?"

"Listen, Imogene"—He half realized that something had slipped away—"let's sit out this dance—you can tell Joe you forgot."

She rose quickly. "Oh, no, I can't!"

Unwillingly Basil followed her inside. It had not gone well —he had talked too much again. He waited moodily for the eleventh dance so that he could behave differently. He believed now that he was in love with Imogene. His self-deception created a tightness in his throat, a counterfeit of longing and desire.

Before the eleventh dance he was aware that some party was being organized from which he was purposely excluded. There were whisperings and arguings among some of the boys, and unnatural silences when he came near. He heard Joe Gorman say to Riply Buckner, "We'll just be gone three days. If Gladys can't go, why don't you ask Connie? The chaperons'll—" he changed his sentence as he saw Basil—"and we'll all go to Smith's for ice-cream soda."

Later, Basil took Riply Buckner aside but failed to elicit any information: Riply had not forgotten Basil's attempt to rob him of Imogene tonight.

"It wasn't about anything," he insisted. "We're going to Smith's, honest. . . . How'd you cut your lip?"

"Cut it shaving."

When his dance with Imogene came she was even vaguer than before, exchanging mysterious communications with various girls as they moved around the room, locked in the convulsive grip of the Grizzly Bear. He led her out to the boat again, but it was occupied, and they walked up and down the pier while he tried to talk to her and she hummed:

"My little lov-in honey man——"

"Imogene, listen. What I wanted to ask you when we were on the boat before was about the night we played Truth. Did you really mean what you said?"

"Oh, what do you want to talk about that silly game for?"

It had reached her ears, not once but several times, that Basil thought he was wonderful—news that was flying about with as much volatility as the rumor of his graces two weeks before.

89

Imogene liked to agree with everyone—and she had agreed with several impassioned boys that Basil was terrible. And it was difficult not to dislike him for her own disloyalty.

But Basil thought that only ill luck ended the intermission before he could accomplish his purpose; though what he had wanted he had not known.

Finally, during the intermission, Margaret Torrence, whom he had neglected, told him the truth.

"Are you going on the touring party up to the St. Croix River?" she asked. She knew he was not.

"What party?"

"Joe Gorman got it up. I'm going with Elwood Leaming."

"No, I'm not going," he said gruffly. "I couldn't go."

"Oh!"

"I don't like Joe Gorman."

"I guess he doesn't like you much either."

"Why? What did he say?"

"Oh, nothing."

"But what? Tell me what he said."

After a minute she told him, as if reluctantly: "Well, he and Hubert Blair said you thought—you thought you were wonderful." Her heart misgave her.

But she remembered he had asked her for only one dance. "Joe said you told him that all the girls thought you were wonderful."

"I never said anything like that," said Basil indignantly, "never!"

He understood—Joe Gorman had done it all, taken advantage of Basil's talking too much—an affliction which his real friends had always allowed for—in order to ruin him. The world was suddenly compact of villainy. He decided to go home.

In the coat room he was accosted by Bill Kampf: "Hello, Basil, how did you hurt your lip?"

"Cut it shaving."

"Say, are you going to this party they're getting up next week?"

"No."

"Well, look, I've got a cousin from Chicago coming to stay with us and mother said I could have a boy out for the week-end. Her name is Minnie Bibble."

"Minnie Bibble?" repeated Basil, vaguely revolted.

"I thought maybe you were going to that party, too, but Riply Buckner said to ask you and I thought——"

"I've got to stay home," said Basil quickly.

"Oh, come on, Basil," he pursued. "It's only for two days, and she's a nice girl. You'd like her."

"I don't know," Basil considered. "I'll tell you what I'll do, Bill. I've got to get the street car home. I'll come out for the week-end if you'll take me over to Wildwood now in your car."

"Sure I will."

Basil walked out on the veranda and approached Connie Davies.

"Good-by," he said. Try as he might, his voice was stiff and proud. "I had an awfully good time."

"I'm sorry you're leaving so early, Basil." But she said to herself: "He's too stuck up to have a good time. He thinks he's wonderful."

From the veranda he could hear Imogene's laughter down at the end of the pier. Silently he went down the steps and along the walk to meet Bill Kampf, giving strollers a wide berth as though he felt the sight of him would diminish their pleasure.

It had been an awful night.

Ten minutes later Bill dropped him beside the waiting trolley. A few last picnickers sauntered aboard and the car bobbed and clanged through the night toward St. Paul.

Presently two young girls sitting opposite Basil began looking over at him and nudging each other, but he took no notice —he was thinking how sorry they would all be—Imogene and Margaret, Joe and Hubert and Riply.

"Look at him now!" they would say to themselves sorrowfully. "President of the United States at twenty-five! Oh, if we only hadn't been so bad to him that night!"

He thought he was wonderful!

IV

Ermine Gilberte Labouisse Bibble was in exile. Her parents had brought her from New Orleans to Southampton in May, hoping that the active outdoor life proper to a girl of fifteen would take her thoughts from love. But North or South, a storm of sapling arrows flew about her. She was "engaged" before the first of June.

Let it not be gathered from the foregoing that the somewhat hard outlines of Miss Bibble at twenty had already begun to appear. She was of a radiant freshness; her head had reminded otherwise not illiterate young men of damp blue violets, pierced with blue windows that looked into a bright soul, with today's new roses showing through.

She was in exile. She was going to Glacier National Park to forget. It was written that in passage she would come to Basil as a sort of initiation, turning his eyes out from himself and giving him a first dazzling glimpse into the world of love.

She saw him first as a quiet handsome boy with an air of consideration in his face, which was the mark of his recent re-discovery that others had wills as strong as his, and more power. It appeared to Minnie—as a few months back it had appeared to Margaret Torrence, like a charming sadness. At dinner he was polite to Mrs. Kampf in a courteous way that he had from his father, and he listened to Mr. Bibble's discussion of the word "Creole" with such evident interest and appreciation that Mr. Bibble thought, "Now here's a young boy with something *to* him."

After dinner, Minnie, Basil and Bill rode into Black Bear village to the movies, and the slow diffusion of Minnie's charm and personality presently became the charm and personality of the affair itself.

It was thus that all Minnie's affairs for many years had a family likeness. She looked at Basil, a childish open look; then opened her eyes wider as if she had some sort of comic misgivings, and smiled—she smiled—

For all the candor of this smile, its effect, because of the special contours of Minnie's face and independent of her mood, was of sparkling invitation. Whenever it appeared Basil seemed to be suddenly inflated and borne upward, a little farther each time, only to be set down when the smile had reached a point where it must become a grin, and chose instead to melt away. It was like a drug. In a little while he wanted nothing except to watch it with a vast buoyant delight.

Then he wanted to see how close he could get to it.

There is a certain stage of an affair between young people when the presence of a third party is a stimulant. Before the second day had well begun, before Minnie and Basil had progressed beyond the point of great gross compliments about each other's surpassing beauty and charm, both of them had begun to think about the time when they could get rid of their host, Bill Kampf.

In the late afternoon, when the first cool of the evening had come down and they were fresh and thin-feeling from swimming, they sat in a cushioned swing, piled high with pillows and shaded by the thick veranda vines; Basil put his arm around her and leaned toward her cheek and Minnie managed it that he touched her fresh lips instead. And he had always learned things quickly.

They sat there for an hour, while Bill's voice reached them, now from the pier, now from the hall above, now from the pagoda at the end of the garden, and three saddled horses chafed their bits in the stable and all around them the bees worked faithfully among the flowers. Then Minnie reached up to reality, and they allowed themselves to be found—

"Why, we were looking for you too."

And Basil, by simply waving his arms and wishing, floated miraculously upstairs to brush his hair for dinner.

"She certainly is a wonderful girl. Oh, gosh, she certainly is a wonderful girl!"

He mustn't lose his head. At dinner and afterward he listened with unwavering deferential attention while Mr. Bibble talked of the boll weevil.

"But I'm boring you. You children want to go off by yourselves."

"Not at all, Mr. Bibble. I was very interested—honestly."

"Well, you all go on and amuse yourselves. I didn't realize time was getting on. Nowadays it's so seldom you meet a young man with good manners and good common sense in his head, that an old man like me is likely to go along forever."

Bill walked down with Basil and Minnie to the end of the pier. "Hope we'll have a good sailing tomorrow. Say, I've got to drive over to the village and get somebody for my crew. Do you want to come along?"

"I reckon I'll sit here for a while and then go to bed," said Minnie.

"All right. You want to come, Basil?"

"Why—why, sure, if you want me, Bill."

"You'll have to sit on a sail I'm taking over to be mended."

"I don't want to crowd you."

"You won't crowd me. I'll go get the car."

When he had gone they looked at each other in despair. But he did not come back for an hour—something happened about the sail or the car that took a long time. There was only the threat, making everything more poignant and breathless, that at any minute he *would* be coming.

By and by they got into the motorboat and sat close together murmuring: "This fall—" "When you come to New Orleans—" "When I go to Yale year after next—" "When I come North to school—" "When I get back from Glacier Park—" "Kiss me once more." . . . "You're terrible. Do you know you're terrible? . . . You're absolutely terrible——"

The water lapped against the posts; sometimes the boat bumped gently on the pier; Basil undid one rope and pushed, so that they swung off and way from the pier, and became a little island in the night . . .

. . . next morning, while he packed his bag, she opened the door of his room and stood beside him. Her face shone with excitement; her dress was starched and white.

"Basil, listen! I have to tell you: Father was talking after breakfast and he told Uncle George that he'd never met such a nice, quiet, level-headed boy as you, and Cousin Bill's got to tutor this month, so father asked Uncle George if he thought your family would let you go to Glacier Park with us for two weeks so I'd have some company." They took hands and danced excitedly around the room. "Don't say anything about it, because I reckon he'll have to write your mother and everything. Basil, isn't it wonderful?"

So when Basil left at eleven, there was no misery in their parting. Mr. Bibble, going into the village for a paper, was going to escort Basil to his train, and till the motor-car moved away the eyes of the two young people shone and there was a secret in their waving hands.

Basil sank back in the seat, replete with happiness. He relaxed—to have made a success of the visit was so nice. He loved her—he loved even her father sitting beside him, her father who was privileged to be so close to her, to fuddle himself at that smile.

Mr. Bibble lit a cigar. "Nice weather," he said. "Nice climate up to the end of October."

"Wonderful," agreed Basil. "I miss October now that I go East to school."

"Getting ready for college?"

"Yes, sir; getting ready for Yale." A new pleasurable thought occurred to him. He hesitated, but he knew that Mr. Bibble, who liked him, would share his joy. "I took my preliminaries this spring and I just heard from them—I passed six out of seven."

"Good for you!"

Again Basil hesitated, then he continued: "I got A in ancient history and B in English history and English A. And I got C in algebra A and Latin A and B. I failed French A."

"Good!" said Mr. Bibble.

"I should have passed them all," went on Basil, "but I didn't study hard at first. I was the youngest boy in my class and I had a sort of swelled head about it."

It was well that Mr. Bibble should know he was taking no dullard to Glacier National Park. Mr. Bibble took a long puff of his cigar.

On second thought, Basil decided that his last remark didn't have the right ring and he amended it a little.

"It wasn't exactly a swelled head, but I never had to study very much, because in English I'd usually read most of the books before, and in history I'd read a lot too." He broke off and tried again: "I mean, when you say swelled head you think of a boy just going around with his head swelled, sort of, saying, 'Oh, look how much I know!' Well, I wasn't like that. I mean, I didn't think I knew everything, but I was sort of——"

As he searched for the elusive word, Mr. Bibble said, "H'm!" and pointed with his cigar at a spot in the lake.

"There's a boat," he said.

"Yes," agreed Basil. "I don't know much about sailing. I never cared for it. Of course I've been out a lot, just tending boards and all that, but most of the time you have to sit with nothing to do. I like football."

"H'm!" said Mr. Bibble. "When I was your age I was out in the Gulf in a catboat every day."

"I guess it's fun if you like it," conceded Basil.

"Happiest days of my life."

The station was in sight. It occurred to Basil that he should make one final friendly gesture.

"Your daughter certainly is an attractive girl, Mr. Bibble," he said. "I usually get along with girls all right, but I don't usually like them very much. But I think your daughter is the most attractive girl I ever met." Then, as the car stopped, a faint misgiving overtook him and he was impelled to add with a disparaging little laugh. "Good-by. I hope I didn't talk too much."

"Not at all," said Mr. Bibble. "Good luck to you. Goo'-by."

A few minutes later, when Basil's train had pulled out, Mr. Bibble stood at the newsstand buying a paper and already drying his forehead against the hot July day.

"Yes, sir! That was a lesson not to do anything in a hurry," he was saying to himself vehemently. "Imagine listening to that fresh kid gabbling about himself all through Glacier Park! Thank the good Lord for that little ride!"

On his arrival home, Basil literally sat down and waited. Under no pretext would he leave the house save for short trips to the drug store for refreshments, whence he returned on a full run. The sound of the telephone or the door-bell galvanized him into the rigidity of the electric chair.

That afternoon he composed a wondrous geographical poem, which he mailed to Minnie:

> Of all the fair flowers of Paris
> Of all the red roses of Rome,

Of all the deep tears of Vienna
   The sadness wherever you roam,
I think of that night by the lakeside,
   The beam of the moon and stars,
And the smell of an aching like perfume,
   The tune of the Spanish guitars.

But Monday passed and most of Tuesday and no word came. Then, late in the afternoon of the second day, as he moved vaguely from room to room looking out of different windows into a barren lifeless street, Minnie called him on the phone.

"Yes?" His heart was beating wildly.

"Basil, we're going this afternoon."

"Going!" he repeated blankly.

"Oh, Basil, I'm so sorry. Father changed his mind about taking anybody West with us."

"Oh!"

"I'm so sorry, Basil."

"I probably couldn't have gone."

There was a moment's silence. Feeling her presence over the wire, he could scarcely breathe, much less speak.

"Basil, can you hear me?"

"Yes."

"We may come back this way. Anyhow, remember we're going to meet this winter in New York."

"Yes," he said, and he added suddenly: "Perhaps we won't ever meet again."

"Of course we will. They're calling me, Basil. I've got to go. Good-by."

He sat down beside the telephone, wild with grief. The maid found him half an hour later bowed over the kitchen table. He knew what had happened as well as if Minnie had told him. He had made the same old error, undone the behavior of three days in half an hour. It would have been no consolation if it had occurred to him that it was just as well. Somewhere on the trip he would have let go and things might have been worse— though perhaps not so sad. His only thought now was that she was gone.

He lay on his bed, baffled, mistaken, miserable but not

beaten. Time after time, the same vitality that had led his spirit to a scourging made him able to shake off the blood like water not to forget, but to carry his wounds with him to new disasters and new atonements—toward his unknown destiny.

Two days later his mother told him that on condition of his keeping the batteries on charge, and washing it once a week, his grandfather had consented to let him use the electric whenever it was idle in the afternoon. Two hours later he was out in it, gliding along Crest Avenue at the maximum speed permitted by the gears and trying to lean back as if it were a Stutz Bearcat. Imogene Bissel waved at him from in front of her house and he came to an uncertain stop.

"You've got a car!"

"It's grandfather's," he said modestly. "I thought you were up on that party at the St. Croix."

She shook her head. "Mother wouldn't let me go—only a few girls went. There was a big accident over in Minneapolis and mother won't even let me ride in a car unless there's someone over eighteen driving."

"Listen, Imogene, do you suppose your mother meant electrics?"

"Why, I never thought—I don't know. I could go and see."

"Tell your mother it won't go over twelve miles an hour," he called after her.

A minute later she ran joyfully down the walk. "I can go, Basil," she cried. "Mother never heard of any wrecks in an electric. What'll we do?"

"Anything," he said in a reckless voice. "I didn't mean that about this bus making only twelve miles an hour—it'll make fifteen. Listen, let's go down to Smith's and have a claret lemonade."

"Why, Basil Lee!"

The Captured Shadow

Basil Duke Lee shut the front door behind him and turned on the dining-room light. His mother's voice drifted sleepily downstairs:

"Basil, is that you?"

"No, mother, it's a burglar."

"It seems to me twelve o'clock is pretty late for a fifteen-year-old boy."

"We went to Smith's and had a soda."

Whenever a new responsibility devolved upon Basil he was "a boy almost sixteen," but when a privilege was in question, he was "a fifteen-year-old boy."

There were footsteps above, and Mrs. Lee, in kimono, descended to the first landing.

"Did you and Riply enjoy the play?"

"Yes, very much."

"What was it about?"

"Oh, it was just about this man. Just an ordinary play."

"Didn't it have a name?"

" 'Are You a Mason?' "

"Oh." She hesitated, covetously watching his alert and eager face, holding him there. "Aren't you coming to bed?"

"I'm going to get something to eat."

"Something more?"

For a moment he didn't answer. He stood in front of a glassed-in bookcase in the living room, examining its contents with an equally glazed eye.

"We're going to get up a play," he said suddenly. "I'm going to write it."

"Well—that'll be very nice. Please come to bed soon. You were up late last night, too, and you've got dark circles under your eyes."

From the bookcase Basil presently extracted "Van Bibber and Others," from which he read while he ate a large plate of strawberries softened with half a pint of cream. Back in the living room he sat for a few minutes at the piano, digesting, and meanwhile staring at the colored cover of a song from "The Midnight Sons." It showed three men in evening clothes and opera hats sauntering jovially along Broadway against the blazing background of Times Square.

Basil would have denied incredulously the suggestion that that was currently his favorite work of art. But it was.

He went upstairs. From a drawer of his desk he took out a composition book and opened it.

BASIL DUKE LEE
St. Regis School
Eastchester, Conn.
Fifth Form French

and on the next page, under Irregular Verbs:

PRESENT

je connais   nous con
tu connais
il connaît

He turned over another page.

MR. WASHINGTON SQUARE
A Musical Comedy by
BASIL DUKE LEE
Music by Victor Herbert

ACT I

[*The porch of the Millionaires' Club, near New York. Opening Chorus,* LEILIA *and* DEBUTANTES:

We sing not soft, we sing not loud
For no one ever heard an opening chorus.
We are a very merry crowd
But no one ever heard an opening chorus.
We're just a crowd of debutantes
As merry as can be
And nothing that there is could ever bore us
We're the wittiest ones, the prettiest ones.
In all society
But no one ever heard an opening chorus.

LEILIA (*stepping forward*): Well, girls, has Mr. Washington Square been around here today?

Basil turned over a page. There was no answer to Leilia's question. Instead in capitals was a brand-new heading:

HIC! HIC! HIC!
A Hilarious Farce in One Act
by
BASIL DUKE LEE

SCENE

[*A fashionable apartment near Broadway, New York City. It is almost midnight. As the curtain goes up there is a knocking at the door and a few minutes later it opens to admit a handsome man in a full evening dress and a companion. He has evidently been imbibing, for his words are thick, his nose is red, and he can hardly stand up. He turns up the light and comes down centre.*]

STUYVESANT: Hic! Hic! Hic!

O'HARA (*his companion*): Begorra, you been sayin' nothing else all this evening.

Basil turned over a page and then another, reading hurriedly, but not without interest.

PROFESSOR PUMPKIN: Now, if you are an educated man, as you claim, perhaps you can tell me the Latin word for "this."
STUYVESANT: Hic! Hic! Hic!
PROFESSOR PUMPKIN: Correct. Very good indeed. I——

At this point Hic! Hic! Hic! came to an end in midsentence. On the following page, in just as determined a hand as if the last two works had not faltered by the way, was the heavily underlined beginning of another:

THE CAPTURED SHADOW
A Melodramatic Farce in Three Acts
by
BASIL DUKE LEE

SCENE

[*All three acts take place in the library of the* VAN BAKERS'
*house in New York. It is well furnished with a red lamp on one
side and some crossed spears and helmets and so on and a
divan and a general air of an oriental den.*
When the curtain rises MISS SAUNDERS, LEILIA VAN BAKER
and ESTELLA CARRAGE *are sitting at a table.* MISS SAUNDERS
is an old maid about forty very kittenish. LEILIA *is pretty with
dark hair.* ESTELLA *has light hair. They are a striking combination.*

"The Captured Shadow" filled the rest of the book and ran
over into several loose sheets at the end. When it broke off
Basil sat for a while in thought. This had been a season of
"crook comedies" in New York, and the feel, the swing, the
exact and vivid image of the two he had seen, were in the
foreground of his mind. At the time they had been enormously
suggestive, opening out into a world much larger and more
brilliant than themselves that existed outside their windows
and beyond their doors, and it was this suggested world rather
than any conscious desire to imitate "Officer 666," that had
inspired the effort before him. Presently he printed ACT II at
the head of a new tablet and began to write.

An hour passed. Several times he had recourse to a collection
of joke books and to an old Treasury of Wit and Humor which
embalmed the faded Victorian cracks of Bishop Wilberforce
and Sydney Smith. At the moment when, in his story, a door
moved slowly open, he heard a heavy creak upon the stairs. He
jumped to his feet aghast and trembling, but nothing stirred;
only a white moth bounced against the screen, a clock struck
the half-hour far across the city, a bird whacked its wings in a
tree outside.

Voyaging to the bathroom at half-past four, he saw with a
shock that morning was already blue at the window. He had
stayed up all night. He remembered that people who stayed
up all night went crazy, and tranfixed in the hall, he tried
agonizingly to listen to himself, to feel whether or not he was

going crazy. The things around him seemed preternaturally unreal, and rushing frantically back into his bedroom, he began tearing off his clothes, racing after the vanishing night. Undressed, he threw a final regretful glance at his pile of manuscript—he had the whole next scene in his head. As a compromise with incipient madness he got into bed and wrote for an hour more.

Late next morning he was startled awake by one of the ruthless Scandinavian sisters who, in theory, were the Lees' servants. "Eleven o'clock!" she shouted. "Five after!"

"Let me alone," Basil mumbled. "What do you come and wake me up for?"

"Somebody downstairs." He opened his eyes. "You ate all the cream last night," Hilda continued. "Your mother didn't have any for her coffee."

"All the cream!" he cried. "Why, I saw some more."

"It was sour."

"That's terrible," he exclaimed, sitting up. "Terrible!"

For a moment she enjoyed his dismay. Then she said, "Riply Buckner's downstairs," and went out, closing the door.

"Send him up!" he called after her. "Hilda, why don't you ever listen for a minute? Did I get any mail?"

There was no answer. A moment later Riply came in.

"My gosh, are you still in bed?"

"I wrote on the play all night. I almost finished Act Two." He pointed to his desk.

"That's what I want to talk to you about," said Riply. "Mother thinks we ought to get Miss Halliburton."

"What for?"

"Just to sort of be there."

Though Miss Halliburton was a pleasant person who combined the occupations of French teacher and bridge teacher, unofficial chaperon and children's friend, Basil felt that her superintendence would give the project an unprofessional ring.

"She wouldn't interfere," went on Riply, obviously quoting his mother. "I'll be the business manager and you'll direct the play, just like we said, but it would be good to have her there

for prompter and to keep order at rehearsals. The girls' mothers'll like it."

"All right," Basil agreed reluctantly. "Now look, let's see
who we'll have in the cast. First, there's the leading man—this
gentleman burglar that's called The Shadow. Only it turns out
at the end that he's really a young man about town doing it on
a bet, and not really a burglar at all."

"That's you."

"No, that's you."

"Come on! You're the best actor," protested Riply.

"No, I'm going to take a smaller part, so I can coach."

"Well, haven't I got to be business manager?"

Selecting the actresses, presumably all eager, proved to be
a difficult matter. They settled finally on Imogene Bissel for
leading lady; Margaret Torrence for her friend, and Connie
Davies for "Miss Saunders, an old maid very kittenish."

On Riply's suggestion that several other girls wouldn't be
pleased at being left out, Basil introduced a maid and a cook,
"who could just sort of look in from the kitchen." He rejected
firmly Riply's further proposal that there should be two or
three maids, "a sort of sewing woman," and a trained nurse. In
a house so clogged with femininity even the most umbrageous
of gentleman burglars would have difficulty in moving about.

"I'll tell you two people we won't have," Basil said medita-
tively—"that's Joe Gorman and Hubert Blair."

"I wouldn't be in it if we had Hubert Blair," asserted Riply.

"Neither would I."

Hubert Blair's almost miraculous successes with girls had
caused Basil and Riply much jealous pain.

They began calling up the prospective cast and immediately
the enterprise received its first blow. Imogene Bissel was going
to Rochester, Minnesota, to have her appendix removed, and
wouldn't be back for three weeks.

They considered.

"How about Margaret Torrence?"

Basil shook his head. He had a vision of Leilia Van Baker as
someone rarer and more spirited than Margaret Torrence. Not
that Leilia had much being, even to Basil—less than the Harri-

son Fisher girls pinned around his wall at school. But she was not Margaret Torrence. She was no one you could inevitably see by calling up half an hour before on the phone.

He discarded candidate after candidate. Finally a face began to flash before his eyes, as if in another connection, but so insistently that at length he spoke the name.

"Evelyn Beebe."

"Who?"

Though Evelyn Beebe was only sixteen, her precocious charms had elevated her to an older crowd and to Basil she seemed of the very generation of his heroine, Leilia Van Baker. It was a little like asking Sarah Bernhardt for her services, but once her name had occurred to him, other possibilities seemed pale.

At noon they rang the Beebe's door-bell, stricken by a paralysis of embarrassment when Evelyn opened the door herself and, with politeness that concealed a certain surprise, asked them in.

Suddenly, through the portière of the living room, Basil saw and recognized a young man in golf knickerbockers.

"I guess we better not come in," he said quickly.

"We'll come some other time," Riply added.

Together they started precipitately for the door, but she barred their way.

"Don't be silly," she insisted. "It's just Andy Lockheart."

Just Andy Lockheart—winner of the Western Golf Championship at eighteen, captain of his freshman baseball team, handsome, successful at everything he tried, a living symbol of the splendid, glamorous world of Yale. For a year Basil had walked like him and tried unsuccessfully to play the piano by ear as Andy Lockheart was able to do.

Through sheer ineptitude at escaping, they were edged into the room. Their plan suddenly seemed presumptuous and absurd.

Perceiving their condition Evelyn tried to soothe them with pleasant banter.

"Well it's about time you came to see me," she told Basil. "Here I've been sitting at home every night waiting for you—

ever since the Davies dance. Why haven't you been here before?"

He stared at her blankly, unable even to smile, and muttered: "Yes, you have."

"I have though. Sit down and tell me why you've been neglecting me! I suppose you've both been rushing the beautiful Imogene Bissel."

"Why, I understand—" said Basil. "Why, I heard from somewhere that she's gone up to have some kind of an appendicitis —that is—" He ran down to a pitch of inaudibility as Andy Lockheart at the piano began playing a succession of thoughtful chords, which resolved itself into the maxixe, an eccentric stepchild of the tango. Kicking back a rug and lifting her skirts a little, Evelyn fluently tapped out a circle with her heels around the floor.

They sat inanimate as cushions on the sofa watching her. She was almost beautiful, with rather large features and bright fresh color behind which her heart seemed to be trembling a little with laughter. Her voice and her lithe body were always mimicking, ceaselessly caricaturing every sound and movement near by, until even those who disliked her admitted that "Evelyn could always make you laugh." She finished her dance now with a false stumble and an awed expression as she clutched at the piano, and Basil and Riply chuckled. Seeing their embarrassment lighten, she came and sat down beside them, and they laughed again when she said: "Excuse my lack of self-control."

"Do you want to be the leading lady in a play we're going to give?" demanded Basil with sudden desperation. "We're going to have it at the Martindale School, for the benefit of the Baby Welfare."

"Basil, this is so sudden."

Andy Lockheart turned around from the piano.

"What're you going to give—a minstrel show?"

"No, it's a crook play named The Captured Shadow. Miss Halliburton is going to coach it." He suddenly realized the convenience of that name to shelter himself behind.

"Why don't you give something like 'The Private Secretary'?" interrupted Andy. "There's a good play for you. We gave it my last year at school."

"Oh, no, it's all settled," said Basil quickly. "We're going to put on this play that I wrote."

"You wrote it yourself?" exclaimed Evelyn.

"Yes."

"My-y gosh!" said Andy. He began to play again.

"Look, Evelyn," said Basil. "It's only for three weeks, and you'd be the leading lady."

She laughed. "Oh, no. I couldn't. Why don't you get Imogene?"

"She's sick, I tell you. Listen——"

"Or Margaret Torrence?"

"I don't want anybody but you."

The directness of this appeal touched her and momentarily she hesitated. But the hero of the Western Golf Championship turned around from the piano with a teasing smile and she shook her head.

"I can't do it, Basil. I may have to go East with the family."

Reluctantly Basil and Riply got up.

"Gosh, I wish you'd be in it, Evelyn."

"I wish I could."

Basil lingered, thinking fast, wanting her more than ever; indeed, without her, it scarcely seemed worth while to go on with the play. Suddenly a desperate expedient took shape on his lips:

"You certainly would be wonderful. You see, the leading man is going to be Hubert Blair."

Breathlessly he watched her, saw her hesitate.

"Good-by," he said.

She came with them to the door and then out on the veranda, frowning a little.

"How long did you say the rehearsals would take?" she asked thoughtfully.

II

On an August evening three days later Basil read the play to the cast on Miss Halliburton's porch. He was nervous and at first there were interruptions of "Louder" and "Not so fast." Just as his audience was beginning to be amused by the repartee of the two comic crooks—repartee that had seen service with Weber and Fields—he was interrupted by the late arrival of Hubert Blair.

Hubert was fifteen, a somewhat shallow boy save for two or three felicities which he possessed to an extraordinary degree. But one excellence suggests the presence of others, and young ladies never failed to respond to his most casual fancy, enduring his fickleness of heart and never convinced that his fundamental indifference might not be overcome. They were dazzled by his flashing self-confidence, by his cherubic ingenuousness, which concealed a shrewd talent for getting around people, and by his extraordinary physical grace. Long-legged, beautifully proportioned, he had that tumbler's balance usually characteristic only of men "built near the ground." He was in constant motion that was a delight to watch, and Evelyn Beebe was not the only older girl who had found in him a mysterious promise and watched him for a long time with something more than curiosity.

He stood in the doorway now with an expression of bogus reverence on his round pert face.

"Excuse me," he said. "Is this the First Methodist Episcopal Church?" Everybody laughed—even Basil. "I didn't know. I thought maybe I was in the right church, but in the wrong pew."

They laughed again, somewhat discouraged. Basil waited until Hubert had seated himself beside Evelyn Beebe. Then he began to read once more, while the others, fascinated, watched Hubert's efforts to balance a chair on its hind legs. This squeaky experiment continued as an undertone to the reading. Not until Basil's desperate "Now, here's where you come in, Hube," did attention swing back to the play.

Basil read for more than an hour. When, at the end, he closed the composition book and looked up shyly, there was a burst of spontaneous applause. He had followed his models closely, and for all its grotesqueries, the result was actually interesting—it was a play. Afterward he lingered, talking to Miss Halliburton, and he walked home glowing with excitement and rehearsing a little by himself into the August night.

The first week of rehearsal was a matter of Basil climbing back and forth from auditorium to stage, crying, "No! Look here, Connie; you come in more like this." Then things began to happen. Mrs. Van Schellinger came to rehearsal one day, and lingering afterward, announced that she couldn't let Gladys be in "a play about criminals." Her theory was that this element could be removed; for instance, the two comic crooks could be changed to "two funny farmers."

Basil listened with horror. When she had gone he assured Miss Halliburton that he would change nothing. Luckily Gladys played the cook, an interpolated part that could be summarily struck out, but her absence was felt in another way. She was tranquil and tractable, "the most carefully brought-up girl in town," and at her withdrawal rowdiness appeared during rehearsals. Those who had only such lines as "I'll ask Mrs. Van Baker, sir," in Act I and "No, ma'am," in Act III showed a certain tendency to grow restless in between. So now it was:

"Please keep that dog quiet or else send him home!" or:

"Where's that maid? Wake up, Margaret, for heaven's sake!" or:

"What is there to laugh at that's so darn funny?"

More and more the chief problem was the tactful management of Hubert Blair. Apart from his unwillingness to learn his lines, he was a satisfactory hero, but off the stage he became a nuisance. He gave an endless private performance for Evelyn Beebe, which took such forms as chasing her amorously around the hall or of flipping peanuts over his shoulder to land mysteriously on the stage. Called to order, he would mutter, "Aw, shut up yourself," just loud enough for Basil to guess, but not to hear.

But Evelyn Beebe was all that Basil had expected. Once on the stage, she compelled a breathless attention, and Basil recognized this by adding to her part. He envied the half-sentimental fun that she and Hubert derived from their scenes together and he felt a vague, impersonal jealousy that almost every night after rehearsal they drove around together in Hubert's car.

One afternoon when matters had progressed a fortnight, Hubert came in an hour late, loafed through the first act and then informed Miss Halliburton that he was going home.

"What for?" Basil demanded.

"I've got some things I got to do."

"Are they important?"

"What business is that of yours?"

"Of course it's my business," said Basil heatedly, whereupon Miss Halliburton interfered.

"There's no use of anybody getting angry. What Basil means, Hubert, is that if it's just some small thing—why, we're all giving up our pleasures to make this play a success."

Hubert listened with obvious boredom.

"I've got to drive downtown and get father."

He looked coolly at Basil, as if challenging him to deny the adequacy of this explanation.

"Then why did you come an hour late?" demanded Basil.

"Because I had to do something for mother."

A group had gathered and he glanced around triumphantly. It was one of those sacred excuses, and only Basil saw that it was disingenuous.

"Oh, tripe!" he said.

"Maybe you think so—Bossy."

Basil took a step toward him, his eyes blazing.

"What'd you say?"

"I said 'Bossy.' Isn't that what they call you at school?"

It was true. It had followed him home. Even as he went white with rage a vast impotence surged over him at the realization that the past was always lurking near. The faces of school were around him, sneering and watching. Hubert laughed.

"Get out!" said Basil in a strained voice. "Go on! Get right out!"

Hubert laughed again, but as Basil took a step toward him he retreated.

"I don't want to be in your play anyhow. I never did."

"Then go on out of this hall."

"Now, Basil!" Miss Halliburton hovered breathlessly beside them. Hubert laughed again and looked about for his cap.

"I wouldn't be in your crazy old show," he said. He turned slowly and jauntily, and sauntered out the door.

Riply Buckner read Hubert's part that afternoon, but there was a cloud upon the rehearsal. Miss Beebe's performance lacked its customary verve and the others clustered and whispered, falling silent when Basil came near. After the rehearsal, Miss Halliburton, Riply and Basil held a conference. Upon Basil flatly refusing to take the leading part, it was decided to enlist a certain Mayall De Bec, known slightly to Riply, who had made a name for himself in theatricals at the Central High School.

But next day a blow fell that was irreparable. Evelyn, flushed and uncomfortable, told Basil and Miss Halliburton that her family's plans had changed—they were going East next week and she couldn't be in the play after all. Basil understood. Only Hubert had held her this long.

"Good-by," he said gloomily.

His manifest despair shamed her and she tried to justify herself.

"Really, I can't help it. Oh, Basil, I'm so sorry!"

"Couldn't you stay over a week with me after your family goes?" Miss Halliburton asked innocently.

"Not possibly. Father wants us all to go together. That's the only reason. If it wasn't for that I'd stay."

"All right," Basil said. "Good-by."

"Basil, you're not mad, are you?" A gust of repentance swept over her. "I'll do anything to help. I'll come to rehearsals this week until you get someone else, and then I'll try to help her all I can. But father says we've got to go."

In vain Riply tried to raise Basil's morale after the rehearsal that afternoon, making suggestions which he waved contemptuously away. Margaret Torrence? Connie Davies? They could hardly play the parts they had. It seemed to Basil as if the undertaking was falling to pieces before his eyes.

It was still early when he got home. He sat dispiritedly by his bedroom window, watching the little Barnfield boy playing a lonesome game by himself in the yard next door.

His mother came in at five, and immediately sensed his depression.

"Teddy Barnfield has the mumps," she said, in an effort to distract him. "That's why he's playing there all alone."

"Has he?" he responded listlessly.

"It isn't at all dangerous, but it's very contagious. You had it when you were seven."

"H'm."

She hesitated.

"Are you worrying about your play? Has anything gone wrong?"

"No, mother. I just want to be alone."

After a while he got up and started after a malted milk at the soda fountain around the corner. It was half in his mind to see Mr. Beebe and ask him if he couldn't postpone his trip East. If he could only be sure that that was Evelyn's real reason.

The sight of Evelyn's nine-year-old brother coming along the street broke in on his thoughts.

"Hello, Ham. I hear you're going away."

Ham nodded.

"Going next week. To the seashore."

Basil looked at him speculatively, as if, through his proximity to Evelyn, he held the key to the power of moving her.

"Where are you going now?" he asked.

"I'm going to play with Teddy Barnfield."

"What!" Basil exclaimed. "Why, didn't you know—" He stopped. A wild, criminal idea broke over him; his mother's words floated through his mind: "It isn't at all dangerous, but it's very contagious." If little Ham Beebe got the mumps, and Evelyn *couldn't* go away—

He came to a decision quickly and coolly.

"Teddy's playing in his back yard," he said. "If you want to see him without going through his house, why don't you go down this street and turn up the alley?"

"All right. Thanks," said Ham trustingly.

Basil stood for a minute looking after him until he turned the corner into the alley, fully aware that it was the worst thing he had ever done in his life.

III

A week later Mrs. Lee had an early supper—all Basil's favorite things: chipped beef, french-fried potatoes, sliced peaches and cream, and devil's food.

Every few minutes Basil said, "Gosh! I wonder what time it is," and went out in the hall to look at the clock. "Does that clock work right?" he demanded with sudden suspicion. It was the first time the matter had ever interested him.

"Perfectly all right. If you eat so fast you'll have indigestion and then you won't be able to act well."

"What do you think of the program?" he asked for the third time. "Riply Buckner, Jr., presents Basil Duke Lee's comedy, 'The Captured Shadow.'"

"I think it's very nice."

"He doesn't really present it."

"It sounds very well though."

"I wonder what time it is?" he inquired.

"You just said it was ten minutes after six."

"Well, I guess I better be starting."

"Eat your peaches, Basil. If you don't eat you won't be able to act."

"I don't have to act," he said patiently. "All I am is a small part, and it wouldn't matter—" It was too much trouble to explain.

"Please don't smile at me when I come on, mother," he requested. "Just act as if I was anybody else."

"Can't I even say how-do-you-do?"

"What?" Humor was lost on him. He said good-by. Trying very hard to digest not his food but his heart, which had somehow slipped down into his stomach, he started off for the Martindale School.

As its yellow windows loomed out of the night his excitement became insupportable; it bore no resemblance to the building he had been entering so casually for three weeks. His footsteps echoed symbolically and portentously in its deserted hall; upstairs there was only the janitor setting out the chairs in rows, and Basil wandered about the vacant stage until someone came in.

It was Mayall De Bec, the tall, clever, not very likeable youth they had imported from Lower Crest Avenue to be the leading man. Mayall, far from being nervous, tried to engage Basil in casual conversation. He wanted to know if Basil thought Evelyn Beebe would mind if he went to see her sometime when the show was over. Basil supposed not. Mayall said he had a friend whose father owned a brewery who owned a twelve-cylinder car.

Basil said, 'Gee!"

At quarter to seven the participants arrived in groups—Riply Buckner with the six boys he had gathered to serve as ticket takers and ushers; Miss Halliburton, trying to seem very calm and reliable; Evelyn Beebe, who came in as if she were yielding herself up to something and whose glance at Basil seemed to say: "Well, it looks as if I'm really going through with it after all."

Mayall De Bec was to make up the boys and Miss Halliburton the girls. Basil soon came to the conclusion that Miss Halliburton knew nothing about make-up, but he judged it diplomatic, in that lady's overwrought condition, to say nothing, but to take each girl to Mayall for corrections when Miss Halliburton had done.

An exclamation from Bill Kampf, standing at a crack in the curtain, brought Basil to his side. A tall bald-headed man in spectacles had come in and was shown to a seat in the middle of the house, where he examined the program. He was the public. Behind those waiting eyes, suddenly so mysterious and incalculable, was the secret of the play's failure or success. He finished the program, took off his glasses and looked around. Two old ladies and two little boys came in, followed immediately by a dozen more.

"Hey, Riply," Basil called softly. "Tell them to put the children down in front."

Riply, struggling into his policeman's uniform, looked up, and the long black mustache on his upper lip quivered indignantly.

"I thought of that long ago."

The hall, filling rapidly, was now alive with the buzz of conversation. The children in front were jumping up and down in their seats, and everyone was talking and calling back and forth save the several dozen cooks and housemaids who sat in stiff and quiet pairs about the room.

Then, suddenly, everything was ready. It was incredible. "Stop! Stop!" Basil wanted to say. "It can't be ready. There must be something—there always has been something," but the darkened auditorium and the piano and violin from Geyer's Orchestra playing "Meet Me in the Shadows" belied his words. Miss Saunders, Leilia Van Baker and Leilia's friend, Estella Carrage, were already seated on the stage, and Miss Halliburton stood in the wings with the prompt book. Suddenly the music ended and the chatter in front died away.

"Oh, gosh!" Basil thought. "Oh, my gosh!"

The curtain rose. A clear voice floated up from somewhere. Could it be from that unfamiliar group on the stage?

I will, Miss Saunders. I tell you I will!

But, Miss Leilia, I don't consider the newspapers proper for young ladies nowadays.

I don't care. I want to read about this wonderful gentleman burglar they call The Shadow.

It was actually going on. Almost before he realized it, a ripple of laughter passed over the audience as Evelyn gave her imitation of Miss Saunders behind her back.

"Get ready, Basil," breathed Miss Halliburton.

Basil and Bill Kampf, the crooks, each took an elbow of Victor Van Baker, the dissolute son of the house, and made ready to aid him through the front door.

It was strangely natural to be out on the stage with all those eyes looking up encouragingly. His mother's face floated past him, other faces that he recognized and remembered.

Bill Kampf stumbled on a line and Basil picked him up quickly and went on.

MISS SAUNDERS: So you are alderman from the Sixth Ward?
RABBIT SIMMONS: Yes, ma'am.
MISS SAUNDERS (*shaking her head kittenishly*): Just what is an alderman?

CHINAMAN RUDD: An alderman is halfway between a politician and a pirate.

This was one of Basil's lines that he was particularly proud of—but there was not a sound from the audience, not a smile. A moment later Bill Kampf absent-mindedly wiped his forehead with his handkerchief and then stared at it, startled by the red stains of make-up on it—and the audience roared. The theatre was like that.

MISS SAUNDERS: Then you believe in spirits, Mr. Rudd.
CHINAMAN RUDD: Yes, ma'am, I certainly do believe in spirits. Have you got any?

The first big scene came. On the darkened stage a window rose slowly and Mayall De Bec, "in a full evening dress," climbed over the sill. He was tiptoeing cautiously from one side of the stage to the other, when Leilia Van Baker came in. For a moment she was frightened, but he assured her that he was a friend of her brother Victor. They talked. She told him naïvely yet feelingly of her admiration for The Shadow, of whose exploits she had read. She hoped, though, that The Shadow would not come here tonight, as the family jewels were all in that safe at the right.

The stranger was hungry. He had been late for his dinner and so had not been able to get any that night. Would he have some crackers and milk? That would be fine. Scarcely had she left the room when he was on his knees by the safe, fumbling at the catch, undeterred by the unpromising word "Cake" stencilled on the safe's front. It swung open, but he heard footsteps outside and closed it just as Leilia came back with the crackers and milk.

They lingered, obviously attracted to each other. Miss Saunders came in, very kittenish, and was introduced. Again Evelyn mimicked her behind her back and the audience roared. Other members of the household appeared and were introduced to the stranger.

What's this? A banging at the door, and Mulligan, a policeman, rushes in.

We have just received word from the Central Office that the notorious Shadow has been seen climbing in the window! No one can leave this house tonight!

The curtain fell. The first rows of the audience—the younger brothers and sisters of the cast—were extravagant in their enthusiasm. The actors took a bow.

A moment later Basil found himself alone with Evelyn Beebe on the stage. A weary doll in her make-up she was leaning against a table.

"Heigh-ho, Basil," she said.

She had not quite forgiven him for holding her to her promise after her little brother's mumps had postponed their trip East, and Basil had tactfully avoided her, but now they met in the genial glow of excitement and success.

"You were wonderful," he said— "Wonderful!"

He lingered a moment. He could never please her, for she wanted someone like herself, someone who could reach her through her senses, like Hubert Blair. Her intuition told her that Basil was of a certain vague consequence; beyond that his incessant attempts to make people think and feel, bothered and wearied her. But suddenly, in the glow of the evening, they leaned forward and kissed peacefully, and from that moment, because they had no common ground even to quarrel on, they were friends for life.

When the curtain rose upon the second act Basil slipped down a flight of stairs and up to another to the back of the hall, where he stood watching in the darkness. He laughed silently when the audience laughed, enjoying it as if it were a play he had never seen before.

There was a second and a third act scene that were very similar. In each of them The Shadow, alone on the stage, was interrupted by Miss Saunders. Mayall De Bec, having had but ten days of rehearsal, was inclined to confuse the two, but Basil was totally unprepared for what happened. Upon Connie's entrance Mayall spoke his third-act line and involuntarily Connie answered in kind.

Others coming on the stage were swept up in the nervousness and confusion, and suddenly they were playing the third act in the middle of the second. It happened so quickly that for a moment Basil had only a vague sense that something was wrong. Then he dashed down one stairs and up another and into the wings, crying:

"Let down the curtain! Let down the curtain!"

The boys who stood there aghast sprang to the rope. In a minute Basil, breathless, was facing the audience.

"Ladies and gentlemen," he said, "there's been changes in the cast and what just happened was a mistake. If you'll excuse us we'd like to do that scene over."

He stepped back in the wings to a flutter of laughter and applause.

"All right, Mayall!" he called excitedly. "On the stage alone. Your line is: 'I just want to see that the jewels are all right,' and Connie's is: 'Go ahead, don't mind me.' All right! Curtain up!"

In a moment things righted themselves. Someone brought water for Miss Halliburton, who was in a state of collapse, and as the act ended they all took a curtain call once more. Twenty minutes later it was over. The hero clasped Leilia Van Baker to his breast, confessing that he was The Shadow, "and a captured Shadow at that"; the curtain went up and down, up and down; Miss Halliburton was dragged unwillingly on the stage and the ushers came up the aisles laden with flowers. Then everything became informal and the actors mingled happily with the audience, laughing and important, congratulated from all sides. An old man whom Basil didn't know came up to him and shook his hand, saying, "You're a young man that's going to be heard from some day," and a reporter from the paper asked him if he was really only fifteen. It might all have been very bad and demoralizing for Basil, but it was already behind him. Even as the crowd melted away and the last few people spoke to him and went out, he felt a great vacancy come into his heart. It was over, it was done and gone—all that work, and interest and absorption. It was a hollowness like fear.

"Good night, Miss Halliburton. Good night, Evelyn."

"Good night, Basil. Congratulations, Basil. Good night."

"Where's my coat? Good night, Basil."

"Leave your costumes on the stage, please. They've got to go back tomorrow."

He was almost the last to leave, mounting to the stage for a moment and looking around the deserted hall. His mother was waiting and they strolled home together through the first cool night of the year.

"Well, I thought it went very well indeed. Were you satisfied?" He didn't answer for a moment. "Weren't you satisfied with the way it went?"

"Yes." He turned his head away.

"What's the matter?"

"Nothing," and then. "Nobody really cares, do they?"

"About what?"

"About anything."

"Everybody cares about different things. I care about you, for instance."

Instinctively he ducked away from a hand extended caressingly toward him: "Oh, don't. I don't mean like that."

"You're just overwrought, dear."

"I am not overwrought. I just feel sort of sad."

"You shouldn't feel sad. Why, people told me after the play——"

"Oh, that's all over. Don't talk about that—don't ever talk to me about that any more."

"Then what are you sad about?"

"Oh, about a little boy."

"What little boy?"

"Oh, little Ham—you wouldn't understand."

"When we get home I want you to take a real hot bath and quiet your nerves."

"All right."

But when he got home he fell immediately into deep sleep on the sofa. She hesitated. Then covering him with a blanket and a comforter, she pushed a pillow under his protesting head and went upstairs.

She knelt for a long time beside her bed.

"God, help him! help him," she prayed, "because he needs help that I can't give him any more."

The Perfect Life

I

When he came into the dining room, a little tired, but with his clothes hanging cool and free on him after his shower, the whole school stood up and clapped and cheered until he slunk down into his seat. From one end of the table to the other, people leaned forward and smiled at him.

"Nice work, Lee. Not your fault we didn't win."

Basil knew that he had been good. Up to the last whistle he could feel his expended energy miraculously replacing itself after each surpassing effort. But he couldn't realize his success all at once, and only little episodes lingered with him, such as when that shaggy Exeter tackle stood up big in the line and said, "Let's get that quarter! He's yellow." Basil shouted back,

"Yellow your gra'mother!" and the linesman grinned good-naturedly, knowing it wasn't true. During that gorgeous hour bodies had no weight or force; Basil lay under piles of them, tossed himself in front of them without feeling the impact, impatient only to be on his feet dominating those two green acres once more. At the end of the first half he got loose for sixty yards and a touchdown, but the whistle had blown and it was not allowed. That was the high point of the game for St. Regis. Outweighed ten pounds to the man, they wilted down suddenly in the fourth quarter and Exeter put over two touchdowns, glad to win over a school whose membership was only one hundred and thirty-five.

When lunch was over and the school was trooping out of the dining hall, the Exeter coach came over to Basil and said:

"Lee, that was about the best game I've ever seen played by a pre-school back, and I've seen a lot of them."

Doctor Bacon beckoned to him. He was standing with two old St. Regis boys, up from Princeton for the day.

"It was a very exciting game, Basil. We are all very proud of the team and—ah—especially of you." And, as if this praise had been an indiscretion, he hastened to add: "And of all the others."

He presented him to the two alumni. One of them, John Granby, Basil knew by reputation. He was said to be a "big man" at Princeton—serious, upright, handsome, with a kindly smile and large, earnest blue eyes. He had graduated from St. Regis before Basil entered.

"That was pretty work, Lee!" Basil made the proper deprecatory noises. "I wonder if you've got a moment this afternoon when we could have a little talk."

"Why, yes, sir." Basil was flattered. "Any time you say."

"Suppose we take a walk about three o'clock. My train goes at five."

"I'd like to very much."

He walked on air to his room in the Sixth Form House. One short year ago he had been perhaps the most unpopular boy at St. Regis—"Bossy" Lee. Only occasionally did people forget and call him "Bossy" now, and then they corrected themselves immediately.

A youngster leaned out of the window of Mitchell House as he passed and cried, "Good work!" The negro gardener, trimming a hedge, chuckled and called, "You almost beatum by y' own self!" Mr. Hicks the housemaster cried, "They ought to have given you that touchdown! That was a crime!" as Basil passed his door. It was a frosty gold October day, tinged with the blue smoke of Indian summer, weather that set him dreaming of future splendors, triumphant descents upon cities, romantic contacts with mysterious and scarcely mortal girls. In his room he floated off into an ambulatory dream in which he walked up and down repeating to himself tag ends of phrases: "by a prep-school back, and I've seen a lot of them." . . . 'Yellow your gra'mother!" . . . 'You get off side again and I'll kick your fat bottom for you!"

Suddenly he rolled on his bed with laughter. The threatened one had actually apologized between quarters—it was Pork Corrigan who only last year had chased him up two flights of stairs.

At three he met John Granby and they set off along the Grunwald Pike, following a long, low red wall that on fair mornings always suggested to Basil an adventurous quest like in "The Broad Highway." John Granby talked awhile about Princeton, but when he realized that Yale was an abstract ideal deep in Basil's heart, he gave up. After a moment a far-away expression, a smile that seemed a reflection of another and brighter world, spread over his handsome face.

"Lee, I love St. Regis School," he said suddenly. "I spent the happiest years of my life here. I owe it a debt I can never repay." Basil didn't answer and Granby turned to him suddenly. "I wonder if you realize what you could do here."

"What? Me?"

"I wonder if you know the effect on the whole school of that wonderful game you played this morning."

"It wasn't so good."

"It's like you to say that," declared Granby emphatically, "but it isn't the truth. However, I didn't come out here to sing your praises. Only I wonder if you realize your power for good. I mean your power of influencing all these boys to lead clean, upright, decent lives."

"I never thought about that," said Basil, somewhat startled; "I never thought about—"

Granby slapped him smartly on the shoulder.

"Since this morning a responsibility has come to you that you can't dodge. From this morning every boy in this school who goes around smoking cigarettes behind the gym and reeking with nicotine is a little bit your responsibility; every bit of cursing and swearing, or of learning to take the property of others by stealing milk and food supplies out of the pantry at night is a little bit your responsibility."

He broke off. Basil looked straight ahead, frowning.

"Gee!" he said.

"I mean it," continued Granby, his eyes shining. "You have the sort of opportunity very few boys have. I'm going to tell you a little story. Up at Princeton I knew two boys who were wrecking their lives with drink. I could have said, 'It's not my affair,' and let them go to pieces their own way, but when I looked deep into my own heart I found I couldn't. So I went to them frankly and put it up to them fairly and squarely, and those two boys haven't—at least one of them hasn't—touched a single drop of liquor from that day to this."

"But I don't think anybody in school drinks," objected Basil. "At least there was a fellow named Bates that got fired last year—"

"It doesn't matter," John Granby interrupted. "Smoking leads to drinking and drinking leads to—other things."

For an hour Granby talked and Basil listened; the red wall beside the road and the apple-heavy branches overhead seemed to become less vivid minute by minute as his thoughts turned inward. He was deeply affected by what he considered the fine unselfishness of this man who took the burdens of others upon his shoulders. Granby missed his train, but he said that didn't matter if he had succeeded in planting a sense of responsibility in Basil's mind.

Basil returned to his room awed, sobered and convinced. Up to this time he had always considered himself rather bad; in fact, the last hero character with which he had been able to identify himself was Hairbreadth Harry in the comic supplement, when he was ten. Though he often brooded, his brooding was dark and nameless and never concerned with moral questions. The real restraining influence on him was fear—the fear of being disqualified from achievement and power.

But this meeting with John Granby had come at a significant moment. After this morning's triumph, life at school scarcely seemed to hold anything more—and here was something new. To be perfect, wonderful inside and out—as Granby had put it, to try to lead the perfect life. Granby had outlined the perfect life to him, not without a certain stress upon its material rewards such as honor and influence at college, and Basil's imagination was already far in the future. When he was tapped last man for Skull and Bones at Yale and shook his head with a sad sweet smile, somewhat like John Granby's, pointing to another man who wanted it more, a burst of sobbing would break from the assembled crowd. Then, out into the world, where, at the age of twenty-five, he would face the nation from the inaugural platform on the Capitol steps, and all around him his people would lift up their faces in admiration and love. . . .

As he thought he absent-mindedly consumed half a dozen soda crackers and a bottle of milk, left from a pantry raid the night before. Vaguely he realized that this was one of the things he was giving up, but he was very hungry. However, he reverently broke off the train of his reflections until he was through.

Outside his window the autumn dusk was split with shafts of lights from passing cars. In these cars were great football players and lovely débutantes, mysterious adventuresses and international spies—rich, gay, glamorous people moving toward brilliant encounters in New York, at fashionable dances and secret cafés, or on roof gardens under the autumn moon. He sighed; perhaps he could blend in these more romantic things later. To be of great wit and conversational powers, and simultaneously strong and serious and silent. To be generous and open and self-sacrificing, yet to be somewhat mysterious and sensitive and even a little bitter with melancholy. To be both light and dark. To harmonize this, to melt all this down into a single man—ah, there was something to be done. The very thought of such perfection crystallized his vitality into an ecstasy of ambition. For a moment longer his soul followed the speeding lights toward the metropolis; then resolutely he arose, put out his cigarette on the window sill, and turning on his reading lamp, began to note down a set of requirements for the perfect life.

II

One month later George Dorsey, engaged in the painful duty of leading his mother around the school grounds, reached the comparative seclusion of the tennis courts and suggested eagerly that she rest herself upon a bench.

Hitherto his conversation had confined itself to a few hoarse advices, such as "That's the gym." . . . "That's Cuckoo Conklin that teaches French. Everybody hates him." . . . "Please don't call me 'Brother' in front of boys." Now his face took on the preoccupied expression peculiar to adolescents in the presence of their parents. He relaxed. He waited to be asked things.

"Now, about Thanksgiving, George. Who is this boy you're bringing home?"

"His name is Basil Lee."

"Tell me something about him."

"There isn't anything to tell. He's just a boy in the Sixth Form, about sixteen."

"Is he a nice boy?"

"Yes. He lives in St. Paul, Minnesota. I asked him a long time ago."

A certain reticence in her son's voice interested Mrs. Dorsey.

"Do you mean you're sorry you asked him? Don't you like him any more?"

"Sure I like him."

"Because there's no use bringing anyone you don't like. You could just explain that your mother has made other plans."

"But I like him," George insisted, and then he added hesitantly: "It's just some funny way he's got to be lately."

"How?"

"Oh, just sort of queer."

"But how, George? I don't want you to bring anyone into the house that's queer."

"He isn't exactly queer. He just gets people aside and talks to them. Then he sort of smiles at them."

Mrs. Dorsey was mystified. "Smiles at them?"

"Yeah. He gets them off in a corner somewheres and talks to them as long as they can stand it, and then he smiles"—his own lips twisted into a peculiar grimace—"like that."

"What does he talk about?"

"Oh, about swearing and smoking and writing home and a lot of stuff like that. Nobody pays any attention except one boy he's got doing the same thing. He got stuck up or something because he was so good at football."

"Well, if you don't want him, don't let's have him."

"Oh, no," George cried in alarm. "I've got to have him. I asked him."

Naturally, Basil was unaware of this conversation when, one morning, a week later, the Dorseys' chauffeur relieved them of their bags in the Grand Central station. There was a slate-pink light over the city and people in the streets carried with them little balloons of frosted breath. About them the buildings broke up through many planes toward heaven, at their base the wintry color of an old man's smile, on through diagonals of diluted gold, edged with purple where the cornices floated past the stationary sky.

In a long, low, English town car—the first of the kind that Basil had ever seen—sat a girl of about his own age. As they came up she received her brother's kiss perfunctorily, nodded stiffly to Basil and murmured, "how-d'y'-do'" without smiling. She said nothing further but seemed absorbed in meditations of her own. At first, perhaps because of her extreme reserve, Basil received no especial impression of her, but before they reached the Dorseys' house he began to realize that she was one of the prettiest girls he had ever seen in his life.

It was a puzzling face. Her long eyelashes lay softly against her pale cheeks, almost touching them, as if to conceal the infinite boredom in her eyes, but when she smiled, her expression was illumined by a fiery and lovely friendliness, as if she were saying, "Go on; I'm listening. I'm fascinated. I've been waiting—oh, ages—for just this moment with you." Then she remembered that she was shy or bored; the smile vanished, the gray eyes half closed again. Almost before it had begun, the moment was over, leaving a haunting and unsatisfied curiosity behind.

The Dorseys' house was on Fifty-third Street. Basil was astonished first at the narrowness of its white stone front and then at the full use to which the space was put inside. The formal chambers ran the width of the house, artificial sunlight bloomed in the dining-room windows, a small elevator navigated the five stories in deferential silence. For Basil there was a new world in its compact luxury. It was thrilling and romantic that a foothold on this island was more precious than the whole rambling sweep of the James J. Hill house at home. In his excitement the feel of school dropped momentarily away from him. He was possessed by the same longing for a new experience, that his previous glimpses of New York had aroused. In the hard bright glitter of Fifth Avenue, in this lovely girl with no words to waste beyond a mechanical "How-d'y'-do," in the perfectly organized house, he recognized nothing, and he knew that to recognize nothing in his surroundings was usually a guaranty of adventure.

But his mood of the last month was not to be thrown off so lightly. There was now an ideal that came first. A day mustn't pass when he wasn't, as John Granby put it, "straight with himself"—and that meant to help others. He could get in a good deal of work on George Dorsey in these five days; other opportunities might turn up, besides. Meanwhile, with the consciousness of making the best of both worlds, he unpacked his grip and got ready for luncheon.

He sat beside Mrs. Dorsey, who found him somewhat precipitately friendly in a Midwestern way, but polite, apparently not unbalanced. He told her he was going to be a minister and immediately he didn't believe it himself; but he saw that it interested Mrs. Dorsey and let it stand.

The afternoon was already planned; they were going dancing—for those were the great days: Maurice was tangoing in "Over the River," the Castles were doing a swift stiff-legged walk in the third act of "The Sunshine Girl"—a walk that gave the modern dance a social position and brought the nice girl into the café, thus beginning a profound revolution in American life. The great rich empire was feeling its oats and was out for some not too plebeian, yet not too artistic, fun.

By three o'clock seven young people were assembled, and they started in a limousine for Emil's. There were two stylish, anaemic girls of sixteen—one bore an impressive financial name—and two freshmen from Harvard who exchanged private jokes and were attentive only to Jobena Dorsey. Basil expected that presently everyone would begin asking each other such familiar questions as "Where do you go to school?" and "Oh, do you know So-and-So?" and the party would become more free and easy, but nothing of the sort happened. The atmosphere was impersonal; he doubted if the other four guests knew his name. "In fact," he thought, "it's just as if everyone's waiting for some one else to make a fool of himself." Here again was something new and unrecognizable; he guessed that it was a typical part of New York.

They reached Emil's. Only in certain Paris restaurants where the Argentines step untiringly through their native coils does anything survive of the dance craze as it existed just before the war. At that time it was not an accompaniment to drinking or love-making or hailing in the dawn—it was an end in itself. Sedentary stockbrokers, grandmothers of sixty, Confederate veterans, venerable statesmen and scientists, sufferers from locomotor ataxia, wanted not only to dance but to dance beautifully. Fantastic ambitions bloomed in hitherto sober breasts, violent exhibitionism cropped out in families modest for generations. Nonentities with long legs became famous overnight, and there were rendezvous where they could renew the dance, if they wished, next morning. Because of a neat glide or an awkward stumble careers were determined and engagements were made or broken, while the tall Englishman and the girl in the Dutch cap called the tune.

As they went into the cabaret sudden anxiety attacked Basil —modern dancing was one of the things upon which John Granby had been most severe.

He approached George Dorsey in the coat room.

"There's an extra man, so do you suppose it'd be all right if

I only danced when there's a waltz? I'm no good at anything else."

"Sure. It's all right with me." He looked curiously at Basil. "Gosh, have you sworn off everything?"

"No, not everything," answered Basil uncomfortably.

The floor was already crowded. All ages and several classes of society shuffled around tensely to the nervous, disturbing beats of "Too Much Mustard." Automatically the other three couples were up and away, leaving Basil at the table. He watched, trying to pretend to himself that he disapproved of it all but was too polite to show it. However, with so much to see, it was difficult to preserve that attitude, and he was gazing with fascination at Jobena's active feet when a good-looking young man of about nineteen sat down beside him at the table.

"Excuse me," he said with exaggerated deference. "This Miss Jobena Dorsey's table?"

"Yes, it is."

"I'm expected. Name's De Vinci. Don't ask me if I'm any relation to the painter."

"My name's Lee."

"All right, Lee. What'll you have? What are you having?" The waiter arrived with a tray, and De Vinci looked at its contents with disgust. "Tea—all tea. . . . Waiter, bring me a double Bronx. . . . How about you, Lee? Another double Bronx?"

"Oh, no, thanks," said Basil quickly.

"One then, waiter."

De Vinci sighed; he had the unmistakable lush look of a man who has been drinking hard for several days.

"Nice dog under that table over there. They oughtn't to let people smoke if they're going to bring dogs in here."

"Why?"

"Hurts their eyes."

Confusedly Basil deliberated this piece of logic.

"But don't talk to me about dogs," said De Vinci with a profound sigh; "I'm trying to keep from thinking of dogs."

Basil obligingly changed the subject for him by asking him if he was in college.

"Two weeks." For emphasis De Vinci held up two fingers.

"I passed quickly through Yale. First man fired out of '15 Sheff."

"That's too bad," said Basil earnestly. He took a deep breath and his lips twisted up in a kindly smile. "Your parents must have felt pretty badly about that."

De Vinci stared at him as if over a pair of spectacles, but before he could answer, the dance ended and the others came back to the table.

"Hello there, Skiddy."

"Well, well, Skiddy!"

They all knew him. One of the freshmen yielded him a place next to Jobena and they began to talk together in lowered voices.

"Skiddy De Vinci," George whispered to Basil. "He and Jobena were engaged last summer, but I think she's through." He shook his head. "They used to go off in his mother's electric up at Bar Harbor; it was disgusting."

Basil glowed suddenly with excitement as if he had been snapped on like an electric torch. He looked at Jobena—her face, infinitely reserved, lightened momentarily, but this time her smile had gone sad; there was the deep friendliness but not the delight. He wondered if Skiddy De Vinci cared about her being through with him. Perhaps, if he reformed and stopped drinking and went back to Yale, she would change her mind.

The music began again. Basil stared uncomfortably into his cup of tea.

"This is a tango," said George. "You can dance the tango, can't you? It's all right; it's Spanish."

Basil considered.

"Sure you can," insisted George. "It's Spanish, I tell you. There's nothing to stop your dancing if it's Spanish, is there?"

One of the freshmen looked at them curiously. Basil leaned over the table and asked Jobena to dance.

She made a last low-voiced remark to De Vinci before she rose; then, to atone for the slight rudeness, she smiled up at Basil. He was light-headed as they moved out on the floor.

Abruptly she made an outrageous remark and Basil started and nearly stumbled, doubtful that he had heard aright.

"I'll bet you've kissed about a thousand girls in your time," she said, "with that mouth."

"What!"

"Not so?"

"Oh, no," declared Basil. "Really, I—"

Her lids and lashes had drooped again indifferently; she was singing the band's tune:

> "Tango makes you warm inside;
> You bend and sway and glide;
> There's nothing far and wide—"

What was the implication—that kissing people was all right; was even admirable? He remembered what John Granby had said: "Every time you kiss a nice girl you may have started her on the road to the devil."

He thought of his own past—an afternoon on the Kampfs' porch with Minnie Bibble, a ride home from Black Bear Lake with Imogene Bissel in the back seat of the car, a miscellany of encounters running back to games of post office and to childish kisses that were consummated upon an unwilling nose or ear.

That was over; he was never going to kiss another girl until he found the one who would become his wife. It worried him that this girl whom he found lovely should take the matter so lightly. The strange thrill he had felt when George spoke of her "behaving disgustingly" with Skiddy De Vinci in his electric, was transformed into indignation—steadily rising indignation. It was criminal—a girl not yet seventeen.

Suddenly it occurred to him that this was perhaps his responsibility, his opportunity. If he could implant in her mind the futility of it all, the misery she was laying up for herself, his visit to New York would not have been in vain. He could go back to school happy, knowing he had brought to one girl the sort of peace she had never known before.

In fact, the more he thought of Jobena and Skiddy De Vinci in the electric, the madder it made him.

At five they left Emil's to go to Castle House. There was a thin rain falling and the streets were gleaming. In the excitement of going out into the twilight Jobena slipped her arm quickly through Basil's.

"There's too many for the car. Let's take the hansom."

She gave the address to a septuagenarian in faded bottle green, and the slanting doors closed upon them, shutting them back away from the rain.

"I'm tired of them," she whispered. "Such empty faces, except Skiddy's, and in another hour he won't be able to even talk straight. He's beginning to get maudlin about his dog Eggshell that died last month, and that's always a sign. Do you ever feel the fascination of somebody that's doomed; who just goes on and on in the way he was born to go, never complaining, never hoping; just sort of resigned to it all?"

His fresh heart cried out against this.

"Nobody has to go to pieces," he assured her. "They can just turn over a new leaf."

"Not Skiddy."

"Anybody," he insisted. "You just make up your mind and resolve to live a better life, and you'd be surprised how easy it is and how much happier you are."

She didn't seem to hear him.

"Isn't it nice, rolling along in this hansom with the damp blowing in, and you and I back here"—she turned to him and smiled—"together."

"Yes," said Basil abstractedly. "The thing is that everybody should try to make their life perfect. They can't start young enough; in fact, they ought to start about eleven or twelve in order to make their life absolutely perfect."

"That's true," she said. "In a way Skiddy's life is perfect. He never worries, never regrets. You could put him back at the time of the—oh, the eighteenth century, or whenever it was they had the bucks and beaux—and he'd fit right in."

"I didn't mean that," said Basil in alarm. "That isn't at all what I mean by the perfect life."

"You mean something more masterful," she supplied. "I thought so, when I saw that chin of yours. I'll bet you just take everything you want."

Again she looked at him, swayed close to him.

"You don't understand—" he began.

She put her hand on his arm. "Wait a minute; we're almost there. Let's not go in yet. It's so nice with all the lights going on and it'll be so hot and crowded in there. Tell him to drive out a few blocks more. I noticed you only danced a few times; I like that. I hate men that pop up at the first sound of music as if their life depended on it. Is it true you're only sixteen?"

"Yes."

"You seem older. There's so much in your face."

"You don't understand—" Basil began again desperately.

She spoke through the trap to the cabby:

"Go up Broadway till we tell you to stop." Sitting back in the cab, she repeated dreamily, "The perfect life. I'd like my life to be perfect. I'd like to suffer, if I could find something worth suffering for, and I'd like to never do anything low or small or mean, but just have big sins."

"Oh, no!" said Basil, aghast. "That's no way to feel; that's morbid. Why, look, you oughtn't to talk like that—a girl sixteen years old. You ought to—to talk things over with yourself—you ought to think more of the after life." He stopped, half expecting to be interrupted, but Jobena was silent. "Why, up to a month ago I used to smoke as many as twelve or fifteen cigarettes a day, unless I was training for football. I used to curse and swear and only write home once in a while, so they had to telegraph sometimes to see if I was sick. I had no sense of responsibility. I never thought I could lead a perfect life until I tried."

He paused, overcome by his emotion.

"Didn't you?" said Jobena, in a small voice.

"Never. I was just like everybody else, only worse. I used to kiss girls and never think anything about it."

"What—what changed you?"

"A man I met." Suddenly he turned to her and, with an effort, caused to spread over his face a caricature of John Granby's sad sweet smile. "Jobena, you—you have the makings of a fine girl in you. It grieved me a lot this afternoon to see you smoking nicotine and dancing modern suggestive dances that are simply savagery. And the way you talk about kissing. What if you meet some man that has kept himself pure and never gone around kissing anybody except his family, and you have to tell him that you went around behaving disgustingly?"

She leaned back suddenly and spoke crisply through the panel.

"You can go back now—the address we gave you."

"You ought to cut it out." Again Basil smiled at her, straining and struggling to lift her up out of herself to a higher plane. "Promise me you'll try. It isn't so hard. And then some day when some upright and straightforward man comes along and says, 'Will you marry me?' you'll be able to say you never danced suggestive modern dances, except the Spanish tango and the Boston, and you never kissed anybody—that is, since you were sixteen, and maybe you wouldn't have to say that you ever kissed anybody at all."

"That wouldn't be the truth," she said in an odd voice. "Shouldn't I tell him the truth?"

"You could tell him you didn't know any better."

"Oh."

To Basil's regret the cab drew up at Castle House. Jobena hurried in, and to make up for her absence, devoted herself exclusively to Skiddy and the Harvard freshmen for the remainder of the afternoon. But doubtless she was thinking hard —as he had done a month before. With a little more time he could have clinched his argument by showing the influence that one leading a perfect life could exert on others. He must find an opportunity tomorrow.

But next day he scarcely saw her. She was out for luncheon and she did not appear at her rendezvous with Basil and George after the matinée; they waited in vain in the Biltmore grill for an hour. There was company at dinner and Basil began to feel a certain annoyance when she disappeared immediately afterwards. Was it possible that his seriousness had frightened her? In that case it was all the more necessary to see her, reassure her, bind her with the invisible cords of high purpose to himself. Perhaps—perhaps she was the ideal girl that he would some day marry. At the gorgeous idea his whole being was flooded with ecstasy. He planned out the years of waiting, each one helping the other to lead the perfect life, neither of them ever kissing anybody else—he would insist on that, absolutely insist on it; she must promise not even to see Skiddy De Vinci—and then marriage and a life of service, perfection, fame and love.

The two boys went to the theatre again that night. When they came home a little after eleven, George went upstairs to say good night to his mother, leaving Basil to make reconnaissance in the ice box. The intervening pantry was dark and as he fumbled unfamiliarly for the light he was startled by hearing a voice in the kitchen pronounce his name:

"—Mr. Basil Duke Lee."

"Seemed all right to me." Basil recognized the drawling tone of Skiddy De Vinci. "Just a kid."

"On the contrary, he's a nasty little prig," said Jobena decisively. "He gave me the old-fashioned moral lecture about nicotine and modern dancing and kissing, and about that upright, straightforward man that was going to come along some day—you know that upright straightforward man they're always talking about. I suppose he meant himself, because he told me he led a perfect life. Oh, it was all so oily and horrible, it made me positively sick. Skiddy. For the first time in my life I was tempted to take a cocktail."

"Oh, he's just a kid," said Skiddy moderately. "It's a phase. He'll get over it."

Basil listened in horror; his face burning, his mouth ajar. He wanted above all things to get away, but his dismay rooted him to the floor.

"What I think of righteous men couldn't be put on paper," said Jobena after a moment. "I suppose I'm just naturally bad, Skiddy; at least, all my contacts with upright young men have affected me like this."

"Then how about it, Jobena?"

There was a long silence.

"This has done something to me," she said finally. "Yesterday I thought I was through with you, Skiddy, but ever since this happened I've had a vision of a thousand Mr. Basil Duke Lees, all grown up and asking me to share their perfect lives. I refuse to—definitely. If you like, I'll marry you in Greenwich tomorrow."

III

At one Basil's light was still burning. Walking up and down his room, he made out case after case for himself, with Jobena in the rôle of villainess, but each case was wrecked upon the rock of his bitter humiliation. "A nasty little prig"—the words, uttered with conviction and scorn, had driven the high principles of John Granby from his head. He was a slave to his own admirations, and in the past twenty-four hours Jobena's personality had become the strongest force in his life; deep in his heart he believed that what she had said was true.

He woke up on Thanksgiving morning with dark circles rimming his eyes. His bag, packed for immediate departure, brought back the debacle of the night before, and as he lay staring at the ceiling, relaxed by sleep, giant tears welled up into his eyes. An older man might have taken refuge behind the virtue of his intentions, but Basil knew no such refuge. For sixteen years he had gone his own way without direction, due to his natural combativeness and to the fact that no older man save John Granby had yet captured his imagination. Now John Granby had vanished in the night, and it seemed the natural thing to Basil that he should struggle back to rehabilitation unguided and alone.

One thing he knew—Jobena must not marry Skiddy De Vinci. That was a responsibility she could not foist upon him. If necessary, he would go to her father and tell what he knew.

Emerging from his room half an hour later, he met her in the hall. She was dressed in a smart blue street suit with a hobble skirt and a ruff of linen at her throat. Her eyes opened a little and she wished him a polite good morning.

"I've got to talk to you," he said quickly.

"I'm terribly sorry." To his intense discomfort she flashed her smile at him, just as if nothing had happened. "I've only a minute now."

"It's something very important. I know you don't like me—"

"What nonsense!" She laughed cheerfully. "Of course I like you. How did you get such a silly idea in your head?"

Before he could answer, she waved her hand hastily and ran down the stairs.

George had gone to town and Basil spent the morning walking through large deliberate snowflakes in Central Park rehearsing what he should say to Mr. Dorsey.

"It's nothing to me, but I cannot see your only daughter throw away her life on a dissipated man. If I had a daughter of my own who was about to throw away her life, I would want somebody to tell me, and so I have come to tell you. Of course, after this I cannot stay in your house, and so I bid you good-by."

At quarter after twelve, waiting anxiously in the drawing-room, he heard Mr. Dorsey come in. He rushed downstairs, but Mr. Dorsey had already entered the lift and closed the door. Turning about, Basil raced against the machine to the third story and caught him in the hall.

"In regard to your daughter," he began excitedly—"in regard to your daughter—"

"Well," said Mr. Dorsey, "is something the matter with Jobena?"

"I want to talk to you about her."

Mr. Dorsey laughed. "Are you going to ask her hand in marriage?"

"Oh, no."

"Well, suppose we have a talk after dinner when we're full of turkey and stuffing, and feeling happy."

He clapped his hand on Basil's shoulder and went on into his room.

It was a large family dinner party, and under cover of the conversation Basil kept an attentive eye on Jobena, trying to determine her desperate intention from her clothes and the expression of her face. She was adept at concealing her real emotions, as he had discovered this morning, but once or twice he saw her eyes wander to her watch and a look of abstraction come into them.

There was coffee afterward in the library, and, it seemed to Basil, interminable chatter. When Jobena arose suddenly and left the room, he moved just as quickly to Mr. Dorsey's side.

"Well, young man, what can I do for you?"

"Why—" Basil hesitated.

"Now is the time to ask me—when I'm well fed and happy."

"Why—" Again Basil stopped.

"Don't be shy. It's something about my Jobena."

But a peculiar thing had happened to Basil. In sudden detachment he saw himself from the outside—saw himself sneaking to Mr. Dorsey, in a house in which he was a guest, to inform against a girl.

"Why—" he repeated blankly.

"The question is: Can you support her?" said Mr. Dorsey jovially. "And the second is: Can you control her?"

"I forgot what it was I wanted to say," Basil blurted out.

He hurried from the library, his brain in a turmoil. Dashing upstairs, he knocked at the door of Jobena's room. There was no answer and he opened the door and glanced inside. The room was empty, but a half-packed suitcase lay on the bed.

"Jobena," he called anxiously. There was no answer. A maid passing along the hall told him Miss Jobena was having a marcel wave in her mother's room.

He hurried downstairs and into his hat and coat, racking his brains for the address where they had dropped Skiddy De Vinci the other afternoon. Sure that he would recognize the building, he drove down Lexington Avenue in a taxi, tried three doors, and trembled with excitement as he found the name "Leonard Edward Davies De Vinci" on a card beside a bell. When he rang, a latch clicked on an inner door.

He had no plan. Failing argument, he had a vague melodramatic idea of knocking him down, tying him up and letting him lie there until it blew over. In view of the fact that Skiddy outweighed him by forty pounds, this was a large order.

Skiddy was packing—the overcoat he tossed hastily over his suitcase did not serve to hide this fact from Basil. There was an open bottle of whisky on his littered dresser, and beside it a half-full glass.

Concealing his surprise, he invited Basil to sit down.

"I had to come and see you"—Basil tried to make his voice calm—"about Jobena."

"Jobena?" Skiddy frowned. "What about her? Did she send you here?"

"Oh, no." Basil swallowed hard, stalling for time. "I thought —maybe you could advise me—you see, I don't think she likes me, and I don't know why."

Skiddy's face relaxed. "That's nonsense. Of course she likes you. Have a drink?"

"No. At least not now."

Skiddy finished his glass. After a slight hesitation he removed his overcoat from the suitcase.

"Excuse me if I go on packing, will you? I'm going out of town."

"Certainly."

"Better have a drink."

"No, I'm on the water wagon—just now."

"When you get worrying about nothing, the thing to do is to have a drink."

The phone rang and he answered it, squeezing the receiver close to his ear:

"Yes.... I can't talk now.... Yes.... At half-past five then. It's now about four.... I'll explain why when I see you.... Goodby." He hung up. "My office," he said with affected nonchalance ... "Won't you have a little drink?"

"No, thanks."

"Never worry. Enjoy yourself."

"It's hard to be visiting in a house and know somebody doesn't like you."

"But she does like you. Told me so herself the other day."

While Skiddy packed they discussed the question. He was a little hazy and extremely nervous, and a single question asked in the proper serious tone would send him rambling along indefinitely. As yet Basil had evolved no plan save to stay with Skiddy and wait for the best opportunity of coming into the open.

But staying with Skiddy was going to be difficult; he was becoming worried at Basil's tenacity. Finally he closed his suitcase with one of those definite snaps, took down a large drink quickly and said:

"Well, guess I ought to get started."

They went out together and Skiddy hailed a taxi.

"Which way are you going?" Basil asked.

"Uptown—I mean downtown."

"I'll ride with you," volunteered Basil. "We might—we might have a drink in the—Biltmore."

Skiddy hesitated. "I'll drop you there," he said.

When they reached the Biltmore, Basil made no move to get out.

"You're coming in with me, aren't you?" he asked in a surprised voice.

Frowning, Skiddy looked at his watch. "I haven't got much time."

Basil's face fell; he sat back in the car.

"Well, there's no use my going in alone, because I look sort of young and they wouldn't give me anything unless I was with an older man."

The appeal succeeded. Skiddy got out, saying, "I'll have to hurry," and they went into the bar.

"What'll it be?"

"Something strong," Basil said, lighting his first cigarette in a month.

"Two stingers," ordered Skiddy.

"Let's have something really strong."

"Two double stingers then."

Out of the corner of his eye Basil looked at the clock. It was twenty after five. Waiting until Skiddy was in the act of taking down his drink he signalled to the waiter to repeat the order.

"Oh, no!" cried Skiddy.

"You'll have to have one on me."

"You haven't touched yours."

Basil sipped his drink, hating it. He saw that with the new alcohol Skiddy had relaxed a little.

"Got to be going," he said automatically. "Important engagement."

Basil had an inspiration.

"I'm thinking of buying a dog," he announced.

"Don't talk about dogs," said Skiddy mournfully. "I had an awful experience about a dog. I've just got over it."

"Tell me about it."

"I don't even like to talk about it; it was awful."

"I think a dog is the best friend a man has," Basil said.

"Do you?" Skiddy slapped the table emphatically with his open hand. "So do I, Lee. So do I."

"Nobody ever loves him like a dog," went on Basil, staring off sentimentally into the distance.

The second round of double stingers arrived.

"Let me tell you about my dog that I lost," said Skiddy. He looked at his watch. "I'm late, but a minute won't make any difference, if you like dogs."

"I like them better than anything in the world." Basil raised his first glass, still half full. "Here's to man's best friend—a dog."

They drank. There were tears in Skiddy's eyes.

"Let me tell you. I raised this dog Eggshell from a pup. He was a beauty—an Airedale, sired by McTavish VI."

"I bet he was a beauty."

"He was! Let me tell you—"

As Skiddy warmed to his subject, Basil pushed his new drink toward Skiddy, whose hand presently closed upon the stem. Catching the bartender's attention, he ordered two more. The clock stood at five minutes of six.

Skiddy rambled on. Ever afterward the sight of a dog story in a magazine caused Basil an attack of acute nausea. At half-past six Skiddy rose uncertainly.

"I've gotta go. Got important date. Be mad."

"All right. We'll stop by the bar and have one more."

The bartender knew Skiddy and they talked for a few minutes, for time seemed of no account now. Skiddy had a drink with his old friend to wish him luck on a very important occasion. Then he had another.

At a quarter before eight o'clock Basil piloted Leonard Edward Davies De Vinci from the hotel bar, leaving his suitcase in care of the bartender.

"Important engagement," Skiddy mumbled as they hailed a taxi.

"Very important," Basil agreed. "I'm going to see that you get there."

When the car rolled up, Skiddy tumbled in and Basil gave the address to the driver.

"Good-by and thanks!" Skiddy called fervently. "Ought to go in, maybe, and drink once more to best friend man ever had."

"Oh, no," said Basil, "it's too important."

"You're right. It's too important."

The car rolled off and Basil followed it with his eye as it turned the corner. Skiddy was going out on Long Island to visit Eggshell's grave.

IV

Basil had never had a drink before and, now with his jubilant relief, the three cocktails that he had been forced to down mounted swiftly to his head. On his way to the Dorseys' house he threw back his head and roared with laughter. The self-respect he had lost last night rushed back to him; he felt himself tingling with the confidence of power.

As the maid opened the door for him he was aware subconsciously that there was someone in the lower hall. He waited till the maid disappeared; then stepping to the door of the coat room, he pulled it open. Beside her suitcase stood Jobena, wearing a look of mingled impatience and fright. Was he deceived by his ebullience or, when she saw him, did her face lighten with relief?

"Hello." She took off her coat and hung it up as if that was her purpose there, and came out under the lights. Her face, pale and lovely, composed itself, as if she had sat down and folded her hands.

"George was looking for you," she said indifferently.

"Was he? I've been with a friend."

With an expression of surprise she sniffed the faint aroma of cocktails.

"But my friend went to visit his dog's tomb, so I came home."

She stiffened suddenly. "You've been with Skiddy?"

"He was telling me about his dog," said Basil gravely. "A man's best friend is his dog after all."

She sat down and stared at him, wide-eyed.

"Has Skiddy passed out?"

"He went to see a dog."

"Oh, the fool!" she cried.

"Were you expecting him? Is it possible that that's your suitcase?"

"It's none of your business."

Basil took it out of the closet and deposited it in the elevator.

"You won't need it tonight," he said.

Her eyes shone with big despairing tears.

"You oughtn't to drink," she said brokenly. "Can't you see what it's made of him?"

"A man's best friend is a stinger."

"You're just sixteen. I suppose all that you told me the other afternoon was a joke—I mean, about the perfect life."

"All a joke," he agreed.

"I thought you meant it. Doesn't anybody ever mean anything?"

"I like you better than any girl I ever knew," Basil said quietly. "I mean that."

"I liked you too, until you said that about my kissing people."

He went and stood over her and took her hand.

"Let's take the bag upstairs before the maid comes in."

They stepped into the dark elevator and closed the door.

"There's a light switch somewhere," she said.

Still holding her hand, he drew her close and tightened his arm around her in the darkness.

"Just for this once we don't need the light."

Going back on the train, George Dorsey came to a sudden resolution. His mouth tightened.

"I don't want to say anything, Basil—" He hesitated. "But look—Did you have something to drink Thanksgiving Day?"

Basil frowned and nodded.

"Sometimes I've got to," he said soberly. "I don't know what it is. All my family died of liquor."

"Gee!" exclaimed George.

"But I'm through. I promised Jobena I wouldn't touch anything more till I'm twenty-one. She feels that if I go on with this constant dissipation it'll ruin my life."

George was silent for a moment.

"What were you and she talking about those last few days? Gosh, I thought you were supposed to be visiting *me*."

"It's—it's sort of sacred," Basil said placidly. . . . "Look here; if we don't have anything fit to eat for dinner, let's get Sam to leave the pantry window unlocked tonight."

Forging Ahead

I

Basil Duke Lee and Riply Buckner, Jr., sat on the Lees' front steps in the regretful gold of a late summer afternoon. Inside the house the telephone sang out with mysterious promise.

"I thought you were going home," Basil said.

"I thought you were."

"I am."

"So am I."

"Well, why don't you go, then?"

"Why don't you, then?"

"I am."

They laughed, ending with yawning gurgles that were not

laughed out but sucked in. As the telephone rang again, Basil got to his feet.

"I've got to study trig before dinner."

"Are you honestly going to Yale this fall?" demanded Riply skeptically.

"Yes."

"Everybody says you're foolish to go at sixteen."

"I'll be seventeen in September. So long. I'll call you up tonight."

Basil heard his mother at the upstairs telephone and he was immediately aware of distress in her voice.

"Yes. . . . Isn't that awful, Everett! . . . Yes. . . . Oh-h my!" After a minute he gathered that it was only the usual worry about business and went on into the kitchen for refreshments. Returning, he met his mother hurrying downstairs. She was blinking rapidly and her hat was on backward—characteristic testimony to her excitement.

"I've got to go over to your grandfather's."

"What's the matter, mother?"

"Uncle Everett thinks we've lost a lot of money."

"How much?" he asked, startled.

"Twenty-two thousand dollars apiece. But we're not sure." She went out.

"Twenty-two thousand dollars!" he repeated in an awed whisper.

His ideas of money were vague and somewhat debonair, but he had noticed that at family dinners the immemorial discussion as to whether the Third Street block would be sold to the railroads had given place to anxious talk of Western Public Utilities. At half-past six his mother telephoned for him to have his dinner; and with growing uneasiness he sat alone at the table, undistracted by The Mississippi Bubble, open beside his plate. She came in at seven, distraught and miserable, and dropping down at the table, gave him his first exact information about finance—she and her father and her brother Everett had lost something more than eighty thousand dollars. She was in a panic and she looked wildly around the dining room as if money were slipping away even here, and she wanted to retrench at once.

"I've got to stop selling securities or we won't have anything," she declared. "This leaves us only three thousand a year—do you realize that, Basil? I don't see how I can possibly afford to send you to Yale."

His heart tumbled into his stomach; the future, always glowing like a comfortable beacon ahead of him, flared up in glory and went out. His mother shivered, and then emphatically shook her head.

"You'll just have to make up your mind to go to the state university."

"Gosh!" Basil said.

Sorry for his shocked, rigid face, she yet spoke somewhat sharply, as people will with a bitter refusal to convey.

"I feel terribly about it—your father wanted you to go to Yale. But everyone says that, with clothes and railroad fare, I can count on it costing two thousand a year. Your grandfather helped me to send you to St. Regis School, but he always thought you ought to finish at the state university."

After she went distractedly upstairs with a cup of tea, Basil sat thinking in the dark parlor. For the present the loss meant only one thing to him—he wasn't going to Yale after all. The sentence itself, divorced from its meaning, overwhelmed him, so many times had he announced casually "I'm going to Yale," but gradually he realized how many friendly and familiar dreams had been swept away. Yale was the far-away East, that he had loved with a vast nostalgia since he had first read books about great cities. Beyond the dreary railroad stations of Chicago and the night fires of Pittsburgh, back in the old states, something went on that made his heart beat fast with excitement. He was attuned to the vast, breathless bustle of New York, to the metropolitan days and nights that were tense as singing wires. Nothing needed to be imagined there, for it was all the very stuff of romance—life was as vivid and satisfactory as in books and dreams.

But first, as a sort of gateway to that deeper, richer life, there was Yale. The name evoked the memory of a heroic team backed up against its own impassable goal in the crisp November twilight, and later, of half a dozen immaculate noblemen with opera hats and canes standing at the Manhattan Hotel bar. And tangled up with its triumphs and rewards, its struggles and glories, the vision of the inevitable, incomparable girl.

Well, then, why not work his way through Yale? In a moment the idea had become a reality. He began walking rapidly up and down the room, declaring half aloud, "Of course, that's the thing to do." Rushing upstairs, he knocked at his mother's door and announced in the inspired voice of a prophet: "Mother, I know what I'm going to do! I'm going to work my way through Yale."

He sat down on her bed and she considered uncertainly. The men in her family had not been resourceful for several generations, and the idea startled her.

"It doesn't seem to me you're a boy who likes to work," she said. "Besides, boys who work their way through college have scholarships and prizes, and you've never been much of a student."

He was annoyed. He was ready for Yale a year ahead of his age and her reproach seemed unfair.

"What would you work at?" she said.

"Take care of furnaces," said Basil promptly. "And shovel snow off sidewalks. I think they mostly do that—and tutor people. You could let me have as much money as it would take to go to the state university?"

"We'll have to think it over."

"Well, don't you worry about anything," he said emphatically, "because my earning my way through Yale will really make up for the money you've lost, almost."

"Why don't you start by finding something to do this summer?"

"I'll get a job tomorrow. Maybe I can pile up enough so you won't have to help me. Good night, mother."

Up in his room he paused only to thunder grimly to the mirror that he was going to work his way through Yale, and going to his bookcase, took down half a dozen dusty volumes of Horatio Alger, unopened for years. Then, much as a postwar young man might consult the George Washington Condensed Business Course, he sat at his desk and slowly began to turn the pages of *Bound to Rise.*

II

Two days later, after being insulted by the doorkeepers, office boys and telephone girls of the Press, the Evening News, the Socialist Gazette and a green scandal sheet called the Courier, and assured that no one wanted a reporter practically seventeen, after enduring every ignominy prepared for a young man in a free country trying to work his way through Yale, Basil Duke Lee, too "stuck-up" to apply to the parents of his friends, got a position with the railroad, through Eddie Parmelee, who lived across the way.

At 6:30 the following morning, carrying his lunch, and a new suit of overalls that had cost four dollars, he strode self-consciously into the Great Northern car shops. It was like entering a new school, except that no one showed any interest in him or asked if he was going out for the team. He punched a time clock, which affected him strangely, and without even an admonition from the foreman to "go in and win," was put to carrying boards for the top of a car.

Twelve o'clock arrived; nothing had happened. The sun was blazing hot and his hands and back were sore, but no real events had ruffled the dull surface of the morning. The president's little daughter had not come by, dragged by a runaway horse; not even a superintendent had walked through the yard and singled him out with an approving eye. Undismayed, he toiled on—you couldn't expect much the first morning.

He and Eddie Parmelee ate their lunches together. For several years Eddie had worked here in vacations; he was sending himself to the state university this fall. He shook his head doubtfully over the idea of Basil's earning his way through Yale.

"Here's what you ought to do," he said: "You borrow two thousand dollars from your mother and buy twenty shares in Ware Plow and Tractor. Then go to a bank and borrow two thousand more with those shares for collateral, and with that two thousand buy twenty more shares. Then you sit on your back for a year, and after that you won't have to think about earning your way through Yale."

"I don't think mother would give me two thousand dollars."

"Well, anyhow, that's what I'd do."

If the morning had been uneventful, the afternoon was distinguished by an incident of some unpleasantness. Basil had risen a little, having been requested to mount to the top of a freight car and help nail the boards he had carried in the morning. He found that nailing nails into a board was more highly technical than nailing tacks into a wall, but he considered that he was progressing satisfactorily when an angry voice hailed him from below:

"Hey, you! Get up!"

He looked down. A foreman stood there, unpleasantly red in the face.

"Yes, you in the new suit. Get up!"

Basil looked about to see if someone was lying down, but the two sullen hunyaks seemed to be hard at work and it grew on him that he was indeed being addressed.

"I beg your pardon, sir," he said.

"Get up on your knees or get out! What the h— do you think this is?"

He had been sitting down as he nailed, and apparently the foreman thought that he was loafing. After another look at the foreman, he suppressed the explanation that he felt steadier sitting down and decided to just let it go. There were probably no railroad shops at Yale; yet, he remembered with a pang the ominous name, New York, New Haven and Hartford.

The third morning, just as he had become aware that his overalls were not where he had hung them in the shop, it was announced that all men of less than six months' service were to be laid off. Basil received four dollars and lost his overalls. Learning that nails are driven from a kneeling position had cost him only carfare.

III

In a large old-fashioned house in the old section of the city lived Basil's great-uncle, Benjamin Reilly, and there Basil presented himself that evening. It was a last resort—Benjamin Reilly and Basil's grandfather were brothers and they had not spoken for twenty years.

He was received in the living room by the small, dumpy old man whose inscrutable face was hidden behind a white poodle beard. Behind him stood a woman of forty, his wife of six months, and her daughter, a girl of fifteen. Basil's branch of the family had not been invited to the wedding, and he had never seen these two additions before.

"I thought I'd come down and see you, Uncle Ben," he said with some embarrassment.

There was a certain amount of silence.

"Your mother well?" asked the old man.

"Oh, yes, thank you."

Mr. Reilly waited. Mrs. Reilly spoke to her daughter, who threw a curious glance at Basil and reluctantly left the room. Her mother made the old man sit down.

Out of sheer embarrassment Basil came to the point. He wanted a summer job in the Reilly Wholesale Drug Company.

His uncle fidgeted for a minute and then replied that there were no positions open.

"Oh."

"It might be different if you wanted a permanent place, but you say you want to go to Yale." He said this with some irony of his own, and glanced at his wife.

"Why, yes," said Basil. "That's really why I want the job."

"Your mother can't afford to send you, eh?" The note of pleasure in his voice was unmistakable. "Spent all her money?"

"Oh, no," answered Basil quickly. "She's going to help me."

To his surprise, aid came from an unpromising quarter. Mrs. Reilly suddenly bent and whispered in her husband's ear, whereupon the old man nodded and said aloud:

"I'll think about it, Basil. You go in there."

And his wife repeated: "We'll think about it. You go in the library with Rhoda while Mr. Reilly looks up and sees."

The door of the library closed behind him and he was alone with Rhoda, a square-chinned, decided girl with fleshy white arms and a white dress that reminded Basil domestically of the lacy pants that blew among the laundry in the yard. Puzzled by his uncle's change of front, he eyed her abstractedly for a moment.

"I guess you're my cousin," said Rhoda, closing her book, which he saw was The Little Colonel, Maid of Honor.

"Yes," he admitted.

"I heard about you from somebody." The implication was that her information was not flattering.

"From who?"

"A girl named Elaine Washmer."

"Elaine Washmer!" His tone dismissed the name scornfully. "That girl!"

"She's my best friend." He made no reply. "She said you thought you were wonderful."

Young people do not perceive at once that the giver of wounds is the enemy and the quoted tattle merely the arrow. His heart smoldered with wrath at Elaine Washmer.

"I don't know many kids here," said the girl, in a less aggressive key. "We've only been here six months. I never saw such a stuck-up bunch."

"Oh, I don't think so," he protested. "Where did you live before?"

"Sioux City. All the kids have much more fun in Sioux City."

Mrs. Reilly opened the door and called Basil back into the living room. The old man was again on his feet.

"Come down tomorrow morning and I'll find you something," he said.

"And why don't you have dinner with us tomorrow night?" added Mrs. Reilly, with a cordiality wherein an adult might have detected disingenuous purpose.

"Why, thank you very much."

His heart, buoyant with gratitude, had scarcely carried him out the door before Mrs. Reilly laughed shortly and called in her daughter.

"Now we'll see if you don't get around a little more," she announced. "When was it you said they had those dances?"

"Thursdays at the College Club and Saturdays at the Lake Club," said Rhoda promptly.

"Well, if this young man wants to hold the position your father has given him, you'll go to them all the rest of the summer."

IV

Arbitrary groups formed by the hazards of money or geography may be sufficiently quarrelsome and dull, but for sheer unpleasantness the condition of young people who have been thrust together by a common unpopularity can be compared only with that of prisoners herded in a cell. In Basil's eyes the guests at the little dinner the following night were a collection of cripples. Lewis and Hector Crum, dullard cousins who were tolerable only to each other; Sidney Rosen, rich but awful; ugly Mary Haupt, Elaine Washmer, and Betty Geer, who reminded Basil of a cruel parody they had once sung to the tune of Jungle Town:

> *Down below the hill*
> *There lives a pill*
> *That makes me ill,*
> *   And her name is Betty Geer.*
> *   We had better stop right here. . . .*
> *She's so fat,*
> *She looks just like a cat,*
> *And she's the queen of pills.*

Moreover, they resented Basil, who was presumed to be "stuck-up," and walking home afterward, he felt dreary and vaguely exploited. Of course, he was grateful to Mrs. Reilly for her kindness, yet he couldn't help wondering if a cleverer boy couldn't have got out of taking Rhoda to the Lake Club next Saturday night. The proposal had caught him unaware; but when he was similarly trapped the following week, and the week after that, he began to realize the situation. It was a part of his job, and he accepted it grimly, unable, nevertheless, to understand how such a bad dancer and so unsociable a person should want to go where she was obviously a burden. "Why doesn't she just sit at home and read a book," he thought disgustedly, "or go away somewhere—or sew?"

It was one Saturday afternoon while he watched a tennis tournament and felt the unwelcome duty of the evening creep up on him, that he found himself suddenly fascinated by a girl's face a few yards away. His heart leaped into his throat and the blood in his pulse beat with excitement; and then, when the crowd rose to go, he saw to his astonishment that he had been staring at a child ten years old. He looked away, oddly disappointed; after a moment he looked back again. The lovely, self-conscious face suggested a train of thought and sensation that he could not identify. As he passed on, forgoing a vague intention of discovering the child's identity, there was beauty suddenly all around him in the afternoon; he could hear its unmistakable whisper, its never-inadequate, ever-failing promise of happiness. "Tomorrow—one day soon now—this fall—maybe tonight." Irresistibly compelled to express himself, he sat down and tried to write to a girl in New York. His words were stilted and the girl seemed cold and far away. The real image on his mind, the force that had propelled him into this state of yearning, was the face of the little girl seen that afternoon.

When he arrived with Rhoda Sinclair at the Lake Club that night, he immediately cast a quick look around to see what boys were present who were indebted to Rhoda or else within his own sphere of influence. This was just before cutting-in arrived, and ordinarily he was able to dispose of half a dozen dances in advance, but tonight an older crowd was in evidence and the situation was unpromising. However, as Rhoda emerged from the dressing room he saw Bill Kampf and thankfully bore down upon him.

"Hello, old boy," he said, exuding personal good will. "How about dancing once with Rhoda tonight?"

"Can't," Bill answered briskly. "We've got people visiting us. Didn't you know?"

"Well, why couldn't we swap a dance anyhow?"

Bill looked at him in surprise.

"I thought you knew," he exclaimed. "Erminie's here. She's been talking about you all afternoon."

"Erminie Bibble!"

"Yes. And her father and mother and her kid sister. Got here this morning."

Now, indeed, the emotion of two hours before bubbled up in Basil's blood, but this time he knew why. It was the little sister of Erminie Gilberte Labouisse Bibble whose strangely familiar face had so attracted him. As his mind swung sharply back to a long afternoon on the Kampfs' veranda at the lake, ages ago, a year ago, a real voice rang in his ear, "Basil!" and a sparkling little beauty of fifteen came up to him with a fine burst of hurry, taking his hand as though she was stepping into the circle of his arm.

"Basil! I'm so glad!" Her voice was husky with pleasure, though she was at the age when pleasure usually hides behind grins and mumbles. It was Basil who was awkward and embarrassed, despite the intention of his heart. He was a little relieved when Bill Kampf, more conscious of his lovely cousin than he had been a year ago, led her out on the floor.

"Who was that?" Rhoda demanded, as he returned in a daze. "I never saw her around."

"Just a girl." He scarcely knew what he was saying.

"Well, I know that. What's her name?"

"Minnie Bibble, from New Orleans."

"She certainly looks conceited. I never saw anybody so affected in my life."

"Hush!" Basil protested involuntarily. "Let's dance."

It was a long hour before Basil was relieved by Hector Crum, and then several dances passed before he could get possession of Minnie, who was now the center of a moving whirl. But she made it up to him by pressing his hand and drawing him out to a veranda which overhung the dark lake.

"It's about time," she whispered. With a sort of instinct she found the darkest corner. "I might have known you'd have another crush."

"I haven't," he insisted in horror. "That's a sort of a cousin of mine."

"I always knew you were fickle. But I didn't think you'd forget me so soon."

She had wriggled up until she was touching him. Her eyes, floating into his, said, "What does it matter? We're alone."

In a curious panic he jumped to his feet. He couldn't possibly kiss her like this—right at once. It was all so different and older than a year ago. He was too excited to do more than walk up and down and say, "Gosh, I certainly am glad to see you," supplementing this unoriginal statement with an artificial laugh.

Already mature in poise, she tried to soothe him: "Basil, come and sit down!"

"I'll be all right," he gasped, as if he had just fainted. "I'm a little fussed, that's all."

Again he contributed what, even to his pounding ears, sounded like a silly laugh.

"I'll be here three weeks. Won't it be fun?" And she added, with warm emphasis: "Do you remember on Bill's veranda that afternoon?"

All he could find to answer was: "I work now in the afternoon."

"You can come out in the evenings, Basil. It's only half an hour in a car."

"I haven't got a car."

"I mean you can get your family's car."

"It's an electric."

She waited patiently. He was still romantic to her—handsome, incalculable, a little sad.

"I saw your sister," he blurted out. Beginning with that, he might bridge this perverse and intolerable reverence she inspired. "She certainly looks like you."

"Does she?"

"It was wonderful," he said. "Wonderful! Let me tell you—"

"Yes, do." She folded her hands expectantly in her lap.

"Well, this afternoon—"

The music had stopped and started several times. Now, in an intermission, there was the sound of determined footsteps on the veranda, and Basil looked up to find Rhoda and Hector Crum.

"I got to go home, Basil," squeaked Hector in his changing voice. "Here's Rhoda."

"Take Rhoda out to the dock and push her in the lake." But only Basil's mind said this; his body stood up politely.

"I didn't know where you were, Basil," said Rhoda in an aggrieved tone. "Why didn't you come back?"

"I was just coming." His voice trembled a little as he turned to Minnie. "Shall I find your partner for you?"

"Oh, don't bother," said Minnie. She was not angry, but she was somewhat astonished. She could not be expected to guess that the young man walking away from her so submissively was at the moment employed in working his way through Yale.

v

From the first, Basil's grandfather, who had once been a regent at the state university, wanted him to give up the idea of Yale, and now his mother, picturing him hungry and ragged in a garret, adjoined her persuasions. The sum on which he could count from her was far below the necessary minimum, and although he stubbornly refused to consider defeat, he consented, "just in case anything happened," to register at the university for the coming year.

In the administration building he ran into Eddie Parmelee, who introduced his companion, a small, enthusiastic Japanese.

"Well, well," said Eddie. "So you've given up Yale!"

"I given up Yale," put in Mr. Utsonomia, surprisingly. "Oh, yes, long time I given up Yale." He broke into enthusiastic laughter. "Oh, sure. Oh, yes."

"Mr. Utsonomia's a Japanese," explained Eddie, winking. "He's a sub-freshman too."

"Yes, I given up Harvard Princeton too," continued Mr. Utsonomia. "They give me choice back in my country. I choose here."

"You did?" said Basil, almost indignantly.

"Sure, more strong here. More peasants come, with strength and odor of ground."

Basil stared at him. "You like that?" he asked incredulously.

Utsonomia nodded. "Here I get to know real American peoples. Girls too. Yale got only boys."

"But they haven't got college spirit here," explained Basil patiently.

Utsonomia looked blankly at Eddie.

"Rah-rah!" elucidated Eddie, waving his arms. "Rah-rah-rah! You know."

"Besides, the girls here—" began Basil, and stopped.

"You know girls here?" grinned Utsonomia.

"No, I don't know them," said Basil firmly. "But I know they're not like the girls that you'd meet down at the Yale proms. I don't think they even have proms here. I don't mean the girls aren't all right, but they're just not like the ones at Yale. They're just coeds."

"I hear you got a crush on Rhoda Sinclair," said Eddie.

"Yes, I have!" said Basil ironically.

"They used to invite me to dinner sometimes last spring, but since you take her around to all the club dances—"

"Good-by," said Basil hastily. He exchanged a jerky bow for Mr. Utsonomia's more formal dip, and departed.

From the moment of Minnie's arrival the question of Rhoda had begun to assume enormous proportions. At first he had been merely indifferent to her person and a little ashamed of her lacy, oddly reminiscent clothes, but now, as he saw how relentlessly his services were commandeered, he began to hate her. When she complained of a headache, his imagination would eagerly convert it into a long, lingering illness from which she would recover only after college opened in the fall. But the eight dollars a week which he received from his great-uncle would pay his fare to New Haven, and he knew that if he failed to hold this position his mother would refuse to let him go.

Not suspecting the truth, Minnie Bibble found the fact that he only danced with her once or twice at each hop, and was then strangely moody and silent, somehow intriguing. Temporarily, at least, she was fascinated by his indifference, and even a little unhappy. But her precociously emotional temperament would not long stand neglect, and it was agony for Basil to watch several rivals beginning to emerge. There were moments when it seemed too big a price to pay even for Yale.

All his hopes centered upon one event. That was a farewell party in her honor for which the Kampfs had engaged the College Club and to which Rhoda was not invited. Given the mood and the moment, he might speed her departure knowing that he had stamped himself indelibly on her heart.

Three days before the party he came home from work at six to find the Kampfs' car before his door and Minnie sitting alone on the front porch.

"Basil, I had to see you," she said. "You've been so funny and distant to me."

Intoxicated by her presence on his familiar porch, he found no words to answer.

"I'm meeting the family in town for dinner and I've got an hour. Can't we go somewhere? I've been frightened to death your mother would come home and think it was fresh for me to call on you." She spoke in a whisper, though there was no one close enough to hear. "I wish we didn't have the old chauffeur. He listens."

"Listens to what?" Basil asked, with a flash of jealousy.

"He just listens."

"I'll tell you," he proposed: "We'll have him drop us by grampa's house and I'll borrow the electric."

The hot wind blew the brown curls around her forehead as they glided along Crest Avenue.

That he contributed the car made him feel more triumphantly astride the moment. There was a place he had saved for such a time as this—a little pigtail of a road left from the excavations of Prospect Park, where Crest Avenue ran obliviously above them and the late sun glinted on the Mississippi flats a mile away.

The end of summer was in the afternoon; it had turned a corner, and what was left must be used while there was yet time.

Suddenly she was whispering in his arms, "You're first, Basil —nobody but you."

"You just admitted you were a flirt."

"I know, but that was years ago. I used to like to be called fast when I was thirteen or fourteen, because I didn't care what people said; but about a year ago I began to see there was something better in life—honestly, Basil—and I've tried to act properly. But I'm afraid I'll never be an angel."

The river flowed in a thin scarlet gleam between the public baths and the massed tracks upon the other side. Booming, whistling, far-away railroad sounds reached them from down there; the voices of children playing tennis in Prospect Park sailed fraily overhead.

"I really haven't got such a line as everybody thinks, Basil, for I mean a lot of what I say way down deep, and nobody believes me. You know how much alike we are, and in a boy it doesn't matter, but a girl has to control her feelings, and that's hard for me, because I'm emotional."

"Haven't you kissed anybody since you've been in St. Paul?"

"No."

He saw she was lying, but it was a brave lie. They talked from their hearts—with the half truths and evasions peculiar to that organ, which has never been famed as an instrument of precision. They pieced together all the shreds of romance they knew and made garments for each other no less warm than their childish passion, no less wonderful than their sense of wonder.

He held her away suddenly, looked at her, made a strained sound of delight. There it was, in her face touched by sun—that promise—in the curve of her mouth, the tilted shadow of her nose on her cheek, the point of dull fire in her eyes—the promise that she could lead him into a world in which he would always be happy.

"Say I love you," he whispered.

"I'm in love with you."

"Oh, no; that's not the same."

She hesitated. "I've never said the other to anybody."

"Please say it."

She blushed the color of the sunset.

"At my party," she whispered. "It'd be easier at night."

When she dropped him in front of his house she spoke from the window of the car:

"This is my excuse for coming to see you. My uncle couldn't get the club Thursday, so we're having the party at the regular dance Saturday night."

Basil walked thoughtfully into the house; Rhoda Sinclair was also giving a dinner at the College Club dance Saturday night.

VI

It was put up to him frankly. Mrs. Reilly listened to his tentative excuses in silence and then said:

"Rhoda invited you first for Saturday night, and she already has one girl too many. Of course, if you choose to simply turn your back on your engagement and go to another party, I don't know how Rhoda will feel, but I know how I should feel."

And the next day his great-uncle, passing through the stock room, stopped and said: "What's all this trouble about parties?"

Basil started to explain, but Mr. Reilly cut him short. "I don't see the use of hurting a young girl's feelings. You better think it over."

Basil had thought it over; on Saturday afternoon he was still expected at both dinners and he had hit upon no solution at all.

Yale was only a month away now, but in four days Erminie Bibble would be gone, uncommitted, unsecured, grievously offended, lost forever. Not yet delivered from adolescence, Basil's moments of foresight alternated with those when the future was measured by a day. The glory that was Yale faded beside the promise of that incomparable hour.

On the other side loomed up the gaunt specter of the university, with phantoms flitting in and out its portals that presently disclosed themselves as peasants and girls. At five o'clock, in a burst of contempt for his weakness, he went to the phone and left word with a maid at the Kampfs' house that he was sick and couldn't come tonight. Nor would he sit with the dull left-overs of his generation—too sick for one party, he was too sick for the other. The Reillys could have no complaint as to that.

Rhoda answered the phone and Basil tried to reduce his voice to a weak murmur:

"Rhoda, I've been taken sick. I'm in bed now," he murmured feebly, and then added: "The phone's right next to the bed, you see; so I thought I'd call you up myself."

"You mean to say you can't come?" Dismay and anger were in her voice.

"I'm sick in bed," he repeated doggedly. "I've got chills and a pain and a cold."

"Well, can't you come anyhow?" she asked, with what to the invalid seemed a remarkable lack of consideration. "You've just got to. Otherwise there'll be two extra girls."

"I'll send someone to take my place," he said desperately. His glance, roving wildly out the window, fell on a house over the way. "I'll send Eddie Parmelee."

Rhoda considered. Then she asked with quick suspicion: "You're not going to that other party?"

"Oh, no; I told them I was sick too."

Again Rhoda considered. Eddie Parmelee was mad at her.

"I'll fix it up," Basil promised. "I know he'll come. He hasn't got anything to do tonight."

A few minutes later he dashed across the street. Eddie himself, tying a bow on his collar, came to the door. With certain reservations, Basil hastily outlined the situation. Would Eddie go in his place?

"Can't do it, old boy, even if I wanted to. Got a date with my real girl tonight."

"Eddie, I'd make it worth your while," he said recklessly. "I'd pay you for your time—say, five dollars."

Eddie considered, there was hesitation in his eyes, but he shook his head.

"It isn't worth it, Basil. You ought to see what I'm going out with tonight."

"You could see her afterward. They only want you—I mean me—because they've got more girls than men for dinner—and listen, Eddie, I'll make it ten dollars."

Eddie clapped him on the shoulder.

"All right, old boy, I'll do it for an old friend. Where's the pay?"

More than a week's salary melted into Eddie's palm, but another sort of emptiness accompanied Basil back across the street—the emptiness of the coming night. In an hour or so the Kampfs' limousine would draw up at the College Club and—time and time again his imagination halted miserably before that single picture, unable to endure any more.

In despair he wandered about the dark house. His mother had let the maid go out and was at his grandfather's for dinner, and momentarily Basil considered finding some rake like Elwood Leaming and going down to Carling's Restaurant to drink whiskey, wines and beer. Perhaps on her way back to the lake after the dance, Minnie, passing by, would see his face among the wildest of the revelers and understand.

"I'm going to Maxim's," he hummed to himself desperately; then he added impatiently: "Oh, to heck with Maxim's!"

He sat in the parlor and watched a pale moon come up over the Lindsays' fence at McKubben Street. Some young people came by, heading for the trolley that went to Como Park. He pitied their horrible dreariness—they were not going to dance with Minnie at the College Club tonight.

Eight-thirty—she was there now. Nine—they were dancing between courses to Peg of My Heart or doing the Castle Walk that Andy Lockheart brought home from Yale.

At ten o'clock he heard his mother come in, and almost immediately the phone rang. For a moment he listened without interest to her voice; then abruptly he sat up in his chair.

"Why, yes; how do you do, Mrs. Reilly. . . . Oh, I see. . . . Oh. . . . Are you sure it isn't Basil you want to speak to? . . . Well, frankly, Mrs. Reilly, I don't see that it's my affair."

Basil got up and took a step toward the door; his mother's voice was growing thin and annoyed: "I wasn't here at the time and I don't know who he promised to send."

Eddie Parmelee hadn't gone after all—well, that was the end.

". . . Of course not. It must be a mistake. I don't think Basil would possibly do that; I don't think he even knows any Japanese."

Basil's brain reeled. For a moment he was about to dash across the street after Eddie Parmelee. Then he heard a definitely angry note come into his mother's voice:

"Very well, Mrs. Reilly. I'll tell my son. But his going to Yale is scarcely a matter I care to discuss with you. In any case, he no longer needs anyone's assistance."

He had lost his position and his mother was trying to put a proud face on it. But her voice continued, soaring a little:

"Uncle Ben might be interested to know that this afternoon we sold the Third Street block to the Union Depot Company for four hundred thousand dollars."

VII

Mr. Utsonomia was enjoying himself. In the whole six months in America he had never felt so caught up in its inner life before. At first it had been a little hard to make plain to the lady just whose place it was he was taking, but Eddie Parmelee had assured him that such substitutions were an American custom, and he was spending the evening collecting as much data upon American customs as possible.

He did not dance, so he sat with the elderly lady until both the ladies went home, early and apparently a little agitated, shortly after dinner. But Mr. Utsonomia stayed on. He watched and he wandered. He was not lonesome; he had grown accustomed to being alone.

About eleven he sat on the veranda pretending to be blowing the smoke of a cigarette—which he hated—out over the city, but really listening to a conversation which was taking place just behind. It had been going on for half an hour, and it puzzled him, for apparently it was a proposal, and it was not refused. Yet, if his eyes did not deceive him, the contracting parties were of an age that Americans did not associate with such serious affairs. Another thing puzzled him even more: obviously, if one substituted for an absent guest, the absent guest should not be among those present, and he was almost sure that the young man who had just engaged himself for marriage was Mr. Basil Lee. It would be bad manners to intrude now, but he would urbanely ask him about a solution of this puzzle when the state university opened in the fall.

Basil and Cleopatra

Wherever she was, became a beautiful and enchanted place to Basil, but he did not think of it that way. He thought the fascination was inherent in the locality, and long afterward a commonplace street or the mere name of a city would exude a peculiar glow, a sustained sound, that struck his soul alert with delight. In her presence he was too absorbed to notice his surroundings; so that her absence never made them empty, but, rather, sent him seeking for her through haunted rooms and gardens that he had never really seen before.

This time, as usual, he saw only the expression of her face, the mouth that gave an attractive interpretation of any emotion she felt or pretended to feel—oh, invaluable mouth—and the rest of her, new as a peach and old as sixteen. He was almost unconscious that they stood in a railroad station and entirely unconscious that she had just glanced over his shoulder and fallen in love with another young man. Turning to walk with the rest to the car, she was already acting for the stranger; no less so because her voice was pitched for Basil and she clung to him, squeezing his arm.

Had Basil noticed this other young man that the train discharged he would merely have been sorry for him—as he had been sorry for the wretched people in the villages along the railroad and for his fellow travelers—they were not entering Yale in a fortnight nor were they about to spend three days in the same town with Miss Erminie Gilberte Labouisse Bibble. There was something dense, hopeless and a little contemptible about them all.

Basil had come to visit here because Erminie Bibble was visiting here. On the sad eve of her departure from his native Western city a month before, she had said, with all the promise one could ask in her urgent voice:

"If you know a boy in Mobile, why don't you make him invite you down when I'll be there?"

He had followed this suggestion. And now with the soft, unfamiliar Southern city actually flowing around him, his excitement led him to believe that Fat Gaspar's car floated off immediately they entered it. A voice from the curb came as a surprise:

"Hi, Bessie Belle. Hi, William. How you all?"

The newcomer was tall and lean and a year or so older than Basil. He wore a white linen suit and a panama hat, under which burned fierce, undefeated Southern eyes.

"Why, Littleboy Le Moyne!" exclaimed Miss Cheever. "When did you get home?"

"Jus' now, Bessie Belle. Saw you lookin' so fine and pretty, had to come and see closer."

He was introduced to Minnie and Basil.

"Drop you somewhere, Littleboy?" asked Fat—on his native heath, William.

"Why—" Le Moyne hesitated. "You're very kind, but the man ought to be here with the car."

"Jump in."

Le Moyne swung his bag on top of Basil's and with courteous formality got in the back seat beside them. Basil caught Minnie's eye and she smiled quickly back, as if to say, "This is too bad, but it'll soon be over."

"Do you happen to come from New Orleans, Miss Bibble?" asked Le Moyne.

"Sure do."

" 'Cause I just came from there and they told me one of their mos' celebrated heartbreakers was visiting up here, and meanwhile her suitors were shooting themselves all over the city. That's the truth. I used to help pick 'em up myself sometimes when they got littering the streets."

"This must be Mobile Bay on the left," Basil thought; "Down Mobile," and the Dixie moonlight and darky stevedores singing. The houses on either side of the street were gently faded behind proud, protecting vines; there had been crinolines on these balconies, and guitars by night in these broken gardens.

It was so warm; the voices were so sure they had time to say everything—even Minnie's voice, answering the banter of the youth with the odd nickname, seemed slower and lazier—he had scarcely ever thought of her as a Southern girl before. They stopped at a large gate where flickers of a yellow house showed through luscious trees. Le Moyne got out.

"I certainly hope you both enjoy your visit here. If you'll permit me I'll call around and see if there's anything I can do to add to your pleasure." He swooped his panama. "I bid you good day."

As they started off, Bessie Belle turned around and smiled at Minnie.

"Didn't I tell you?" she demanded.

"I guessed it in the station, before he came up to the car," said Minnie. "Something told me that was him."

"Did you think he was good-looking?"

"He was divine," Minnie said.

"Of course he's always gone with an older crowd."

To Basil, this prolonged discussion seemed a little out of place. After all, the young man was simply a local Southerner who lived here; add to that, that he went with an older crowd, and it seemed that his existence was being unnecessarily insisted upon.

But now Minnie turned to him, said, "Basil," wriggled invitingly and folded her hands in a humble, expectant way that invariably caused disturbances in his heart.

"I loved your letters," she said.

"You might have answered them."

"I haven't had a minute, Basil. I visited in Chicago and then in Nashville. I haven't even been home." She lowered her voice. "Father and mother are getting a divorce, Basil. Isn't that awful?"

He was startled; then, after a moment, he adjusted the idea to her and she became doubly poignant; because of its romantic connection with her, the thought of divorce would never shock him again.

"That's why I didn't write. But I've thought of you so much. You're the best friend I have, Basil. You always understand."

This was decidedly not the note upon which they had parted in St. Paul. A dreadful rumor that he hadn't intended to mention rose to his lips.

"Who is this fellow Bailey you met at Lake Forest?" he inquired lightly.

"Buzz Bailey!" Her big eyes opened in surprise. "He's very attractive and a divine dancer, but we're just friends." She frowned. "I bet Connie Davies has been telling tales in St. Paul. Honestly, I'm so sick of girls that, just out of jealousy or nothing better to do, sit around and criticize you if you have a good time."

He was convinced now that something had occurred in Lake Forest, but he concealed the momentary pang from Minnie.

"Anyhow, you're a fine one to talk." She smiled suddenly. "I guess everybody knows how fickle you are, Mr. Basil Duke Lee."

Generally such an implication is considered flattering, but the lightness, almost the indifference, with which she spoke increased his alarm—and then suddenly the bomb exploded.

"You needn't worry about Buzz Bailey. At present I'm absolutely heartwhole and fancy free."

Before he could even comprehend the enormity of what she

had said, they stopped at Bessie Belle Cheever's door and the two girls ran up the steps, calling back, "We'll see you this afternoon."

Mechanically Basil climbed into the front seat beside his host.

"Going out for freshman football, Basil?" William asked.

"What? Oh, sure. If I can get off my two conditions." There was no if in his heart; it was the greatest ambition of his life.

"You'll probably make the freshman team easy. That fellow Littleboy Le Moyne you just met is going to Princeton this fall. He played end at V. M. I."

"Where'd he get that crazy name?"

"Why, his family always called him that and everybody picked it up." After a moment he added, "He asked them to the country-club dance with him tonight."

"When did he?" Basil demanded in surprise.

"Right then. That's what they were talking about. I meant to ask them and I was just leading up to it gradually, but he stepped in before I could get a chance." He sighed, blaming himself. "Well, anyhow, we'll see them there."

"Sure; it doesn't matter," said Basil. But was it Fat's mistake? Couldn't Minnie have said right out: "But Basil came all this way to see me and I ought to go with him on his first night here."

What had happened? One month ago, in the dim, thunderous Union Station at St. Paul, they had gone behind a baggage truck and he had kissed her, and her eyes had said: "Again." Up to the very end, when she disappeared in a swirl of vapor at the car window, she had been his—those weren't things you thought; they were things you knew. He was bewildered. It wasn't like Minnie, who, for all her glittering popularity, was invariably kind. He tried to think of something in his letters that might have offended her, and searched himself for new shortcomings. Perhaps she didn't like him the way he was in the morning. The joyous mood in which he had arrived was vanishing into air.

She was her familiar self when they played tennis that afternoon; she admired his strokes and once, when they were close at the net, she suddenly patted his hand. But later, as they drank lemonade on the Cheevers' wide, shady porch, he couldn't seem to be alone with her even for a minute. Was it by accident that, coming back from the courts, she had sat in front with Fat? Last summer she had made opportunities to be alone with him—made them out of nothing. It was in a state that seemed to border on some terrible realization that he dressed for the country-club dance.

The club lay in a little valley, almost roofed over by willows, and down through their black silhouettes, in irregular blobs and patches, dripped the light of a huge harvest moon. As they parked the car, Basil's tune of tunes, Chinatown, drifted from the windows and dissolved into its notes which thronged like elves through the glade. His heart quickened, suffocating him; the throbbing tropical darkness held a promise of such romance as he had dreamed of; but faced with it, he felt himself too small and impotent to seize the felicity he desired. When he danced with Minnie he was ashamed of inflicting his merely mortal presence on her in this fairyland whose unfamiliar figures reached towering proportions of magnificence and beauty. To make him king here, she would have to reach forth and draw him close to her with soft words; but she only said, "Isn't it wonderful, Basil? Did you ever have a better time?"

Talking for a moment with Le Moyne in the stag line, Basil was hesitantly jealous and oddly shy. He resented the tall form that stooped down so fiercely over Minnie as they danced, but he found it impossible to dislike him or not to be amused by the line of sober-faced banter he kept up with passing girls. He and William Gaspar were the youngest boys here, as Bessie Belle and Minnie were the youngest girls, and for the first time in his life he wanted passionately to be older, less impressionable, less impressed. Quivering at every scent, sight or tune, he wanted to be blasé and calm. Wretchedly he felt the whole world of beauty pour down upon him like moonlight, pressing on him, making his breath now sighing, now short, as he wallowed helplessly in a superabundance of youth for which a hundred adults present would have given years of life.

Next day, meeting her in a world that had shrunk back to reality, things were more natural, but something was gone and he could not bring himself to be amusing and gay. It would be like being brave after the battle. He should have been all that the night before. They went downtown in an unpaired foursome and called at a photographer's for some pictures of Minnie. Basil liked one proof that no one else liked—somehow, it reminded him of her as she had been in St. Paul—so he ordered two—one for her to keep and one to send after him to Yale. All afternoon she was distracted and vaguely singing, but back at the Cheevers' she sprang up the steps at the sound of the phone inside. Ten minutes later she appeared, sulky and lowering, and Basil heard a quick exchange between the two girls:

"He can't get out of it."

"—a pity."

"—back Friday."

It could only be Le Moyne who had gone away, and to Minnie it mattered. Presently, unable to endure her disappointment, he got up wretchedly and suggested to William that they go home. To his surprise, Minnie's hand on his arm arrested him.

"Don't go, Basil. It doesn't seem as if I've seen you a minute since you've been here."

He laughed unhappily.

"As if it mattered to you."

"Basil, don't be silly." She bit her lip as if she were hurt. "Let's go out to the swing."

He was suddenly radiant with hope and happiness. Her tender smile, which seemed to come from the heart of freshness, soothed him and he drank down her lies in grateful gulps like cool water. The last sunshine touched her cheeks with the unearthly radiance he had seen there before, as she told him how she hadn't wanted to accept Le Moyne's invitation, and how surprised and hurt she had been when he hadn't come near her last night.

"Then do one thing, Minnie," he pleaded: "Won't you let me kiss you just once?"

"But not here," she exclaimed, "you silly!"

"Let's go in the summerhouse, for just a minute."

"Basil, I can't. Bessie Belle and William are on the porch. Maybe some other time."

He looked at her distraught, unable to believe or disbelieve in her, and she changed the subject quickly:

"I'm going to Miss Beecher's school, Basil. It's only a few hours from New Haven. You can come up and see me this fall. The only thing is, they say you have to sit in glass parlors. Isn't that terrible?"

"Awful," he agreed fervently.

William and Bessie Belle had left the veranda and were out in front, talking to some people in a car.

"Minnie, come into the summerhouse now—for just a minute. They're so far away."

Her face set unwillingly.

"I can't, Basil. Don't you see I can't?"

"Why not? I've got to leave tomorrow."

"Oh, no."

"I have to. I only have four days to get ready for my exams. Minnie—"

He took her hand. It rested calmly enough in his, but when he tried to pull her to her feet she plucked it sharply away. The swing moved with the little struggle and Basil put out his foot and made it stop. It was terrible to swing when one was at a disadvantage.

She laid the recovered hand on his knee.

"I've stopped kissing people, Basil. Really. I'm too old; I'll be seventeen next May."

"I'll bet you kissed Le Moyne," he said bitterly.

"Well, you're pretty fresh—"

Basil got out of the swing.

"I think I'll go."

Looking up, she judged him dispassionately, as she never had before—his sturdy, graceful figure; the high, warm color through his tanned skin; his black, shining hair that she had once thought so romantic. She felt, too—as even those who disliked him felt—that there was something else in his face— a mark, a hint of destiny, a persistence that was more than will, that was rather a necessity of pressing its own pattern on the world, of having its way. That he would most probably succeed at Yale, that it would be nice to go there this year as his girl, meant nothing to her. She had never needed to be calculating.

Hesitating, she alternatingly drew him toward her in her mind and let him go. There were so many men and they wanted her so much. If Le Moyne had been here at hand she wouldn't have hesitated, for nothing must interfere with the mysterious opening glory of that affair; but he was gone for three days and she couldn't decide quite yet to let Basil go.

"Stay over till Wednesday and I'll—I'll do what you want," she said.

"But I can't. I've got these exams to study for. I ought to have left this afternoon."

"Study on the train."

She wriggled, dropped her hands in her lap and smiled at him. Taking her hand suddenly, he pulled her to her feet and toward the summerhouse and the cool darkness behind its vines.

II

The following Friday Basil arrived in New Haven and set about crowding five days' work into two. He had done no studying on the train; instead he sat in a trance and concentrated upon Minnie, wondering what was happening now that Le Moyne was there. She had kept her promise to him, but only literally—kissed him once in the playhouse, once, grudgingly, the second evening; but the day of his departure there had been a telegram from Le Moyne, and in front of Bessie Belle she had not even dared to kiss him good-by. As a sort of amend she had given him permission to call on the first day permitted by Miss Beecher's school.

The opening of college found him rooming with Brick Wales and George Dorsey in a suite of two bedrooms and a study in Wright Hall. Until the result of his trigonometry examination was published he was ineligible to play football, but watching the freshmen practice on Yale field, he saw that the quarterback position lay between Cullum, last year's Andover captain, and a man named Danziger from a New Bedford high school. There was a rumor that Cullum would be moved to halfback. The other quarterbacks did not appear formidable and Basil felt a great impatience to be out there with a team in his hands to move over the springy turf. He was sure he could at least get in some of the games.

Behind everything, as a light showing through, was the image of Minnie; he would see her in a week, three days, tomorrow. On the eve of the occasion he ran into Fat Gaspar, who was in Sheff, in the oval by Haughton Hall. In the first busy weeks they had scarcely met; now they walked along for a little way together.

"We all came North together," Fat said. "You ought to have been along. We had some excitement. Minnie got in a jam with Littleboy Le Moyne."

Basil's blood ran cold.

"It was funny afterward, but she was pretty scared for a while," continued Fat. "She had a compartment with Bessie Belle, but she and Littleboy wanted to be alone; so in the afternoon Bessie Belle came and played cards in ours. Well, after about two hours Bessie Belle and I went back, and there were Minnie and Littleboy standing in the vestibule arguing with the conductor; Minnie white as a sheet. Seems they locked the door and pulled down the blinds, and I guess there was a little petting going on. When he came along after the tickets and knocked on the door, they thought it was us kidding them, and wouldn't let him in at first, and when they did, he was pretty upset. He asked Littleboy if that was his compartment, and whether he and Minnie were married that they locked the door, and Littleboy lost his temper trying to explain that there was nothing wrong. He said the conductor had insulted Minnie and he wanted him to fight. But that conductor could have made trouble, and believe me, I had an awful time smoothing it all over."

With every detail imagined, with every refinement of jealousy beating in his mind, including even envy for their community of misfortune as they stood together in the vestibule, Basil went up to Miss Beecher's next day. Radiant and glowing, more mysteriously desirable than ever, wearing her very sins like stars, she came down to him in her plain white uniform dress, and his heart turned over at the kindness of her eyes.

"You were wonderful to come up, Basil. I'm so excited having a beau so soon. Everybody's jealous of me."

The glass doors hinged like French windows, shutting them in on all sides. It was hot. Down through three more compartments he could see another couple—a girl and her brother, Minnie said—and from time to time they moved and gestured soundlessly, as unreal in these tiny human conservatories as the vase of paper flowers on the table. Basil walked up and down nervously.

"Minnie, I want to be a great man some day and I want to do everything for you. I understand you're tired of me now. I don't know how it happened, but somebody else came along —it doesn't matter. There isn't any hurry. But I just want you to—oh, remember me in some different way—try to think of me as you used to, not as if I was just another one you threw over. Maybe you'd better not see me for a while—I mean at the dance this fall. Wait till I've accomplished some big scene or deed, you know, and I can show it to you and say I did that all for you."

It was very futile and young and sad. Once, carried away by the tragedy of it all, he was on the verge of tears, but he controlled himself to that extent. There was sweat on his forehead. He sat across the room from her, and Minnie sat on the couch, looking at the floor, and said several times: "Can't we be friends, Basil? I always think of you as one of my best friends."

Toward the end she rose patiently.

"Don't you want to see the chapel?"

They walked upstairs and he glanced dismally into a small dark space, with her living, sweet-smelling presence half a yard from his shoulder. He was almost glad when the funereal business was over and he walked out of the school into the fresh autumn air.

Back in New Haven he found two pieces of mail on his desk. One was a notice from the registrar telling him that he had failed his trigonometry examination and would be ineligible for football. The second was a photograph of Minnie—the picture that he had liked and ordered two of in Mobile. At first the inscription puzzled him: "L. L. from E. G. L. B. Trains are bad for the heart." Then suddenly he realized what had

175

happened, and threw himself on his bed, shaken with wild laughter.

III

Three weeks later, having requested and passed a special examination in trigonometry, Basil began to look around him gloomily to see if there was anything left in life. Not since his miserable first year at school had he passed through such a period of misery; only now did he begin for the first time to be aware of Yale. The quality of romantic speculation reawoke, and, listlessly at first, then with growing determination, he set about merging himself into this spirit which had fed his dreams so long.

"I want to be chairman of the News or the Record," thought his old self one October morning, "and I want to get my letter in football, and I want to be in Skull and Bones."

Whenever the vision of Minnie and Le Moyne on the train occurred to him, he repeated this phrase like an incantation. Already he thought with shame of having stayed over in Mobile, and there began to be long strings of hours when he scarcely brooded about her at all.

He had missed half of the freshman football season, and it was with scant hope that he joined the squad on Yale field. Dressed in his black and white St. Regis jersey, amid the motley of forty schools, he looked enviously at the proud two dozen in Yale blue. At the end of four days he was reconciling himself to obscurity for the rest of the season when the voice of Carson, assistant coach, singled him suddenly out of a crowd of scrub backs.

"Who was throwing those passes just now?"

"I was, sir."

"I haven't seen you before, have I?"

"I just got eligible."

"Know the signals?"

"Yes, sir."

"Well, you take this team down the field—ends, Krutch and Bispam; tackles—"

A moment later he heard his own voice snapping out on the crisp air: "Thirty-two, sixty-five, sixty-seven, twenty-two—"

There was a ripple of laughter.

"Wait a minute! Where'd you learn to call signals like that?" said Carson.

"Why, we had a Harvard coach, sir."

"Well, just drop the Haughton emphasis. You'll get everybody too excited."

After a few minutes they were called in and told to put on headgears.

"Where's Waite?" Carson asked. "Test, eh? Well, you then —what's your name?—in the black and white sweater?"

"Lee."

"You call signals. And let's see you get some life into this outfit. Some of you guards and tackles are big enough for the varsity. Keep them on their toes, you—what's your name?"

"Lee."

They lined up with possession of the ball on the freshmen's twenty-yard line. They were allowed unlimited downs, but when, after a dozen plays, they were in approximately that same place, the ball was given to the first team.

"That's that!" thought Basil. "That finishes me."

But an hour later, as they got out of the bus, Carson spoke to him:

"Did you weigh this afternoon?"

"Yes. Hundred and fifty-eight."

"Let me give you a tip—you're still playing prep-school football. You're still satisfied with stopping them. The idea here is that if you lay them down hard enough you wear them out. Can you kick?"

"No, sir."

"Well, it's too bad you didn't get out sooner."

A week later his name was read out as one of those to go to Andover. Two quarterbacks ranked ahead of him, Danziger and a little hard rubber ball of a man, named Appleton, and Basil watched the game from the sidelines, but when, the following Tuesday, Danziger splintered his arm in practice, Basil was ordered to report to training table.

On the eve of the game with the Princeton freshmen, the egress of the student body to Princeton for the Varsity encounter left the campus almost deserted. Deep autumn had set in, with a crackling wind from the west, and walking back to his room after final skull practice, Basil felt the old lust for glory sweep over him. Le Moyne was playing end on the Princeton freshmen and it was probable that Minnie would be in the stands, but now, as he ran along the springy grass in front of Osborne, swaying to elude imaginary tacklers, the fact seemed of less importance than the game. Like most Americans, he was seldom able really to grasp the moment, to say: "This, for me, is the great equation by which everything else will be measured; this is the golden time," but for once the present was sufficient. He was going to spend two hours in a country where life ran at the pace he demanded of it.

The day was fair and cool; an unimpassioned crowd, mostly townsmen, was scattered through the stands. The Princeton freshmen looked sturdy and solid in their diagonal stripes, and Basil picked out Le Moyne, noting coldly that he was exceptionally fast, and bigger than he had seemed in his clothes. On an impulse Basil turned and searched for Minnie in the crowd, but he could not find her. A minute later the whistle blew; sitting at the coach's side, he concentrated all his faculties on the play.

The first half was played between the thirty-yard lines. The main principles of Yale's offense seemed to Basil too simple; less effective than the fragments of the Haughton system he had learned at school, while the Princeton tactics, still evolved in Sam White's long shadow, were built around a punter and the hope of a break. When the break came, it was Yale's. At the start of the second half Princeton fumbled and Appleton sent over a drop kick from the thirty-yard line.

It was his last act of the day. He was hurt on the next kick-off and, to a burst of freshmen cheering, assisted from the game.

With his heart in a riot, Basil sprinted out on the field. He felt an overpowering strangeness, and it was someone else in his skin who called the first signals and sent an unsuccessful play through the line. As he forced his eyes to take in the field slowly, they met Le Moyne's, and Le Moyne grinned at him.

Basil called for a short pass over the line, throwing it himself for a gain of seven yards. He sent Cullum off tackle for three more and a first down. At the forty, with more latitude, his mind began to function smoothly and surely. His short passes worried the Princeton fullback, and, in consequence, the running gains through the line were averaging four yards instead of two.

At the Princeton forty he dropped back to kick formation and tried Le Moyne's end, but Le Moyne went under the interfering halfback and caught Basil by a foot. Savagely Basil tugged himself free, but too late—the halfback bowled him over. Again Le Moyne's face grinned at him, and Basil hated it. He called the same end and, with Cullum carrying the ball, they rolled over Le Moyne six yards, to Princeton's thirty-two. He was slowing down, was he? Then run him ragged! System counseled a pass, but he heard himself calling the end again. He ran parallel to the line, saw his interference melt away and Le Moyne, his jaw set, coming for him. Instead of cutting in, Basil turned full about and tried to reverse his field. When he was trapped he had lost fifteen yards.

A few minutes later the ball changed hands and he ran back to the safety position thinking: "They'd yank me if they had anybody to put in my place."

The Princeton team suddenly woke up. A long pass gained thirty yards. A fast new back dazzled his way through the line for another first down. Yale was on the defensive, but even before they had realized the fact, the disaster had happened. Basil was drawn on an apparently developed play; too late he saw the ball shoot out of scrimmage to a loose end; saw, as he was neatly blocked, that the Princeton substitutes were jumping around wildly, waving their blankets. They had scored.

He got up with his heart black, but his brain cool. Blunders could be atoned for—if they only wouldn't take him out. The whistle blew for the quarter, and squatting on the turf with the exhausted team, he made himself believe that he hadn't lost their confidence, kept his face intent and rigid, refusing no man's eye. He had made his errors for today.

On the kick-off he ran the ball back to the thirty-five, and a steady rolling progress began. The short passes, a weak spot inside tackle, Le Moyne's end. Le Moyne was tired now. His face was drawn and dogged as he smashed blindly into the interference; the ball carrier eluded him—Basil or another.

Thirty more to go—twenty—over Le Moyne again. Disentangling himself from the pile, Basil met the Southerner's weary glance and insulted him in a crisp voice:

"You've quit, Littleboy. They better take you out."

He started the next play at him and, as Le Moyne charged in furiously, tossed a pass over his head for the score. Yale 10, Princeton 7. Up and down the field again, with Basil fresher every minute and another score in sight, and suddenly the game was over.

Trudging off the field, Basil's eye ranged over the stands, but he could not see her.

"I wonder if she knows I was pretty bad," he thought, and then bitterly: "If I don't, he'll tell her."

He could hear him telling her in that soft Southern voice— the voice that had wooed her so persuasively that afternoon on the train. As he emerged from the dressing room an hour later he ran into Le Moyne coming out of the visitors' quarters next door. He looked at Basil with an expression at once uncertain and angry.

"Hello, Lee." After a momentary hesitation he added: "Good work."

"Hello, Le Moyne," said Basil, clipping his words.

Le Moyne turned away, turned back again.

"What's the matter?" he demanded. "Do you want to carry this any further?"

Basil didn't answer. The bruised face and the bandaged hand assuaged his hatred a little, but he couldn't bring himself to speak. The game was over, and now Le Moyne would meet Minnie somewhere, make the defeat negligible in the victory of the night.

"If it's about Minnie, you're wasting your time being sore," Le Moyne exploded suddenly. "I asked her to the game, but she didn't come."

"Didn't she?" Basil was startled.

"That was it, eh? I wasn't sure. I thought you were just trying to get my goat in there." His eyes narrowed. "The young lady kicked me about a month ago."

"Kicked you?"

"Threw me over. Got a little weary of me. She runs through things quickly."

Basil perceived that his face was miserable.

"Who is it now?" he asked in more civil tone.

"It seems to be a classmate of yours named Jubal—and a mighty sad bird, if you ask me. She met him in New York the day before her school opened, and I hear it's pretty heavy. She'll be at the Lawn Club Dance tonight."

IV

Basil had dinner at the Taft with Jobena Dorsey and her brother George. The Varsity had won at Princeton and the college was jubilant and enthusiastic; as they came in, a table of freshmen by the door gave Basil a hand.

"You're getting very important," Jobena said.

A year ago Basil had thought for a few weeks that he was in love with Jobena; when they next met he knew immediately that he was not.

"And why was that?" he asked her now, as they danced. "Why did it all go so quick?"

"Do you really want to know?"

"Yes."

"Because I let it go."

"You let it go?" he repeated. "I like that!"

"I decided you were too young."

"Didn't I have anything to do with it?"

She shook her head.

"That's what Bernard Shaw says," Basil admitted thoughtfully. "But I thought it was just about older people. So you go after the men."

"Well, I should say not!" Her body stiffened indignantly in his arms. "The men are usually there, and the girl blinks at them or something. It's just instinct."

"Can't a man make a girl fall for him?"

"Some men can—the ones who really don't care."

He pondered this awful fact for a moment and stowed it away for future examination. On the way to the Lawn Club he brought forth more questions. If a girl who had been "crazy about a boy" became suddenly infatuated with another, what ought the first boy to do?

"Let her go," said Jobena.

"Supposing he wasn't willing to do that. What ought he to do?"

"There isn't anything to do."

"Well, what's the best thing?"

Laughing, Jobena laid her head on his shoulder.

"Poor Basil," she said, "I'll be Laura Jean Libbey and you tell me the whole story."

He summarized the affair. "You see," he concluded, "if she was just anybody I could get over it, no matter how much I loved her. But she isn't—she's the most popular, most beautiful girl I've ever seen. I mean she's like Messalina and Cleopatra and Salome and all that."

"Louder," requested George from the front seat.

"She's sort of an immortal woman," continued Basil in a lower voice. "You know, like Madame du Barry and all that sort of thing. She's not just—"

"Not just like me."

"No. That is, you're sort of like her—all the girls I've cared about are sort of the same. Oh, Jobena, you know what I mean."

As the lights of the New Haven Lawn Club loomed up she became obligingly serious:

"There's nothing to do. I can see that. She's more sophisticated than you. She staged the whole thing from the beginning, even when you thought it was you. I don't know why she got tired, but evidently she is, and she couldn't create it again, even if she wanted to, and you couldn't because you're—"

"Go on. What?"

"You're too much in love. All that's left for you to do is to show her you don't care. Any girl hates to lose an old beau; so she may even smile at you—but don't go back. It's all over."

In the dressing room Basil stood thoughtfully brushing his

hair. It was all over. Jobena's words had taken away his last faint hope, and after the strain of the afternoon the realization brought tears to his eyes. Hurriedly filling the bowl, he washed his face. Someone came in and slapped him on the back.

"You played a nice game, Lee."

"Thanks, but I was rotten."

"You were great. That last quarter—"

He went into the dance. Immediately he saw her, and in the same breath he was dizzy and confused with excitement. A little dribble of stags pursued her wherever she went, and she looked up at each one of them with the bright-eyed, passionate smile he knew so well. Presently he located her escort and indignantly discovered it was a flip, blatant boy from Hill School he had already noticed and set down as impossible. What quality lurked behind those watery eyes that drew her? How could that raw temperament appreciate that she was one of the immortal sirens of the world?

Having examined Mr. Jubal desperately and in vain for the answers to these questions, he cut in and danced all of twenty feet with her, smiling with cynical melancholy when she said:

"I'm so proud to know you, Basil. Everybody says you were wonderful this afternoon."

But the phrase was precious to him and he stood against the wall repeating it over to himself, separating it into its component parts and trying to suck out any lurking meaning. If enough people praised him it might influence her. "I'm proud to know you, Basil. Everybody says you were wonderful this afternoon."

There was a commotion near the door and someone said, "By golly, they got in after all!"

"Who?" another asked.

"Some Princeton freshmen. Their football season's over and three or four of them broke training at the Hofbrau."

And now suddenly the curious specter of a young man burst out of the commotion, as a back breaks through a line, and neatly straight-arming a member of the dance committee, rushed unsteadily onto the floor. He wore no collar with his dinner coat, his shirt front had long expelled its studs, his hair and eyes were wild. For a moment he glanced around as if blinded by the lights; then his glance fell on Minnie Bibble and an unmistakable love light came into his face. Even before he reached her he began to call her name aloud in a strained, poignant Southern voice.

Basil sprang forward, but others were before him, and Littleboy Le Moyne, fighting hard, disappeared into the coatroom in a flurry of legs and arms, many of which were not his own. Standing in the doorway, Basil found his disgust tempered with a monstrous sympathy; for Le Moyne, each time his head emerged from under the faucet, spoke desperately of his rejected love.

But when Basil danced with Minnie again, he found her frightened and angry; so much so that she seemed to appeal to Basil for support, made him sit down.

"Wasn't he a fool?" she cried feelingly. "That sort of thing gives a girl a terrible reputation. They ought to have put him in jail.'

"He didn't know what he was doing. He played a hard game and he's all in, that's all."

But her eyes filled with tears.

"Oh, Basil," she pleaded, "am I just perfectly terrible? I never want to be mean to anybody; things just happen."

He wanted to put his arm around her and tell her she was the most romantic person in the world, but he saw in her eyes that she scarcely perceived him; he was a lay figure—she might have been talking to another girl. He remembered what Jobena had said—there was nothing left except to escape with his pride.

"You've got more sense." Her soft voice flowed around him like an enchanted river. "You know that when two people aren't—aren't crazy about each other any more, the thing is to be sensible."

"Of course," he said, and forced himself to add lightly: "When a thing's over, it's over."

"Oh, Basil, you're so satisfactory. You always understand." And now suddenly, for the first time in months, she was actually thinking of him. He would be an invaluable person in any girl's life, she thought, if that brain of his, which was so annoying sometimes, was really used "to sort of understand."

He was watching Jobena dance, and Minnie followed his eyes.

"You brought a girl, didn't you? She's awfully pretty."

"Not as pretty as you."

"Basil."

Resolutely he refused to look at her, guessing that she had wriggled slightly and folded her hands in her lap. And as he held on to himself an extraordinary thing happened—the world around, outside of her, brightened a little. Presently more freshmen would approach him to congratulate him on the game, and he would like it—the words and the tribute in their eyes. There was a good chance he would start against Harvard next week.

"Basil!"

His heart made a dizzy tour of his chest. Around the corner of his eyes he felt her eyes waiting. Was she really sorry? Should he seize the opportunity to turn to her and say: "Minnie, tell this crazy nut to go jump in the river, and come back to me." He wavered, but a thought that had helped him this afternoon returned: He had made all his mistakes for this time. Deep inside of him the plea expired slowly.

Jubal the impossible came up with an air of possession, and Basil's heart went bobbing off around the ballroom in a pink silk dress. Lost again in a fog of indecision, he walked out on the veranda. There was a flurry of premature snow in the air and the stars looked cold. Staring up at them he saw that they were his stars as always—symbols of ambition, struggle and glory. The wind blew through them, trumpeting that high white note for which he always listened, and the thin-blown clouds, stripped for battle, passed in review. The scene was of an unparalleled brightness and magnificence, and only the practiced eye of the commander saw that one star was no longer there.

II. *Josephine*

First Blood

I

"I remember your coming to me in despair when Josephine was about three!" cried Mrs. Bray. "George was furious because he couldn't decide what to go to work at, so he used to spank little Josephine."

"I remember," said Josephine's mother.

"And so this is Josephine."

This was, indeed, Josephine. She looked at Mrs. Bray and smiled, and Mrs. Bray's eyes hardened imperceptibly. Josephine kept on smiling.

"How old are you, Josephine?"

"Just sixteen."

"Oh-h. I would have said you were older."

At the first opportunity Josephine asked Mrs. Perry, "Can I go to the movies with Lillian this afternoon?"

"No, dear; you have to study." She turned to Mrs. Bray as if the matter were dismissed—but: "You darn fool," muttered Josephine audibly.

Mrs. Bray said some words quickly to cover the situation, but, of course, Mrs. Perry could not let it pass unreproved.

"What did you call mother, Josephine?"

"I don't see why I can't go to the movies with Lillian."

Her mother was content to let it go at this.

"Because you've got to study. You go somewhere every day, and your father wants it to stop."

"How crazy!" said Josephine, and she added vehemently, "How utterly insane! Father's got to be a maniac I think. Next thing he'll start tearing his hair and think he's Napoleon or something."

"No," interposed Mrs. Bray jovially as Mrs. Perry grew rosy. "Perhaps she's right. Maybe George *is* crazy—I'm sure my husband's crazy. It's this war."

But she was not really amused; she thought Josephine ought to be beaten with sticks.

They were talking about Anthony Harker, a contemporary of Josephine's older sister.

"He's divine," Josephine interposed—not rudely, for, despite the foregoing, she was not rude; it was seldom even that she appeared to talk too much, though she lost her temper, and swore sometimes when people were unreasonable. "He's perfectly——"

"He's very popular. Personally, I don't see very much to him. He seems rather superficial."

"Oh, no, mother," said Josephine. "He's far from it. Everybody says he has a great deal of personality—which is more than you can say of most of these jakes. Any girl would be glad to get their hands on him. I'd marry him in a minute."

She had never thought of this before; in fact, the phrase had been invented to express her feeling for Travis de Coppet. When, presently, tea was served, she excused herself and went to her room.

It was a new house, but the Perrys were far from being new

people. They were Chicago Society, and almost very rich, and not uncultured as things went thereabouts in 1914. But Josephine was an unconscious pioneer of the generation that was destined to "get out of hand."

In her room she dressed herself for going to Lillian's house, thinking meanwhile of Travis de Coppet and of riding home from the Davidsons' dance last night. Over his tuxedo, Travis had worn a loose blue cape inherited from an old fashioned uncle. He was tall and thin, an exquisite dancer, and his eyes had often been described by female contemporaries as "very dark"—to an adult it appeared that he had two black eyes in the collisional sense, and that probably they were justifiably renewed every night; the area surrounding them was so purple, or brown, or crimson, that they were the first thing you noticed about his face, and, save for his white teeth, the last. Like Josephine, he was also something new. There were a lot of new things in Chicago then, but lest the interest of this narrative be divided, it should be remarked that Josephine was the newest thing of all.

Dressed, she went down the stairs and through a softly opening side door, out into the street. It was October and a harsh breeze blew her along under trees without leaves, past houses with cold corners, past caves of the wind that were the mouths of residential streets. From that time until April, Chicago is an indoor city, where entering by a door is like going into another world, for the cold of the lake is unfriendly and not like real northern cold—it serves only to accentuate the things that go on inside. There is no music outdoors, or love-making, and even in prosperous times the wealth that rolls by in limousines is less glamorous than embittering to those on the sidewalk. But in the houses there is a deep, warm quiet, or else an excited, singing noise, as if those within were inventing things like new dances. That is part of what people mean when they say they love Chicago.

Josephine was going to meet her friend Lillian Hammel, but their plan did not include attending the movies. In comparison to it, their mothers would have preferred the most objectionable, the most lurid movie. It was no less than to go for a long auto ride with Travis de Coppet and Howard Page, in the course of which they would kiss not once but a lot. The four of them had been planning this since the previous Saturday, when unkind circumstances had combined to prevent its fulfillment.

Travis and Howard were already there—not sitting down, but still in their overcoats, like symbols of action, hurrying the girls breathlessly into the future. Travis wore a fur collar on his overcoat and carried a gold-headed cane; he kissed Josephine's hand facetiously yet seriously, and she said, "Hel*lo*, Travis!" with the warm affection of a politician greeting a prospective vote. But for a minute the two girls exchanged news aside.

"I saw him," Lillian whispered, "just now."

"Did you?"

Their eyes blazed and fused together.

"Isn't he di*vine*?" said Josephine.

They were referring to Mr. Anthony Harker, who was twenty-two, and unconscious of their existence, save that in the Perry house he occasionally recognized Josephine as Constance's younger sister.

"He has the most beautiful nose," cried Lillian, suddenly laughing. "It's—" She drew it on the air with her finger and they both became hilarious. But Josephine's face composed itself as Travis' black eyes, conspicuous as if they had been freshly made the previous night, peered in from the hall.

"Well!" he said tensely.

The four young people went out, passed through fifty bitter feet of wind and entered Page's car. They were all very confident and knew exactly what they wanted. Both girls were expressly disobeying their parents, but they had no more sense of guilt about it than a soldier escaping from an enemy prison camp. In the back seat, Josephine and Travis looked at each other; she waited as he burned darkly.

"Look," he said to his hand; it was trembling. "Up till five this morning. Girls from the Follies."

"Oh, Travis!" she cried automatically, but for the first time a communication such as this failed to thrill her. She took his hand, wondering what the matter was inside herself.

It was quite dark, and he bent over her suddenly, but as suddenly she turned her face away. Annoyed, he made cynical nods with his head and lay back in the corner of the car. He became engaged in cherishing his dark secret—the secret that always made her yearn toward him. She could see it come into his eyes and fill them, down to the cheek bones and up to the brows, but she could not concentrate on him. The romantic mystery of the world had moved into another man.

Travis waited ten minutes for her capitulation; then he tried again, and with this second approach she saw him plain for the first time. It was enough. Josephine's imagination and her desires were easily exploited up to a certain point, but after that her very impulsiveness protected her. Now, suddenly, she found something real against Travis, and her voice was modulated with lowly sorrow.

"I heard what you did last night. I heard very well."

"What's the matter?"

"You told Ed Bement you were in for a big time because you were going to take me home in your car."

"Who told you that?" he demanded, guilty but belittling.

"Ed Bement did, and he told me he almost hit you in the face when you said it. He could hardly keep restraining himself."

Once more Travis retired to his corner of the seat. He accepted this as the reason for her coolness, as in a measure it was. In view of Doctor Jung's theory that innumerable male voices argue in the subconscious of a woman, and even speak through her lips, then the absent Ed Bement was probably speaking through Josephine at that moment.

"I've decided not to kiss any more boys, because I won't have anything left to give the man I really love."

"Bull!" replied Travis.

"It's true. There's been too much talk around Chicago about me. A man certainly doesn't respect a girl he can kiss whenever he wants to, and I want to be respected by the man I'm going to marry some day."

Ed Bement would have been overwhelmed had he realized the extent of his dominance over her that afternoon.

Walking from the corner, where the youths discreetly left her, to her house, Josephine felt that agreeable lightness which comes with the end of a piece of work. She would be a good girl now forever, see less of boys, as her parents wished, try to be what Miss Benbower's school denominated An Ideal Benbower Girl. Then next year, at Breerly, she could be an Ideal Breerly Girl. But the first stars were out over Lake Shore Drive, and all about her she could feel Chicago swinging around its circle at a hundred miles an hour, and Josephine knew that she only wanted to want such wants for her soul's sake. Actually, she had no desire for achievement. Her grandfather had had that, her parents had had the consciousness of it, but Josephine accepted the proud world into which she was born. This was easy in Chicago, which, unlike New York, was a city state, where the old families formed a caste—intellect was represented by the university professors, and there were no ramifications, save that even the Perrys had to be nice to half a dozen families even richer and more important than themselves. Josephine loved to dance, but the field of feminine glory, the ballroom floor, was something you slipped away from with a man.

As Josephine came to the iron gate of her house, she saw her sister shivering on the top steps with a departing young man; then the front door closed and the man came down the walk. She knew who he was.

He was abstracted, but he recognized her for just a moment in passing.

"Oh, hello," he said.

She turned all the way round so that he could see her face by the street lamp; she lifted her face full out of her fur collar and toward him, and then smiled.

"Hello," she said modestly.

They passed. She drew in her head like a turtle.

"Well, now he knows what I look like, anyhow," she told herself excitedly as she went on into the house.

II

Several days later Constance Perry spoke to her mother in a serious tone:

"Josephine is so conceited that I really think she's a little crazy."

"She's very conceited," admitted Mrs. Perry. "Father and I

were talking and we decided that after the first of the year she should go East to school. But you don't say a word about it until we know more definitely."

"Heavens, mother, it's none too soon! She and that terrible Travis de Coppet running around with his cloak, as if they were about a thousand years old. They came into the Blackstone last week and my *spine* crawled. They looked just like two maniacs—Travis slinking along, and Josephine twisting her mouth around as if she had St. Vitus dance. *Honestly*——"

"What did you begin to say about Anthony Harker?" interrupted Mrs. Perry.

"That she's got a crush on him, and he's about old enough to be her grandfather."

"Not quite."

"Mother, he's twenty-two and she's sixteen. Every time Jo and Lillian go by him, they giggle and stare——"

"Come here, Josephine," said Mrs. Perry.

Josephine came into the room slowly and leaned her backbone against the edge of the opened door, teetering upon it calmly.

"What, mother?"

"Dear, you don't want to be laughed at, do you?"

Josephine turned sulkily to her sister. "Who laughs at me? You do, I guess. You're the only one that does."

"You're so conceited that you don't see it. When you and Travis de Coppet came into the Blackstone that afternoon, my *spine* crawled. Everybody at our table and most of the other tables laughed—the ones that weren't shocked."

"I guess they were more shocked," guessed Josephine complacently.

"You'll have a fine reputation by the time you come out."

"Oh, shut your mouth!" said Josephine.

There was a moment's silence. Then Mrs. Perry whispered solemnly, "I'll have to tell your father about this as soon as he comes home."

"Go on, tell him." Suddenly Josephine began to cry. "Oh, why can't anybody ever leave me alone? I wish I was dead."

Her mother stood with her arm around her, saying, "Josephine—now, Josephine"; but Josephine went on with deep, broken sobs that seemed to come from the bottom of her heart.

"Just a lot—of—of ugly and jealous girls who get mad when anybody looks at m-me, and make up all sorts of stories that are absolutely untrue, just because I can get anybody I want. I suppose that Constance is mad about it because I went in and sat for *five* minutes with Anthony Harker while he was waiting last night."

"Yes, I was *ter*ribly jealous! I sat up and cried all night about it. Especially because he comes to talk to me about Marice Whaley. Why!—you got him so crazy about you in that five minutes that he couldn't stop laughing all the way to the Warrens."

Josephine drew in her breath in one last gasp, and stopped crying. "If you want to know, I've decided to give him up."

"Ha-ha!" Constance exploded. "Listen to *that*, mother! She's going to give him up—as if he ever looked at her or knew she was al*ive!* Of all the conceited——"

But Mrs. Perry could stand no more. She put her arm around Josephine and hurried her to her room down the hall.

"All your sister meant was that she didn't like to see you laughed at," she explained.

"Well, I've given him up," said Josephine gloomily.

She had given him up, renouncing a thousand kisses she had never had, a hundred long, thrilling dances in his arms, a hundred evenings not to be recaptured. She did not mention the letter she had written him last night—and had not sent, and now would never send.

"You musn't think about such things at your age," said Mrs. Perry. "You're just a child."

Josephine got up and went to the mirror.

"I promised Lillian to come over to her house. I'm late now."

Back in her room, Mrs. Perry thought: "Two months to February." She was a pretty woman who wanted to be loved by everyone around her; there was no power of governing in her. She tied up her mind like a neat package and put it in the post office, with Josephine inside it safely addressed to the Breerly School.

An hour later, in the tea room at the Blackstone Hotel, Anthony Harker and another young man lingered at table. Anthony was a happy fellow, lazy, rich enough, pleased with his current popularity. After a brief career in an Eastern university, he had gone to a famous college in Virgina and in its less exigent shadow completed his education; at least, he had absorbed certain courtesies and mannerisms that Chicago girls found charming.

"There's that guy Travis de Coppet," his companion had just remarked. "What's he think he is, anyhow?"

Anthony looked remotely at the young people across the room, recognizing the little Perry girl and other young females whom he seemed to have encountered frequently in the street of late. Although obviously much at home, they seemed silly and loud; presently his eyes left them and searched the room for the party he was due to join for dancing, but he was still sitting there when the room—it had a twilight quality, in spite of the lights within and the full dark outside—woke up to confident and exciting music. A thickening parade drifted past him. The men in sack suits, as though they had just come from portentous affairs, and the women in hats that seemed about to take flight, gave a special impermanence to the scene. This implication that this gathering, a little more than uncalculated, a little less than clandestine, would shortly be broken into formal series, made him anxious to seize its last minutes, and he looked more and more intently into the crowd for the face of anyone he knew.

One face emerged suddenly around a man's upper arm not five feet away, and for a moment Anthony was the object of the saddest and most tragic regard that had ever been directed upon him. It was a smile and not a smile—two big gray eyes with bright triangles of color underneath, and a mouth twisted into a universal sympathy that seemed to include both him and herself—yet withal, the expression not of a victim, but rather of the very *de*mon of tender melancholy—and for the first time Anthony really saw Josephine.

His immediate instinct was to see with whom she was dancing. It was a young man he knew, and with this assurance he was on his feet giving a quick tug to his coat, and then out upon the floor.

"May I cut in, please?"

Josephine came close to him as they started, looked up into his eyes for an instant, and then down and away. She said nothing. Realizing that she could not possibly be more than sixteen, Anthony hoped that the party he was to join would not arrive in the middle of the dance.

When that was over, she raised eyes to him again; a sense of having been mistaken, of her being older than he had thought, possessed him. Just before he left her at her table, he was moved to say:

"Couldn't I have another later?"

"Oh, sure."

She united her eyes with his, every glint a spike—perhaps from the railroads on which their family fortunes were founded, and upon which they depended. Anthony was disconcerted as he went back to his table.

One hour later, they left the Blackstone together in her car.

This had simply happened—Josephine's statement, at the end of their second dance, that she must leave, then her request, and his own extreme self-consciousness as he walked beside her across the empty floor. It was a favor to her sister to take her home—but he had that unmistakable feeling of expectation.

Nevertheless, once outside and shocked into reconsideration by the bitter cold, he tried again to allocate his responsibilities in the matter. This was hard going with Josephine's insistent dark and ivory youth pressed up against him. As they got in the car he tried to dominate the situation with a masculine stare, but her eyes, shining as if with fever, melted down his bogus austerity in a whittled second.

Idly he patted her hand—then suddenly he was inside the radius of her perfume and kissing her breathlessly. . . .

"So that's that," she whispered after a moment. Startled, he wondered if he had forgotten something—something he had said to her before.

"What a cruel remark," he said, "just when I was getting interested."

"I only meant that any minute with you may be the last one," she said miserably. "The family are going to send me away to school—they think I haven't found that out yet."

"Too bad."

"—and today they got together—and tried to tell me that you didn't know I was al*ive*!"

After a long pause, Anthony contributed feebly. "I hope you didn't let them convince you."

She laughed shortly. "I just laughed and came down here."

Her hand burrowed its way into his; when he pressed it, her eyes, bright now, not dark, rose until they were as high as his, and came toward him. A minute later he thought to himself: "This is a rotten trick I'm doing."

He was sure he was doing it.

"You're so sweet," she said.

"You're a dear child."

"I hate jealousy worse than anything in the world," Josephine broke forth, "and *I* have to suffer from it. And my own sister worse than all the rest."

"Oh, no," he protested.

"I couldn't help it if I fell in love with you. I tried to help it. I used to go out of the house when I knew you were coming."

The force of her lies came from her sincerity and from her simple and superb confidence that whomsoever she loved must love her in return. Josephine was never either ashamed or plaintive. She was in the world of being alone with a male, a world through which she had moved surely since she was eight years old. She did not plan; she merely let herself go, and the overwhelming life in her did the rest. It is only when youth is gone and experience has given us a sort of cheap courage that most of us realize how simple such things are.

"But you couldn't be in love with me," Anthony wanted to say, and couldn't. He fought with a desire to kiss her again, even tenderly, and began to tell her that she was being unwise, but before he got really started at this handsome project, she was in his arms again, and whispering something that he had to accept, since it was wrapped up in a kiss. Then he was alone, driving away from her door.

What had he agreed to? All they had said rang and beat in his ear like an unexpected temperature—tomorrow at four o'clock on that corner.

"Good God!" he thought uneasily. "All that stuff about giving me up. She's a crazy kid, she'll get into trouble if somebody looking for trouble comes along. *Big* chance of my meeting her tomorrow!"

But neither at dinner nor the dance that he went to that night could Anthony get the episode out of his mind; he kept looking around the ballroom regretfully, as if he missed some-one who should be there.

III

Two weeks later, waiting for Marice Whaley in a meagre, indefinable down-stairs "sitting room," Anthony reached in his pocket for some half-forgotten mail. Three letters he replaced; the other—after a moment of listening—he opened quickly and read with his back to the door. It was the third of a series —for one had followed each of his meetings with Josephine— and it was exactly like the others—the letter of a child. What-ever maturity of emotion could accumulate in her expression, when once she set pen to paper was snowed under by inepti-tude. There was much about "your feeling for me" and "my feeling for you," and sentences began, "Yes, I know I am senti-mental," or more gawkily, "I have always been sort of pash, and I can't help that," and inevitably much quoting of lines from current popular songs, as if they expressed the writer's state of mind more fully than verbal struggles of her own.

The letter disturbed Anthony. As he reached the postscript, which coolly made a rendezvous for five o'clock this afternoon, he heard Marice coming down-stairs, and put it back in his pocket.

Marice hummed and moved about the room. Anthony smoked.

"I saw you Tuesday afternoon," she said suddenly. "You seemed to be having a fine time."

"Tuesday," he repeated, as if thinking. "Oh, yeah. I ran into some kids and we went to a tea dance. It was amusing."

"You were *al*most alone when I saw you."

"What are you getting at?"

Marice hummed again. "Let's go out. Let's go to a matinée."

On the way Anthony explained how he had happened to be

with Connie's little sister; the necessity of the explanation somehow angered him. When he had done, Marice said crisply:

"If you wanted to rob the cradle, why did you have to pick out that little devil? Her reputation's so bad already that Mrs. McRae didn't want to invite her to dancing class this year—she only did it on account of Constance."

"Why is she so awful?" asked Anthony, disturbed.

"I'd rather not discuss it."

His five-o'clock engagement was on his mind throughout the matinée. Though Marice's remarks served only to make him dangerously sorry for Josephine, he was nevertheless determined that this meeting should be the last. It was embarassing to have been remarked in her company, even though he had tried honestly to avoid it. The matter could very easily develop into a rather dangerous little mess, with no benefit either to Josephine or to himself. About Marice's indignation he did not care; she had been his for the asking all autumn, but Anthony did not want to get married; did not want to get involved with anybody at all.

It was dark when he was free at 5:30, and turned his car toward the new Philanthrophilogical Building in the maze of reconstruction in Grant Park. The bleakness of place and time depressed him, gave a further painfulness to the affair. Getting out of his car, he walked past a young man in a waiting roadster —a young man whom he seemed to recognize—and found Josephine in the half darkness of the little chamber that the storm doors formed.

With an indefinable sound of greeting, she walked determinedly into his arms, putting up her face.

"I can only stay for a sec" she protested, just as if he had begged her to come. "I'm supposed to go to a wedding with sister, but I had to see you."

When Anthony spoke, his voice froze into a white mist, obvious in the darkness. He said things he had said to her before but this time firmly and finally. It was easier, because he could scarcely see her face and because somewhere in the middle she irritated him by starting to cry.

"I knew you were supposed to be fickle," she whispered,

"but I didn't expect this. Anyhow I've got enough pride not to bother you any further." She hesitated. "But I wish we could meet just once more to try and arrive at a more different settlement."

"No."

"Some jealous girl has been talking to you about me."

"No." Then, in despair, he struck at her heart. "I'm *not* fickle. I've never loved you and I *never* told you I did."

Guessing at the forlorn expression that would come into her face, Anthony turned away and took a purposeless step; when he wheeled nervously about, the storm door had just shut—she was gone.

"Josephine!" he shouted in helpless pity, but there was no answer. He waited, heart in his boots, until presently he heard a car drive away.

At home, Josephine thanked Ed Bement, whom she had used, with a tartlet of hope, went in by a side door and up to her room. The window was open and, as she dressed hurriedly for the wedding she stood close to it so that she would catch cold and die.

Seeing her face in the bathroom mirror, she broke down and sat on the edge of the tub, making a small choking sound like a struggle with a cough, and cleaning her finger nails. Later she could cry all night in bed when every one else was asleep, but now it was still afternoon.

The two sisters and their mother stood side by side at the wedding of Mary Jackson and Jackson Dillon. It was a sad and sentimental wedding—an end to the fine, glamorous youth of a girl who was universally admired and loved. Perhaps to no onlooker were there its details symbolical of the end of a period, yet from the vantage point of a decade, certain things that happened are already powdered with yesterday's ridiculousness, and even tinted with the lavender of the day before. The bride raised her veil, smiling that grave sweet smile that made her "adored," but with tears pouring down her cheeks, and faced dozens of friends hands outheld as if embracing all of them for the last time. Then she turned to a husband as serious and immaculate as herself, and looked at him as if to say, "That's done. All this that I am is yours forever and ever."

In her pew, Constance, who had been at school with Mary Jackson, was frankly weeping, from a heart that was a ringing vault. But the face of Josephine beside her was a more intricate study watched intently. Once or twice, though her eyes lost none of their level straight intensity, an isolated tear escaped, and, as if startled by the feel of it, the face hardened slightly and the mouth remained in defiant immobility, like a child well warned against making a disturbance. Only once did she move; hearing a voice behind her say: "That's the little Perry girl. Isn't she lovely looking?" she turned presently and gazed at a stained-glass window lest her unknown admirers miss the sight of the side face.

Josephine's family went on to the reception, so she dined alone—or rather with her little brother and his nurse, which was the same thing.

She felt all empty. Tonight Anthony Harker, "so deeply lovable—so sweetly lovable—so deeply, sweetly lovable" was making love to someone new, kissing her ugly, jealous face; soon he would have disappeared forever, together with all the men of his generation, into a loveless matrimony, leaving only a world of Travis de Coppets and Ed Bements—people so easy as to scarcely be worth the effort of a smile.

Up in her room, she was excited again by the sight of herself in the bathroom mirror. Oh, what if she should die in her sleep tonight?

"Oh, what a shame," she whispered.

She opened the window, and holding her only souvenir of Anthony, a big initialed linen handkerchief, crept desolately into bed. While the sheets were still cold, there was a knock at the door.

"Special-delivery letter," said the maid.

Putting on the light, Josephine opened it, turned to the signature, then back again, her breast rising and falling quickly under her nightgown.

DARLING LITTLE JOSEPHINE: It's no use, I can't help it, I can't lie about it. I'm desperately, terribly in love with you. When you went away this afternoon, it all rushed over me, and I knew I couldn't give you up. I drove home, and I couldn't eat or sit still, but only walk up and down thinking of your darling face and your darling tears, there in that vestibule. And now I sit writing this letter—

It was four pages long. Somewhere it disposed of their disparate ages as unimportant, and the last words were:

I know how miserable you must be, and I would give ten years of my life to be there to kiss your sweet lips good night.

When she had read it through, Josephine sat motionless for some minutes; grief was suddenly gone, and for a moment she was so overwhelmed that she supposed joy had come in its stead. On her face was a twinkling frown.

"Gosh!" she said to herself. She read over the letter once more.

Her first instinct was to call up Lillian, but she thought better of it. The image of the bride at the wedding popped out at her —the reproachless bride, unsullied, beloved and holy with a sweet glow. An adolescence of uprightness, a host of friends, then the appearance of the perfect lover, the Ideal. With an effort, she recalled her drifting mind to the present occasion. Certainly Mary Jackson would never have kept such a letter. Getting out of bed, Josephine tore it into little pieces and, with some difficulty, caused by an unexpected amount of smoke, burned it on a glass-topped table. No well-brought up girl would have answered such a letter; the proper thing was to simply ignore it.

She wiped up the table top with the man's linen handkerchief she held in her hand, threw it absently into a laundry basket and crept into bed. She suddenly was very sleepy.

IV

For what ensued, no one, not even Constance, blamed Josephine. If a man of twenty-two should so debase himself as to pay frantic court to a girl of sixteen against the wishes of her parents and herself, there was only one answer—he was a person who shouldn't be received by decent people. When Travis de Coppet made a controversial remark on the affair at a dance, Ed Bement beat him into what was described as "a pulp," down in the washroom, and Josephine's reputation rose to normal and stayed there. Accounts of how Anthony had called time and time again at the house, each time denied admittance, how he had threatened Mr. Perry, how he had tried to bribe a maid to deliver letters, how he had attempted to waylay Josephine on her way back from school—these things pointed to the fact that he was a little mad. It was Anthony Harker's own family who insisted that he should go West.

All this was a trying time for Josephine. She saw how close she had come to disaster, and by constant consideration and implicit obedience, tried to make up to her parents for the trouble she had unwittingly caused. At first she decided she didn't want to go to any Christmas dances, but she was persuaded by her mother, who hoped she would be distracted by boys and girls home from school for the holidays. Mrs. Perry was taking her East to the Breerly School early in January, and in the buying of clothes and uniforms, mother and daughter were much together, and Mrs. Perry was delighted at Josephine's new feeling of responsibility and maturity.

As a matter of fact, it was sincere, and only once did Josephine do anything that she could not have told the world. The day after New Year's she put on her new travelling suit and her new fur coat and went out by her familiar egress, the side door, and walked down the block to the waiting car of Ed Bement. Downtown she left Ed waiting at a corner and entered a drug store opposite the old Union Station on LaSalle Street. A man with an unhappy mouth and desperate, baffled eyes was waiting for her there.

"Thank you for coming," he said miserably.

She didn't answer. Her face was grave and polite.

"Here's what I want—just one thing," he said quickly: "Why did you change? What did I do that made you change so suddenly? Was it something that happened, something I did? Was it what I said in the vestibule that night?"

Still looking at him, she tried to think, but she could only think how unattractive and rather terrible she found him now, and try not to let him see it. There would have been no use saying the simple truth—that she could not help what she had done, that great beauty has a need, almost an obligation, of trying itself, that her ample cup of emotion had spilled over on its own accord, and it was an accident that it had destroyed him and not her. The eyes of pity might follow Anthony Harker in his journey West, but most certainly the eyes of destiny followed Josephine as she crossed the street through the falling snow to Ed Bement's car.

She sat quiet for a minute as they drove away, relieved and yet full of awe. Anthony Harker was twenty-two, handsome, popular and sought after—and how he had loved her—so much that he had to go away. She was as impressed as if they had been two other people.

Taking her silence for depression, Ed Bement said:

"Well, it did one thing anyhow—it stopped that other story they had around about you."

She turned to him quickly. "What story?"

"Oh, just some crazy story."

"What was it?" she demanded.

"Oh, nothing much," he said hesitantly, "but there was a story around last August that you and Travis de Coppet were married."

"Why, how perfectly terrible!" she exclaimed. "Why, I never heard of such a lie. It—" She stopped herself short of saying the truth—that though she and Travis had adventurously driven twenty miles to New Ulm, they had been unable to find a minister willing to marry them. It all seemed ages behind her, childish, forgotten.

"Oh, how perfectly terrible!" she repeated. "That's the kind of story that gets started by jealous girls."

"I know," agreed Ed. "I'd just like to hear any boy try to repeat it to me. Nobody believed it anyhow."

It was the work of ugly and jealous girls. Ed Bement, aware of her body next to him, and of her face shining like fire through the half darkness, knew that nobody so beautiful could ever do anything really wrong.

A Nice Quiet Place

All that week she couldn't decide whether she was a lollipop or a roman candle—through her dreams, dreams that promised uninterrupted sleep through many vacation mornings, drove a series of long, incalculable murmuring in tune with the put-put-put of their cut-outs, "I love you—I love you," over and over. She wrote in the evening:

DEAR RIDGE: When I think of not being able to come to the freshman dance with you this June, I could lie down and *die,* but mother is sort of narrow-minded in some ways, and she feels that sixteen is too young to go to a prom; and Lil Hammel's mother feels the same way. When I think of you dancing around with *some other girl* and hear you handing her a line, like you do to everybody, I could lie down and *scream*. Oh, I *know*—because a girl here at school met you after I left Hot Springs at Easter. Anyhow, if you start rushing some other kid when you come out to Ed Bement's house party this summer, I intend to *cut her throat*, or my own, or something desperate. And probably no one will even be sorry I'm dead. Ha-ha—

Summer, summer, summer—bland inland sun and friendly rain. Lake Forest, with its thousand enchanted verandas, the dancing on the outdoor platform at the club, and always the boys, centaurs, in new cars. Her mother came East to meet her, and as they walked together out of the Grand Central Station, the symphony of promise became so loud that Josephine's face was puckered and distorted, as with the pressure of strong sunshine.

"We've got the best plans," her mother said.

"Oh, what? What, mother?"

"A real change. I'll tell you all about it when we get to the hotel."

There was a sudden discord; a shadow fell upon Josephine's heart.

"What do you mean? Aren't we going to Lake Forest?"

"Some place much better"—her mother's voice was alarmingly cheerful. "I'm saving it till we get to the hotel."

Before Mrs. Perry had left Chicago, she and Josephine's father had decided, from observations of their own and some revelations on the part of their elder daughter, Constance, that Josephine knew her way around Lake Forest all too well. The place had changed in the twenty years that it had been the summer rendezvous of fashionable Chicago; less circumscribed children of new families were resoundingly in evidence and, like most parents, Mrs. Perry thought of her daughter as one easily led into mischief by others. The more impartial eyes of other members of the colony had long regarded Josephine herself as the principal agent of corruption. But, preventive or penalty, the appalling thing to Josephine was that the Perrys were going to a "nice quiet place" this summer.

"Mother, I simply can't go to Island Farms. I simply—"

"Father feels—"

"Why don't you take me to a reform school if I'm so awful? Or to state's penitentiary? I simply can't go to a horrible old farm with a lot of country jakes and no fun and no friends except a lot of hicks."

"But, dear, it's not like that at all. They just call it Island Farms. In fact, your aunt's place isn't a farm; it's really a nice little resort up in Michigan where lots of people spend the summer. Tennis and swimming and—and fishing."

"Fishing?" repeated Josephine incredulously. "Do you call *that* something to do?" She shook her head in mute incomprehension. "I'll just be forgotten, that's all. When it's my year to come out nobody will know who I am. They'll just say, 'Who in heck is this Josephine Perry? I never saw her around here.' 'Oh, she's just some hick from a horrible old farm up in Michigan. Let's not invite her.' Just when everybody else is having a wonderful time—"

"Nobody'll forget you in one summer, dear."

"Yes, they will. Everybody'll have new friends and know new dances, and I'll be up there in the backwoods, full of hayseed, forgetting everything I know. If it's so wonderful why isn't Constance coming?"

Lying awake in their drawing-room on the Twentieth Century, Josephine brooded upon the terrible injustice of it all. She knew that her mother was going on her account, and mostly because of the gossip of a few ugly and jealous girls. These ugly and jealous girls, her relentless enemies, were not entirely creatures of Josephine's imagination. There was something in the frank sensuousness of her beauty that plain women found absolutely intolerable; they stared at her in a frightened, guarded way.

It was only recently that gossip had begun to worry Josephine. Her own theory was that, though at thirteen or fourteen she had been "speedy"—a convenient word that lacked the vulgar implication of "fast"—she was now trying to do her best, and a difficult enough business it was, without the past being held against her; for the only thing she cared about in the world was being in love and being with the person she currently loved.

Toward midnight her mother spoke to her softly and found that she was asleep. Turning on the berth light, she looked for a moment at the flushed young face, smoothed now of all its disappointment by a faint, peculiar smile. She leaned over and kissed Josephine's brow, behind which, doubtless, were passing in review those tender and eagerly awaited orgies of which she was to be deprived this summer.

II

Into Chicago, resonant with shrill June clamor; out to Lake Forest, where her friends moved already in an aura of new boys, new tunes, parties and house parties yet to be. One concession was granted her—she was to come back from Island Farms in time for Ed Bement's house party—which is to say, for Ridgeway Saunders' visit, the first of September.

Then northward, leaving all gayety behind, to the nice quiet place, implicit in its very station, which breathed no atmosphere of hectic arrivals or feverish partings: there was her aunt, her fifteen-year-old cousin, Dick, with the blank resentful stare of youth in spectacles, there were the dozen or so estates with tired people asleep inside them and the drab village three miles away. It was worse, even, than Josephine had imagined; to her the vicinity was literally unpopulated, for, as a representative of her generation, she stood alone. In despair, she buried herself in ceaseless correspondence with the outer world or, as a variant, played tennis with Dick and carried on a slow indifferent quarrel at his deliberately spiteful immaturity.

"Are you going to be this way always?" she demanded, breaking down at his stupidity one day. "Can't you do anythng about it? Does it hurt?"

"What way?" Dick shambled around the tennis net in the way that so offended her.

"Oh, such a pill! You ought to be sent away to some good school."

"I am going to be."

"Why, at your age, most of the boys in Chicago have cars of their own."

"Too many," he responded.

"How do you mean?" Josephine flared up.

"I heard my aunt say there was too much of that there. That's why they made you come up here. You're too much for that sort of thing."

Josephine flushed. "Couldn't you *help* being such a pill, if you honestly tried?"

"I don't know, " admitted Dick. "I don't even think that maybe I *am* one."

"Oh, yes, you are. I can assure you of that."

It occurred to her, not very hopefully, that under proper supervision something might be made of him. Perhaps she could teach him to dance or have him learn to drive his mother's car. She went to the extent of trying to smarten him up, to make him wash his hands bidiurnally and to soak his hair and cleave it down the middle. She suggested that he would be more beautiful without his spectacles, and he obediently bumped around without them for several afternoons. But when he developed a feverish headache one night and confessed to his mother why he had been "so utterly insane," Josephine gave him up without a pang.

But she could have cared for almost anyone. She wanted to hear the mystical terminology of love, to feel the lift and pull inside herself that each one of a dozen affairs had given her. She had written, of course, to Ridgeway Saunders. He answered. She wrote again. He answered—but after two weeks. On the first of August, with one month gone and one to go, came a letter from Lillian Hammel, her best friend in Lake Forest.

DEAREST Jo: You said to write you every single thing, and I will, but some of it will be sort of a fatal blow to you—about Ridgeway Saunders. Ed Bement visited him in Philadelphia, and he says he is so crazy about a girl there that he wants to leave Yale and get married. Her name is Evangeline Ticknor and she was fired from Foxcroft last year for smoking; quite a speed and said to be beautiful and something like you, from what I hear. Ed said that Ridgeway was so crazy about her that he wouldn't even come out here in September unless Ed invited her, too; so Ed did. Probably a lot you care!

You've probably had lots of crushes up there where you are, or aren't there any attractive boys—

Josephine walked slowly up and down her room. Her parents had what they wanted now; the plot against her was complete. For the first time in her life she had been thrown over, and by the most attractive, the most desirable boy she had ever known, cut out by a girl "very much like herself." Josephine wished passionately that she had been fired from school—then the family might have given up and let her alone.

She was not so much humiliated as full of angry despair, but for the sake of her pride, she had a letter to write immediately. Her eyes were bright with tears as she began:

DEAREST LIL: I was not surprised when I heard that about R.S. I knew he was fickle and never gave him a second *thought* after school closed in June. As a matter of fact, you know how fickle I am myself, darling, and you can imagine that I haven't had time to let it worry *me*. Everybody has a right to do what they want, say I. Live and let live is my motto. I wish you could have been here this summer. More *wonderful* parties—

She paused, knowing that she should invent more circumstantial evidence of gayety. Pen in air, she gazed out into the deep, still mass of northern trees. Inventing was delicate work, and having dealt always in realities, her imagination was ill-adapted to the task. Nevertheless, after several minutes a vague, synthetic figure began to take shape in her mind. She dipped the pen and wrote: "One of the darlingest—" hesitated and turned again for inspiration to the window.

Suddenly she started and bent forward, the tears drying in her eyes. Striding down the road, not fifty feet from her window, was the handsomest, the most fascinating boy she had ever seen in her life.

III

He was about nineteen and tall, with a blond viking head; the fresh color in his slender, almost gaunt cheeks was baked warm and dry by the sun. She had a glimpse of his eyes—enough to know that they were "sad" and of an extraordinary glistening blue. His model legs were in riding breeches, above which he wore a soft sweater jacket of blue chamois, and as he walked he swung a crop acrimoniously at the overhanging leaves.

For a moment the vision endured; then the path turned into a clump of trees and he was gone, save for the small crunch of his boots on the pine needles.

Josephine did not move. The dark green trees that had seemed so lacking in promise were suddenly like a magic wall that had opened and revealed a short cut to possible delight; the trees gave forth a great trembling rustle. For another instant she waited; then she threw herself at the unfinished letter:

—he usually wears the best-looking riding clothes. He has the *most* beautiful eyes. On top he usually wears a blue chamois thing that is simply *divine*.

IV

When her mother came in, half an hour later, she found Josephine getting into her best afternoon dress with an expression that was at once animated and far away.

"I thought—" she said. "I don't suppose you'd want to come with me and pay a few calls?"

"I'd adore to," said Josephine unexpectedly.

Her mother hesitated. "I'm afraid it's been a rather stupid month for you. I didn't realize that there wouldn't be anyone your age. But something nice has happened that I can't tell you about yet, and perhaps I'll soon have some news for you."

Josephine did not appear to hear.

"Who shall we call on?" she demanded eagerly. "Let's just call on everybody, even if it takes until ten o'clock tonight. Let's start at the nearest house and just keep going until we've killed everybody off."

"I don't know whether we can do that."

"Come on." Josephine was putting on her hat. "Let's get going, mother."

Perhaps, Mrs. Perry thought, the summer was really making a difference in her daughter; perhaps it was developing in her a more gently social vein. At each house they visited she positively radiated animation, and displayed sincere disappointment when they found no one home. When her mother called it a day, the light in her eyes went out.

"We can try again tomorrow," she said impatiently. "We'll kill the rest of them off. We'll go back to those houses where there was no one home."

It was almost seven—a nostalgic hour, for it had been the loveliest of all at Lake Forest a year ago. Bathed and positively shining, one had intruded then for a last minute into the departing day, and, sitting alone on the veranda, turned over the romantic prospects of the night, while lighted windows sprang out on the blurring shapes of houses, and cars flew past with people late home from tea.

But tonight the murmurous Indian twilight of the lake country had a promise of its own, and strolling out into the lane that passed the house, Josephine broke suddenly into a certain walk, rather an externallized state of mind, that had been hitherto reserved for more sophisticated localities. It implied, through a skimming lift of the feet, through an impatience of the moving hips, through an abstracted smile, lastly through a glance that fell twenty feet ahead, that this girl was about to cross some material threshold where she was eagerly awaited; that, in fact, she had already crossed it in her imagination and left her surroundings behind. It was just at that moment she heard a strong clear whistle in front of her and the sound as of a stick swishing through leaves:

> "Hel-lo,
> Fris-co,
> Hello!
>
> How do you do, my dear?
> I only wish that you were here."

Her heart beat a familiar tattoo; she realized that they would pass each other just where a last rift of sunset came down through the pines.

"Hello,
Fris-co,
Hel-lo!"

There he was, a fine shape against the foreground. His gallant face, drawn in a single dashing line, his chamois vest, so blue—she was near enough that she could have touched it. Then she realized with a shock that he had passed without noticing her proximity by a single flicker of his unhappy eyes.

"The conceited pill!" she thought indignantly. "Of all the conceited—"

She was silent during dinner; at the end she said to her aunt, with small preliminary:

"I passed the most conceited-looking young man today. I wonder who he could have been."

"Maybe it was the nephew of old Dorrance," offered Dick, "or the fellow staying at old Dorrance's. Somebody said it was his nephew or some sort of relation."

His mother said pointedly to Josephine: "We don't see the Dorrances. Mr. Charles Dorrance considered that my husband was unjust to him about our boundary some years ago. Old Mr. Dorrance was a very stubborn man indeed."

Josephine wondered if that was why he had failed to respond this afternoon. It was a silly reason.

But next day, at the same place, at the same hour, he literally jumped at her soft "Good evening"; he stared at her with unmistakable signs of dismay. Then his hand went up as if to remove a hat, found none, and he bowed instead and went on by.

But Josephine turned swiftly and walked at his side, smiling.

"You might be more sociable. You really shouldn't be so exclusive, since we're the only two people in this place. I do think it's silly to let older people influence young people."

He was walking so fast that she could scarcely keep up with him.

"Honestly, I'm a nice girl," she persisted, still smiling. "Quite a few people rush me at dances and I once had a blind man in love with me."

They were almost at her aunt's gate, still walking furiously.

"Here's where I live," she said.

"Then I'll say good-by."

"What *is* the matter?" she demanded. "How *can* you be so rude?"

His lips formed the words, "I'm sorry."

"I suppose you've got to hurry home so you can stare at yourself at the mirror."

She knew this was untrue. He wore his good looks in almost an apologetic way. But it reached him, for he came to a precipitate halt, immediately moving off a little.

"Excuse my rudeness," he exploded. "But I'm not used to girls."

She was too winded to answer. But as her shaken composure gradually returned, she became aware of an odd weariness in his face.

"At least you might talk to me for a minute, if I don't come any nearer."

After a moment's hesitation he hoisted himself tentatively onto a fence rail.

"If you're so frightened of females, isn't it time something was done about it?" she inquired.

"It's too late."

"Never," she said positively. "Why, you're missing half of life. Don't you want to marry and have children and make some woman a fine wife—I mean, a fine husband?"

In answer he only shivered.

"I used to be terribly timid myself," she lied kindly. "But I saw that I was missing half of life."

"It isn't a question of will power. It's just that I'm a little crazy on the subject. A minute ago I had an instinct to throw a stone at you. I know it's terrible, so if you'll excuse me—"

He jumped down off the fence, but she cried quickly: "Wait! Let's talk it all over."

He lingered reluctantly.

"Why, in Chicago," she said, "any man as good-looking as

you could have any girl he wanted. Everyone would simply pursue him."

The idea seemed to distress him still further; his face grew so sad that impulsively she moved nearer, but he swung one leg over the fence.

"All right. We'll talk about something else," she conceded. "Isn't this the most dismal place you ever saw? I was supposed to be a speed in Lake Forest, so the family sentenced me to this, and I've had the most *kill*ing month, just sitting and twirling my thumbs. Then yesterday I looked out the window and saw you."

"What do you mean you were a speed?" he inquired.

"Just sort of speedy—you know, sort of pash."

He got up—this time with an air of finality.

"You really must excuse me. I know I'm an idiot on this woman question, but there's nothing to do about it."

"Will you meet me here tomorrow?"

"Heavens, no!"

Josephine was suddenly angry; she had humbled herself enough for one afternoon. With a cold nod, she started homeward down the lane.

"Wait!"

Now that there was thirty feet between them, his timidity had left him. She was tempted to go back, resisted the impulse with difficulty.

"I'll be here tomorrow," she said coolly.

Walking slowly home, she saw, by instinct rather than logic, that there was something here she failed to understand. In general, a lack of self-confidence was enough to disqualify any boy from her approval; it was the unforgivable sin, the white flag, the refusal of battle. Yet now that this young man was out of sight, she saw him as he had appeared the previous afternoon—unself-conscious, probably arrogant, utterly debonair. Again she wondered if the unpleasantness between the families could be responsible for his attitude.

In spite of their unsatisfactory conversation, she was happy. In the soft glow of the sunset it seemed certain that it would all come right tomorrow. Already the oppressive sense of being wasted had deserted her. The boy who had passed her window yesterday afternoon was capable of anything—love, drama, or even that desperate recklessness that she loved best of all.

Her mother was waiting on the veranda.

"I wanted to see you alone," she said, "because I thought Aunt Gladys would be offended if you looked too delighted. We're going back to Lake Forest tomorrow."

"Mother!"

"Constance is announcing her engagement tomorrow and getting married in ten days. Malcolm Libby is in the State Department and he's ordered abroad. Isn't it wonderful? Your sister's opening up the Lake Forest house today."

"It'll be marvellous." After a moment Josephine repeated, with more conviction: "Perfectly marvellous."

Lake Forest—she could feel the fast-beating excitement of it already. Yet there was something missing, as if the note of an essential trumpet had become separated from the band. For five weeks she had passionately hated Island Farms, but glancing around her in the gathering dusk, she felt rather sorry for it, a little ashamed of her desertion.

Throughout dinner the odd feeling persisted. She would be deep in exciting thoughts that began, "Won't it be fun to—" then the imminent brilliance would fade and there would be a stillness inside her like the stillness of these Michigan nights. That was what was lacking in Lake Forest—a stillness for things to happen in, for people to walk into.

"We'll be terribly busy," her mother said. "Next week there'll be bridesmaids in the house, and parties, and the wedding itself. We should have left tonight."

Josephine went up to her room immediately and sat looking out into the darkness. Too bad; a wasted summer after all. If yesterday had happened sooner she might have gone away with some sense of having lived after all. Too late. "But there'll be lots of boys," she told herself—"Ridgeway Saunders."

She could hear their confident lines, and somehow they rang silly on her ears. Suddenly she realized that what she was regretting was not the lost past but the lost future, not what had not been but what would never be. She stood up, breathing quickly.

A few minutes later she left the house by a side door and crossed the lawn to the gardener's gate. She heard Dick call after her uncertainly, but she did not answer. It was dark and cool, and the feeling that the summer was rushing away from her. As if to overtake it, she walked faster, and in ten minutes turned in at the gate of the Dorrance house, set behind the jagged silhouettes of many trees. Someone on the veranda hailed her as she came near:

"Good evening. I can't see who it is."

"It's the girl who was so fresh this afternoon."

She heard him catch his breath suddenly.

"May I sit here on the steps for a moment? See? Quite safe and far away. I came to say good-by, because we're going home tomorrow."

"Are you really?" She could not tell whether his tone showed concern or relief. "It'll be very quiet."

"I want to explain about this afternoon, because I don't want you to think I was just being fresh. Usually I like boys with more experience, but I just thought that since we were the only ones here, we might manage to have a good time, and there weren't any days to waste."

"I see." After a moment he asked, "What will you do in Lake Forest? Be a—a speed?"

"I don't much care what I do. I've wasted the whole six weeks."

She heard him laugh.

"I gather from your tone that someone is going to have to pay for it," he said.

"I hope so," she answered rather grimly. She felt tears rise in her eyes. Everything was wrong. Everything seemed to be fixed against her.

"Please let me come up there on the settee," she asked suddenly.

There was a creak as it stopped swinging.

"Please don't. I hate to ask you, but really I'll have to go if you do. Let's talk about— Do you like horses?"

She got up swiftly, mounted the steps and walked toward the corner where he sat.

"No," she said, "I think that what I'd like would be to be liked by you."

In the light of the moon just lifting over the woods his face was positively haggard. He jumped to his feet; then his hands were on her arms and he was drawing her slowly toward him.

"You simply want to be kissed," he was saying through scarcely opened lips. "I knew it the first time I saw that mouth of yours—that perfectly selfish, self-sufficient look that—"

Suddenly he dropped his arms and stepped away from her with a gesture of horror.

"Don't stop!" she cried. "Do anything, tell me anything, even if it isn't complimentary. I don't care."

But he had vaulted swiftly over the railing and, with his hands clasping the back of his head, was walking across the lawn. In a minute she overtook him and stood beseechingly in his path, her small bosom rising and falling.

"Why do you suppose I'm here?" he demanded suddenly. "Do you think I'm alone?"

"What—"

"My wife is with me."

Josephine shivered.

"Oh—oh—then why doesn't anybody know?"

"Because my wife is—my wife is colored."

If it had not been so dark Josephine would have seen that for an instant he was laughing silently and uncontrollably.

"Oh," she repeated.

"I didn't know," he continued.

In spite of a subconscious scepticism, an uncanny feeling stole over Josephine.

"What dealings could I have with a girl like you?"

She began to weep softly.

"Oh, I'm sorry. If I could only help you."

"You can't help me." He turned gruffly away.

"You want me to go."

He nodded.

"All right. I'll go."

Still sobbing, she half walked, half backed away from him, intimidated now, yet still hoping he would call to her. When she saw him for the last time from the gate, he was standing where she had left him, his fine thin face clear and handsome in the suddenly streaming light of an emergent moon.

She had gone a quarter of a mile down the road when she became conscious of running footsteps behind her. Before she could do more than start and turn anxiously, a figure sprang out at her. It was her cousin, Dick.

"Oh!" she cried. "You frightened me!"

"I followed you here. You had no business going out at night like this."

"What a sneaky thing!" she said contemptuously.

They walked along side by side.

"I heard you with that fellow. You had a crush on him, didn't you?"

"Will you be quiet! What does a horrible little pill like you know about anything?"

"I know a lot," said Dick glumly. "I know there's too much of that sort of thing at Lake Forest."

She scorned to answer; they reached her aunt's gate in silence.

"I tell you one thing," he said uncertainly. "I'll bet you wouldn't want your mother to know about this."

"You mean you're going to my mother?"

"Just hold your horses. I was going to say I wouldn't say anything about it—"

"I should hope not."

"—on one condition."

"Well?"

"The condition is—" He fidgeted uncomfortably. "You told me once that a lot of girls at Lake Forest had kissed boys and never thought anything about it."

"Yes." Suddenly she guessed what was coming, and an astonished laugh rose to her lips.

"Well, will you, then—kiss me?"

A vision of her mother arose—of a return to Lake Forest in chains. Deciding quickly, she bent toward him. Less than a minute later she was in her room, almost hysterical with tears and laughter. That, then, was the kiss with which destiny had seen fit to crown the summer.

v

Josephine's sensational return to Lake Forest that August marked a revision of opinion about her; it can be compared to the moment when the robber bandit evolved through sheer power into the feudal seignior.

To the three months of nervous energy conserved since Easter beneath the uniform of her school were added six weeks of resentment—added, that is, as the match might be said to be added to the powder. For Josephine exploded with an audible, visible bang; for weeks thereafter pieces of her were gathered up from Lake Forest's immaculate lawns.

It began quietly; it began with the long-awaited house party, on the first evening of which she was placed next to the unfaithful Ridgeway Saunders at dinner.

"I certainly felt pretty badly when you threw me over," Josephine said indifferently—to rid him of any lingering idea that he had thrown her over. Once she had chilled him into wondering if, after all, he had come off best in the affair, she turned to the man on the other side. By the time the salad was served, Ridgeway was explaining himself to her. And his girl from the East, Miss Ticknor, was becoming increasingly aware of what an obnoxious person Josephine Perry was. She made the mistake of saying so to Ridgeway. Josephine made no such mistake; toward the end of dinner she merely asked him the innocent question as to who was his friend with the high button shoes.

By ten o'clock Josephine and Ridgeway were out in somebody's car—far out where the colony becomes a prairie. As minute by minute she grew wearier of his softness, his anguish increased. She let him kiss her, just to be sure; and it was a desperate young man who returned to his host's that night.

All next day his eyes followed her about miserably; Miss Ticknor was unexpectedly called East the following afternoon. This was pathetic, but certainly someone had to pay for Josephine's summer. That score settled, she returned her attention to her sister's wedding.

Immediately on her return she had demanded a trousseau in keeping with the splendor of a maid of honor, and under cover of the family rush had so managed to equip herself as to add a charming year to her age. Doubtless this contributed to the change of attitude toward her, for though her emotional maturity, cropping out of a schoolgirl dress, had seemed not quite proper, in more sophisticated clothes she was an incontestable little beauty; and as such she was accepted by at least the male half of the wedding party.

Constance was openly hostile. On the morning of the wedding itself, she unburdened herself to her mother.

"I do hope you'll take her in hand after I'm gone, mother. It's really unendurable the way she's behaving. None of the bridesmaids have had a good time."

"Let's not worry," Mrs Perry urged. "After all, she's had a very quiet summer."

"I'm not worrying about *her*," said Constance indignantly.

The wedding party were lunching at the club, and Josephine found herself next to a jovial usher who had arrived inebriated and remained in that condition ever since. However, it was early enough in the day for him to be coherent.

"The belle of Chicago, the golden girl of the golden West. Oh, why didn't I come out here this summer?"

"I wasn't here. I was up in a place called Island Farms."

"Ah!" he exclaimed. "Ah-ha! That accounts for a lot of things —that accounts for the sudden pilgrimage of Sonny Dorrance."

"Of who?"

"The famous Sonny Dorrance, the shame of Harvard, but the maiden's prayer. Now don't tell me you didn't exchange a few warm glances with Sonny Dorrance."

"But isn't he," she demanded faintly—"isn't he supposed to be—married?"

He roared with laughter.

"Married—sure, married to a mulatto! You didn't fall for *that* old line. He always pulls it when he's reacting from some violent affair—that's to protect himself while he recovers. You see, his whole life has been cursed by that fatal beauty."

In a few minutes she had the story. Apart from everything else, Sonny Dorrance was fabulously rich—women had pursued him since he was fifteen—married women, débutantes, chorus girls. It was legendary.

There actually had been plots to entangle him into marriage, to entangle him into anything. There was the girl who tried to kill herself, there was the one who tried to kill him. Then, this spring, there was the annulled marriage business that had cost him an election to Porcellian at Harvard, and was rumored to have cost his father fifty thousand dollars.

"And now," Josephine asked tensely, "you say he doesn't like women?"

"Sonny? I tell you he's the most susceptible man in America. This last thing shook him, and so he keeps off admirers by telling them anything. But by this time next month he'll be involved again."

As he talked, the dining room faded out like a scene in a moving picture, and Josephine was back at Island Farms, staring out the window, as a young man appeared between the pine trees.

"He was afraid of me," she thought to herself, her heart tapping like a machine gun. "He thought I was like the others."

Half an hour later she interrupted her mother in the midst of the wedding's last and most violent confusion.

"Mother, I want to go back to Island Farms for the rest of the summer," she said at once.

Mrs. Perry looked at her in a daze, and Josephine repeated her statement.

"Why, in less than a month you'll be starting back to school."

"I want to go anyhow."

"I simply can't understand you. In the first place, you haven't been invited, and in the second place, I think a little gayety is good for you before you go back to school, and in the third place, I want you here with me."

"Mother," Josephine wailed, "don't you understand? I want to go! You take me up there all summer when I don't want to go, and just when I *do* want to, you make me stay in this ghastly place. Let me tell you this isn't any place for a sixteen-year-old girl, if you knew everything."

"What nonsense to be bothering me with just at this time!"

Josephine threw up her hands in despair; the tears were streaming down her cheeks.

"It's ruining me here!" she cried. "Nobody thinks of anything but boys and dances from morning till night. They go out in their cars and kiss them from morning till night."

"Well, I know my little girl doesn't do anything like that."

Josephine hesitated, taken a little aback.

"Well, I will," she announced. "I'm weak. You told me I was. I always do what anybody tells me to do, and all these boys are just simply immoral, that's all. The first thing you know I'll be entirely ruined, and then you'll be sorry you didn't let me go to Island Farms. You'll be sorry—"

She was working herself into hysteria. Her distracted mother took her by the shoulders and forced her down into a chair.

"I've never heard such silly talk. If you weren't so old I'd spank you. If you keep this up you'll be punished."

Suddenly dry-eyed, Josephine got up and stalked out of the room. Punished! They had been punishing her all summer, and now they refused to punish her, refused to send her away. Oh, she was tired of trying. If she could think of something really awful to do, so that they would send her away forever—

Mr. Malcolm Libby, the prospective bridegroom, happened upon her fifteen minutes later, in an obscure corner of the garden. He was pacing restlessly about, steadying himself for the rehearsal at four o'clock and for the ceremony two hours later.

"Why, hello!" he cried. "Why, what's the matter? You've been crying."

He sat down on the bench, full of sympathy for Constance's little sister.

"I'm not crying," she sobbed. "I'm just angry."

"About Constance going away? Don't you think I'll take good care of her?"

Leaning over, he patted her hand. If he had seen the look that flashed suddenly across her face it would have alarmed him, for it was curiously like the expression associated with a prominent character in Faust.

When she spoke, her voice was calm, almost cool, and yet tenderly sad:

"No that wasn't it. It was something else."

"Tell me about it. Maybe I can help."

"I was crying"—she hesitated delicately—"I was crying because Constance has all the luck."

Half an hour later when, with the rehearsal twenty minutes late, the frantic bride-to-be came searching through the garden and happened upon them suddenly, Malcolm Libby's arm was around Josephine, who seemed dissolved in uncontrollable grief, and on his face was a wildly harassed expression she had never seen there before. Constance gave a little gasping cry and sank down upon the pebbled path.

The next hour passed in an uproar. There was a doctor; there were shut doors; there was Mr. Malcolm Libby in an agonized condition, the sweat pouring off his brow, explaining to Mrs. Perry over and over that he could explain if he could only see Constance. There was Josephine, tight-lipped, in a room, being talked to coldly by various members of the family. There was the clamor of arriving guests; then frantic last minutes' patching up of things, with Constance and Malcolm in each other's arms and Josephine, unforgiven, being bundled into her dress.

Then a solemn silence fell and, moving to music, the maid of honor, her head demurely bowed, followed her sister up the two aisles of people that crowded the drawing-room. It was a lovely, sad wedding; the two sisters, light and dark, were a lovely contrast; there was as much interest in one as in the other. Josephine had become a great beauty and the prophets were busy; she stood for the radiant future, there at her sister's side.

The crush was so great at the reception that not until it was over was Josephine missed. And long before nine o'clock, before Mrs. Perry had time to be uneasy, a note from the station had been handed in at the door:

MY DEAREST MOTHER: Ed Bement brought me here in his car, and I am catching the train to Island Farms at seven. I have wired the housekeeper to meet me, so don't worry. I feel I have behaved *terribly* and am ashamed to *face* anyone, and I am punishing myself as I deserve by going back to the *simple* life. It is, after all, better for a girl of sixteen, I feel, and when you think it over you will agree. With dearest love.

JOSEPHINE.

After all, thought Mrs. Perry, perhaps it was just as well. Her husband was really angry, and she herself was exhausted and didn't feel up to another problem at the moment. Perhaps a nice quiet place was best.

A Woman with a Past

Driving slowly through New Haven, two of the young girls became alert. Josephine and Lillian darted soft frank glances into strolling groups of three or four undergraduates, into larger groups on corners, which swung about as one man to stare at their receding heads. Believing that they recognized an acquaintance in a solitary loiterer, they waved wildly, whereupon the youth's mouth fell open, and as they turned the next corner he made a dazed dilatory gesture with his hand. They laughed, "We'll send him a post card when we get back to school tonight, to see if it really was him."

Adele Craw, sitting on one of the little seats, kept on talking to Miss Chambers, the chaperone. Glancing sideways at her,

Lillian winked at Josephine without batting an eye, but Josephine had gone into a reverie.

This was New Haven—city of her adolescent dreams, of glittering proms where she would move on air among men as intangible as the tunes they danced to. City sacred as Mecca, shining as Paris, hidden as Timbuctoo. Twice a year the life-blood of Chicago, her home, flowed into it, and twice a year flowed back, bringing Christmas or bringing summer. Bingo, bingo, bingo, that's the lingo; love of mine, I pine for one of your glances; the darling boy on the left there; underneath the stars I wait.

Seeing it for the first time, she found herself surprisingly unmoved—the men they passed seemed young and rather bored with the possibilities of the day, glad of anything to stare at; seemed undynamic and purposeless against the background of bare elms, lakes of dirty snow and buildings crowded together under the February sky. A wisp of hope, a well-turned-out derby-crowned man, hurrying with stick and suitcase toward the station, caught her attention, but his reciprocal glance was too startled, too ingenuous. Josephine wondered at the extent of her own disillusionment.

She was exactly seventeen and she was blasé. Already she had been a sensation and a scandal; she had driven mature men to a state of disequilibrium; she had, it was said, killed her grandfather, but as he was over eighty at the time perhaps he just died. Here and there in the Middle West were discouraged little spots which upon inspection turned out to be the youths who had once looked full into her green and wistful eyes. But her love affair of last summer had ruined her faith in the all-sufficiency of men. She had grown bored with the waning September days—and it seemed as though it had happened once too often. Christmas with its provocative shortness, its travelling glee clubs, had brought no one new. There remained to her only a persistent, a physical hope; hope in her stomach that there was someone whom she would love more than he loved her.

They stopped at a sporting-goods store and Adele Craw, a pretty girl with clear honorable eyes and piano legs, purchased the sporting equipment which was the reason for their trip—

they were the spring hockey committee for the school. Adele was in addition the president of the senior class and the school's ideal girl. She had lately seen a change for the better in Josephine Perry—rather as an honest citizen might guilelessly approve a peculator retired on his profits. On the other hand, Adele was simply incomprehensible to Josephine—admirable, without doubt, but a member of another species. Yet with the charming adaptability that she had hitherto reserved for men, Josephine was trying hard not to disillusion her, trying to be honestly interested in the small, neat, organized politics of the school.

Two men who had stood with their backs to them at another counter turned to leave the store, when they caught sight of Miss Chambers and Adele. Immediately they came forward. The one who spoke to Miss Chambers was thin and rigid of face. Josephine recognized him as Miss Brereton's nephew, a student at New Haven, who had spent several week ends with his aunt at the school. The other man Josephine had never seen before. He was tall and broad, with blond curly hair and an open expression in which strength of purpose and a nice consideration were pleasantly mingled. It was not the sort of face that generally appealed to Josephine. The eyes were obviously without a secret, without a sidewise gambol, without a desperate flicker to show that they had a life of their own apart from the mouth's speech. The mouth itself was large and masculine; its smile was an act of kindness and control. It was rather with curiosity as to the sort of man who would be attentive to Adele Craw that Josephine continued to look at him, for his voice that obviously couldn't lie greeted Adele as if this meeting was the pleasant surprise of his day.

In a moment Josephine and Lillian were called over and introduced.

"This is Mr. Waterbury"—that was Miss Brereton's nephew —"and Mr. Dudley Knowleton."

Glancing at Adele, Josephine saw on her face an expression of tranquil pride, even of possession. Mr. Knowleton spoke politely, but it was obvious that though he looked at the younger girls he did not quite see them. But since they were friends of Adele's he made suitable remarks, eliciting the fact that they were both coming down to New Haven to their first prom the following week. Who were their hosts? Sophomores; he knew them slightly. Josephine thought that was unnecessarily superior. Why, they were the charter members of the Loving Brothers' Association—Ridgeway Saunders and George Davey—and on the glee-club trip the girls they picked out to rush in each city considered themselves a sort of élite, second only to the girls they asked to New Haven.

"And oh, I've got some bad news for you," Knowleton said to Adele. "You may be leading the prom. Jack Coe went to the infirmary with appendicitis, and against my better judgment I'm the provisional chairman." He looked apologetic. "Being one of these stone-age dancers, the two-step king, I don't see how I ever got on the committee at all."

When the car was on its way back to Miss Brereton's school, Josephine and Lillian bombarded Adele with questions.

"He's an old friend from Cincinnati," she explained demurely. "He's captain of the baseball team and he was last man for Skull and Bones."

"You're going to the prom with him?"

"Yes. You see, I've known him all my life."

Was there a faint implication in this remark that only those who had known Adele all her life knew her at her true worth?

"Are you engaged?" Lillian demanded.

Adele laughed. "Mercy, I don't think of such matters. It doesn't seem to be time for that sort of thing yet, does it?" ["Yes," interpolated Josephine silently.] "We're just good friends. I think there can be a perfectly healthy friendship between a man and a girl without a lot of——"

"Mush," supplied Lillian helpfully.

"Well, yes, but I don't like that word. I was going to say without a lot of sentimental romantic things that ought to come later."

"Bravo, Adele!" said Miss Chambers somewhat perfunctorily.

But Josephine's curiosity was unappeased.

"Doesn't he say he's in love with you, and all that sort of thing?"

"Mercy, no! Dud doesn't believe in such stuff any more than

I do. He's got enough to do at New Haven serving on the committees and the team."

"Oh!" said Josephine.

She was oddly interested. That two people who were attracted to each other should never even say anything about it but be content to "not believe in such stuff," was something new in her experience. She had known girls who had no beaus, others who seemed to have no emotions, and still others who lied about what they thought and did; but here was a girl who spoke of the attentions of the last man tapped for Skull and Bones as if they were two of the limestone gargoyles that Miss Chambers had pointed out on the just completed Harkness Hall. Yet Adele seemed happy—happier than Josephine, who had always believed that boys and girls were made for nothing but each other, and as soon as possible.

In the light of his popularity and achievements, Knowleton seemed more attractive. Josephine wondered if he would remember her and dance with her at the prom, or if that depended on how well he knew her escort, Ridgeway Saunders. She tried to remember whether she had smiled at him when he was looking at her. If she had really smiled he would remember her and dance with her. She was still trying to be sure of that over her two French irregular verbs and her ten stanzas of the Ancient Mariner that night; but she was still uncertain when she fell asleep.

II

Three gay young sophomores, the founders of the Loving Brothers' Association, took a house together for Josephine, Lillian and a girl from Farmington and their three mothers. For the girls it was a first prom, and they arrived at New Haven with all the nervousness of the condemned; but a Sheffield fraternity tea in the afternoon yielded up such a plethora of boys from home, and boys who had visited there, and friends of those boys, and new boys with unknown possibilities but obvious eagerness, that they were glowing with self-confidence as they poured into the glittering crowd that thronged the armory at ten.

It was impressive; for the first time Josephine was at a function run by men upon men's standards—an outward projection of the New Haven world from which women were excluded and which went on mysteriously behind the scenes. She perceived that their three escorts, who had once seemed the very embodiments of worldliness, were modest fry in this relentless microcosm of accomplishment and success. A man's world! Looking around her at the glee-club concert, Josephine had felt a grudging admiration for the good fellowship, the good feeling. She envied Adele Craw, barely glimpsed in the dressing-room, for the position she automatically occupied by being Dudley Knowleton's girl tonight. She envied her more stepping off under the draped bunting through a gateway of hydrangeas at the head of the grand march, very demure and faintly unpowdered in a plain white dress. She was temporarily the centre of all attention, and at the sight something that had long lain dormant in Josephine awakened—her sense of a problem, a scarcely defined possibility.

"Josephine," Ridgeway Saunders began, "you can't realize how happy I am now that it's come true. I've looked forward to this so long, and dreamed about it——"

She smiled up at him automatically, but her mind was elsewhere, and as the dance progressed the idea continued to obsess her. She was rushed from the beginning; to the men from the tea were added a dozen new faces, a dozen confident or timid voices, until, like all the more popular girls, she had her own queue trailing her about the room. Yet all this had happened to her before, and there was something missing. One might have ten men to Adele's two, but Josephine was abruptly aware that here a girl took on the importance of the man who had brought her.

She was discomforted by the unfairness of it. A girl earned her popularity by being beautiful and charming. The more beautiful and charming she was, the more she could afford to disregard public opinion. It seemed absurd that simply because Adele had managed to attach a baseball captain, who mightn't know anything about girls at all, or be able to judge their attractions, she should be thus elevated in spite of her thick ankles, her rather too pinkish face.

Josephine was dancing with Ed Bement from Chicago. He was her earliest beau, a flame of pigtail days in dancing school when one wore white cotton stockings, lace drawers with a waist attached and ruffled dresses with the inevitable sash.

"What's the matter with me?" she asked Ed, thinking aloud. "For months I've felt as if I were a hundred years old, and I'm just seventeen and that party was only seven years ago."

"You've been in love a lot since then," Ed said.

"I haven't," she protested indignantly. "I've had a lot of silly stories started about me, without any foundation, usually by girls who were jealous."

"Jealous of what?"

"Don't get fresh," she said tartly. "Dance me near Lillian."

Dudley Knowleton had just cut in on Lillian. Josephine spoke to her friend; then waiting until their turns would bring them face to face over a space of seconds, she smiled at Knowleton. This time she made sure that smile intersected as well as met glance, that he passed beside the circumference of her fragrant charm. If this had been named like French perfume of a later day it might have been called "Please." He bowed and smiled back; a minute later he cut in on her.

It was in an eddy in a corner of the room and she danced slower so that he adapted himself, and for a moment they went around in a slow circle.

"You looked so sweet leading the march with Adele," she told him. "You seemed so serious and kind, as if the others were all a lot of children. Adele looked sweet too." And she added on an inspiration, "At school I've taken her for a model."

"You have!" She saw him conceal his sharp surprise as he said, "I'll have to tell her that."

He was handsomer than she had thought, and behind his cordial good manners there was a sort of authority. Correctly attentive to her, she saw his eyes search the room quickly to see if all went well; he spoke quietly, in passing, to the orchestra leader, who came down deferentially to the edge of his dais. Last man for Bones. Josephine knew what that meant—her father had been Bones. Ridgeway Saunders and the rest of the Loving Brothers' Association would certainly not be Bones. She wondered, if there had been a Bones for girls, whether she would be tapped—or Adele Craw with her ankles, symbol of solidity.

> Come on o-ver here,
> Want to have you near;
> Come on join the part-y,
> Get a wel-come heart-y.

"I wonder how many boys here have taken you for a model," she said. "If I were a boy you'd be exactly what I'd like to be. Except I'd be terribly bothered having girls falling in love with me all the time."

"They don't," he said simply. "They never have."

"Oh, yes—but they hide it because they're so impressed with you, and they're afraid of Adele."

"Adele wouldn't object." And he added hastily, "—if it ever happened. Adele doesn't believe in being serious about such things."

"Are you engaged to her?"

He stiffened a little. "I don't believe in being engaged till the right time comes."

"Neither do I," agreed Josephine readily. "I'd rather have one good friend than a hundred people hanging around being mushy all the time."

"Is that what that crowd does that keep following you around tonight?"

"What crowd?" she asked innocently.

"The 50 per cent of the sophomore class that's rushing you."

"A lot of parlor snakes," she said ungratefully.

Josephine was radiantly happy now as she turned beautifully through the newly enchanted hall in the arms of the chairman of the prom committee. Even this extra time with him she owed to the awe which he inspired in her entourage; but a man cut in eventually and there was a sharp fall in her elation. The man was impressed that Dudley Knowleton had danced with her; he was more respectful, and his modulated admiration bored her. In a little while, she hoped, Dudley Knowleton would cut back, but as midnight passed, dragging on another hour with it, she wondered if after all it had only been a courtesy to a girl from Adele's school. Since then Adele had probably painted him a neat little landscape of Josephine's past. When finally he approached her she grew tense and watchful, a state which made her exteriorly pliant and tender and quiet. But instead of dancing he drew her into the edge of a row of boxes.

"Adele had an accident on the cloakroom steps. She turned her ankle a little and tore her stocking on a nail. She'd like to borrow a pair from you because you're staying near here and we're way out at the Lawn Club."

"Of course."

"I'll run over with you—I have a car outside."

"But you're busy, you mustn't bother."

"Of course I'll go with you."

There was thaw in the air; a hint of thin and lucid spring hovered delicately around the elms and cornices of buildings whose bareness and coldness had so depressed her the week before. The night had a quality of asceticism, as if the essence of masculine struggle were seeping everywere through the little city where men of three centuries had brought their energies and aspirations for winnowing. And Dudley Knowleton sitting beside her, dynamic and capable, was symbolic of it all. It seemed that she had never met a man before.

"Come in, please," she said as he went up the steps of the house with her. "They've made it very comfortable."

There was an open fire burning in the dark parlor. When she came downstairs with the stockings she went in and stood beside him, very still for a moment, watching it with him. Then she looked up, still silent, looked down, looked at him again.

"Did you get the stockings?" he asked, moving a little.

"Yes," she said breathlessly. "Kiss me for being so quick."

He laughed as if she had said something witty and moved toward the door. She was smiling and her disappointment was deeply hidden as they got into the car.

"It's been wonderful meeting you," she told him. "I can't tell you how many ideas I've gotten from what you said."

"But I haven't any ideas."

"You have. All that about not getting engaged till the proper time comes. I haven't had much opportunity to talk to a man like you. Otherwise my ideas would be different, I guess. I've just realized that I've been wrong about a lot of things. I used to want to be exciting. Now I want to help people."

"Yes," he agreed, "that's very nice."

He seemed about to say more when they arrived at the armory. In their absence supper had begun; and crossing the great floor by his side, conscious of many eyes regarding them, Josephine wondered if people thought that they had been up to something.

"We're late," said Knowleton when Adele went off to put on the stockings. "The man you're with has probably given you up long ago. You'd better let me get you something here."

"That would be too divine."

Afterward, back on the floor again, she moved in a sweet aura of abstraction. The followers of several departed belles merged with hers until now no girl on the floor was cut in on with such frequency. Even Miss Brereton's nephew, Ernest Waterbury, danced with her in stiff approval. Danced? With a tentative change of pace she simply swung from man to man in a sort of hands-right-and-left around the floor. She felt a sudden need to relax, and as if in answer to her mood a new man was presented, a tall, sleek Southerner with a persuasive note:

"You lovely creacha. I been strainin my eyes watchin your cameo face floatin round. You stand out above all these othuz like an Amehken Beauty Rose over a lot of field daisies."

Dancing with him the second time, Josephine hearkened to his pleadings.

"All right. Let's go outside."

"It wasn't outdaws I was considerin," he explained as they left the floor. "I happen to have a mortgage on a nook right hee in the building."

"All right."

Book Chaffee, of Alabama, led the way through the cloak-room, through a passage to an inconspicuous door.

"This is the private apartment of my friend Sergeant Boone, instructa of the battery. He wanted to be particularly sure it'd be used as a nook tonight and not a readin room or anything like that."

Opening the door he turned on a dim light; she came in and he shut it behind her, and they faced each other.

"Mighty sweet," he murmured. His tall face came down, his long arms wrapped around her tenderly, and very slowly, so that their eyes met for quite a long time, he drew her up to him. Josephine kept thinking that she had never kissed a Southern boy before.

They started apart at the sudden sound of a key turning in the lock outside. Then there was a muffled snicker followed by retreating footsteps, and Book sprang for the door and wrenched at the handle, just as Josephine noticed that this was not only Sergeant Boone's parlor, it was his bedroom as well.

"Who was it?" she demanded. "Why did they lock us in?"

"Some funny boy. I'd like to get my hands on him."

"Will he come back?"

Book sat down on the bed to think. "I couldn't say. Don't even know who it was. But if somebody on the committee came along it wouldn't look too good, would it?"

Seeing her expression change, he came over and put his arm around her. "Don't you worry, honey. We'll fix it."

She returned his kiss, briefly but without distraction. Then she broke away and went into the next apartment, which was hung with boots, uniform coats and various military equipment.

"There's a window up here," she said. It was high in the wall and had not been opened for a long time. Book mounted on a chair and forced it ajar.

"About ten feet down," he reported, after a moment, "but there's a big pile of snow just underneath. You might get a nasty fall and you'll sure soak your shoes and stockin's."

"We've got to get out," Josephine said sharply.

"We'd better wait and give this funny man a chance——"

"I won't wait. I want to get out. Look—throw out all the blankets from the bed and I'll jump on that; or you jump first and spread them over the pile of snow."

After that it was merely exciting. Carefully Book Chaffee wiped the dust from the window to protect her dress; then they were struck silent by a footstep that approached—and passed the outer door. Book jumped, and she heard him kicking profanely as he waded out of the soft drift below. He spread the blankets. At the moment when Josephine swung her legs out the window, there was the sound of voices outside the door and the key turned again in the lock. She landed softly, reaching for his hand, and convulsed with laughter they ran and skidded down the half block toward the corner, and reaching the entrance to the armory, they stood panting for a moment, breathing in the fresh night. Book was reluctant to go inside.

"Why don't you let me conduct you where you're stayin? We can sit around and sort of recuperate."

She hesitated, drawn toward him by the community of their late predicament; but something was calling her inside, as if the fulfillment of her elation awaited her there.

"No," she decided.

As they went in she collided with a man in a great hurry, and looked up to recognize Dudley Knowleton.

"So sorry," he said. "Oh, hello——"

"Won't you dance me over to my box?" she begged him impulsively. "I've torn my dress."

As they started off he said abstractedly: "The fact is, a little mischief has come up and the buck has been passed to me. I was going along to see about it."

Her heart raced wildly and she felt the need of being another sort of person immediately.

"I can't tell you how much it's meant meeting you. It would be wonderful to have one friend I could be serious with without being all mushy and sentimental. Would you mind if I wrote you a letter—I mean, would Adele mind?"

"Lord, no." His smile had become utterly unfathomable to her. As they reached the box she thought of one more thing:

"Is it true that the baseball team is training at Hot Springs during Easter?"

"Yes. You going there?"

"Yes. Good night, Mr. Knowleton."

But she was destined to see him once more. It was outside the men's coat room, where she waited among a crowd of other pale survivors and their paler mothers, whose wrinkles had doubled and tripled with the passing night. He was explaining something to Adele, and Josephine heard the phrase. "The door was locked, and the window open——"

Suddenly it occurred to Josephine that, meeting her coming in damp and breathless, he must have guessed at the truth—and Adele would doubtless confirm his suspicion. Once again the spectre of her old enemy, the plain and jealous girl, arose before her. Shutting her mouth tight together she turned away.

But they had seen her, and Adele called to her in her cheerful ringing voice:

"Come say good night. You were *so* sweet about the stockings. Here's a girl you won't find doing shoddy, silly things, Dudley." Impulsively she leaned and kissed Josephine on the cheek. "You'll see I'm right, Dudley—next year she'll be the most respected girl in school."

III

As things go in the interminable days of early March, what happened next happened quickly. The annual senior dance at Miss Brereton's school came on a night soaked through with spring, and all the junior girls lay awake listening to the sighing tunes from the gymnasium. Between the numbers, when boys up from New Haven and Princeton wandered about the grounds, cloistered glances looked down from dark open windows upon the vague figures.

Not Josephine, though she lay awake like the others. Such vicarious diversions had no place in the sober pattern she was spinning now from day to day; yet she might as well have been in the forefront of those who called down to the men and threw notes and entered into conversations, for destiny had suddenly turned against her and was spinning a dark web of its own.

> Lit-tle lady, don't be depressed and blue,
> After all we're both in the same
> can-noo——

Dudley Knowleton was over in the gymnasium fifty yards away, but proximity to a man did not thrill her as it would have done a year ago—not, at least, in the same way. Life, she saw now, was a serious matter, and in the modest darkness a line of a novel ceaselessly recurred to her: "He is a man fit to be the father of my children." What were the seductive graces, the fast lines of a hundred parlor snakes compared to such realities. One couldn't go on forever kissing comparative strangers behind half-closed doors.

Under her pillow now were two letters, answers to her letters. They spoke in a bold round hand of the beginning of baseball practice; they were glad Josephine felt as she did about things; and the writer certainly looked forward to seeing her at Easter. Of all the letters she had ever received they were the most difficult from which to squeeze a single drop of heart's blood—one couldn't even read the "Yours" of the subscription as "Your"—but Josephine knew them by heart. They were precious because he had taken the time to write them; they were eloquent in the very postage stamp because he used so few.

She was restless in her bed—the music had begun again in the gymnasium:

> Oh, my love, I've waited so long for you,
> Oh, my love, I'm singing this song for
> you—
>   Oh-h-h-h—

From the next room there was light laughter, and then from below a male voice, and a long interchange of comic whispers. Josephine recognized Lillian's laugh and the voices of two other girls. She could imagine them as they lay across the window in their nightgowns, their heads just showing from the open window. "Come right down," one boy kept saying. "Don't be formal—come just as you are."

There was a sudden silence, then a quick crunching of footsteps on gravel, a suppressed snicker and a scurry, and the sharp, protesting groan of several beds in the next room and the banging of a door down the hall. Trouble for somebody, maybe. A few minutes later Josephine's door half opened, she caught a glimpse of Miss Kwain against the dim corridor light, and then the door closed.

The next afternoon Josephine and four other girls, all of whom denied having breathed so much as a word into the night, were placed on probation. There was absolutely nothing to do about it. Miss Kwain had recognized their faces in the window and they were all from two rooms. It was an injustice, but it was nothing compared to what happened next. One week before Easter vacation the school motored off on a one-day trip to inspect a milk farm—all save the ones on probation. Miss Chambers, who sympathized with Josephine's misfortune, enlisted her services in entertaining Mr. Ernest Waterbury, who was spending a week-end with his aunt. This was only vaguely better than nothing, for Mr. Waterbury was a very dull, very priggish young man. He was so dull and so priggish that the following morning Josephine was expelled from school.

It had happened like this: They had strolled in the grounds, they had sat down at a garden table and had tea. Ernest Waterbury had expressed a desire to see something in the chapel, just a few minutes before his aunt's car rolled up the drive. The chapel was reached by descending winding mock-medieval stairs; and, her shoes still wet from the garden, Josephine had slipped on the top step and fallen five feet directly into Mr. Waterbury's unwilling arms, where she lay helpless, convulsed with irresistible laughter. It was in this position that Miss Brereton and the visiting trustee had found them.

"But I had nothing to do with it!" declared the ungallant Mr. Waterbury. Flustered and outraged, he was packed back to New Haven, and Miss Brereton, connecting this with last week's sin, proceeded to lose her head. Josephine, humiliated and furious, lost hers, and Mr. Perry, who happened to be in New York, arrived at the school the same night. At his passionate indignation, Miss Brereton collapsed and retracted, but the damage was done, and Josephine packed her trunk. Unexpectedly, monstrously, just as it had begun to mean something, her school life was over.

For the moment all her feelings were directed against Miss

Brereton, and the only tears she shed at leaving were of anger and resentment. Riding with her father up to New York, she saw that while at first he had instinctively and whole-heartedly taken her part, he felt also a certain annoyance with her misfortune.

"We'll all survive," he said. "Unfortunately, even that old idiot Miss Brereton will survive. She ought to be running a reform school." He brooded for a moment. "Anyhow, your mother arrives tomorrow and you and she can go down to Hot Springs as you planned."

"Hot Springs!" Josephine cried, in a choked voice. "Oh, no!"

"Why not?" he demanded in surprise. "It seems the best thing to do. Give it a chance to blow over before you go back to Chicago."

"I'd rather go to Chicago," said Josephine breathlessly. "Daddy, I'd much rather go to Chicago."

"That's absurd. Your mother's started East and the arrangements are all made. At Hot Springs you can get out and ride and play golf and forget that old she-devil—"

"Isn't there another place in the East we could go? There's people I know going to Hot Springs who'll know all about this, people that I don't want to meet—girls from school."

"Now, Jo, you keep your chin up—this is one of those times. Sorry I said that about letting it blow over in Chicago; if we hadn't made other plans we'd go back and face every old shrew and gossip in town right away. When anybody slinks off in a corner they think you've been up to something bad. If anybody says anything to you, you tell them the truth—what I said to Miss Brereton. You tell them she said you could come back and I damn well wouldn't let you go back."

"They won't believe it."

There would be, at all events, four days of respite at Hot Springs before the vacations of the schools. Josephine passed this time taking golf lessons from a professional so newly arrived from Scotland that he surely knew nothing of her misadventure; she even went riding with a young man one afternoon, feeling almost at home with him after his admission that he had flunked out of Princeton in February—a confidence, however, which she did not recriprocate in kind. But in the evenings, despite the young man's importunity, she stayed with her mother, feeling nearer to her than she ever had before.

But one afternoon in the lobby Josephine saw by the desk two dozen good-looking young men waiting by a stack of bat cases and bags, and knew that what she dreaded was at hand. She ran upstairs and with an invented headache dined there that night, but after dinner she walked restlessly around their apartment. She was ashamed not only of her situation but of her reaction to it. She had never felt any pity for the unpopular girls who skulked in dressing-rooms because they could attract no partners on the floor, or for girls who were outsiders at Lake Forest, and now she was like them—hiding miserably out of life. Alarmed lest already the change was written in her face, she paused in front of the mirror, fascinated as ever by what she found there.

"The darn fools," she said aloud. And as she said it her chin went up and the faint cloud about her eyes lifted. The phrases of the myraid love letters she had received passed before her eyes; behind her, after all, was the reassurance of a hundred lost and pleading faces, of innumerable tender and pleading voices. Her pride flooded back into her till she could see the warm blood rushing up into her cheeks.

There was a knock at the door—it was the Princeton boy.

"How about slipping downstairs?" he proposed. "There's a dance. It's full of Ee-lies, the whole Yale baseball team. I'll pick up one of them and introduce you and you'll have a big time. How about it?"

"All right, but I don't want to meet anybody. You'll just have to dance with me all evening."

"You know that suits *me.*"

She hurried into a new spring evening dress of the frailest fairy blue. In the excitement of seeing herself in it, it seemed as if she had shed the old skin of winter and emerged a shining chrysalis with no stain; and going downstairs her feet fell softly just off the beat of the music from below. It was a tune from a play she had seen a week ago in New York, a tune with a future—ready for gayeties as yet unthought of, lovers not yet met. Dancing off, she was certain that life had innumerable beginnings. She had hardly gone ten steps when she was cut in upon by Dudley Knowleton.

"Why, Josephine!" He had never used her first name before —he stood holding her hand. "Why, I'm so glad to see you. I've been hoping and hoping you'd be here."

She soared skyward on a rocket of surprise and delight. He was actually glad to see her—the expression on his face was obviously sincere. Could it be possible that he hadn't heard?

"Adele wrote me you might be here. She wasn't sure."

—Then he knew and didn't care; he liked her anyhow.

"I'm in sackcloth and ashes." she said.

"Well, they're very becoming to you."

"You know what happened—" she ventured.

"I do. I wasn't going to say anything, but it's generally agreed that Waterbury behaved like a fool—and it's not going to be much help to him in the elections next month. Look— I want you to dance with some men who are just starving for a touch of beauty."

Presently she was dancing with, it seemed to her, the entire team at once. Intermittently Dudley Knowleton cut back in, as well as the Princeton man, who was somewhat indignant at this unexpected competition. There were many girls from many schools in the room, but with an admirable team spirit the Yale men displayed a sharp prejudice in Josephine's favor; already she was pointed out from the chairs along the wall.

But interiorly she was waiting for what was coming, for the moment when she would walk with Dudley Knowleton into the warm, Southern night. It came naturally, just at the end of a number, and they strolled along an avenue of early-blooming lilacs and turned a corner and another corner . . .

"You were glad to see me, weren't you?" Josephine said.

"Of course."

"I was afraid at first. I was sorriest about what happened at school because of you. I'd been trying so hard to be different —because of you."

"You mustn't think of that school business any more. Everybody that matters knows you got a bad deal. Forget it and start over."

"Yes," she agreed tranquilly. She was happy. The breeze and

the scent of lilacs—that was she, lovely and intangible; the rustic bench where they sat and the trees—that was he, rugged and strong beside her, protecting her.

"I'd thought so much of meeting you here," she said after a minute. "You'd been so good for me, that I thought maybe in a different way I could be good for you—I mean I know ways of having a good time that you don't know. For instance, we've certainly got to go horseback riding by moonlight some night. That'll be fun."

He didn't answer.

"I can really be very nice when I like somebody—that's really not often," she interpolated hastily, "not seriously. But I mean when I do feel seriously that a boy and I are really friends I don't believe in having a whole mob of other boys hanging around taking up time. I like to be with him all the time, all day and all evening, don't you?"

He stirred a little on the bench; he leaned forward with his elbows on his knees, looking at his strong hands. Her gently modulated voice sank a note lower.

"When I like anyone I don't even like dancing. It's sweeter to be alone."

Silence for a moment.

"Well, you know"—he hesitated, frowning—"as a matter of fact, I'm mixed up in a lot of engagements made some time ago with some people." He floundered about unhappily. "In fact, I won't even be at the hotel after tomorrow. I'll be at the house of some people down the valley—a sort of house party. As a matter of fact, Adele's getting here tomorrow."

Absorbed in her own thoughts, she hardly heard him at first, but at the name she caught her breath sharply.

"We're both to be at this house party while we're here, and I imagine it's more or less arranged what we're going to do. Of course, in the daytime I'll be here for baseball practice."

"I see." Her lips were quivering. "You won't be—you'll be with Adele."

"I think that—more or less—I will. She'll—want to see you, of course."

Another silence while he twisted his big fingers and she helplessly imitated the gesture.

"You were just sorry for me," she said. "You like Adele—much better."

"Adele and I understand each other. She's been more or less my ideal since we were children together."

"And I'm not your kind of girl." Josephine's voice trembled with a sort of fright. "I suppose because I've kissed a lot of boys and got a reputation for a speed and raised the deuce."

"It isn't that."

"Yes, it is," she declared passionately. "I'm just paying for things." She stood up. "You better take me back inside so I can dance with the kind of boys that like me."

She walked quickly down the path, tears of misery streaming from her eyes. He overtook her by the steps, but she only shook her head and said, "Excuse me for being so fresh. I'll grow up —I got what was coming to me—it's all right."

A little later when she looked around the floor for him he had gone—and Josephine realized with a shock that for the first time in her life she had tried for a man and failed. But, save in the very young, only love begets love, and from the moment Josephine had perceived that his interest in her was merely kindness she realized the wound was not in her heart but in her pride. She would forget him quickly, but she would never forget what she had learned from him. There were two kinds of men, those you played with and those you might marry. And as this passed through her mind, her restless eyes wandered casually over the group of stags, resting very lightly on Mr. Gordon Tinsley, the current catch of Chicago, reputedly the richest young man in the Middle West. He had never paid any attention to young Josephine until tonight. Ten minutes ago he had asked her to go driving with him tomorrow.

But he did not attract her—and she decided to refuse. One mustn't run through people, and, for the sake of a romantic half-hour, trade a possibility that might develop—quite seriously—later, at the proper time. She did not know that this was the first mature thought that she had ever had in her life, but it was.

The orchestra were packing their instruments and the Princeton man was still at her ear, still imploring her to walk out with him into the night. Josephine knew without cogitation which sort of man he was—and the moon was bright even on the windows. So with a certain sense of relaxation she took his arm and they strolled out to the pleasant bower she had so lately quitted, and their faces turned toward each other, like little moons under the great white one which hovered high over the Blue Ridge; his arm dropped softly about her yielding shoulder.

"Well?" he whispered.

"Well?"

A Snobbish Story

I

It is difficult for young people to live things down. We will tolerate vice, grand larceny and the quieter forms of murder in our contemporaries, because we are so strong and incorruptible ourselves, but our children's friends must show a blank service record. When young Josephine Perry was "removed" by her father from the Brereton School, where she had accidentally embraced a young man in the chapel, some of the best people in Chicago would have liked to have seen her drawn and quartered. But the Perrys were rich and powerful, so that friends rallied to their daughter's reputation—and Josephine's lovely face with its expression of just having led the children from a burning orphan asylum did the rest.

Certainly there was no consciousness of disgrace in it when she entered the grand stand at Lake Forest on the first day of the tennis tournament. Same old crowd, she seemed to say, turning, without any curiosity, half left, half right—not that I object, but you can't expect me to get excited.

It was a bright day, with the sun glittering on the crowd; the white figures on the courts threw no shadow. Over in Europe the bloody terror of the Somme was just beginning, but the war had become second-page news and the question agitating the crowd was who would win the tournament. Dresses were long and hats were small and tight, and America, shut in on itself, was bored beyond belief.

Josephine, representing in her own person the future, was not bored; she was merely impatient for a change. She gazed about until she found friends; they waved and she joined them. Only as she sat down did she realize that she was also next to a lady whose lips, in continual process of masking buck teeth, gave her a deceptively pleasant expression. Mrs. McRae belonged to the drawing-and-quartering party. She hated young people, and by some perverse instinct was drawn into contact with them, as organizer of the midsummer vaudeville at Lake Forest and of dancing classes in Chicago during the winter. She chose rich, plain girls and brought them along, bullying boys into dancing with them and comparing them to their advantage with the more popular black sheep—the most prominent representative of this flock being Josephine.

But Josephine was stiffened this afternoon by what her father had said the night before: "If Jenny McRae raises a finger against you, heaven help Jim." This was because of a rumor that Mrs. McRae, as an example for the public weal, was going to omit Josephine's usual dance with Travis de Coppet from the vaudeville that summer.

As a matter of fact, Mrs. McRae had, upon her husband's urgent appeal, reconsidered; she was one large, unconvincing smile. After a short but obvious conference behind her own eyes, she said:

"Do you see that young man on the second court, with the headband?" And as Josephine gazed apathetically, "That's my nephew from Minneapolis. They say he has a fine chance to

win here. I wonder if you'd be a sweet girl and be nice to him
and introduce him to the young people."

Again she hesitated. "And I want to see you about the vaudeville soon. We expect you and Travis to do that marvelous,
marvelous maxixe for us."

Josephine's inner response was the monosyllable "Huh!"

She realized that she didn't want to be in the vaudeville, but
only to be invited. And another look at Mrs. McRae's nephew
decided her that the price was too high.

"The maxixe is stale now," she answered, but her attention
had already wandered. Someone was staring at her from near
by, someone whose eyes burned disturbingly, like an un-
charted light.

Turning to speak to Travis de Coppet, she could see the pale
lower half of a face two rows behind, and during the burst of
clapping at the end of a game she turned and made a cerebral
photograph of the entire individual as her eyes wandered casually down the row.

He was a tall, even a high young man, with a rather small
head set on enormous round shoulders. His face was pale; his
eyes were nearly black, with an intense, passionate light in
them; his mouth was sensitive and strongly set. He was poorly
dressed—green shine on his suit, a shabby string of a necktie
and a bum cap. When she turned he looked at her with rigid
hunger, and kept looking at her after she had turned away, as
if his eyes could burn loopholes through the thin straw of her
hat.

Suddenly Josephine realized what a pleasant scene it was,
and, relaxing, she listened to the almost regular pat-smack,
smack-pat-pat of the balls, the thud of a jump and the overtone
of the umpire's "Fault"; "Out"; "Game and set, 6–2, Mr.
Oberwalter." The sun moved slowly westward off the games
and gossip. The day's matches ended.

Rising, Mrs. McRae said to Josephine: "Then shall I bring
Donald to you when he's dressed? He doesn't know a soul. I
count on you. Where will you be?"

Josephine accepted the burden patiently: "I'll wait right
here."

Already there was music on the outdoor platform beside the

club, and there was a sound of clinking waiters as the crowd swayed out of the grand stand. Josephine refused to go and dance, and presently the three young men, each of whom had loved and lost her, moved on to other prospects, and Josephine picked them out presently below a fringe by their well-known feet—Travis de Coppet's deft, dramatic feet; Ed Bement's stern and uncompromising feet; Elsie Kerr's warped ankles; Lillian's new shoes; the high, button shoes of some impossible girl. There were more feet; the stands were almost empty now, and canvas was being spread over the lonely courts. She heard someone coming clumsily down the plank behind her and landing with a plunk upon the board on which she sat, lifting her an abrupt inch into the air.

"D' I jar you?"

It was the man she had noticed and forgotten. He was still very tall.

"Don't you go in for dancing?" he asked, lingering. "I picked you out for the belle of the ball."

"You're rather fresh, aren't you?"

"My error," he said. "I should have known you were too swell to be spoken to."

"I never saw you before."

"I never saw you either, but you looked so nice in your hat, and I saw you smiling to your friends, so I thought I'd take a chance."

"Like you do downstate, hey, Si?" retorted Josephine insolently.

"What's the matter with downstate? I come from Abe Lincoln's town, where the boys are big and brilliant."

"What are you—a dance-hall masher?"

He was extraordinarily handsome, and she liked his imperviousness to insult.

"Thanks. I'm a reporter—not sports, or society either. I came to do the atmosphere—you know, a fine day with the sun sizzling on high and all the sporting world as well as the fashionable world of Lake Forest out in force."

"Hadn't you better go along and write it then?"

"Finished; another fellow took it. Can I sit down for a minute, or do you soil easily? A mere breath of wind and poof!

Listen, Miss Potterfield-Swiftcormick, or whatever your name is. I come from good people and I'm going to be a great writer some day." He sat down. "If anybody comes you can say I was interviewing you for the paper. What's your name?"

"Perry."

"Herbert T. Perry?"

She nodded and he looked at her hard for a moment.

"Well, well," he sighed, "most attractive girl I've met for months turns out to be Herbert T. Perry's daughter. As a rule, you society nuts aren't much to look at. I mean, you pass more pretty girls in the Loop in one hour than I've seen here this afternoon, and the ones here have the advantage of dressing and all that. What's your first name?"

She started to say "Miss," but suddenly it seemed pointless, and she answered "Josephine."

"My name's John Boynton Bailey." He handed her his card with CHICAGO TRIBUNE printed in the corner. "Let me inform you I'm the best reporter in this city. I've written a play that ought to be produced this fall. I'm telling you that to prove I'm not just some bum, as you may judge from my old clothes. I've got some better clothes home, but I didn't think I was going to meet you."

"I just thought you were sort of fresh to speak to me without being introduced."

"I take what I can get," he admitted moodily.

At the sudden droop of his mouth, thoughtful and unhappy, Josephine knew that she liked him. For a moment she did not want Mrs. McRae and her nephew to see her with him; then, abruptly, she did not care.

"It must be wonderful to write."

"I'm just getting started, but you'll be proud to know me sometime." He changed the subject. "You've got wonderful features—you know it? You know what features are—the eyes and the mouth together, not separately—the triangle they make. That's how people decide in a flash whether they like other people. A person's nose and shape of the face are just things he's born with and can't change. They don't matter, Miss Gotrocks."

"Please cut out the Stong Age slang."

"All right; but you've got nice features. Is your father good-looking?"

"Very," she answered, appreciating the compliment.

The music started again. Under the trees the wooden floor was red in the sun. Josephine sang softly:

> "'Lisibeth Ann-n,
> I'm wild a-bow-ow-out you, a-bow-ow-out you——"

"Nice here," he murmured. "Just this time of day and that music under the trees. . . . It's hot in Chicago!"

She was singing to him; the remarked triangle of her eyes and mouth was turned on him, faintly and sadly smiling, her low voice wooed him casually from some impersonal necessity of its own. Realizing it, she broke off, saying: "I've got to go to the city tomorrow. I've been putting it off."

"I bet you have a lot of men worried about you."

"Me? I just sit home and twirl my thumbs all day."

"Yes, you do."

"Everybody hates me and I return the compliment, so I'm going into a convent or else to be a trained nurse in the war. Will you enlist in the French Army and let me nurse you?"

Her words died away; his eyes, following hers, saw Mrs. McRae and her nephew coming in at the gate. "I'll go now," he said quickly. "You wouldn't have lunch with me if you come to Chicago tomorrow? I'll take you to a German place with fine food."

She hesitated; Mrs. McRae's insincerely tickled expression grew larger on the near distance.

"All right."

He wrote swiftly on a piece of paper and handed it to her. Then, lifting his big body awkwardly, he gallumped down the tier of seats, receiving a quick but inquisitive glance from Mrs. McRae as he lumbered past her.

II

It was easy to arrange. Josephine phoned the aunt with whom she was to lunch, dropped the chauffeur and, not without a certain breathlessness, approached Hoftzer's Rathskeller Garten on North State Street. She wore a blue crêpe-de-chine dress sprinkled with soft brown leaves that were the color of her eyes.

John Boynton Bailey was waiting in front of the restaurant, looking distracted, yet protective, and Josephine's uneasiness departed.

He said, "We don't want to eat in this place. It seemed all right when I thought about it, but I just looked inside, and you might get sawdust in your shoes. We better go to some hotel."

Agreeably she turned in the direction of a hotel sacred to tea dancing, but he shook his head.

"You'd meet a lot of your friends. Let's go to the old La Grange."

The old La Grange Hotel, once the pride of the Middle West, was now a rendezvous of small-town transients and a forum for traveling salesmen. The women in the lobby were either hard-eyed types from the Loop or powderless, transpiring mothers from the Mississippi Valley. There were spittoons in patient activity and a busy desk where men mouthed cigars grotesquely and waited for telephone calls.

In the big dining room, John Bailey and Josephine ordered grapefruit, club sandwiches and julienne potatoes. Josephine put her elbows on the table and regarded him as if to say: "Well, now I'm temporarily yours; make the most of your time."

"You're the best-looking girl I ever met," he began. "Of course you're tangled up in all this bogus society hokum, but you can't help that. You think that's sour grapes, but I'll tell you; when I hear people bragging about their social position and who they are, and all that, I just sit back and laugh. Because I happen to be descended directly from Charlemagne. What do you think of that?"

Josephine blushed for him, and he grew a little ashamed of his statement and qualified it:

"But I believe in men, not their ancestors. I want to be the best writer in the world, that's all."

"I love good books," Josephine offered.

"It's the theater that interests me. I've got a play now that I think would go big if the managers would bother to read it. I've got all the stuff—sometimes I walk along the streets so full of it that I feel I could just sail out over the city like a balloon." His mouth drooped suddenly. "It's because I haven't got anything to show yet that I talk like that."

"Mr. Bailey, the great playwright. You'll send me tickets to your plays, won't you?"

"Sure," he said abstractedly, "but by that time you'll be married to some boy from Yale or Harvard with a couple of hundred neckties and a good-looking car, and you'll get to be dumbbell like the rest."

"I guess I am already—but I simply love 'poetry. Did you ever read The Passing of Arthur?"

"There's more good poetry being written now right in Chi than during the whole last century. There's a man named Carl Sandburg that's as great as Shakspere."

She was not listening; she was watching him. His sensitive face was glowing with the same strange light as when she had first seen him.

"I like poetry and music better than anything in the world," she said. "They're wonderful."

He believed her, knowing that she spoke of her liking for him. She felt that he was distinguished, and by this she meant something definite and real; the possession of some particular and special passion for life. She knew that she herself was superior in something to the girls who criticized her—though she often confused her superiority with the homage it inspired —and she was apathetic to the judgments of the crowd. The distinction that at fifteen she had found in Travis de Coppet's ballroom romantics she discovered now in John Bailey, in spite of his assertiveness and his snobbishness. She wanted to look at life through his glasses, since he found it so absorbing and exciting. Josephine had developed early and lived hard—if that can be said of one whose face was cousin to a fresh, damp rose—and she had begun to find men less than satisfactory.

The strong ones were dull, the clever ones were shy, and all too soon they were responding to Josephine with a fatal sameness, a lack of temperament that blurred their personalities.

The club sandwiches arrived and absorbed them; there was activity from an orchestra placed up near the ceiling in the fashion of twenty years before. Josephine, chewing modestly, looked around the room; just across from them a man and woman were getting up from table, and she started and made one big swallow. The woman was what was called a peroxide blonde, with doll's eyes boldly drawn on a baby-pink face. The sugary perfume that exuded from her garish clothes was almost visible as she preceded her escort to the door. Her escort was Josephine's father.

"Don't you want your potatoes?" John Bailey asked after a minute.

"I think they're very good," she said in a strained voice.

Her father, the cherished ideal of her life—handsome, charming Herbert Perry. Her mother's lover—through so many summer evenings had Josephine seen them in the swinging settee of the veranda, with his head on her lap, smoothing his hair. It was the promise of happiness in her parents' marriage that brought a certain purposefulness into all Josephine's wayward seeking.

Now to see him lunching safely out of the zone of his friends with such a woman! It was different with boys—she rather admired their loud tales of conquest in the nether world, but for her father, a grown man, to be like that. She was trembling; a tear fell and glistened on a fried potato.

"Yes, I'd like very much to go there," she heard herself saying.

"Of course, they are all very serious people," he explained defensively. "I think they've decided to produce my play in their little theater. If they haven't I'll give one or two of them a good sock on the jaw, so that next time they strike any literature they'll recognize it."

In the taxi Josephine tried to put out of her mind what she had seen at the hotel. Her home, the placid haven from which she had made her forays, seemed literally in ruins, and she dreaded her return. Awful, awful, awful!

In a panic she moved close to John Bailey, with the necessity of being near something strong. The car stopped before a new building of yellow stucco from which a blue-jowled, fiery-eyed young man came out.

"Well, what happened?" John demanded.

"The trap dropped at 11:30."

"Yes?"

"I wrote out his farewell speech like he asked me to, but he took too long and they wouldn't let him finish it."

"What a dirty trick on you."

"Wasn't it? . . . Who's your friend?" The man indicated Josephine.

"Lake Forest stuff," said John, grinning. "Miss Perry, Mr. Blacht."

"Here for the triumph of the Springfield Shakspere? But I hear they may do Uncle Tom's Cabin instead." He winked at Josephine. "So long."

"What did he mean?" she demanded as they went on.

"Why, he's on the Tribune and he had to cover a hanging this morning. What's more, he and I caught the fellow ourselves. . . . Do you think these cops ever catch anybody?"

"This isn't a jail, is it?"

"Lord, no; this is the theater workshop."

"What did he mean about a speech?"

"He wrote the man a dying speech to sort of make up for having caught him."

"How perfectly hectic!" cried Josephine, awed.

They were in a long, dimly lit hall with a stage at one end; upon it, standing about in the murkiness of a few footlights, were a dozen people. Almost at once Josephine realized that everybody there except herself was crazy. She knew it incontrovertibly, although the only person of outward eccentricity was a robust woman in a frock coat and gray morning trousers. And in spite of the fact that of those present seven were later to attain notoriety, and four, actual distinction, Josephine was, for the moment, right. It was their intolerable inadjustability to their surroundings that had plucked them from lonely normal schools, from the frame rows of Midwestern towns and the respectability of shoddy suburbs, and brought them to Chicago in 1916—ignorant, wild with energy, doggedly sensitive and helplessly romantic, wanderers like their pioneer ancestors upon the face of the land.

"This is Miss ——," said John Bailey, "and Mrs. —— and Caroline —— and Mr. —— and ——"

Their frightened eyes lifted to the young girl's elegant clothes, her confident, beautiful face, and they turned from her rudely in self-protection. Then gradually they came toward her, hinting of their artistic or economic ideals, naïve as freshmen, unreticent as Rotarians. All but one, a handsome girl with a dirty neck and furtive eyes—eyes which, from the moment of Josephine's entrance, never left her face. Josephine listened to a flow of talk, rapt of expression, but only half comprehending and thinking often with sharp pain of her father. Her mind wandered to Lake Forest as if it were a place she had left long ago, and she heard the crack-pat-crack of the tennis balls in the still afternoon. Presently the people sat down on kitchen chairs and a gray-haired poet took the floor.

"The meeting of the committee this morning was to decide on our first production. There was some debate. Miss Hammerton's drama"—he bowed in the direction of the trousered lady —"received serious consideration, but since one of our benefactors is opposed to representations of the class war, we have postponed consideration of Miss Hammerton's powerful play until later."

At this point Josephine was startled to hear Miss Hammerton say "Boo!" in a large, angry voice, give a series of groans, varied as if to express the groans of many people—then clap on a soft gray hat and stride angrily from the room.

"Elsie takes it hard," said the chairman. "Unhappily, the benefactor I spoke of, whose identity you have doubtless guessed, is adamant on the subject—a thorough reactionary. So your committee have unanimously voted that our production shall be Race Riot, by John Boynton Bailey."

Josephine gasped congratulations. In the applause the girl with the furtive eyes brought her chair over and sat down beside Josephine.

"You live at Lake Forest," she said challengingly.

"In the summer."

"Do you know Emily Kohl?"

"No, I don't."

"I thought you were from Lake Forest."

"I live at Lake Forest," said Josephine, still pleasantly. "but I don't know Emily Kohl."

Rebuffed only for a moment, the girl continued, "I don't suppose all this means much to you."

"It's a sort of dramatic club, isn't it?" said Josephine.

"Dramatic club! Oh, gosh!" cried the girl. "Did you hear that? She thinks it's a dramatic club, like Miss Pinkerton's school." In a moment her uninfectious laughter died away, and she turned to the playwright. "How about it? Have you picked your cast?"

'Not yet," he said shortly, annoyed at the baiting of Josephine.

"I suppose you'll have Mrs. Fiske coming on from New York," the girl continued. "Come on, we're all on pins and needles. Who's going to be in it?"

"I'll tell you one thing, Evelyn. You're not."

She grew red with astonishment and anger. "Oho! When did you decide that?"

"Some time ago."

"Oho! How about all the lines I gave you for Clare?"

"I'll cut them tonight; there were only three. I'd rather not produce the thing than have you play Clare."

The others were listening now.

"Far be it from me," the girl began, her voice trembling a little, "far be it from me——"

Josephine saw that John Bailey's face was even whiter than usual. His mouth was hard and cold. Suddenly the girl got up, cried out, "You fool!" and hurried from the room.

With this second temperamental departure a certain depression settled on those remaining; presently the meeting broke up, convoked for next day.

"Let's take a walk," John said to Josephine as they came out into a different afternoon; the heat had lifted with the first breeze from Lake Michigan.

"Let's take a walk," John suggested. "That made me sort of sick—her talking to you like that."

"I didn't like her, but now I'm sorry for her. Who is she?"

"She's a newspaper woman," he answered vaguely. "Listen. How would you like to be in this play?"

"Oh, I couldn't—I've got to be in a play out at the Lake."

"Society stuff," he said, scornfully mimicking: " 'Here come the jolly, jolly golfing girls. Maybe they'll sing us a song.' If you want to be in this thing of mine you can have the lead."

"But how do you know I could act?"

"Come on! With that voice of yours? Listen. The girl in the play is like you. This race riot is caused by two men, one black and one white. The black man is fed up with his black wife and in love with a high-yellow girl, and that makes him bitter, see? And the white man married too young and he's in the same situation. When they both get their domestic affairs straightened the race riot dies down, too, see?"

"It's very original," said Josephine breathlessly. "Which would I be?"

"You'd be the girl the married man was in love with."

"Is that the part that girl was going to play?"

"Yes." He frowned, and then added, "She's my wife."

"Oh—you're married?"

"I married young—like the man in my play. In one way it isn't so bad, because neither of us believed in the old-fashioned bourgeois marriage, living in the same apartment and all. She kept her own name. But we got to hate each other anyhow."

After the first shock was over, it did not seem so strange to Josephine that he was married; there had been a day two years before when only the conscientiousness of a rural justice had prevented Josephine from becoming Mrs. Travis de Coppet.

"We all get what's coming to us," he remarked.

They turned up the boulevard, passing the Blackstone, where faint dance music clung about the windows.

On the street the plate glass of a hundred cars, bound for the country or the North Shore, took the burning sunset, but the city would make shift without them, and Josephine's imagination rested here instead of following the cars; she thought of electric fans in little restaurants with lobsters on ice in the windows, and of pearly signs glittering and revolving against the obscure, urban sky, the hot, dark sky. And pervading ev-

A Snobbish Story

erything, a terribly strange, brooding mystery of roof tops and
empty apartments, of white dresses in the paths of parks, and
fingers for stars and faces instead of moons, and people with
strange people scarcely knowing one another's names.

A sensuous shiver went over Josephine, and she knew that
the fact that John Bailey was married simply added to his
attraction for her. Life broke up a little; barred and forbidden
doors swung open, unmasking enchanted corridors. Was it that
which drew her father, some call to adventure that she had
from him?

"I wish there was some place we could go and be alone
together," John Bailey said, and suddenly, "I wish I had a car."

But they were already alone, she thought. She had spun him
out a background now that was all his—the summer streets of
the city. They were alone here; when he kissed her, finally,
they would be less alone. That would be his time; this was hers.
Their mutually clinging arms pulled her close to his tall side.

A little later, sitting in the back of a movie with the yellow
clock in the corner creeping fatally toward six, she leaned into
the hollow of his rounded shoulder and his cool white cheek
bent down to hers.

"I'm letting myself in for a lot of suffering," he whispered.
She saw his black eyes thinking in the darkness and met them
reassuringly with hers.

"I take things pretty hard," he went on. "And what in hell
could we ever be to each other?"

She didn't answer. Instead she let the familiar lift and float
and flow of love close around them, pulling him back from his
far-away uniqueness with the pressure of her hand.

"What will your wife think if I take that part in your play?"
she whispered.

At the same moment Josephine's wayward parent was being
met by her mother at the Lake Forest Station.

"It's deathly hot in town," he said. "What a day!"

"Did you see her?"

"Yes, and after one look I took her to the La Grange for
lunch. I wanted to preserve a few shreds of my reputation."

"Is it settled?"

"Yes. She's agreed to leave Will alone and stop using his name for three hundred a month for life. I wired your highly discriminating brother in Hawaii that he can come home."

"Poor Will," sighed Mrs. Perry.

III

Three days later, in the cool of the evening, Josephine spoke to her father as he came out on the veranda.

"Daddy, do you want to back a play?"

"I never thought about it. I'd always thought I'd like to write one. Is Jenny McRae's vaudeville on the rocks?"

Josephine ticked impatiently with her tongue. "I'm not even going to be in the vaudeville. I'm talking about an attempt to do something fine. What I want to ask is: What would be your possible objections to backing it?"

"My objections?"

"What would they be?"

"You haven't given me time to drum up any."

"I should think you'd want to do something decent with your money."

"What's the play?" He sat down beside her, and she moved just slightly away from him.

"Mother knows some of the patronesses and it's absolutely all right. But the man who was going to be the backer is very narrow and wants to make a lot of changes that would ruin the whole thing; so they want to find another backer."

"What's it about?"

"Oh, the play's all right, don't you worry," she assured him. "The man that wrote it is still alive, but the play is a part of English literature."

He considered. "Well, if you're going to be in it, and your mother thinks it all right, I'd put up a couple of hundred."

"A couple of hundred!" she exclaimed. "A man who goes around throwing away his money like you do! They need at least a thousand."

"Throwing away my money?" he repeated. "What on earth are you talking about?"

"You know what I'm talking about." It seemed to her that he winced slightly, that his voice was uncertain as he said:

"If you mean the way we live, it doesn't seem quite tactful to reproach me about that."

"I don't mean that." Josephine hesitated; then without premeditation took a sudden plunge into blackmail: "I should think you'd rather not have me soil my hands by discussing——"

Mrs. Perry's footsteps sounded in the hall, and Josephine rose quickly. The car rolled up the drive.

"I hope you'll go to bed early," her mother said.

"Lillian and some kids are coming over."

Josephine and her father exchanged a short, hostile glance before the machine drove off.

It was a harvest night, bright enough to read by. Josephine sat on the veranda steps listening to the tossing of sleepless birds, the rattle of a last dish in the kitchen, the sad siren of the Chicago-Milwaukee train. Composed and tranquil, she sat waiting for the telephone; he could not see her there, so she saw herself for him—it was almost the same.

She considered the immediate future in all its gorgeous possibilities—the first night, with the audience whispering: "Do you realize that's the Perry girl?" With the final curtain, tumultuous applause and herself, with arms full of flowers, leading forth a tall, shy man who would say: "I owe it all to her." And Mrs. McRae's furious face in the audience, and the remorseful face of Miss Brereton, of the Brereton School, who happened to be in town. "Had I but known her genius, I wouldn't have acted as I did." Comments jubilant and uproarious from every side: "The greatest young actress on the American stage!"

Then the move to a larger theater; great, staring, electric letters, JOSEPHINE PERRY in RACE RIOT. "No, father, I'm not going back to school. This is my education and my debut." And her father's answer:

"Well, little girl, I'll have to admit it was a lucky speculation for me to put up that money."

If the figure of John Bailey became a little dim during the latter part of this reverie, it was because the reverie itself opened out to vaguer and vaguer horizons, to return always to that opening night from which it started once more.

Lillian, Travis and Ed came, but she was hardly aware of them, listening for the telephone. They sat, as they had so often, in a row on the steps, surrounded, engulfed, drowned in summer. But they were growing up and the pattern was breaking; they were absorbed in secret destinies of their own, no matter how friendly their voices or how familiar their laughter in the silence. Josephine's boredom with a discussion of the tournament turned to irascibility; she told Travis de Coppet that he smelled of onions.

"I won't eat any onions when we rehearse for the vaudeville," he said.

"You won't be rehearsing with me, because I'm not being in it. I've got a little tired of 'Here come the jolly golfing girls. Hurray!' "

The phone rang and she excused herself.

"Are you alone?"

"There're some people here—that I've known all my life."

"Don't kiss anybody. I don't mean that—go kiss anybody you want to."

"I don't want to." She felt her own lips' warmth in the mouthpiece of the phone.

"I'm out in a pay station. She came up to my room in a crazy humor and I got out."

Josephine didn't answer; something went out of her when he spoke of his wife.

When she went back on the porch her guests, sensing her abstraction, were on their feet.

"No. We want to go. You bore us too."

Her parents' car pursued Ed's around the circular drive. Her father motioned that he wanted to see her alone.

"I didn't quite understand about my spending my money. Is this a Socialist bunch?"

"I told you that mother knew some of the——"

"But who is it you know? The fellow who wrote the play?"

"Yes."

"Where did you meet him?"

"Just around."

"He asked you to raise the money?"

"No."

"I'd certainly like to have a talk with him before you go into this any further. Invite him out to luncheon Saturday?"

"All right," she agreed unwillingly. "If you don't taunt him about his poverty and his ragged clothes."

"What a thing to accuse me of!"

It was with a deep uneasiness that, next Saturday, Josephine drove her roadster to the station. She was relieved to see that he had had a haircut, and he looked very big and powerful and distinguished among the tennis crowd as he got off the train. But finding him nervous, she drove around Lake Forest for half an hour.

"Whose house is that?" he kept asking. "Who are these two people you just spoke to?"

"Oh, I don't know; just somebody. There'll be nobody at lunch but the family and a boy named Howard Page I've known for years."

"These boys you've known for years," he sighed. "Why wasn't I one?"

"But you don't want to be that. You want to be the best writer in the world."

In the Perrys' living room John Bailey stared at a photograph of bridesmaids at her sister's wedding the previous summer. Then Howard Page, a junior at New Haven, arrived and they talked of the tennis: Mrs. McRae's nephew had done brilliantly and was conceded a chance in the finals this afternoon. When Mrs. Perry came downstairs, just before luncheon, John Bailey could not help turning his back on her suddenly and walking up and down to pretend he was at home. He knew in his heart he was better than these people, and he couldn't bear that they should not know it.

The maid called him to the telephone, and Josephine overheard him say, "I can't help it. You have no right to call me here." It was because of the existence of his wife that she had not let him kiss her, but had fitted him, instead, into her platonic reverie, which should endure until Providence set him free.

At luncheon she was relieved to see John Bailey and her

father take a liking to each other. John was expert and illuminating about the race riots, and she saw how thin and meager Howard Page was beside him.

Again John Bailey was summoned to the phone; this time he left the room with an exclamation, said three words into the mouthpiece and hung up with a sharp click.

Back at table, he whispered to Josephine: "Will you tell the maid to say I'm gone if she calls again?"

Josephine was in argument with her mother: "I don't see the use of coming out if I could be an actress instead."

"Why should she come out?" her father agreed. "Hasn't she done enough rushing around?"

"But certainly she's to finish school. There's a course in dramatic art and every year they give a play."

"What do they give?" demanded Josephine scornfully. "Shakspere or something like that! Do you realize there are at least a dozen poets right here in Chicago that are better than Shakspere?"

John Bailey demurred with a laugh. "Oh, no. One maybe."

"I think a dozen," insisted the eager convert.

"In Billy Phelps' course at Yale——" began Howard Page, but Josephine said vehemently:

"Anyhow, I don't think you ought to wait till people are dead before you recognize them. Like mother does."

"I do no such thing," objected Mrs. Perry. "Did I say that, Howard?"

"In Billy Phelps' course at Yale——" began Howard again, but this time Mr. Perry interrupted:

"We're getting off the point. This young man wants my daughter in his play. If there's nothing disgraceful in the play I don't object."

"In Billy——"

"But I don't want Josephine in anything sordid."

"Sordid!" Josephine glared at him. "Don't you think there are plenty of sordid things right here in Lake Forest, for instance?"

"But they don't touch you," her father said.

"Don't they, though?"

"No," he said firmly. "Nothing sordid touches you. If it does, then it's your own fault." He turned to John Bailey. "I understand you need money."

John flushed. "We do. But don't think——"

"That's all right. We've stood behind the opera here for many years and I'm not afraid of things simply because they're new. We know some women on your committee and I don't suppose they'd stand for any nonsense. How much do you need?"

"About two thousand dollars."

"Well, you raise half and I'll raise half—on two conditions: First, my name kept entirely out of it and my daughter's name not played up in any way; second, you assure me personally that she doesn't play any questionable part or have any speeches to make that might offend her mother."

John Bailey considered. "That last is a large order," he said. "I don't know what would offend her mother. There wouldn't be any cursing to do, for instance. There's not a bit in the whole damn play."

He flushed slowly at their laughter.

"Nothing sordid is going to touch Josephine unless she steps into it herself," said Mr. Perry.

"I see your point," John Bailey said.

Lunch was over. For some moments Mrs. Perry had been glancing toward the hall, where some loud argument was taking place.

"Shall we——"

They had scarcely crossed the threshold of the living room when the maid appeared, followed by a local personage in a vague uniform of executive blue.

"Hello, Mr. Kelly. You going to take us into custody?"

Kelly hesitated awkwardly. "Is there a Mr. Bailey?"

John, who had wandered off, swung about sharply. "What?"

"There's an important message for you. They've been trying to get you here, but they couldn't, so they telephoned the constable—that's me." He beckoned him, and then, talking to him, tried at the same time to urge him, with nods of his head, toward the privacy of outdoors; his voice, though lowered, was perfectly audible to everybody in the room.

"The St. Anthony's Hospital—your wife slashed both her

wrists and turned the gas on—they want you as soon as you can get there." The voice pitched higher as they went through the door: "They don't know yet——If there's no train, you can get a car——" They were both outside now, walking fast down the path. Josephine saw John trip and grasp clumsily at the hedge that bordered the gate, and then go on with great strides toward the constable's flivver. The constable was running to keep up with him.

IV

After a few minutes, when John Bailey's trouble had died away in the distance, they all stopped being stunned and behaved like people again. Mr. and Mrs. Perry were panicky as to how far Josephine was involved; then they became angry at John Bailey for coming there with disaster hanging over him.

Mr. Perry demanded: "Did you know he was married?"

Josephine was crying; her mouth was drawn; he looked away from her.

"They lived separately," she whispered.

"She seemed to know he was out here."

"Of course he's a newspaperman," said her mother, "so he can probably keep it out of the papers. Or do you think you ought to do something, Herbert?"

"I was just wondering."

Howard Page got up awkwardly, not wanting to say he was now going to the tennis finals. Mr. Perry went to the door and talked earnestly for a few minutes, and Howard nodded.

Half an hour passed. Several callers drifted by in cars, but received word that no one was at home. Josephine felt something throbbing on the heat of the summer afternoon; and at first she thought it was pity and then remorse, but finally she knew what the throbbing was. "I must push this thing away from me," it said; "this thing must not touch me. I hardly met his wife. He told me——"

And now John Bailey began slipping away. Who was he but a chance encounter, someone who had spoken to her a week before about a play he had written? He had nothing to do with her.

At four o'clock Mr. Perry went to the phone and called St. Anthony's Hospital; only when he asked for an official whom he knew did he get the information: In the actual face of death, Mrs. Bailey had phoned for the police, and it now seemed that they had reached her in time. She had lost blood, but barring complications——

Now, in the relief, the parents grew angry with Josephine as with a child who has toddled under galloping horses.

"What I can't understand is why you should have to know people like that. Is it necessary to go into the back streets of Chicago?"

"That young man had no business here," her father thundered grimly, "and he knew it."

"But who was he?" wailed Mrs. Perry.

"He told me he was a descendant of Charlemagne," said Josephine.

Mr. Perry grunted. "Well, we want no more of Charlemagne's descendants here. Young people had better stay with their own kind until they can distinguish one from another. You let married men alone."

But now Josephine was herself again. She stood up, her eyes hardening.

"Oh, you make me sick," she cried— "a married man! As if there weren't a lot of married men who met other women besides their wives."

Unable to bear another scene, Mrs. Perry withdrew. Once she was out of hearing, Josephine came out into the open at last: "You're a fine one to talk to me."

"Now look here; you said that the other night, and I don't like it now any better than I did then. What do you mean?"

"I suppose you've never been to lunch with anybody at the La Grange Hotel."

"The La Grange——" The truth broke over him slowly. "Why——" He began laughing. Then he swore suddenly, and going quickly to the foot of the stairs, called his wife.

"You sit down," he said to Josephine. "I'm going to tell you a story."

Half an hour later Miss Josephine Perry left her house and set off for the tennis tournament. She wore one of the new autumn gowns with the straight line, but having a looped effect at the sides of the skirt, and fluffy white cuffs. Some people she met just outside the stands told her that Mrs. McRae's nephew was weakening to the veteran, and this started her thinking of Mrs. McRae and of her decision about the vaudeville with a certain regret. People would think it odd if she wasn't in it.

There was a sudden burst of wild clapping as she went in; the tournament was over. The crowd was swarming around victor and vanquished in the central court, and gravitating with it, she was swept by an eddy to the very front of it, until she was face to face with Mrs. McRae's nephew himself. But she was equal to the occasion. With her most sad and melting smile, as if she had hoped for him from day to day, she held out her hand and spoke to him in her clear, vibrant voice:

"We are all awfully sorry."

For a moment, even in the midst of the excited crowd, a hushed silence fell. Modestly, conscious of her personality, Josephine backed away, aware that he was staring after her, his mouth stupidly open, aware of a burst of laughter around her. Travis de Coppet appeared beside her.

"Well, of all the nuts!" he cried.

"What's the matter? What——"

"Sorry! Why, he won! It was the greatest come-back I ever saw."

So, at the vaudeville, Josephine sat with her family after all. Looking around during the show, she saw John Bailey standing in the rear. He looked very sad, and she felt very sorry, realizing that he had come in hopes of a glimpse of her. He would see, at least, that she was not up there on the stage debasing herself with such inanities.

Then she caught her breath as the lights changed, the music quickened and at the head of the steps, Travis de Coppet in white-satin football suit swung into the spotlight a shimmering blonde in a dress of autumn leaves. It was Madelaine Danby, and it was the rôle Josephine would have played. With the warm rain of intimate applause, Josephine decided something: That any value she might have was in the immediate, shimmering present—and thus thinking, she threw in her lot with the rich and powerful of this world forever.

Emotional Bankruptcy

I

"There's that nut with the spyglass again," remarked Jose-phine. Lillian Hammel unhooked a lace sofa cushion from her waist and came to the window. "He's standing back so we can't see him. He's looking at the room above."

The peeper was working from a house on the other side of narrow Sixty-eighth Street, all unconscious that his activities were a matter of knowledge and, lately, of indifference to the pupils of Miss Truby's finishing school. They had even iden-tified him as the undistinguished but quite proper young man who issued from the house with a brief case at eight every morning, apparently oblivious of the school across the street.

"What a horrible person," said Lillian.

"They're all the same," Josephine said. "I'll bet almost every man we know would do the same thing, if he had a telescope and nothing to do in the afternoon. I'll bet Louie Randall would, anyhow."

"Josephine, is he actually following you to Princeton?" Lillian asked.

"Yes, dearie."

"Doesn't he think he's got his nerve?"

"He'll get away with it," Josephine assured her.

"Won't Paul be wild?"

"I can't worry about that. I only know half a dozen boys at Princeton, and with Louie I know I'll have at least one good dancer to depend on. Paul's too short for me, and he's a bum dancer anyhow."

Not that Josephine was very tall; she was an exquisite size for seventeen, and of a beauty that was flowering marvelously day by day into something richer and warmer. People gasped nowadays, whereas a year ago they would merely have stared, and scarcely glanced at her a year before that. She was manifestly to be the spectacular debutante of Chicago next year, in spite of the fact that she was an egotist who played not for popularity but for individual men. While Josephine always recovered, the men frequently didn't—her mail from Chicago, from New Haven, from the Yale Battery on the border, averaged a dozen letters a day.

This was in the fall of 1916, with the thunder of far-off guns already growing louder on the air. When the two girls started for the Princeton prom two days later, they carried with them the Poems of Alan Seeger, supplemented by copies of Smart Set and Snappy Stories, bought surreptitiously at the station news stand. When compared to a seventeen-year-old girl of today, Lillian Hammel was an innocent; Josephine Perry, however, belonged to the ages.

They read nothing en route save a few love epigrams beginning: "A woman of thirty is——" The train was crowded and a sustained, excited chatter flowed along the aisles of the coaches. There were very young girls in a gallantly concealed state of terror; there were privately bored girls who would never see twenty-five again; there were unattractive girls, blandly unconscious of what was in store; and there were little, confident parties who felt as though they were going home.

"They say it's not like Yale," said Josephine. "They don't do things so elaborately here. They don't rush you from place to place, from one tea to another, like they do at New Haven."

"Will you ever forget that divine time last spring?" exclaimed Lillian.

They both sighed.

"At least there'll be Louie Randall," said Josephine.

There would indeed be Louie Randall, whom Josephine had seen fit to invite herself, without the formality of telling her Princeton escort that he was coming. The escort, at that moment pacing up and down at the station platform with many other young men, was probably under the impression that it was his party. But he was wrong; it was Josephine's party; even Lillian was coming with another Princeton man, named Martin Munn, whom Josephine had thoughtfully provided. "Please ask her," she had written. "We'll manage to see a lot of each other, if you do, because the man I'm coming with isn't really very keen about me, so he won't mind."

But Paul Dempster cared a lot; so much so that when the train came puffing up from the Junction he gulped a full pint of air, which is a mild form of swooning. He had been devoted to Josephine for a year—long after her own interest had waned —he had long lost any power of judging her objectively; she was become simply a projection of his own dreams, a radiant, nebulous mass of light.

But Josephine saw Paul clearly enough as they stepped off the train. She gave herself up to him immediately, as if to get it over with, to clear the decks for more vital action.

"So thrilled—so thrilled! So darling to ask me!" Immemorial words, still doing service after fifteen years.

She took his arm snugly, settling it in hers with a series of little readjustments, as if she wanted it right because it was going to be there forever.

"I bet you're not glad to see me at all," she whispered. "I'll bet you've forgotten me. I know you."

Rudimentary stuff, but it sent Paul Dempster into a confused and happy trance. He had the adequate surface of nineteen, but, within, all was still in a ferment of adolescence.

He could only answer gruffly: "Big chance." And then: "Martin had a chemistry lab. He'll meet us at the club."

Slowly the crowd of youth swirled up the steps and beneath Blair arch, floating in an autumn dream and scattering the yellow leaves with their feet. Slowly they moved between stretches of greensward under the elms and cloisters, with breath misty upon the crisp evening, following the hope that lay just ahead, the goal of happiness almost reached.

They sat before a big fire in the Witherspoon Club, the largest of those undergraduate mansions for which Princeton is famous. Martin Munn, Lillian's escort, was a quiet, handsome boy whom Josephine had met several times, but whose sentimental nature she had not explored. Now, with the phonograph playing Down Among the Sheltering Palms, with the soft orange light of the great room glowing upon the scattered groups, who seemed to have brought in the atmosphere of infinite promise from outside, Josephine looked at him appraisingly. A familiar current of curiosity coarsed through her; already her replies to Paul had grown abstracted. But still in the warm enchantment of the walk from the station, Paul did not notice. He was far from guessing that he had already been served his ration; of special attention he would get no more. He was now cast for another rôle.

At the exact moment when it was suggested that they dress for dinner the party became aware of an individual who had just entered the club and was standing by the entrance looking not exactly at home, for he blinked about unfamiliarly, but not in the least ill at ease. He was tall, with long, dancing legs, and his face was that of an old, experienced weasel to whom no henhouse was impregnable.

"Why, Louie Randall!" exclaimed Josephine in a tone of astonishment.

She talked to him for a moment as if unwillingly, and then introduced him all around, meanwhile whispering to Paul: "He's a boy from New Haven. I never dreamed he'd follow me down here."

Randall within a few minutes was somehow one of the party. He had a light and witty way about him; no dark suspicions had penetrated Paul's mind.

"Oh, by the way," said Louie Randall, "I wonder if I can find a place to change my clothes. I've got a suitcase outside."

There was a pause. Josephine was apparently uninterested. The pause grew difficult, and Paul heard himself saying: "You can change in my room if you want to."

"I don't want to put you out."

"Not at all."

Josephine raised her eyebrows at Paul, disclaiming responsibility for the man's presumption; a moment later, Randall said: "Do you live near here?"

"Pretty near."

"Because I have a taxi and I could take you there if you're going to change, and you could show me where it is. I don't want to put you out."

The repetition of this ambiguous statement suggested that otherwise Paul might find his belongings in the street. He rose unwillingly; he did not hear Josephine whisper to Martin Munn: "Please don't you go yet." But Lillian did, and without minding at all. Her love affairs never conflicted with Josephine's, which is why they had been intimate friends so long. When Louie Randall and his involuntary host had departed, she excused herself and went to dress upstairs.

"I'd like to see all over the clubhouse," suggested Josephine. She felt the old excitement mounting in her pulse, felt her cheeks begin to glow like an electric heater.

"These are the private dining rooms," Martin explained as they walked around. . . . "The billiard room. . . . The squash courts. . . . This library is modeled on something in a Cercersion monastery in—in India or somewhere. . . . This"—he opened a door and peered in—"this is the president's room, but I don't know where the light is."

Josephine walked in with a little laugh. "It's very nice in here," she said. "You can't see anything at all. Oh, what have I run into? Come and save me!"

When they emerged a few minutes later, Martin smoothed back his hair hurriedly.

"You darling!" he said.

Josephine made a funny little clicking sound.

"What is it?" he demanded. "Why have you got such a funny look on your face?"

Josephine didn't answer.

"Have I done something? Are you angry? You look as if you'd seen a ghost," he said.

"You haven't done anything," she answered, and added, with an effort: "You were—sweet." She shuddered. "Show me my room, will you?"

"How strange," she was thinking. "He's so attractive, but I didn't enjoy kissing him at all. For the first time in my life— even when it was a man I didn't especially care for—I had no feeling about him at all. I've often been bored afterward, but at the time it's always meant something."

The experience depressed her more than she could account for. This was only her second prom, but neither before nor after did she ever enjoy one so little. She had never been more enthusiastically rushed, but through it all she seemed to float in a detached dream. The men were not individuals tonight, but dummies; men from Princeton, men from New Haven, new men, old beaus—were all as unreal as sticks. She wondered if her face wore that bovine expression she had often noted on the faces of stupid and apathetic girls.

"It's a mood," she told herself. "I'm just tired."

But next day, at a bright and active luncheon, she seemed to herself to have less vivacity than the dozen girls who boasted wanly that they hadn't gone to bed at all. After the football game she walked with Paul Dempster to the station, trying contritely to give him the last end of the week-end, as she had given him the beginning.

"Then why won't you go to the theater with us tonight?" he was pleading. "That was the understanding in my letter. We. were to come to New York with you and all go to the theater."

"Because," she explained patiently, "Lillian and I have to be back at school by eight. That's the only condition on which we were allowed to come."

"Oh, hell," he said. "I'll bet you're doing something tonight with that Randall."

She denied this scornfully, but Paul was suddenly realizing that Randall had dined with them, Randall had slept upon his couch, and Randall, though at the game he had sat on the Yale side of the field, was somehow with them now.

His was the last face that Paul saw as the train pulled out for the Junction. He had thanked Paul very graciously and asked him to stay with him if he was ever in New Haven.

Nevertheless, if the miserable Princetonian had witnessed a scene in the Pennsylvania Station an hour later, his pain would have been moderated, for now Louie Randall was arguing bitterly:

"But why not take a chance? The chaperon doesn't know what time you have to be in."

"We do."

When finally he had accepted the inevitable and departed, Josephine sighed and turned to Lillian.

"Where are we going to meet Wallie and Joe? At the Ritz?"

"Yes, and we'd better hurry," said Lillian. "The Follies begin at nine."

II

It had been like that for almost a year—a game played with technical mastery, but with the fire and enthusiasm gone—and Josephine was still a month short of eighteen. One evening during Thanksgiving vacation, as they waited for dinner in the library of Christine Dicer's house on Gramercy Park, Josephine said to Lillian:

"I keep thinking how excited I'd have been a year ago. A new place, a new dress, meeting new men."

"You've been around too much, dearie; you're blasé."

Josephine bridled impatiently: "I hate that word, and it's not true. I don't care about anything in the world except men, and you know it. But they're not like they used to be. . . . What are you laughing at?"

"When you were six years old they were different?"

"They were. They used to have more spirit when we played drop-the-handkerchief—even the little Ikeys that used to come in the back gate. The boys at dancing school were so exciting; they were all so sweet. I used to wonder what it would be like to kiss every one of them, and sometimes it was wonderful. And then came Travis and Tony Harker and Ridge Saunders and Ralph and John Bailey, and finally I began to realize that I was doing it all. They were nothing, most of them —not heroes or men of the world or anything I thought. They were just easy. That sounds conceited, but it's true."

She paused for a moment.

"Last night in bed I was thinking of the sort of man I really could love, but he'd be different from anybody I've ever met. He'd have to have certain things. He wouldn't necessarily be very handsome, but pleasant looking; and with a good figure, and strong. Then he'd have to have some kind of position in the world, or else not care whether he had one or not; if you see what I mean. He'd have to be a leader, not just like everybody else. And dignified, but very pash, and with lots of experience, so I'd believe everything he said or thought was right. And every time I looked at him I'd have to get that thrill I sometimes get out of a new man; only with him I'd have to get it over and over every time I looked at him, all my life."

"And you'd want him to be very much in love with you. That's what I'd want first of all."

"Of course," said Josephine abstractedly, "but principally I'd want to be always sure of loving him. It's much more fun to love someone than to be loved by someone."

There were footsteps in the hall outside and a man walked into the room. He was an officer in the uniform of the French aviation—a glove-fitting tunic of horizon blue, and boots and belt that shone like mirrors in the lamplight. He was young, with gray eyes that seemed to be looking off into the distance, and a red-brown military mustache. Across his left breast was a line of colored ribbons, and there were gold-embroidered stripes on his arms and wings on his collar.

"Good evening," he said courteously. "I was directed in here. I hope I'm not breaking into something."

Josephine did not move; from head to foot she saw him, and as she watched he seemed to come nearer, filling her whole vision. She heard Lillian's voice, and then the officer's voice, saying:

"My name's Dicer; I'm Christine's cousin. Do you mind if I smoke a cigarette?"

He didn't sit down. He moved about the room and turned over a magazine, not oblivious to their presence, but as if respecting their conversation. But when he saw that silence had fallen, he sat against a table near them with his arms folded and smiled at them.

"You're in the French army," Lillian ventured.

"Yes, I've just got back, and very glad to be here."

He didn't look glad, Josephine noticed. He looked as if he wanted to get out now, but had no place to go to.

For the first time in her life she felt no confidence. She had absolutely nothing to say. She hoped the emptiness that she had felt ever since her soul poured suddenly out toward his beautiful image didn't show in her face. She made her lips into a smile, and kept thinking how once, long ago, Travis de Coppet had worn his uncle's opera cloak to dancing school and suddenly seemed like a man out of the great world. So, now, the war overseas had gone on so long, touched us so little, save for confining us to our own shores, that it had a legendary quality about it, and the figure before her seemed to have stepped out of a gigantic red fairy tale.

She was glad when the other dinner guests came and the room filled with people, strangers she could talk to or laugh with or yawn at, according to their deserts. She despised the girls fluttering around Captain Dicer, but she admired him for not showing by a flicker of his eye that he either enjoyed it or hated it. Especially she disliked a tall, possessive blonde who once passed, her hand on his arm; he should have flicked away with a handkerchief the contamination of his immaculateness.

They went in to dinner; he was far away from her, and she was glad. All she could see of him was his blue cuff farther up the table when he reached for a glass, but she felt that they were alone together, none the less because he did not know.

The man next to her gave her the superfluous information that he was a hero:

"He's Christine's cousin, brought up in France, and joined at the beginning of the war. He was shot down behind the German lines and escaped by jumping off a train. There was a lot about it in the papers. I think he's over here on some kind of propaganda work. . . . Great horseman too. Everybody likes him."

After dinner she sat quietly while two men talked over her, sat persistently willing him to come to her. Ah, but she would be so nice, avoiding any curiosity or sentimentality about his experiences, avoiding any of the things that must have bored and embarrassed him since he had been home. She heard the voices around him:

"Captain Dicer. . . . Germans crucify all the Canadian soldiers they capture. . . . How much longer do you think the war . . . to be behind the enemy lines. . . . Were you frightened?" And then a heavy, male voice telling him about it, between puffs of a cigar: "The way I see it, Captain Dicer, neither side is getting anywhere. It strikes me they're afraid of each other."

It seemed a long time later that he came over to her, but at just the right moment, when there was a vacant seat beside her and he could slip into it.

"I wanted to talk to the prettiest girl for a while. I've wanted to all evening; it's been pretty heavy going."

Josephine wanted to lean against the shining leather of his belt, and more, she wanted to take his head in her lap. All her life had pointed toward this moment. She knew what he wanted, and gave it to him; not words, but a smile of warmth and delight—a smile that said, "I'm yours for the asking; I'm won." It was not a smile that undervalued herself, because through its beauty it spoke for both of them, expressed all the potential joy that existed between them.

"Who are you?" he asked.

"I'm a girl."

"I thought you were a flower. I wondered why they put you on a chair."

"Vive la France," answered Josephine demurely. She dropped her eyes to his chest. "Do you collect stamps, too, or only coins?"

He laughed. "It's good to meet an American girl again. I hoped they'd at least put me across from you at table, so I could rest my eyes on you."

"I could see your cuff."

"I could see your arm. At least—yes, I thought it was your green bracelet."

Later he suggested: "Why couldn't you come out with me one of these evenings?"

"It's not done. I'm still in school."

"Well, some afternoon then. I'd like to go to a tea-dance place and hear some new tunes. The newest thing I know is Waiting for the Robert E. Lee."

"My nurse used to sing me to sleep with it."

"When could you?"

"I'm afraid you'll have to make up a party. Your aunt, Mrs. Dicer, is very strict."

"I keep forgetting," he agreed. "How old are you?"

"Eighteen," she said, anticipating by a month.

That was the point at which they were interrupted and the evening ended for her. The other young men in dinner coats looked like people in mourning beside the banner of his uniform. Some of them were persistent about Josephine, but she was in a reverie of horizon blue and she wanted to be alone.

"This is it at last," something whispered inside her.

Later that night and next day, she still moved in a trance. Another day more and she would see him—forty-eight hours, forty, thirty. The very word "blasé" made her laugh; she had never known such excitement, such expectation. The blessed day itself was a haze of magic music and softly lit winter rooms, of automobiles where her knee trembled against the top lacing of his boot. She was proud of the eyes that followed them when they danced; she was proud of him even when he was dancing with another girl.

"He may think I'm too young," she thought anxiously. "That's why he won't say anything. If he did, I'd leave school; I'd run away with him tonight."

School opened next day and Josephine wrote home:

> *Dear Mother:*
> *I wonder if I can't spend part of the vacation in New York. Christine Dicer wants me to stay a week with her, which would still leave me a full ten days in Chicago. One reason is that the Metropolitan is putting on Wagner's Der Ring des Nibelungen*

and if I come home right away I can only see the Rheingold. Also there are two evening dresses that aren't finished——

The answer came by return post:

. . . because, in the first place, your eighteenth birthday falls then, and your father would feel very badly, because it would be the first birthday you hadn't passed with us; and, in the second place, I've never met the Dicers; and, thirdly, I've planned a little dance for you and I need your help; and, lastly, I can't believe that the reasons you give are your real ones. During Christmas week the Chicago Grand Opera Company is giving——

Meanwhile Capt. Edward Dicer had sent flowers and several formal little notes that sounded to her like translations from the French. She was self-conscious, answering them; so she did it in slang. His French education and his years in the war while America was whirling toward the Jazz Age had made him, though he was only twenty-three, seem of a more formal, more courteous generation than her own. She wondered what he would think of such limp exotics as Travis de Coppet, or Book Chaffee, or Louie Randall. Two days before vacation he wrote asking when her train left for the West. That was something, and for seventy-two hours she lived on it, unable to turn her attention to the masses of Christmas invitations and unheeded letters that she had meant to answer before leaving. But on the day itself, Lillian brought her a marked copy of Town Tattle that, from its ragged appearance, had already been passed around the school.

It is rumored that a certain Tuxedo papa who was somewhat irrasticable about the marital choice of a previous offspring views with equanimity the fact that his remaining daughter is so often in company with a young man fresh from his exploits in the French army.

Captain Dicer did not come to the train. He sent no flowers. Lillian, who loved Josephine like part of herself, wept in their compartment.

Josephine comforted her, saying: "But listen, darling; it's all the same to me. I didn't have a chance, being in school like we were. It's all right." But she was awake hours and hours after Lillian was asleep.

III

Eighteen—it was to have meant so many things: When I'm eighteen I can——Until a girl's eighteen——You'll see things differently when you're eighteen.

That, at least, was true. Josephine saw her vacation invitations as so many overdue bills. Abstractedly she counted them as she always had before—twenty-eight dances, nineteen dinner and theater parties, fifteen tea dances and receptions, a dozen luncheons, a few miscellaneous bids, ranging from early breakfast for the Yale Glee Club to a bob party at Lake Forest —seventy-eight in all, and with the small dance she was giving herself, seventy-nine. Seventy-nine promises of gayety, seventy-nine offers to share fun with her. Patiently she sat down, choosing and weighing, referring doubtful cases to her mother.

"You seem a little white and tired," her mother said.

"I'm wasting away. I've been jilted."

"That won't worry you very long. I know my Josephine. Tonight at the Junior League german you'll meet the most marvelous men."

"No, I won't, mother. The only hope for me is to get married. I'll learn to love him and have his children and scratch his back——"

"Josephine!"

"I know two girls who married for love who told me they were supposed to scratch their husbands' backs and send out the laundry. But I'll go through with it, and the sooner the better."

"Every girl feels like that sometimes," said her mother cheerfully. "Before I was married I had three or four beaus, and I honestly liked each one of them as well as the others. Each one had certain qualities I liked, and I worried about it so long that it didn't seem worth while; I might as well have counted eenie, meenie, mynie, mo. Then one day when I was feeling lonely your father came to take me driving, and from that day I never had a single doubt. Love isn't like it is in books."

"But it is," said Josephine gloomily. "At least for me it always has been."

For the first time it seemed to her more peaceful to be with a crowd than to be alone with a man. The beginning of a line wearied her; how many lines had she listened to in three years? New men were pointed out as exciting, were introduced, and she took pleasure in freezing them to unhappiness with languid answers and wandering glances. Ancient admirers looked favorably upon the metamorphosis, grateful for a little overdue time at last. Josephine was glad when the holiday drew to a close. Returning from a luncheon one gray afternoon, the day after New Year's, she thought that for once it was nice to think she had nothing to do until dinner. Kicking off her overshoes in the hall, she found herself staring at something on the table that at first seemed a projection of her own imagination. It was a card fresh from a case—MR. EDWARD DICER.

Instantly the world jerked into life, spun around dizzily and came to rest on a new world. The hall where he must have stood throbbed with life; she pictured his straight figure against the open door, and thought how he must have stood with his hat and cane in hand. Outside the house, Chicago, permeated with his presence, pulsed with the old delight. She heard the phone ring in the downstairs lounge and, still in her fur coat, ran for it.

"Hello!"

"Miss Josephine, please."

"Oh, hello!"

"Oh. This is Edward Dicer."

"I saw your card."

"I must have just missed you."

What did the words matter when every word was winged and breathless?

"I'm only here for the day. Unfortunately, I'm tied up for dinner tonight with the people I'm visiting."

"Can you come over now?"

"If you like."

"Come right away."

She rushed upstairs to change her dress, singing for the first time in weeks. She sang:

> *"Where's my shoes?*
> *Where's my new gray shoes, shoes, shoes?*
> *I think I put them here,*
> *But I guess—oh, where the deuce——"*

Dressed, she was at the head of the stairs when the bell rang.

"Never mind," she called to the maid; "I'll answer."

She opened upon Mr. and Mrs. Warren Dillon. They were old friends and she hadn't seen them before, this Christmas.

"Josephine! We came to meet Constance here, but we hoped we'd have a glimpse of you; but you're rushing around so."

Aghast, she led the way into the library. "What time is sister meeting you?" she asked when she could.

"Oh, in half an hour, if she isn't delayed."

She tried to be especially polite, to atone in advance for what impoliteness might be necessary later. In five minutes the bell rang again; there was the romantic figure on the porch, cut sharp and clear against the bleak sky; and up the steps behind him came Travis de Coppet and Ed Bement.

"Stay!" she whispered quickly. "These people will all go."

"I've two hours," he said. "Of course, I'll wait if you want me to."

She wanted to throw her arms around him then, but she controlled herself, even her hands. She introduced everyone, she sent for tea. The men asked Edward Dicer questions about the war and he parried them politely but restlessly.

After half an hour he asked Josephine: "Have you the time? I must keep track of my train."

They might have noticed the watch on his own wrist and taken the hint, but he fascinated them all, as though they had isolated a rare specimen and were determined to find out all about it. Even had they realized Josephine's state of mind, it would have seemed to them that she was selfish to want something of such general interest for her own.

The arrival of Constance, her married sister, did not help matters; again Dicer was caught up into the phenomenon of human curiosity. As the clock in the hall struck six, he shot a desperate glance at Josephine. With a belated appreciation of the situation, the group broke itself up. Constance took the Dillons upstairs to the other sitting room, the two young men went home.

Silence, save for the voices fading off on the stairs, the automobile crunching away on the snow outside. Before a word was said, Josephine rang for the maid, and instructing her that she was not at home, closed the door into the hall. Then she went and sat down on the couch next to him and clasped her hands and waited.

"Thank God," he said. "I thought if they stayed another minute——"

"Wasn't it terrible?"

"I came out here because of you. The night you left New York I was ten minutes late getting to the train because I was detained at the French propaganda office. I'm not much good at letters. Since then I've thought of nothing but getting out here to see you."

"I felt sad." But not now; now she was thinking that in a moment she would be in his arms, feeling the buttons of his tunic press bruisingly against her, feeling his diagonal belt as something that bound them both and made her part of him. There were no doubts, no reservations, he was everything she wanted.

"I'm over here for six months more—perhaps a year. Then, if this damned war goes on, I'll have to go back. I suppose I haven't really got the right——"

"Wait—wait!" she cried. She wanted a moment longer to taste, to feel fully her happiness. "Wait," she repeated, putting her hand on his. She felt every object in the room vividly; she saw the seconds passing, each one carrying a load of loveliness toward the future. "All right; now tell me."

"Just that I love you," he whispered. She was in his arms, her hair against his cheek. "We haven't known each other long, and you're only eighteen, but I've learned to be afraid of waiting."

Now she leaned her head back until she was looking up at him, supported by his arm. Her neck curved gracefully, full and soft, and she leaned in toward his shoulder, as she knew how, so that her lips were every minute closer to him. "Now," she thought. He gave a funny little sigh and pulled her face up to his.

After a minute she leaned away from him and twisted herself upright.

"Darling—darling—darling," he said.

She looked at him, stared at him. Gently he pulled her over again and kissed her. This time, when she sat up, she rose and went across the room, where she opened a dish of almonds and dropped some in her mouth. Then she came back and sat beside him, looking straight ahead, then darting a sudden glance at him.

"What are you thinking, darling, darling Josephine?" She didn't answer; he put both hands over hers. "What are you feeling, then?"

As he breathed, she could hear the faint sound of his leather belt moving on his shoulder; she could feel his strong, kind handsome eyes looking at her; she could feel his proud self feeding on glory as others feed on security; she heard the jingle of spurs ring in his strong, rich, compelling voice.

"I feel nothing at all," she said.

"What do you mean?" He was startled.

"Oh, help me!" she cried. "Help me!"

"I don't understand what you mean."

"Kiss me again."

He kissed her. This time he held on to her and looked down into her face.

"What do you mean?" he demanded. "You mean you don't love me?"

"I don't feel anything."

"But you did love me."

"I don't know."

He let her go. She went across the room and sat down.

"I don't understand," he said after a minute.

"I think you're perfect," she said, her lips quivering.

"But I'm not—thrilling to you?"

"Oh, yes, very thrilling. I was thrilled all afternoon."

"Then what is it, darling?"

"I don't know. When you kissed me I wanted to laugh." It made her sick to say this, but a desperate, interior honesty drove her on. She saw his eyes change, saw him withdrawing a little from her. "Help me," she repeated.

"Help you how? You'll have to be more definite. I love you; I thought perhaps you loved me. That's all. If I don't please you——"

"But you do. You're everything—you're everything I've always wanted." Her voice continued inside herself: "But I've had everything."

"But you simply don't love me."

"I've got nothing to give you. I don't feel anything at all."

He got up abruptly. He felt her vast, tragic apathy pervading the room, and it set up an indifference in him now, too—a lot of things suddenly melted out of him.

"Good-by."

"You won't help me," she murmured abstractedly.

"How in the devil can I help you?" he answered impatiently. "You feel indifferent to me. You can't change that, but neither can I. Good-by."

"Good-by."

She was very tired and lay face downward on the couch with that awful, awful realization that all the old things are true. One cannot both spend and have. The love of her life had come by, and looking in her empty basket, she had found not a flower left for him—not one. After a while she wept.

"Oh, what have I done to myself?" she wailed. "What have I done? What have I done?"

ABOUT THE AUTHOR

Francis Scott Key Fitzgerald was born in St. Paul, Minnesota, in 1896, and was educated at St. Paul Academy, the Newman School, and Princeton University. In 1917, he left Princeton to join the army, and shortly after his demobilization, sold his first short story to the *Smart Set*, edited by H. L. Mencken and George Jean Nathan. Encouraged by his early success, Fitzgerald went on to write his first novel, *This Side of Paradise* (1920), which was published by Scribners when he was just twenty-three. An exuberant and unconventional novel of undergraduate life at Princeton, it immediately established him as the bright light of his era—the spokesman for the "jazz age." That same year, Scott married Zelda Sayre, and the notorious couple divided their time among New York, Paris, the Riviera, and Rome, becoming a part of the American expatriate circle that included Gertrude Stein, Ernest Hemingway, John Dos Passos, and Thomas Wolfe.

The crowning achievement of his career was his novel *The Great Gatsby* (1925), but Fitzgerald's popularity waned thereafter. In 1930 Zelda suffered a nervous breakdown that required her to be institutionalized. Beset as he was by his wife's illness and his own drinking problems, Fitzgerald was having a difficult time writing *Tender Is the Night* (1934), for which he drew on both his own experiences and Zelda's fifteen months in a Swiss sanitarium. To accommodate the high life-style to which he was accustomed, he came to rely more and more on his commercial short story writing for *The Saturday Evening Post*, *Scribner's Magazine*, and *Esquire*, earning, at his peak, more than $36,000 a year.

Fitzgerald died of a heart attack at the age of forty-four, while working on his unfinished novel of Hollywood, *The Last Tycoon*, which Edmund Wilson considered his most mature work. For his keen social insight, glib sophistication, and breathtaking lyricism, Fitzgerald stands as one of the most important American writers of the first half of the twentieth century. His other works include *Flappers and Philosophers* (1920); *The Beautiful and Damned* (1922); *Tales of the Jazz Age* (1922); a play, *The Vegetable* (1923); *All the Sad Young Men* (1926); *Taps at Reveille* (1935); and a posthumous selection of short stories, essays, and autobiographical reflections, *Afternoon of an Author*, all of which are available in Collier Scribner editions.